Praise for Andrea Dunlop's *Losing the Light*
One of *Redbook*'s Best Books of 2016

"Dunlop infuses *She Regrets Nothing* with insight into family dynamics, which makes it especially rich, multifaceted, and engrossing. Fans of Becky Sharp and Brenda Walsh, this is your lucky day."

—Caroline Kepnes, bestselling author of
Hidden Bodies and *You*

"Dunlop has created unforgettable characters and a setting so richly drawn, the reader is immersed in the drama until the last engaging page. *She Regrets Nothing* is an entertaining, compelling story of family, class, and the yearning to belong."

—Amy Poeppel, author of *Small Admissions*

"Laila Lawrence and her family are people I am thrilled not to know personally and was equally thrilled to spend a few hours following around New York City in all the best clothes and shoes to all the best clubs and parties. *She Regrets Nothing* is addictive, dark, and twisty and, like its characters, delightfully conniving."

—Laurie Frankel, author of *This Is How It Always Is*

"A complicated friendship, a disastrous affair with a professor, and intoxicating relationships factor in making this an unforgettable trip."

—BuzzFeed

"Who doesn't fantasize about a sexy and passionate romance with a hot foreigner?"

—PopSugar

"A haunting story of betrayal within a beautiful portrait of youth."

—*Kirkus Reviews*

"Dunlop's smart and suspenseful debut follows the lead of Katie Crouch's *Abroad* (2014) and Jennifer duBois's *Cartwheel* (2013), but delves more deeply into the repercussions beyond a shocking incident during a year abroad. Dunlop richly evokes the heady emotions of friendship, lust, and betrayal."

—*Booklist*

"A heady cocktail of nostalgia, a seductive Frenchman, a passionate love triangle, a mysterious disappearance: Seattle author Andrea Dunlop weaves an intriguing story about 30-year-old Brooke, now newly engaged, and her recollections of student days a decade earlier in France with her bubbly, blond buddy Sophie. . . . *Losing the Light* is a love letter to France—the cafes, the language, the 'fierce elegance' of Parisiennes, the sun-drenched beauty of Cap Ferrat. Dunlop brilliantly recreates the tempestuous, 'anything is possible' whirlwind of emotions that accompany Brooke's coming of age, with the dizzying heights and depths of feeling. . . . A thoughtful, assured debut."

—*The Seattle Times*

"Good wine, dark chocolate, a French love triangle, and the perfect best friend—at first—are only a handful of the decadences awaiting you in *Losing the Light*—not to mention the shocking twist that kept this succulent debut lingering long after the final page."

—Miranda Beverly-Whittemore, *New York Times* bestselling author of *Bittersweet*

"Dunlop's writing is effervescent, but wise . . . the story, which is as much about love, lust and longing as it is about the intricacies and potential pitfalls of close, obsessive friendship, also offers a truly lovely depiction of France."

—*The Globe and Mail*

"In her debut, Dunlop writes of a fizzy, decadent world, filled with the intense relationships that young love brings, whether that feeling is for a person or for a beautiful location."

—*Library Journal*

"Love triangles can haunt you forever. This gorgeously written debut novel centers around one woman being seduced by European high life while on a study abroad trip in France. It's an exotic escape and a literary escape at the same time."

—*Redbook*

"The story of a young girl studying abroad in France who gets sucked into a world of love and lust. This unraveling tale is absolutely haunting."

—*SheKnows*

"There are so many coming-of-age novels in the world about the young, innocent girl making her way in the world. And yet, *Losing the Light* is really something special. Andrea Dunlop has a keen sense of what a modern woman on the cusp of her twenties might truly desire, fear, and be tempted by. Her characters are unapologetic and troublesome, yet intensely likable. On top of that, she sets the book in a French town and feeds you wine and men the whole way through. Oh, and there's a murder mystery. Seduced yet? You should be. This is a lovely debut."

—Katie Crouch, *New York Times* bestselling author of
Girls in Trucks and *Abroad*

"It's got Gainsbourg's 'Sea, Sex, and Sun' plus red wine and betrayal—a compulsively readable debut about forever friendships that can't last."

—Courtney Maum, bestselling author of
I Am Having So Much Fun Here Without You

"*Losing the Light* is a smart, sexy, thrilling novel. Andrea Dunlop's debut brilliantly captures the tension and sharp edges of female friendships, infatuation, and life abroad. You will feel transported to France, as if you yourself are speaking French and drinking a little too much wine with your best friend and a dangerously handsome man."

—Taylor Jenkins Reid, author of *One True Loves*

"Andrea Dunlop's captivating debut ardently delivers the thrill and joy and exquisite pain of being young and in love: with a friend, with a lover, with a country, with a life, with the future. I felt myself twenty and in France with nothing but heady enchantment before me. *Losing the Light* is utterly transporting."

—Laurie Frankel, author of *The Atlas of Love*

"This delicious literary indulgence is consuming and addictive . . . the perfect partner for every beach day this summer."

—*Sunset*

"In *Losing the Light*, Andrea Dunlop takes readers on an intense, smart, sexy adventure, giving major *The Talented Mr. Ripley* vibes."

—*Working Mother*

Also by Andrea Dunlop

Losing the Light
Broken Bay (a novella)

She Regrets Nothing

a novel

ANDREA DUNLOP

WASHINGTON SQUARE PRESS

—

ATRIA

New York   London   Toronto   Sydney   New Delhi

Washington Square Press
An Imprint of Simon & Schuster, Inc.
1230 Avenue of the Americas
New York, NY 10020

First Washington Square Press trade paperback edition February 2018

WASHINGTON SQUARE PRESS and colophon are registered
trademarks of Simon & Schuster, Inc.

For information about special discounts for bulk purchases,
please contact Simon & Schuster Special Sales at 1-866-506-1949 or
business@simonandschuster.com.

The Simon & Schuster Speakers Bureau can bring authors to your live
event. For more information or to book an event, contact the Simon &
Schuster Speakers Bureau at 1-866-248-3049 or visit our website at
www.simonspeakers.com.

Manufactured in the United States of America

10   9   8   7   6   5   4   3   2   1

Library of Congress Cataloging-in-Publication Data

Names: Dunlop, Andrea, author.
Title: She regrets nothing : a novel / Andrea Dunlop.
Description: First Washington Square Press trade paperback edition. | New
York : Washington Square Press, 2018.
Identifiers: LCCN 2017006868 (print) | LCCN 2017011097 (ebook) | ISBN
9781501155987 (pbk.) | ISBN 9781501155994 (ebook) | ISBN
9781501155994 (eBook)
Classification: LCC PS3604.U5554 S54 2018 (print) | LCC PS3604.U5554 (ebook) |
DDC 813/.6--dc23
LC record available at https://lccn.loc.gov/2017006868

ISBN 978-1-5011-5598-7
ISBN 978-1-5011-5599-4 (ebook)

For Derek.

She Regrets Nothing

1

"ARE YOU sure we should have come?" Nora whispered to her sister. "I feel like everyone is staring at us."

Liberty briefly considered telling her that perhaps the sky-high black patent-leather heels she was wearing, flashing their gaudy red soles as she walked, paired with her tight black dress and a pillbox hat with a veil—honestly, she looked like a 1940s mob widow—were not helping her be inconspicuous at the midwestern service. Though Nora had traveled the world, she remained in New York no matter her physical location. Her New York–ness wrapped around her like a protective gauze, even here at a funeral in the Grosse Pointe Memorial Church. The place was more beautiful, somehow, than Liberty had expected, with its white stone walls, Tudor arches, and ornate stained-glass windows. It felt at least a hundred years old. A comfort, somehow.

"I should hope so," Leo said, flashing a smile at an older woman who had her eyes glued to him as she passed the pew toward the back where the three Lawrence siblings had settled in, Liberty futilely hoping they could keep a low profile. "I mean, the day I *don't* stand out from a crowd like this? Euthanasia, I beg you." Leo was Nora's twin (Leonardo and Leonora: they were named after royalty and so they behaved), though they hardly resembled each other.

"Leo." Liberty shot him a warning look.

"A joke," he whispered back. "Trying to lighten the mood."

"The mood is meant to be somber, Leo. Just . . . please." Liberty wrapped her arms tighter around herself and faced forward.

"Sorry. Jesus."

"Is that her?" Nora said, leaning over Leo's lap toward Liberty, who was sitting on the aisle.

Liberty looked up as a young woman (she was twenty-three, the same age as the twins) walked by to the front pew that was reserved for family. Laila—their cousin, a stranger, the person they had come to see—seemed to be the only person in the church who hadn't noticed the three of them. Though this was the first time they would meet, Liberty recognized her immediately. She was distinctive: petite and lovely, with green eyes and long red hair. She was fine-boned (as Liberty and her siblings were) and appeared delicate to the point of breakable against the backdrop of the sturdy midwesterners who surrounded her.

"That's her."

She clung to the arm of a tall, broad-shouldered man who was wearing a suit that appeared made for someone much smaller, the lip of his boxy white shirt peeking out from the bottom of his jacket as he moved—could this really be her boyfriend? He looked like a high school jock who'd gone to seed but had failed to notice. Laila appeared to be in a fog, eyes straight ahead as she made her way to the pew. Liberty wondered if she'd taken a sedative to get through her mother's funeral. In her Internet scouring, she'd not been able to find much information on Laila. A Facebook profile, of course, and some photos of her on the website of a local high-end cosmetic dentist's office. At first, Liberty thought she might be a model—and was struck by the irony of this, that her faraway midwestern cousin would be a model just as she and her own mother had been—but upon further inspection, it appeared that Laila worked at the office. They'd simply taken advantage of having such a comely staff member by putting her front and center on the website. She was not a dentist, it seemed; perhaps a hygienist or receptionist.

"It's so weird that they both went in car accidents, so many years apart," Leo said. Their uncle—their father's brother—had died thusly thirteen years before. The two families had grown up estranged from each other. Now Laila was an orphan.

"Tragic," Nora said. "Dickensian," she added dramatically.

"What is our actual plan here?" Leo asked. He was clearly losing patience with the whole idea, which at the outset, he'd found amusing enough. He was bored now and wanted to be back in Manhattan. Organ music boomed through the church and Liberty hushed her brother. The service was beginning.

Betsy Lawrence was eulogized by her older sister, Jennifer, a short, round woman with whispers of Laila's green-eyed wholesome prettiness. It was a strange speech, containing nothing specific about Betsy herself or what the world had lost in her passing. "'The body that is sown is perishable, it is raised imperishable,'" she quoted from Corinthians. "'It is sown in dishonor, it is raised in glory; it is sown in weakness, it is raised in power.' And so Betsy goes home to the Lord. I know my niece Laila wanted to speak about her mother today. I know she loved her dearly. But the shock . . . I'm afraid . . ." She was twisting a tissue in her hands and appeared overcome, standing at the pulpit as though she had no idea how she'd gotten there. After a moment, a man (her husband?) came to collect her, draping his arm around her and shepherding her off the stage. It was an odd moment, but then, it was a funeral. The Lawrence siblings had not been to many—only their grandmother's and an older family friend or two.

The service was brief, and before long, the organ was once again sounding its dirge, and people were standing up and filing out. Before Liberty could come up with a plan, the three of them were pulled along in a tide of people to the church basement where the reception was being held. It was an altogether more modern and sterile space than the grandeur of the hall above, fit for Sunday school and AA meetings. There was subdued string music playing, and officious church ladies were ferrying a large spread—tea, cookies, various hot dishes, and, mercifully, several bottles of wine. Now that the funeral-goers were no longer restrained by the pews, they gawked openly at the Lawrence siblings.

"Is this the mom?" Nora said, picking up one of several framed photos arranged on the table closest to the door. The shot was of a young woman who, if not for the teased hair and color-block 1980s sweater, could have easily been mistaken for Laila.

"Must be," Liberty said. "God, Laila's a dead ringer."

They made their way down the line of photos. Even Leo was hushed by seeing these images of the family that had been kept from them. Liberty felt tears coming to her eyes when she got to her aunt and uncle's wedding photos from twenty-five years earlier. She could see so much of her father in his younger brother's face, a man she'd supposedly met but had no clear memories of.

Their father, Ben Lawrence, never spoke of his brother, Gregory. He'd been gone now thirteen years and all Liberty knew had been gleaned from the occasional overheard conversation in her childhood and what she could discover online, which was not much more than the basics: her uncle had owned a number of luxury car dealerships throughout Michigan, and he and his wife had one daughter, Laila, who was the same age as the twins. Liberty was seventeen when her uncle died; her father hadn't been an especially warm man to begin with, and the death of his brother had made him even more remote, causing him to retreat further into his work. Repeated searches yielded little more, but Liberty set up a Google Alert with Laila's name, which was how she'd discovered Betsy's recent death. And that had brought them here.

The three of them moved on to the food and drinks. Liberty poured red wine into the small, sad plastic cups for each of them. Nora examined the food from a distance, as though even coming near it might make her fat. There were piles of cookie bars with numerous layers and frostings, great platters of potato salad with what appeared to be hot dogs mixed in, several varieties of mac and cheese.

"This is so weird," Nora said, taking a sip of her wine and peering around at the men in their khakis and the women whose collective bulk was covered in many layers of scarves and cardigans. "It's . . . America."

"Like a TLC show or something," Leo added.

Liberty rolled her eyes and just at that moment felt a hand on her elbow.

"Excuse me?"

She turned and the glassy green eyes of her cousin looked up at her. She was small, a half foot shorter than Liberty at least. There was something familiar about her still: the nose, the set of her eyes; she was a stranger, but she was their family.

"I don't mean to be rude," Laila said hesitantly, "but who *are* you? This is my mother's funeral."

Liberty felt sick to her stomach. A moment before, she'd been contemplating telling her siblings that they should just leave, get in touch later. But now it was too late for that.

"Um . . . oh. I'm Liberty, and this is Leo and Nora."

Nora—who didn't have good boundaries on her best day—flung herself at her unsuspecting cousin, who blankly accepted her into her arms. "You poor thing! We just had to come."

Liberty gently pulled her sister away from Laila, who was now smiling nervously.

"Thank you." She looked at them as though searching for clues. "But who are you? Why are you *here*?"

The siblings quickly glanced at each other, amazed. Their names had triggered nothing; she knew even less than they did.

"Well . . ." Liberty weighed the option of coming up with some alternate cover story so as not to distract from the occasion, which their visit seemed certain to do. She dismissed this. "We're your cousins. Ben is our dad."

She looked incredulous. "Ben doesn't have kids," Laila said uncertainly, as if she was asking a question. For a moment the three siblings were quiet, because they hadn't precisely been *told* about Laila either. Liberty had eavesdropped and eventually told the twins.

"He does," Leo said at last, his voice kind. "We're them."

Laila continued to stare at them uncomprehendingly. A moment later, the man she was with—her fiancé, although their engagement was still a secret—appeared at her side. Liberty watched him subtly lock on her brother as though thinking, Oh thank goodness, a man.

"Nathan Jansen," he said, introducing himself to Leo with a hearty handshake.

"Leo Lawrence," he smiled with relish as surprise came over the man's pale features.

"And I'm Nora Lawrence."

"Liberty," she followed as Nathan's eyes ricocheted over to her.

"Lawrence? As in . . ." He looked over at Laila.

"We're her cousins," Liberty said, feeling suddenly helpless.

Laila turned to him, still bewildered. "I didn't know."

Oh, why had they come? Liberty was mortified to ever be the cause of drama. And at a funeral! Tacky.

"We just came to pay our respects, and actually, we'd probably better get going. Laila, you can call me anytime." Liberty pressed a card into her hand, adding, "My cell is on there. And I would love to hear from you." Liberty began to shepherd her siblings in the direction of the door.

"Wait," Laila said. "Where are you staying?"

"The Atheneum."

"Okay. I'll call you later, maybe," Laila said, before being pulled away by funeral-goers who had been waiting nearby.

❧

"It is so messed up that her parents didn't even tell her we *existed*." Nora leaned her head wearily on her brother's shoulder. They were fitted snuggly in the back of a town car, three across for the twenty-minute drive along the Lake Shore Road to their hotel.

"Well, our parents didn't tell us about her either, at least not willingly."

"Do you think Beau knows about her?"

Liberty shrugged. Of the three of them, she was closest with their eldest half brother, Beau, but she didn't hear from him for months at a time and hadn't told him about their trip. He lived in Banff, a tiny town near Alberta, Canada.

"Beau barely speaks to Dad, so I don't know that he would have made the effort to get to know Laila even if he did. I'll ask him whenever he reappears, though."

"She's really pretty. I wonder why she lives here," Nora said.

"Well, she grew up here," Leo said, "and at least the neighborhood is nice. Look at the houses. We could practically be in Connecticut."

"But that guy she was with. Was that really her boyfriend?" Nora pulled at the waistband of her dress. Her clothes were always a size too small, as though she imagined herself thinner when she bought them.

"I don't know," Liberty said, "it seemed that way."

Nora made a face.

Just then Liberty felt her phone buzz with a text message.

Hi Liberty - it's Laila. When are you leaving? I thought we might meet up tomorrow. Would it be okay if it was just you and me though? I'm feeling overwhelmed.

"What is it?"

"Just Reece checking in." Liberty felt strangely protective of Laila. She thought of her standing there next to her boyfriend in the church, looking fragile and faraway. Was that strange aunt with the Bible verses the only family she had left?

"I can't believe we have to spend the night in *Detroit*," Nora said as they were getting out of the car.

"Nora, hush," Liberty said, feeling the eyes of the hotel's doorman on them. She smiled at him warmly and his expression said that she, at least, was forgiven.

"I like it here," Leo said, just to be contrary. "It's so much edgier than New York, so much more *real*. And this hotel," he said, stretching his arms wide, smiling up at the dramatic frescos and expanse of marble that engulfed the lobby, "it's like Vegas or something."

"Or something," Nora muttered.

"My good man!" Leo said, strolling up to the concierge desk where a thin twentysomething who swam in his dark suit lifted his gaze from his computer.

"How can I help you, sir?"

"Tell me," Leo said, leaning over the counter, his convivial charm working on the young man, "where should we go for dinner? We're only in town for a night."

"Well," the concierge said, straightening his spine, "were we thinking fine dining or . . ."

"Oh, God, no," Leo said.

"Can you imagine what passes for fine dining in this hellhole?" Nora said under her breath to Liberty, who gave her a sharp look.

"Something authentic," Leo said, "what's your favorite spot?"

"Pizza okay?"

"We have pizza in New York," Nora said, "amazing pizza."

"Not like this," the concierge said, "I promise you. No one has pizza like Papalis."

"I'm intrigued," Leo said. "Girls?"

They both nodded, Liberty smiling, Nora sulking as the concierge showed Leo the restaurant's location on a map.

❧

They were seated in a booth toward the front of Papalis as Leo watched other patrons as if they were performing a cabaret for his amusement. "It's like being on safari! I should write about this in my column," he said, meaning his weekly missive for *New York* magazine's Man About Town where he mostly chronicled the parties he went to—he'd even sold a book to a publisher off the concept.

When their pizza arrived, it was a monstrous thing, like five pizzas crammed together and covered with extra cheese and sauce.

"Ugh," Nora said, "no wonder everyone here is so fat."

"This actually smells pretty delicious," Liberty said.

"I'm ordering a salad," Nora said, "if they even *have* such a thing here."

"So," Leo said, taking a generous bite of his slice and rolling his eyes in ecstasy, "God, this is good. What's the plan now with Laila? Just the funeral drive-by or what?"

"Maybe she can come visit us in New York! The poor thing," Nora said.

Liberty knew it was best if she kept her meeting with their cousin a secret for now. Like all siblings—particularly those with nearly a decade's difference in age—she and the twins had grown up both in the same and completely different households. Their parents had been much stricter with Liberty, imparted different lessons about money and work and privilege. She loved the twins, but they were so woefully naive. She didn't want to lose her cousin's trust if they said or did the wrong thing at such a delicate time, which she somehow knew they would.

"That's a great idea, Nora, why don't we invite her once we've given her a few days to recover from the funeral?"

Nora, a bit unaccustomed to having good ideas, beamed.

"I'm not surprised Dad never told *me* anything about this family imbroglio," Leo said to Liberty. It was true Ben wasn't one for cozy father-son chats. "But you really don't know what happened with them?"

"I really don't, but it must have been big. Mom knows something, I'm just not sure how much."

"A mystery," Nora said.

⁓⁓

Their flight to New York wasn't until the next afternoon. That morning, Liberty told her siblings she was going to check out a rare bookstore nearby that she'd read about, thereby ensuring they wouldn't want to come. At any rate, they were settled into their favorite activity, hotel movies and room service. They were already in robes and unlikely to move for hours, giving Liberty ample time to meet Laila for coffee.

Liberty felt stares trailing her as she made her way to a small two-top table in the corner of a nearby café to wait for Laila. It was always worse outside New York. In Manhattan, she wasn't so out of place, but here she was like another species, so tall and slender, with her miles of legs, high cheekbones, and dramatic brows. She stared at her phone while she waited, avoiding fervent glances and hoping no one would see the open chair opposite her as an invitation. A few moments later, she felt the energy of the room shift and raised her eyes to see her cousin come through the door. She was wearing a royal-blue peacoat that she shook off upon entering. Underneath she had on a tight sweater and jeans, her lovely red hair splashed out across her shoulders; she looked revived since the previous afternoon.

Liberty leaned forward and waved to her. She had the impulse to stand and embrace her, but then remembered Laila's bewildered grimace at Nora's hug. Laila spotted her and strode toward the table.

"Thanks for meeting me." Laila gave her a weak smile as she settled into her chair, draping her coat over the back. Laila scrutinized her. Liberty realized that her presence was being met with something besides curiosity. Suspicion.

"Of course. I'm glad you texted. I'm sorry we just showed up like that. Maybe that wasn't the right way to . . . ," she fell off, embarrassed.

"Trust me, there's no right way for anyone to do anything for me right now." Laila took off her hat and shook out her hair. "Jesus," she said, looking back at Liberty, "you're so pretty." Liberty thanked her, though it sounded more like an accusation than a compliment.

"It makes sense. I gather my uncle married a supermodel; I read up on you guys this morning. I can't believe I'd never done it before. But I guess I had no real reason to—I didn't even know you existed—let alone that you'd be this interesting. You guys are, like, famous."

Just then the waiter came by and took their coffee orders. Liberty asked for black; Laila ordered a latte, skim, just a dusting of nutmeg. Thank you so much.

Liberty laughed off the previous comment, "Hardly. I mean, you'd never heard of us."

"Yeah, but there's all this stuff in the tabloids," she smiled. "Lots of people seem to care who you date and what you wear."

"Well, New York is like that." Liberty shrugged. She didn't think they were in the press that much, but she supposed if you Googled it, if it all came up together, it might seem they were. "Have you ever visited?" The idea that her cousin might have come, worn the touristy path from Times Square to the Empire State Building to South Street Seaport, without ever knowing she had family there, struck Liberty as inexpressibly sad.

Laila shook her head, "No reason to, I guess. I mean, I've always wanted to see it, like everyone. But I don't travel much."

"You really didn't know anything about us?" It hurt Liberty that her uncle had taken such pains to deny her very existence. But then, her own father had done the same. What must have happened between the two brothers to have caused such a rift?

"You know how that is: your parents tell you something from the time you're a little kid. You believe it. My dad said he had a brother he didn't get along with; he never said anything about cousins. He died before I was old enough to start asking serious questions. My mom didn't say anything about Ben having children, but then, maybe she didn't know?"

Liberty nodded, wishing they'd not started in the deep end. Better to revert to less serious topics, maybe. "So, tell me about yourself. What do you do?"

"I'm a dental hygienist. I work for my boyfriend, who you met. I mean, he wasn't my boyfriend when I started working for him." Laila smiled. "And I guess he's not really my boyfriend anymore."

Liberty tilted her head, waited for her to continue. Had they broken up? They'd certainly seemed like an item the day before.

"We're getting married."

Liberty breathed a sigh of relief that yet another misfortune had not landed on her cousin.

"That's wonderful! He seems really lovely, by the way." And he had—the vigorous handshake, the warm smile—in their brief interaction, he'd exuded goodness. "When is the wedding?"

Laila let out a big sigh. The waiter reappeared with their coffees, and Laila shot him a sparkling smile that made him nearly lose his footing. "Not sure. But we're going to keep it supersmall. It might be just the two of us. After my mom . . . I don't have . . ."

"Yeah, of course. Well, that's some happy news, anyway. So how . . . how are you doing?"

Laila shrugged. "I'm just numb still, I think. I wake up and I think, Maybe today it won't be true. That probably sounds nuts. Nathan has been such a support."

"I'm glad you have him. I wish . . . our families . . ." Liberty didn't know what she meant to say but Laila seemed to understand and smiled kindly at her.

"It's just such a stupid thing, you know? She was out playing bingo like she always does on Sunday nights and . . ."

Liberty finally found the courage to reach across the table and take her cousin's hand, which happily, she accepted and squeezed.

"What a *boring* way to die, you know? A car accident." Laila said.

Liberty looked at her, confused, resisting the urge to withdraw her hand.

"Senseless, I mean. You understand."

Liberty nodded. It was unfair to expect eloquence from her cousin, in her grief. "You two were close?"

"It's complicated. My mother was a very difficult woman, and I'm fairly sure she was never totally enthused about the whole motherhood thing. But I spent a lot of time with her, so in that way we were close, I guess. But mostly it was because she had no one else, and what was I going to do?"

"But there were all those people at the funeral?"

"My aunts' friends. The two of them did more for Betsy last night than they did in the last ten years of her life," she said with a rueful smile. "My mother didn't really have friends of her own. God, sorry," she said, shaking her head. "Why am I telling you all of this?"

"It's okay." Liberty felt relieved that her cousin would confide in her. "I'm glad you feel like you can share."

"Well, Nathan doesn't like talking about it. His mother is, like, the polar opposite of Betsy, she has these four jock-y sons that she still babies, and she's always baking something. She wears sweatshirts with cats on them, remembers the mailman's birthday. That kind of mom."

"She sounds sweet." Liberty's mother, Petra, also bore no resemblance to this paragon. She loved her children and was devoted to her family, but she'd grown up poor in Russia before emigrating and becoming a top-tier model. She was all hard edges: no baking and *certainly* no cat sweatshirts.

"She is, but . . . anyway. Tell me about New York!" Laila's eyes lit up, her posture straightened as though shaking off the burdens she'd just enumerated.

"Well, it's the only place I've ever lived, so it's home." Liberty shrugged. "I love it."

"You must have traveled all over the world for your modeling career, though?"

Liberty smiled, "Not as much as you'd think. I did mostly local stuff because I was really young when I was working." Her cousin must have gone back a ways with her research. Liberty hadn't modeled since she was a teenager, and she was thirty now.

"And now you're a literary agent. You didn't like modeling?"

Liberty shook her head, "Wasn't for me. I love working with books."

"That sounds cool. And are you seeing anyone? A boyfriend?" Laila's expression was girlish; she suddenly looked years younger, the cloud of her grief clearing.

Liberty shook her head. "Too busy!" she said cheerfully, the usual answer, the simplest. She was charmed by the childlike bluntness of her cousin's questioning.

The two chatted for another half hour, as Laila peppered her with excited questions about New York. Liberty figured she was desperate to talk about anything other than her mom's death. At last Laila excused herself. "I have to meet my aunts Jennifer and Lisa to go through the stuff at my mom's condo."

"Today?" Liberty said. The task seemed brutal so soon after the funeral.

"Honestly, I just want to get it over with. You can't even imagine the amount of random shit there is to deal with when someone dies unexpectedly."

"I could change my flight if you need help."

"That's really sweet of you, but no, it's okay. Aunt Jen has all her church ladies coming, so we'll have plenty of hands."

"Okay, then." Liberty stood and this time hugged her cousin, who smelled like vanilla.

They promised to keep in touch, and Liberty walked back in the direction of the hotel. The early-October sun was out and it warmed her face. She texted her best friend, Reece, to see if she could talk, but there was no response. Liberty thought of calling her mother, who didn't even know they were out of town, just to hear her voice. She was reminded by meeting her cousin that you only had so much time with people, only so many chances to make things right. Holding grudges—as her own father had obviously done with his brother—was never worthwhile.

❧

Aunt Jen (the eldest) and Aunt Lisa (the middle sister) had been at her mother's condo since 9:00 a.m. with a half dozen of their interchangeable dowdy church friends, and they were busy pawing through the remnants of Betsy's life.

"Do you need me today?" Nathan had asked her before she'd set off to meet Liberty—a part of her day's itinerary that she hadn't shared with him. His tone made it quite clear that if he was required to help, it would be as a brave martyr on his fiancée's behalf, rather than out of any genuine desire to be there. It was a Saturday, which meant hours upon hours of college football blaring from the massive, vulgar television that dominated their living room. It meant the house steadily crowding with his brothers—both biological and fraternity—their voices growing ever louder as they consumed more and more beer.

"No," Laila had replied flatly, "it's fine."

"Okay, I'll just leave you ladies to it, then," he said, his relief palpable. As though the tossing out of dozens of take-out menus, the sorting of her mother's vast collection of stretchy pants to determine which were fit for donation and which should just be thrown away, were some fun girly outing his male presence would impinge upon. Not that Laila wanted him to come; there was something deeply humiliating about going through the effects of a middle-aged woman who'd lived alone. She'd succumbed to the sort of squalor in the past several years that showed she'd given up: the fridge full of take-out leftovers and condiment packets; the crusty, expired cosmetics jumbled in the bathroom drawers, long since unused, inexplicably held on to; the trashy romance novels and self-help tomes piled on the window sill.

The church ladies squawked around Laila as they sifted through the unfortunate detritus. How was she doing? Did she need anything? They'd brought a massive platter of cookies with them, as though refined carbohydrates could somehow make this task more pleasant.

"Honey, there's a little pile of some nice things we found, some jewelry you might want to hang on to." One of the ladies pointed her to the dresser in the corner.

Laila smiled sweetly and made her way through the chaos. The dresser was in a corner of the room that had already been dealt with and was consequently cleaner than Laila had ever seen it while her mother was alive. There was another version of Betsy buried somewhere in Laila's memory: the one featured in the photographs at the memorial service. This was the incarnation of her mother whose prettiness and smarts had helped her—for a time, at least—rise above her circumstances by landing a scholarship to the University of Michigan where she met, and soon married, Gregory Lawrence. But that version had lapsed after her husband's death. The Betsy of the rancid condo where Laila too had spent her teenage years was doomed to be the one who endured in her memory. There were many women who rose to the occasion of single motherhood—in truth, the world would grind to a halt without such women—but Betsy was not one of them. After Gregory's death, their family was like a rulerless nation—a vacuum that impressed upon Laila the dangerous notion that women were powerless alone.

Laila picked through the pile of so-called nice things the church ladies had set aside. Her mother had developed an unfortunate QVC habit in her later years and had accumulated a massive amount of junky costume jewelry. But then it caught her eye—the red enamel pendant with the two golden birds, both of them with diamonds for eyes. It was the one beautiful thing Laila's mother had owned, and she was shocked to find it here, having assumed that her mother would find a way to take it with her to the grave. Laila didn't know anything about its provenance, but it was her mother's treasured possession: Laila had already looked through the apartment once and not found it. Somehow the church ladies had unearthed it.

As the day following her mother's death had dawned, Laila had snuck from Nathan's bed in silence. She always woke before him, and this morning she'd risen at 5:00 a.m. She didn't know what exactly she was looking for: only that her mother had been lording some secret over her for years. It was her method of keeping Laila close. "Oh, if you'd only known the life I could have had. But I chose you, my little sweetheart," she'd say, venomous and sly. Or: "Someday, I'll tell you everything. Someday you'll understand what your poor mother has been through." Laila knew her mother could have easily been bluffing; it was a bit of theater that the two of them went through. Laila continued to see her mother— making sure she took her diabetes meds and keeping her from turning completely feral in her disgusting condo—not because she genuinely thought her mother might have something to offer her one day, but out of a filial duty that she didn't so much feel as know was expected of her. As much as Nathan wanted no part of this duty, he would have judged her harshly if she'd rejected it herself. And Laila had done well thus far positioning herself as the caretaker Nathan expected her to be: the one who cooked their dinners, folded his laundry, and remembered not only her own mother's birthday but his mother's as well. But Laila had woken with a start that morning; if there *was* something to find, it was she who must find it. And now would be her best chance.

And she *had* found something. Secreted away in an old jewelry box on the top shelf of the bedroom closet was a fragile and crumbling cache of letters from Frederick Lawrence, Laila's grandfather. She'd not yet read through them—she'd wanted to return to the house before Nathan could realize she'd left and then hadn't, it seemed, had a moment to herself since then. But the very fact of their existence was revelatory. And the fact that the church ladies had managed to unearth the pendant, the one possession of her mother's that she'd admired, felt like a small miracle.

Out of the corner of her eye, Laila could see her pious Aunt Jen rooting around her dead sister's things, sorting, *judging*. These women were no longer all she had left, Laila realized. She had family: an exciting and beautiful family. She'd not been prepared for them to swan into the little Michigan suburb in all of their glory: the dark mane of Liberty's hair; Leo's extraordinary green eyes; the flash of red on Nora's expensive shoes; the shock of them standing next to Nathan. How different he seemed to her throughout the course of that long day of the funeral. That morning, she'd woken next to a savior—a man who'd taken her into his own family when hers had disintegrated. Here was a man who would allow her to quit her dreadful job upon having children. And yet, she'd fallen asleep that night next to an anchor. Someone who would pin her to a place she'd never truly belonged. She'd felt it with a rush upon seeing her cousins. She'd never had a sibling, never had the experience of looking into someone's face and seeing a shadow of her own. It could not be a coincidence that they'd shown up now, she decided. That they'd come for her. And she felt it even more deeply that morning at the condo, with its cigarette funk that hung in the air, the stained beige carpet, the fussy, fat church ladies bustling around industriously; New York was coming slowly into view, an unanticipated escape hatch. As she headed for the door, she felt a wild fantasy well up: a desire to break every dish and piece of glassware in the place, to set fire to the curtains and leave them blazing in her wake.

She would never set foot in here again. Her mother was dead. At last.

2

LIBERTY LAWRENCE had a distinct memory of the moment she became aware of what her family was, of the distance between them and others in the world. Like any very young child, she started off thinking that the reality of her daily life was all that existed, the sum total of the universe. She saw the occasional homeless person while walking through the vast reaches of Central Park just beyond their doorstep, but she couldn't be sure that they were real. When she would pass one, with hand outstretched, entreating her mother or her nanny, Esperanza, for money or food, the grown-up clutching her hand would ignore them so entirely that Liberty became convinced that she was the only one who could see them. This worried her a great deal, for if only she could see them, wasn't she the only one who could come to their aid? They obviously needed help. Then one night, Esperanza came to check on her and finally coaxed out of her what was wrong when she was discovered thrashing around in her bedclothes, whimpering.

"Oh, don't worry, pretty girl," she said. Her nanny, a strict but exceedingly gentle woman from Ecuador, was the primary voice of Liberty's childhood. *But did she see them too?* young Liberty asked. She was well aware how fond adults were of telling children that things were "only in their imagination." Esperanza confirmed that she also saw the homeless people, that they were as real as the two of them sitting in this room.

"We have to help!" Liberty cried, getting out of bed that moment to search for her pink rain boots.

"Such a sweet child," Esperanza said, gathering her onto her lap. "But this is not a job for little girls."

But shouldn't they do something? They had plenty of food, a very big house. Her nanny sighed and stroked her head. "You are a good girl, but this is not the way it works."

But why, Liberty wanted to know, why did they not have homes? Why were they out there with no food?

"Oh, *mi niña*. Drugs. Crazy," she said with a pronounced shrug, growing visibly uncomfortable at having to answer these questions. "Okay, *mi amor*, no more worrying. Off to bed."

Liberty was not satisfied but knew that this was the best answer she was likely to get. Esperanza was her main source of wisdom from the adult world; these were not questions Liberty could ask her parents.

But it was not the destitute men and women—so numerous on the streets of her childhood, long before Giuliani came and swept them all away—who cemented Liberty's awareness of her family's place in the world. That defining moment occurred on a Saturday afternoon when she was with her grandfather, Frederick. She must have been five at the time; it was before the twins were born. Her grandmother Helen, whom Liberty had no real memory of, had passed two years earlier from ovarian cancer, leaving Frederick a widower. Her opa, as she called him, came to pick her up at the town house on East Seventy-Third Street, and as they exited the front door, Frederick waved the driver, Geoffrey, away, telling him they would walk. It was a sunny, crisp autumn day, and Liberty was happy to be outside. She normally spent Saturdays with her mother who never wanted to walk anywhere because of her shoes. Liberty asked her what the point of wearing shoes was if not to walk in them, and her mother had laughed as if the girl had said the funniest thing, telling her she'd understand one day, which Liberty doubted very much.

"Where are we going, Opa?" Liberty had asked her grandfather that day.

"To get the best sandwich you'll ever have in your life!"

Well, that was exciting; she liked sandwiches.

"Like the ones Mummy and I have with tea?" The tiny cucumber ones were her favorite.

"Oh, kiddo, no," he said, laughing. Frederick was wiry and strong, dapper in his suits, always suits. He would never seem old to Liberty, even when he reached his nineties. His laugh could fill a room; his steely gaze could make grown men unravel. He'd been harsh as a father, unforgiving and exacting, but he was indulgent as a grandfather. "Like a hundred of those stacked on top of each other! I'm taking you to the Second Avenue Deli."

They took the 6 train down to the East Village, where the famous kosher deli was. Liberty would remember many things about that day: the sandwiches with their menacing names like Instant Heart Attack—which her opa explained would not *literally* give you a heart attack—the way they'd laughed and laughed as Liberty tried to get her tiny mouth around the massive pastrami he'd ordered her. But she would remember the subway ride most vividly of all.

She recalled descending into the mouth of the subway, hearing the roaring trains and the cacophony of voices, clutching her opa's hand fiercely, wide-eyed and delighted, knowing instinctively that this was an addition to the long list of adventures with Opa that would have horrified her parents, alongside a ride on the Coney Island Cyclone and a street fair in Harlem. But the subway! This was unprecedented. Everywhere she looked there were people darting from one place to another, there were buskers playing overturned buckets like drums, and more people of different races than she had seen during the rest of her short life.

It was there, sitting on the bench of the train with her grandfather, that she realized—watching families scolding and joking with and cuddling children her age and younger in ways that seemed exciting and entirely alien to her—that there was another world out there that she was not a part of, an enormous universe of which her family occupied one very narrow slice in their town house on the quiet, tree-lined street. She thought of the immaculate mothers of her schoolmates, all thin, like facsimiles of each other. She thought of the horseback lessons, the drivers, the school uniforms—all ordinary parts of her life and those of her peers, but not of so many other children.

For the rest of her girlhood, Liberty kept a keen eye on this other world, and once aware, she saw it everywhere. She knew that in addition to her aunt Birdie, her father had a brother, but he and his wife had disappeared, gone off to this other world perhaps. According to her mother, Liberty had met them a few times, but she couldn't recall much about them. Once, she overheard her parents talking about the fact that her aunt was pregnant, just like her own mother was at the time, with the twins.

"Why can't we visit them?" Liberty had asked. So long an only child, she was desperate for company. Her father looked at Petra in a way he often did when exasperated by his daughter; the child was her domain, why was she not handling her?

"It's grown-up stuff, honey," Ben said.

"Surely Frederick will relent now that there is a little one on the way."

He'd given Petra a stern look. The estrangement was fresh

then; only six months had gone by. No one, including Ben, imagined that it might become permanent.

"Opa doesn't like your brother?" Liberty wasn't about to let the moment pass without getting at least some information.

Her father, a tall, broad-shouldered man—not handsome but rather imposing, even dashing, like his father but larger, a natural consequence of being born and raised in the United States rather than wartime Germany—leaned down and cupped Liberty's chin affectionately.

"It's complicated, kiddo."

"But why can't we see them?"

At this, her father had stiffened and looked down at his watch. "I don't have time for this," he said with a huff. And with that, he was out the door. There were a great many things her father didn't have time for. Liberty's interactions with him were always fleeting. He seemed never to have the patience for anything beyond a kiss on her forehead and perhaps a few minutes of quotidian chitchat about what she was learning in school. Encouragingly, he did seem to enjoy showing her off to colleagues when the opportunity arose, presenting her as though she were living proof of . . . something.

In this moment, Liberty looked to her mother for further explanation. Petra turned in her chair to face her daughter, shifting heavily under the enormously pregnant belly that engulfed her tall but slender frame.

"Your opa," she began, appearing to choose her words extremely carefully even without her husband's watchful gaze, "he worked very hard to give his family a good life. Sometimes I think I understand this part better than your father."

"Because of growing up in Russia?"

Petra smiled. On the infrequent occasions when Liberty misbehaved or complained, her mother would admonish her with tales of growing up in Communist Russia. She'd come from a big family, and there was never enough to go around: not enough food or money or clothes, least of all patience from her parents. It had sealed in Petra a cold, hard ambition, which had led her here.

"Yes, my darling, that is part of it. He wanted his sons to be just like him. He was disappointed when your uncle didn't want the life he'd worked so hard for."

"Why didn't he want it?"

One of the chief tenets of Liberty's childhood was that *everyone* wanted what they had, and that they must always be grateful for it. *Not* wanting to be a Lawrence was a new concept entirely.

"I don't know. But that's enough questions for now. I need to rest."

That was the last Liberty heard of her other family until many years later, when she was seventeen and her uncle Gregory died. It was a time of closed doors and hushed phone calls, but no détente, no opening of hearts. As for Gregory's wife, Laila's mother, Liberty would never know her beyond those unremembered childhood meetings. Liberty had always been plagued by the sense that her immense privilege meant that she owed some substantial debt. But *what* exactly she owed, and to whom, was never clear.

So when Laila called her one day, not quite two years after her mother was laid to rest, to tell her that the fragile life she'd pulled together in the wake of the tragedy had fallen apart, Liberty was moved. Her cousin, whose life had diverged from her own by a twist of fate, and who had endured so much, needed her. It was an opportunity to set right some misalignment in the universe. Liberty would do whatever she needed to help her.

After all, Laila was a Lawrence. And wasn't keeping family close what mattered most of all?

3

"DO YOU think that this room will do?" Nora asked Liberty. She hung the moon on her sister's opinion, always had. She'd spent hours the day before wandering the glittering aisles of ABC Carpet & Home, and now the guest bedroom looked like something between a pricey hotel and a high-end French brothel, which rather encapsulated Nora's style. A stark contrast with that of her twin brother, Leo, who lived in the adjoining penthouse; his decor was so sleek and modern, you were always in danger of sliding off one piece of furniture and impaling yourself on the next.

"I think she'll love it," Liberty said encouragingly. Though who knew what Laila would love? None of them had spent very much time with her. The few times that she'd visited in the two years since they'd met her, she seemed so roundly dazzled by everything she laid eyes on that all they'd seen of her personality was blissful and overwhelmed. It had thrilled Nora, made her feel like New York was hers to share with her cousin, whom she imagined as having been, until that moment, deprived of all luxuries and excitement. Laila always wanted to know more, more, more about New York and what growing up there had been like. And now she was on her way to join them.

Nora was intent on giving her cousin—who had sensibly

27

ended her marriage with that dentist—the perfect welcome. She'd thought through every detail—buying brand-new guest towels and sheets (though those she already owned were barely used), even a candy-pink silk robe with Laila's name embroidered on it, which she hung on the hook in the bathroom, a delightful little surprise for her. She filled the bathroom with scented candles and Kérastase hair products. The vases in the bedroom she filled with pink roses (her personal favorite) and white dahlias. It was always good for Nora to have a project, something to drive her energies into, lest they start to turn on her.

Nora was a true New York hothouse flower who had not, at twenty-five, managed to blossom into any ambition beyond socializing and doing some disjointed charity work—this week for the Lymphoma Society, next week for rescue dogs—she was not organized enough to take one of the board positions that would lend the event-hopping an air of legitimacy.

Laila had become of particular fascination to her, since the two were the same age and had lived what seemed to be completely opposite lives. Her cousin was an orphan and now a divorcée. The combination nearly blew Nora's mind and made Laila seem like an exotic species. People in New York, at least the people Nora knew, did not marry in their early twenties, and if they did, they did not marry dentists. It was true that a girl she knew from Spence had eloped with a pop star she'd known for two weeks (the marriage hadn't lasted much longer), but that wasn't the same thing at all. Though of course Laila's marriage had been practically an elopement—and also brief, less than two years from start to finish.

Nora found herself captivated by her cousin's looks too; Laila was beautiful in a way that was unlike what Nora was used to comparing herself to in Manhattan: she had a big smile and thick red hair, and was as petite and curvy as a forties pinup girl. Nora felt the sickening pull that she always did around the beautiful: the vain hope that if she could only get close enough, she might absorb some of what they had for herself. She was the only sibling who did not take after her mother—and could never wrap her head around the idea that the beauty she felt was her due had been denied her. It seemed impossible that this thing she wanted couldn't be bought, cultivated, or somehow procured for her. After a nose job, a boob job, and several rounds of liposuction, she had acquired a Barbie doll sort of sex appeal; men now responded to her in a Pavlovian way, yet she was doomed to always be not only the less pretty sister but the less pretty twin, outshone by her brother with his cherubic lips, his soft wavy hair, and his mother's green eyes, bordered by impossibly thick lashes. Laila also had green eyes, from her own mother's side. To Nora, this seemed fated, a sign that Laila was meant to be more of a sister than a cousin.

"Will she want to go out tomorrow night, do you think? I don't want to make plans unless she wants to come along." Nora sat on the bed, exhausted from her domestic efforts.

"I don't know, honey," Liberty said, sitting beside her. "Why don't you just ask her when she gets here? She might want to relax. She's starting at the agency on Monday."

"Right. Oh, I just want her to be happy here! She's been through so much." In Nora's mind, Laila's string of tragedies had a romantic sheen; they made her compelling and mysterious. And perhaps it was natural for someone so unused to struggle to fetishize it.

It had occurred to all three siblings that whatever share of bad luck the universe had meant for the Lawrence family had landed squarely on Laila. Not only had she now lost both of her parents, there was nothing in the way of inheritance. There was no money left, period, Laila had at last confessed to Liberty; Betsy had not even taken out a life insurance policy. Liberty had relayed this to her siblings—thinking they ought to know, lest they drag Laila somewhere expensive and leave her with her half of the check—and it made Nora swoon. The drama of it: Orphaned! Impoverished! It all seemed inexplicably, poignantly cruel.

"She's had a hard few years," Liberty agreed.

"And can you imagine being *divorced*? I don't know anyone our age who is even married."

"I think she was still grieving when they got married," said Liberty, absentmindedly fluffing a pillow. "People are vulnerable when they've just been through a trauma." Nora knew that Liberty thought the less of Nathan for asking Laila to marry him when he had. She imagined that he'd sensed an opening in the death of Laila's mother, a chance to lock in the local dream girl who might otherwise say no. No one was surprised that it hadn't worked out.

"Should we have gone to meet her at the airport instead of sending a car? I don't want her to get lost." Nora was back on her feet now, pacing.

"Relax," Liberty said, wrapping her arm around her sister, enveloping her like a mother bird. "She'll be fine. She's been to New York before. And she can call us if she gets lost. But I think that she'll find her way."

4

LAILA SETTLED into her seat in the second row of the plane, the wide leather chair dwarfing her petite frame. She pushed her sunglasses—Yves Saint Laurent, classic tortoiseshell, purchased on her last visit to New York—up onto her head, only to reconsider and pull them back over her eyes. She didn't want to invite conversation from her seatmate, nor did she want to betray her nervousness. She'd flown infrequently, and the takeoff always made her panic. Laila had been in first class once before: en route to her honeymoon in Hawaii. Her now ex-husband— ex-husband!—wanted to make up for the hurried nature of their wedding and had sprung for first-class tickets and a week at the Grand Wailea on Maui. She'd drunk three mai tais, one after the other, as the gravity of her mistake in marrying Nathan had sunk in over the many hours of connecting flights from Detroit to the island. The effects of her mother's death, and the insult of discovering that she was left with exactly nothing financially, had not even begun to evaporate. For many reasons, the loss of her mother did not feel exactly tragic, but it had been a shock. Laila, who'd forever been locked in Betsy's orbit, felt like an astronaut who'd come untethered from her vessel, careening into space looking for anything to ground her. And all of her mother's warnings had faded from her memory until this very moment: *Do not marry the wrong man, Laila; do not get pregnant by the wrong man. These will be the only decisions in your life that will matter in the end.*

Laila felt a familiar twinge of bitterness thinking of her late father, for his decisions had led to all of it, beginning with his choice to attend the University of Michigan, to distance himself from Frederick, Laila's grandfather. Gregory had loved the Midwest—he'd made his home there after only a brief postcollege stint back in New York—and this was how Laila had ended up in the wrong life. Whatever traits Gregory might've inherited from his father, business acumen wasn't among them. He'd set out to prove he could be a success without his father's help and had ended up demonstrating just the opposite. This all became painfully clear as various debts and disasters had revealed themselves following his untimely death.

And what of the secrets her mother's death had brought to light? The bundle of letters Laila had found were actually a collection of little notes, cards that had accompanied gifts or flowers, dashed off missives on stationery from the Carlyle Hotel. These mementos that Betsy had kept for all of these years—softened from being taken out and read time and again—were, at first, incomprehensible to Laila. *Thanks for a lovely evening, Beautiful B! xo Frederick*; *Make yourself comfortable and meet me in our booth at 7pm.* Several of the notes included dates, and all were from the late eighties, during the two years Betsy and Gregory had lived in New York. The only conclusion Laila could come to was that her mother and grandfather had had an affair—a possibility that shocked and thrilled her—but the letters offered no context, no details. In an instant, her memory of her mother shifted. She'd been not a mere bystander in this family feud but its very impetus.

But why had her mother remained quiet about it all of these years? Why never mention her cousins? Laila might have not met any of them if Liberty hadn't shown up in Grosse Pointe that day. Betsy had always seemed to harbor bitterness for these mysterious rich relations, who had not only cut her husband off but refused to come to her aid in the wake of his death. Now, knowing she'd had this trump card all along, it made even less sense to Laila.

Laila's last two years—the death of her mother, the disastrous marriage, the insipid job in Nathan's dental office that left her with an unmistakable chemical scent in her hair, the ten pounds gained under the influence of coworkers who grew fat beneath formless scrubs and brought an endless parade of doughnuts, cookies, and dessert bars to the office—it was all meant to break her down so that she might begin again. Her cousins' visit, the discovery of the letters, hadn't changed her life's direction right away. At first, the cousins returned to New York, and Laila's life went on as it would otherwise have. But not indefinitely. Laila was like a ship that had been steered just a few degrees off course; it would take some time for anyone to notice, but in the end, she would land very far from her original destination. The ugly truth that had her parents not died young, she wouldn't be on her way to New York, was one she could live with. And she would never have discovered that cache of letters. It horrified her still, the memory of going through her mother's abandoned earthly belongings. A sudden death, though preferable in many ways to a drawn-out one, leaves no chance to hide anything.

"Would you like a glass of champagne, miss?" Laila looked up. Even the flight attendants were prettier in first class. A harbinger that she would be surrounded by beauty from now on, she thought.

"Oh, I shouldn't," Laila said in a tone indicating that yes, in fact, she would. The attendant smiled at her and inched the bottle suggestively forward. "Oh, well, just one," Laila said. Free-flowing champagne. The life of her cousins, she imagined. Hers now too.

Laila had been to New York twice in the two years since she'd met her cousins. Nathan had been worried about her going alone— he'd been right to worry, just not for the reasons he imagined—but Laila had convinced him she should, she wanted to bond with her family. *They were all she had left*, she would remind him, and that would do the trick. And though this wasn't strictly true—there were the dreadful aunties, their multitudinous and criminally dull offspring—Laila indeed felt she'd been robbed of knowing this other side of her family. How might have her childhood world been expanded by having had them in her life? She'd longed for an older sister growing up, and Liberty seemed every bit the living version of those dreams. The world of the Lawrences dazzled her: Liberty with her sophisticated job and cool apartment, and the twins! They lived in a *penthouse* (actually, two connected penthouses) and were able to breeze into any nightclub in town, it seemed. Since meeting them, Laila had developed a voracious habit of consuming Manhattan gossip blogs as well as *Vogue*, *Vanity Fair*, and the *New York Post*'s infamous Page Six. When she visited her cousins, it seemed to her she had landed on the very pages she'd made a study of.

A year earlier, Laila had begun emerging from the fog that had followed her mother's death and her hasty marriage, and she'd felt her life tugging at the seams, needing to come apart. By then, she was talking to, or at least texting with, Liberty and Nora nearly every day.

"I'm asking Nathan for a divorce," she'd told Nora one afternoon, sequestered in the guest bedroom in the attic, the only place in the house Laila felt she could go to be remotely alone.

"Good!" came the reply. "Yay! Now you can move to New York! Oh my God, we'll have so much fun! You can live in the penthouse with us." Nora had needed no explanation other than Laila's wish to no longer be married, so she spared her the trumped-up story of Nathan's affair with one of the other hygienists that she'd recounted to Liberty. This tale, she knew, would likely preclude further questions.

Ultimately, the divorce wasn't big news to anyone, as Laila had been considering it in one way or another since the day she'd married Nathan. Despite the blurry haze that spread over her in the weeks following her mother's funeral, she remembered feeling a persistent wrongness on the day of the marriage: a throbbing *no, no, no* that she ignored as she put on her white shift dress from J.Crew. A coworker she wasn't even terribly close to—but who Nathan inexplicably thought was one of her best friends—pinned baby's breath in her hair. (For good measure, she later positioned this same coworker as the harlot in her fabricated cheating drama.) She ignored the *no* as she came downstairs to the small crowd of twenty friends gathered in Nathan's—now their—backyard. Not a face among them that Laila cared for. She ignored it, for what else was there to do but marry Nathan? She knew everyone else in Grosse Pointe and there was no one better. She had no money, no savings, and where else would she find someone? Detroit? No. The best you could hope for was to try to land one of the professional athletes: to be one of those desperate girls on the hunt for Lions, Tigers, and Red Wings—tits spilling out of the neckline of a tight jersey, blond extensions piled on. *Go team!* No.

At first, her cousins had been like an apparition; something she couldn't wrap her fingers around, with the momentum of the marriage already carrying her along. But then New York had emerged on the horizon, solid and real and beckoning. And now she was on her way.

5

WHEN LAILA arrived at last at the doorway of the twins' Tribeca building, her cheeks were flushed from the mid-September heat: she'd worn a sweet, lilac-colored jersey dress that at least would not have become too rumpled by the journey. The doorman knew her on sight, a fact that thrilled her.

"Welcome, Ms. Lawrence!" he said, a brilliant smile beaming from beneath his dark mustache. He swooped in and relieved Laila of her suitcase and the small shabby duffle bag that had served as her carry-on. He looked cool and crisp in his uniform despite the humidity of the day.

"It's so good to see you!" Nora said, throwing her arms around her cousin as she came through their door. She seemed beside herself with excitement. Liberty thanked the doorman, Louis, as they swept her inside. Laila hugged Liberty.

"Oh no," Laila said, realizing that Louis had left. "Should I have tipped him?"

Nora let out a delighted little laugh. "Silly goose! But then, why would you know the first thing about doormen? You're too adorable! Are the rest of your things being shipped?" Nora asked, gazing upon Laila's suitcase and duffle.

"I'm . . . traveling light. This is all I brought."

When Laila had packed for her move to New York, she'd been

ruthless. Living with her mother, then, briefly, roommates, then Nathan (with whom she had lived right up until the move), she'd never had much of anything in the way of furniture or household items. And her clothes! As she went through them they seemed all wrong. She'd long had a fondness for tight-fitting dresses and tops from Bebe and Forever 21. But after all her months of poring over *Vogue* and dreaming of her New York life, she'd wanted to burn these clothes. She'd come to feel that some parallel version of herself was already living in Manhattan, wearing chic dresses with a polished haircut and perhaps taking a town car back and forth to some glossy media job, the vague variety of which characters in movies always seemed to have. Now Laila had only to catch up to her phantom self. And clothes from the Twelve Oaks Mall were *not* going to help. She'd brought only the basics. She'd also brought virtually no mementos—save the letters and the pendant—for what about her former life was worth remembering?

"What a good idea! A fresh start," Nora chirped. "We'll go to Bergdorf's tomorrow and start building your wardrobe from scratch. Oh, this will be so much fun!"

◦❦◦

The next day they sat drinking champagne in a decadent and quiet section of Bergdorf's that was unlike anything Laila had ever seen before. Everything about the interior of the store whispered luxury: from the calming neutral tones and the soft lighting to the plush seating stationed everywhere for women shopping in towering heels to sit and rest while an attendant brought them all the things they never knew they needed.

"I can't wait to see Aunt Petra and Uncle Ben," Laila said. They were meeting them in the café in an hour. She'd met Petra during her previous visits, and while Ben had always promised to come, he'd been pulled away by mysterious and pressing work matters each time. Though Laila was assured that this happened regularly, she wondered if he wasn't so keen to reconnect with her. She suspected that he knew about what had happened between Betsy and Frederick: that he had chosen sides and that had led to the rift. It seemed likely that Petra also knew, but perhaps the uncomfortable history Laila represented was a bit less personal; she could only speculate. "When will I get to meet grandfather?"

Nora giggled. "Opa?"

She inexplicably seemed to think everything that came out of Laila's mouth was adorable. Laila knew she must seem gauche against the backdrop of Nora's New York where everyone she knew was coated with a lifetime's worth of polish. She felt Nora regarding her as a *Pygmalion*-like project, which she did not object to. It was better to be what people needed you to be, especially when it cost you nothing. And in truth, she wanted to be made new.

"He's coming back from Europe next week. I know he is excited to see you." Laila suspected that last part was a fib, but then, it seemed clear that the siblings did not know the history, that Laila's shameful parents had successfully removed themselves from the equation.

"What is he like? Opa, I mean," Laila asked. The word felt strange on her tongue, stranger still because this person—her own grandfather—was unknown to her. A hazy image of him was materializing in her mind—not of the old man pictured in the framed photos in the twins' penthouses, photos conspicuously placed so that the patriarch was certain not to miss them on his occasional visits—but of a younger, more dashing Frederick. The man who had, evidently, seduced her mother with stolen nights at the Carlyle Hotel.

Nora scrunched her face as though she'd tasted something sour. "He's very serious. Harsh with Daddy. The only one he approves of is Liberty. He *adores* her. He thinks Leo should fall in line to run the business one day."

"He doesn't like that Leo's a writer?"

"He doesn't find it masculine. I mean I guess if Leo was Hemingway, writing about hunting and bullfights, but he thinks Leo's column is silly. I don't; I think Leo is the most brilliant person in the world." Nora seemed dazzled by her brother and, truthfully, a little in love with him.

"It's easier for me and Liberty. We're women; he doesn't expect as much. He's old school: for women, being beautiful is enough. Of course, I'm a disappointment on that front," Nora said flatly.

"Nora," Laila scolded. "Stop it! You're gorgeous." If such traits were awarded based on effort, Laila thought, she would be.

"And of course Liberty is so beautiful *and* smart," Nora continued, ignoring Laila's objection. "I know he wishes she'd get married; he's obsessed with the idea of meeting his greatgrandchildren."

"What about you?"

"Well, I'm young still, but yes, I suppose that's one way I could win him over. Though if I did it out of wedlock, he'd disown me!"

So the old man was a hypocrite too. For Laila, her grandfather was key to putting her life back on the course it was always meant for: he was the originator of the fortune she was meant to benefit from, which she'd been kept from. And he, for many reasons, owed her.

"What's he doing in Europe?" Laila asked.

"Oh, no one knows," Nora said, distracted, her eyes locking on the handsome shoe salesman who was making his way toward them carrying a tower of boxes as colorful and decadent as layers of a cake. "He left suddenly, but that's not unlike him. He travels all the time."

Laila and Nora had already done an impressive amount of shopping that morning. Nora had gleefully pooh-poohed most of what Laila had deemed acceptable from her Michigan wardrobe. "It's not that these clothes are *bad* or anything, but you're in New York now! You're one of us." Laila luxuriated in being treated like her cousin's living doll. Why not be kept? Why not be cared for?

"We're about the same size!" Nora exclaimed. "So you can share my clothes too!"

At Bergdorf's, they were like children playing dress up, the indulgent shop assistant looking on as though she were a nanny. The thousand-dollar-plus price tags flashed before Laila's eyes as she tried on brands she'd coveted in *Vogue* and observed hanging in Nora's closet: Céline, Hervé Léger, Derek Lam, Narciso Rodriguez. Nora made all the decisions and several times vetoed dresses Laila loved, leaving her to wonder what her error in liking them had been. When Nora enumerated to the shop assistant which items they would take, Laila felt a creeping panic. Would she be presented with a bill? Asked for a credit card? She had no concept of how much it had all added up to, only that it had been a lot.

Fortunately, no bill appeared and the clothes were sent directly to Nora's apartment. Laila was relieved on both accounts, as she did not want to see her aunt and uncle while lugging bags with thousands of dollars' worth of clothes she did not pay for. She didn't want to look like a freeloader. Besides, she was a part of this family, not a barnacle clinging to it.

Laila's eyes widened as she followed her cousin into the restaurant on the seventh floor: the opulent setting was bordered by windows that opened up on sweeping views of Central Park. She had never seen women who looked so polished and pristine; she was overcome by their shiny hair, their crisp outfits; the glittering jewels of the older women in brocade Chanel jackets, the massive diamond engagement rings on the hands of the younger ones. There was the occasional tourist in the crowd, and they were glaringly obvious—because of their clothes, certainly, but also their faces: hyperaware, full of wonder. Laila realized she must be mindful of what her expressions gave away.

The girls were seated, and ten minutes later, as they were perusing the menu for tea service, Nora's mother, Petra, arrived. Laila watched her entrance. Petra was almost sixty but was still so striking that even the grandes dames lunching in the corner—otherwise nearly pickled in ennui—stopped to look at her as she made her way to the table. She wore her dark hair long, past her shoulders just as she'd done in her heyday; she was still slim and still dressed to show off her legendary long legs. Her face was, it must be said, a little unnaturally tight, but this could only be seen close-up. Between her undoubtedly good genes, a lifetime of the best self-care, and expert styling, she simply appeared to be the eternal Petra Lawrence, as unchanging as a well-preserved and constantly polished diamond.

"Hello, darlings," she said, leaning over to kiss first her daughter and then Laila.

"Where's Dad?" Nora asked.

"Couldn't make it, my love. Work." Petra was long an American but had retained some typically Russian tendencies, stoicism in particular. Laila wondered if this conservation of emotion was one of the secrets to her appearance. Her aunt's graceful aging

41

couldn't be further from the rapid decline of Laila's own mother. Of course, Betsy hadn't been a supermodel to begin with, but she had been gorgeous when she was young. Laila did not remember a version of her mother as a slim woman, but she knew from pictures that had once been the case. She had steadily put on weight after her husband's death, most of which had concentrated itself in her lower half. One could be under the illusion that she was normal-size if you saw her sitting behind a table, but once she was standing, lumbering heavily across a room, her gait as though she were dragging shackles, the damage was revealed. Her face maintained a certain buried loveliness until the day she died, shimmering like a memory, as though obscured below the surface of a swift-moving river. Laila wondered if the weight had functioned as a protective carapace to ward off the attentions of men—even though she was always vowing to lose it, was always messing around with the idea of some fad diet or another. Laila was grateful her mother had remained single; having to spend her teenage years around various boyfriends and perhaps even a step-father seemed a fate likely worse than coming of age with only her mother for company. Men had reacted to Laila everywhere she'd gone from the time she was thirteen. Why would a stranger her mother brought home have been different?

"Laila, my dear, are you enjoying your first day in New York?" Petra asked. Laila shifted in her seat, finding it difficult not to stare at her; those green eyes—which both Leo and Liberty had inherited—were mesmerizing.

"It's like a dream," she said. "I'm so excited to be here."

"We're happy to have you. To have all the family in one place, it's a blessing."

Nora had given Laila the rundown on Petra's background,

a story so well-worn it had the cadence of a fairy tale. She'd left her own family at sixteen—she'd married a Mormon missionary who'd visited her appallingly poor town in the Siberian peninsula. She'd lied about her age and come back with him to Salt Lake City, where she was stopped by a local talent agent within weeks of landing. It was not long before she'd left her husband and moved to New York. The missionary remarried and was now a father of ten. Petra talked about him with kindness, for the truth remained that he had solved her horrible bad luck of being born in the wrong place. She had sent money to her parents early in her career, but they had died before she could bring them to the US.

So Petra was an orphan too. That word: so heavy, so loaded. Laila saw that this could work for her; seen in a certain light, it could be exotic. And more important, it meant that she had something in common with her otherworldly aunt, something that could unite them. They'd ordered the champagne tea, an extravagant setup that would take the place of lunch—but which neither Nora nor Petra would do anything more than pick at. Laila, ravenous, had to restrain herself from falling upon the trays of tiny, buttery sandwiches the moment they were placed on the table. She knew that her mother's figure—which had looked just like hers at her age—lay in wait to emerge and spoil all her chances.

"Mother, I meant to tell you. I got an invitation to the Operation Smile benefit next week," Nora said excitedly.

"That's marvelous," Petra said. "From Lydia?"

"Yes! Well, her assistant, but still! But I sent her an e-mail personally with my RSVP telling her how passionate I am about the cause. Can you imagine these poor babies with the cleft palates? I just try to put myself in that position. I mean, really! Dating is hard enough as it is."

"Indeed," Petra said. "Well, I'm sure she appreciates your enthusiasm. By the way, you're looking lovely, my darling."

A look of surprise passed over Nora's face. Laila suspected Petra was not one to offer false compliments, and nor did it seem she doled them out frequently.

"Thank you, Mother. I've been working out with Antoine three times a week; I think it's really helping," Nora said, a hint of color rising in her cheeks. *Helping*, Laila thought, as though Nora's body were a problem to be solved. Antoine, she knew from reading his name in interviews, was Petra's longtime personal trainer. He had several bestselling books and a series of DVDs.

"Well," Petra continued on brusquely, "twenty-five is a perfect age. You are as lovely as you will ever be, still young but no puppy fat," she said, letting her fingers skitter over her own sharp cheekbones. Laila noticed that other diners in the restaurant were surreptitiously sneaking looks at their table. She knew it was because of Petra, but she felt a proximate thrill. A memory passed over her of being included for a brief moment with the popular girls in high school, of the feeling of sitting at their table in the cafeteria. But of course, it had not lasted. Initially, they'd recruited her because she was beautiful, but then when her appeal to the boys became inconvenient, they'd turned on her—which was all too easy to do given her embarrassing mother and their diminished circumstances. Suddenly, she'd become a slut. *Girls will always do that*, her mother had reminded her. *Women are inherently jealous creatures.*

"I am taking you to see Oxana."

"Mother!" Nora's face had fallen, as though someone had played a nasty trick on her.

"Who is Oxana?" Laila asked.

"A *matchmaker*," Nora said.

"Don't take that tone," Petra said. "You girls today think you have all the time in the world. But you *don't*; all men want a twenty-five-year-old, and that, right now, is what you are. Your options won't get better from here."

"Mother, things are different now; it's not like it was when you were our age," Nora rolled her eyes like a pouting teenager.

"It is. Everyone pretending it isn't changes nothing."

"You never give Liberty a hard time." Nora's posture had curled into itself slightly.

"You don't know what I discuss with your sister," Petra said curtly. Laila had sensed some tension between Liberty and her mother but did not yet know its source. "I was already married to your father by your age," Petra continued.

"But that was fate! You didn't meet Daddy through a matchmaker."

"But you can't always leave things to fate. And besides which, I was already looking. The career of a model barely lasts to twenty-five. Just meet with her; what could it hurt? Oxana is the best."

"You like her because she's Russian. You all stick together," Nora said.

"Russians are more sensible about marriage than Americans. None of these delusions that feminism has fixed everything—poof! All better."

"I didn't realize that matchmakers still existed," Laila said gingerly. She was unsure if she was meant to be only a witness to the conversation or a participant, but she was intrigued. Truthfully, she admired Petra's pragmatism.

"Welcome to New York," Nora said. "How do you think all those gross old men find their hot young wives?"

Now it was Petra's turn to roll her eyes. "In a few years, you're going to want her help, but then it will be too late. Look at your poor aunt Birdie."

Nora seemed to consider this for a moment and shuddered. "Oh, just wait until you meet her!" she said, glancing at Laila.

Laila looked bewildered. She had no idea who they were talking about.

Nora and Petra turned to look at her. "Oh, you poor thing, you don't even know about Birdie? She's our aunt, our dads' older sister."

Laila smiled blankly. How many other relatives were there?

"She lives upstate, by our house there. She's, like . . . completely batshit."

"Don't be disrespectful," Petra said.

"I'm sorry, Mother. Birdie is *eccentric.* Anyway, she's definitely single. In, like, a permanent capacity."

Nora stared into her teacup for a long moment, as though considering a similar fate for herself.

"Okay, Mother, I'll meet with Oxana."

"Good, we'll go when we've finished here." Petra patted her lips delicately with the corner of her napkin.

"You want to go *now*?"

"I told you, I made an appointment."

Nora closed her eyes and took a deep breath, as though steeling herself.

"Laila, you have your keys?"

Laila nodded, realizing only now that the excursion wouldn't include her. Not that she necessarily wanted to visit a matchmaker; she just wasn't sure what she'd do with her afternoon. She'd been in New York barely a day and had not been left to her own devices even for a moment.

She thought first to take herself out for a glass of wine and, perhaps, something to eat. She was still hungry, having been unwilling to scarf down the tea service that her aunt and cousin had barely touched. There were innumerable cafés on the block next to the twins' building, and on this sunny September Sunday, all were packed. As she walked down the bustling sidewalks, Laila felt the overwhelm of being on a street with so many people, a sensation she was not nearly accustomed to. Looking at the groups of girls her age—sculpted bare shoulders, hair piled on top of their heads in intentionally unruly topknots—she felt a pang of sudden loneliness. She gathered her courage and approached the elegant, rail-thin man at the host stand of a trendy-looking café who looked dressed for boating in his salmon shorts and light-blue Top-Siders.

"Hi there," she said, stepping forth.

"How many?" he said, not even looking up at her. In the face of his indifference, she lost her nerve. "Um, oh, just . . . two. I'm waiting for my friend."

"It'll be at least forty-five minutes, and we can't seat you until everyone in your party has arrived. Name?"

She gave him Nora's name and then slunk away back to the penthouse.

~§~

Upstairs, Laila was alone in the apartment for the first time. Nora and Leo's penthouses were separate but connected by a hidden door behind a pivoting bookcase. On Nora's side it was filled with candy-colored hardcovers: *The Shopaholic*, *The Devil Wears Prada*, *Bergdorf Blondes* (of course). Leo's side was serious, leather bound, exclusively male: Hemingway, Steinbeck, Fitzgerald. The apartments were mirror images of each other, and they shared a patio that included a Jacuzzi. Laila peeked her head through the connecting door and called Leo's name; when there was no answer she pushed the bookcase back into place and wandered into Nora's kitchen, which was decorated to look like it belonged in a French country house: the cabinets were pale blue with filigreed edges, a small chandelier hung over the center island, and fresh flowers were placed in a vase atop the pristine white marble of the countertop. Laila was still a little buzzed from the champagne they'd had at tea—and on an empty stomach. She looked in the fridge, but it was bare, other than several bottles of wine and champagne that were chilling there. After a few more moments of scrounging, Laila unearthed a box of organic granola and unceremoniously crammed a few handfuls in her mouth. Her stomach settled, and she pulled a bottle of champagne from the fridge. She had come upon an open case of Veuve Clicquot in the cabinet during her search for food, so she knew she could easily replace it. She popped the cork—what a satisfying sound it was!—and poured herself a glass. "To my new life!" she said aloud, holding her glass in the air.

To Laila's pleasant surprise, the packages from Bergdorf's had been delivered while they'd been at tea. She turned on the built-in stereo that piped music throughout the apartment, and a Taylor Swift song came on. Nora's taste in music was naturally sweet, girly, adolescent. Swifty. It was not Laila's style, but she could get on board for a moment. She needed something to shake off her encounter with the restaurant host, which had left a lingering film of mortification. Laila made her way to Nora's slightly nauseating bedroom. Laila thought the enormous, gilt-edged, pink damask bed must terrify any man who dared enter (if any, in fact, did;

Laila wasn't sure). There was a massive mirror—also gilt-edged—that took up most of one wall. Laila went back to the kitchen to retrieve the bottle of champagne, having quickly finished her first glass. She fetched the Bergdorf's packages and did a little fashion show for herself, trying on her new rag & bone jeans, her Hervé Léger dress. She admired herself in the skintight dress—her perky breasts and taut stomach; not her mother. Not yet. Not ever. Soon she'd gone through the clothes they'd bought her and, after a moment's hesitation, pulled Nora's new clothes out of the shiny lavender bags. She continued to analyze herself as she drank more champagne and flew through Nora's new purchases. What lives could be lived in these dresses? What trouble could ever befall someone in these delicate Italian sandals with their slender, flared heels and their soles of buttery suede—it was footwear that seemed to promise one would never have to run after, or away from, anything while wearing them.

Laila thought she could stand to lose a little weight—the women here were like whippets —but she knew she was beautiful. It was really the one thing she could be certain of: her beauty. And until now, she'd been wasting it. Well, there was no real use for it in Michigan, was there? People there considered a reasonably attractive dentist a catch.

When she was finished trying on all the new clothes, she ventured into Nora's closet, which was nearly the size of the guest bedroom Laila was staying in. It had tall, built-in shelves that showcased an impressive array of shoes and handbags under soft lighting. There were racks and racks of designer dresses, piles of expensive denim, and buttery cashmere sweaters, which Laila ran her fingers over. She had reached Shangri-la, and she intended to stay. Nora wouldn't be home anytime soon, and she *had* said that because they were the same size, they could share everything. Laila began plucking dresses from their hangers and trying them on. Nora's style could be charitably described as eclectic, but in truth, it was more that she had lots of money and a short attention span, which resulted in an enviable but inconsistent wardrobe.

As Laila continued to make her way through the bottle, memories of her recently abandoned life began to swirl up and take hold. She and Nathan had lived in a four-bedroom house on a quiet leafy street in Grosse Pointe. Their furniture had mostly been from Crate & Barrel, and every room but the kitchen had been carpeted. She remembered the monotony of coming home each night after a day of staring into the lurid caverns of other people's mouths, of inevitably getting some bodily fluids on her clothes, or worse, her skin. Of seeing Nathan going back and forth all day like a king in his castle among the giggling hygienists and that slutty receptionist he'd hired. Then at home, there he was again, always cracking a beer and watching "the game," whatever the game was: football in the fall and winter; hockey and basketball in the spring; baseball in the summer; "the game" was a nebulous but unending commitment.

When she'd left Nathan, Laila had lost what few friends she had in Grosse Pointe, as they'd of course sided with him. In their eyes, she was simply screwing over a good man. She was alone and hurtling toward a new future that would have nothing at all to do with her past. She was home.

6

"WELL," LEO said as Nora stifled a giggle, "darling sister, your closet appears to have exploded and knocked out our cousin in the blast."

The two of them gazed upon the sleeping figure of Laila, curled up on the pale pink velvet chaise longue, an empty bottle of Veuve Clicquot turned on its side on the floor beside her. Dresses were draped on the back of the chair and the center island, shoes taken out of their tiny, well-lit warrens, purses piled askew.

"She looks so sweet," Nora said, sitting gingerly at her cousin's feet on the chaise.

"Sweet? She looks like she was trying to rob the place and got drunk on the job," Leo smirked. He, unlike his sisters, had not cared much whether his cousin moved to New York. But now that he could see the potential for mischief—evidenced by the champagne guzzling and ransacking of his sister's closet—he was glad she had. Leo's chief concern in life was not growing bored. And the arrival of this cousin seemed to promise that, for at least a time, he would not.

"Stop it." Nora reached over and pinched her brother's side. "She just got here. I shouldn't have left her alone all afternoon."

"Should we get a nanny for her?" he asked. He looked at her sleeping. She was awfully pretty, though she didn't resemble his sisters at all. She was like a contestant in one of the beauty pageants Nora loved to watch—wholesome-looking, not a shred of chic or cool. And like most men, because he found her beautiful, he also found her much more sympathetic. Poor thing: her parents, the bad marriage. Poor, poor thing.

"Laila, honey," Nora said softly, leaning forward to shake her cousin's shoulder.

Laila awoke with a snort; it took her a moment to gain her bearings, but as she came to, she appeared overwhelmed by humiliation.

"Oh God," she said, "I'm so sorry, Nora, I fell asleep . . . and I was just . . ."

"Playing dress up?" Leo suggested. She was delightful, he thought; so guileless.

Laila blushed crimson and looked like she might cry.

"Cut it out, Leo."

"Nora, I . . ."

"Honey, it's *fine*. I said you could borrow my clothes, didn't I?"

"I know, but I'm embarrassed. I was just feeling lonely and bored, I guess." She sat up abruptly and then immediately lowered herself back down again. "Oh, my head."

"One of Leo's sidecars will fix that. Come on, let's go downstairs."

"You go; let me just clean all this up."

"Don't worry about it," Nora said, "Maggie will be in tomorrow; she can do it."

"Are you sure?"

"Of course!"

Soon the three of them were settled in the plush couches and armchair that surrounded Nora's automatic fireplace. The day had been pleasant, but a cold snap was descending as the sun went down, a harbinger of autumn. Leo had made them cocktails, wheeling out Nora's beloved copper bar cart with its mirrored trays.

"Is it really Sunday evening already?" Leo wondered aloud. "Ah, tomorrow the mines."

Laila looked at him curiously. Neither of the twins worked, at least not in any traditional sense, and she was curious about how they spent their days.

"I promised Brian I'd get him pages by the end of the week," Leo said by way of explanation, Brian being his long-suffering literary agent. Of course, he'd told himself this every week since they'd sold the book a year ago. His original deadline had come and gone, and he still didn't have much beyond the original proposal—which had been heavily edited by Brian, who had suggested simply hiring a ghostwriter to complete the book, but Leo was appalled by the suggestion.

"Why don't you go out to the house in East? It would be so quiet, and you could focus. I could come with you so you wouldn't be lonely! At least until Thursday, but then I have to be back for the Operation Smile luncheon. Did I tell you?"

"Yes, you know I love Lydia." Leo smiled approvingly, "But see, if I go isolate myself in my little writer's garret, how can I write Man About Town? Which is the whole *essence* of the book. It's a Catch-22!"

Laila had read through the online archive of Leo's columns. It was mostly a collection of names, places, and events in bold typeface—none of which meant anything to her, with the exception of the occasional famous actor or model who popped up. She felt as though she were reading coded messages, the details decipherable only to those in the know.

Leo vowed to tackle his manuscript in monastic seclusion early the next morning, but for now, he wished only to distract himself from the task that awaited him.

"How was the matchmaker?" he asked his sister.

"Oh God," Nora said. "Awful, what do you think? She *appraised* me, like I was going up for auction at Christie's or something. And she and Mom kept talking back and forth in Russian. Ugh. Be glad you're a boy and Mother doesn't pull this bullshit on you."

"I'm a lost cause anyway." Leo's brief attention span was as consistent in his love life as it was in the rest of his endeavors.

"No, you're a man," Laila said. "You can wait as long as you want to get married." He gave her a surprised little smile. The beauty queen had bite.

"So can you!" he said, directing his words back to his sister, whom he hated to see in distress for any reason.

"Mother doesn't think so."

Leo rolled his eyes. "What's the point in money if you can't marry whomever you want? Haven't those always been the rules?"

"Yes, but I don't want someone to marry *me* for my money."

"That's not what I mean. You want someone who loves you for *you*, obviously. I just don't think you *need* to get married at all if you don't want to." Leo had tried, on occasion, to set Nora up, but the few young men Leo felt were suitable for his sister had not shown interest. In his love for his twin, he sweetly overestimated her appeal.

"I hate to agree with Petra on this," Laila began. Leo and Nora turned their heads to look at her. "But it's true that most men want women in their twenties."

She suddenly seemed world-weary for her age, and Leo thought, not for the first time, that twenty-five meant something very different where she came from. "Well, I love older women," he said.

"Yes, but . . . ," Laila began then stopped short.

Leo looked at her expectantly, an amused smile on his lips. "But?" he said, sweeping his hand before him with a flourish.

"Just . . . don't you think that's a novelty? Like, once you get married, you really think it will be to someone older than you?"

"Leo, married!" Nora squealed.

Leo made a mock-hurt face at her. "I'll get married someday!"

"Oh? To whom? A unicorn princess who slides down a rainbow right onto your lap?" Nora asked.

"Unfair! I'll get married when I find the right girl." Leo did not like to think of himself as mercurial and easily bored with women. Instead, he fancied himself a romantic who found something to love in a great many women, but who would be humbled into monogamy when the right one appeared.

"My ex-husband, Nathan," Laila said, "was ten years older, and he confessed once to me how much fun it was to have a younger woman on his arm. I'm just saying, Nora, at our age, we have the most options we're ever going to have. It's just a numbers game."

"Does this mean I have to go on a date with *Larry*?" Nora said as though she expected them to follow this.

"Who is Larry?" Leo and Laila asked in unison.

Nora groaned. "The guy Oxana wants to set me up with. He owns a clothing company."

"Well, that sounds okay," Leo said, "at least he's not a *banker*." Bankers, to Leo's mind, were the worst of the worst. There were so many of them in the city—rich and gauche, every last one—they were without nuance, without taste, they were the antithesis of everything Leo held dear. Ironically, they made up the majority of the readership of his Man About Town column and would be the first to buy his prospective book to display proudly on their hulking onyx coffee tables.

Nora made a face. "He's forty-one."

"That's horrifying," Leo said. "He could be our dad."

"Only in the technical sense," Laila said.

"Would *you* date someone that age?" Nora was incredulous.

"Of course," Laila said, "if it was the right person."

"George Clooney?" Leo said. He dearly hoped his cousin was not simply a gold digger. It wasn't that he had a moral quandary with this, but then she would be boring. And Leo did not want to think she was boring.

"Clooney is way older than forty-one; not that that would stop me or anyone else."

"Well *Larry* is not George Clooney," Nora said. "I just wish Mother didn't have to be so pushy. She never does this with Liberty."

"That's because she wants Liberty to continue speaking to her."

"Liberty didn't talk to my mother for six months one time," Nora explained to her cousin.

"What happened?"

"This was when Liberty was still modeling. Our mother kind of pushed her into it; it was never . . . it just didn't really work out."

"But she was so good," Laila said.

"She was, but she never liked it." Leo was aware they shouldn't even be discussing this with Laila just yet. In general, this wasn't a period of time that any of them discussed.

"Why did she ever get into it, then?"

This part of the story was well-worn, unlike the shadowy events that followed it. "Mother was shooting a story for *Elle*

Decor," Nora began, "and Liberty came home from school while the photographer and his team were still there. My mother called her into the room for a kiss hello, and the photographer kept shooting. They used one of the images in the story, and everyone became *obsessed* with Liberty. So she started modeling."

"It was Mother's doing. Liberty hates being the center of attention," Leo said.

"Is that why she stopped speaking to her?"

"No, when she was sixteen there was a lingerie shoot that my mother wanted her to do. . . ."

Leo flashed a stern look at Nora. Even the twins didn't know the details of the shoot that had upset Liberty so much. They were only ten at the time, and their glamorous teenage sister was a mystery to them. When she became withdrawn and stopped speaking to their mother, they only knew something bad had happened, never exactly what. In the years that followed, it became crystal clear that Liberty never wanted to speak of the incident. Of course, the twins were sophisticated enough to know how sordid the modeling industry could get, and they too wanted to look no closer at what might have befallen their sister. Needless to say, the whole matter felt like it ought to be off-limits with Laila.

"Anyway, Liberty was mad at her," Nora said, waving her hand in front of her face, "it was a whole thing. So now my mom doesn't interfere in her life, and they get along fine."

"But she kept modeling after that," Laila said.

"Yes, but she fired her agent, hired her own team. She did it till college and then dropped it," Leo said.

"But wasn't she doing really well?"

"She just liked making her own money. I never got why that made any difference. Like, whatever *any* of us could make from

57

working, it's not going to matter, you know? It's a drop in the bucket." It was something about his older sister that genuinely confounded Leo: the way she seemed to want to pretend that the family's money didn't exist, as though it was a burden to her. She lived in a modest one-bedroom in the East Village, and although the neighborhood had gentrified around her, she'd originally bought it for a song with her modeling money. He knew others admired her for it, but he couldn't understand her motives. It's not as though they were the children of an arms dealer; why should they be ashamed of their wealth?

"Now she gets paid to have her nose in a book all day!" Nora said. "She loves it."

Laila nodded and took a long sip from her cocktail. "And she's very close with our grandfather?"

Leo and Nora both let out a groan. "The golden grand-daughter," Leo said. Their grandfather held standards for each of his progeny that were both impossible to divine and even more impossible to live up to. He had wanted his son to follow him, but then seemed to disdain him for his lack of originality. His daughter was an obvious lost cause, and God only knew what had happened with Laila's father. As far as Leo went, Frederick always asked him when he would find a "real" job or join his own father at Lawrence Holdings. Leo hoped that in making himself an author, he might win him over. Only Liberty seemed to meet with Fredrick's approval. Nora just seemed to baffle him, though there was a certain affection in his tolerance of her.

It struck Laila how the twins seemed to envy their sister without malice. Here in the Lawrences' world, could it simply be that there was enough for all?

7

Dear Mr. Haegal,

Thank you for your submission to Gerard Mills & Co. We recognize the hard work that goes into writing a novel of this length—

Two hundred and ten thousand words, to be exact!

and we appreciate your giving us the opportunity to read it.

Laila rifled back through her notes to find anything positive to say about the intergalactic western she was rejecting on behalf of the agency. Her eyes landed squarely on a space in the margin where she'd written, in all caps, *EWWW!* It was a graphic sex scene between the middle-aged earthling hero and a buxom blond alien (qualities that existed irrespective of humanity in this author's reality).

While we appreciate your vivid attention to detail, we don't feel that Fear and Loathing and Space Pirates *is a good fit for us. We wish you the best of luck in finding representation.*

Sincerely,
Liberty Lawrence

Laila sent the e-mails from the main address but signed them with Liberty's name. She'd been told this made authors feel as if their work were being taken seriously and discouraged them from calling in about it. It didn't *prevent* them from doing so: in the first two weeks of her internship, she'd had a dozen calls from writers the agency did not represent—some "just checking in" to see when their manuscript might be read, others irate that they'd been rejected. At first Laila had felt sympathetic to the nicer ones, but she was quickly tiring of all of them. Did they not understand how repellent desperation was?

She'd feigned a passion for books when Liberty had offered her the intern gig—managing to pull some details of classics she'd read in high school out of the ether—figuring she could cultivate her interests as needed. This was something Laila had become good at: mirroring. It was the secret to making men feel loved and making them love you in return (if they could even tell the difference, which so many could not): be into things they liked, be the girl they'd always imagined, a perfect projection of themselves. She'd discovered this when she was coming into herself around the age of fourteen, and it was amazing how true it still was. But women were harder to crack. Women were cannier. Laila longed to be close to her cousins, to Petra. Her mother hadn't had women friends, didn't believe in them. It didn't mean it had to be the same for her, did it? This was a new life. This was another chance.

When she'd first arrived at the beautiful old brick building near Gramercy Park that housed the agency, and climbed the stairs gazing at the framed book covers that decorated the walls, Laila imagined that the job might be rather glamorous. After all, Liberty herself was the chicest person Laila knew. She had been shocked to find out how hard her cousin worked, often staying at the office long after Laila left at five. You would have thought she actually needed the money! She was beloved by her boss, Gerard Mills—that giant, lumbering publishing titan—and had easily secured Laila a spot as an intern, which, evidently, was a coveted position. Now that she was here, though, Laila couldn't imagine why. It was a curious thing about New York: the fierce scramble to gain a foothold permeated everything. There were droves of young women who lived in shoe boxes with eight roommates in order to work such internships. Laila swung between feeling lucky—after all, she lived in the resplendent luxury of what had to be one of the nicest penthouses in lower Manhattan—and also entitled, by her very birth, to be exactly where she was.

At the end of her first week, two of the assistants were already in Liberty's office by the time Laila arrived for the day. She was late because she'd taken the subway. Nora had taken the car that morning for some errand or other, and when Laila asked how she ought to get to the office—hoping that Nora would simply offer to drop her off—she'd told her to just take a cab. She ought to have just done this; it was a short ride and would not have made much of a dent in her admittedly small cash reserves, but she'd gotten it in her head that it might be fun to take the subway. She'd chosen the right line to get her to Gramercy but had gotten on the R train to Whitehall Street and was several stops in the wrong direction before she realized her mistake. By the time she'd arrived at the office, she was frazzled. On that morning, the city felt like a giant and seething beast threatening to devour her.

"Good morning, sweets," Liberty said when Laila had at last made it to the sanctuary of the air-conditioned office, "are you okay?"

"I'm sorry I'm late," Laila said. "I got lost on the subway."

The assistants gave each other a knowing smile, and Laila wanted to smack them. She did not need their patronizing sympathy.

"It's fine. Hey, Kim and Daphne offered to take you to lunch this afternoon." Liberty nodded at the two young women hovering at her office door.

"That's so sweet," Laila said, turning to them and smiling. Though she would rather eat at her desk—or with Liberty in the small kitchen as she had the day before, the two of them snugly sitting at the tiny table chatting about books—than make conversation for an hour with Kim and Daphne, who were of little interest to her.

"It's so hard when you first move here," Daphne—Asian, and the prettier of the two—said.

"I got lost all the time!" Kim added. She was pale and a little chubby with sporadic freckles and dishwater blond hair. Laila had noticed her grating laugh echoing from Liberty's office the day before. She was the assistant who directly supported her cousin, and her adoration was plain. But both assistants seemed keen to suck up to Liberty, hence the lunch invitation.

They took her to a nearby restaurant called Bite.

"Order whatever you want!" Kim said, "Liberty gave us her agency card. Your cousin is the best, you know?"

Laila smiled at her. "Thanks."

All three studied the menus as Kim tortured herself with her desire for an eggplant panini before at last ordering a salad with the dressing on the side. Daphne then smoothly ordered the eggplant panini—which garnered a look of betrayal from Kim. "It sounded so good, I had to!"

Laila saw this for the power move it was and one-upped her by ordering the roast-beef sandwich.

"So Liberty said you're from Michigan? Were you working in books there too?"

Laila briefly considered lying, but it seemed too likely that Liberty might have already told them what she did, or would at some point.

"Uh, no, I was a dental hygienist."

"Oh," Daphne said flatly, as though she had no idea how to respond to such information. Neither girl was especially glamorous in their H&M cardigans and Zara pencil skirts. At least Daphne wore ballet flats for her commute rather than the dreadful sneakers Kim could be seen in on her way in and out of the office each day. But despite their shabbiness, they were both Ivy League grads—Daphne from Harvard, Kim from Princeton. They had spent their lives on the ascent.

"Only while I was putting myself through school, though," Laila said, layering the truth with a nicer-looking lie. "Once I'd graduated U of M, I came out here."

She could see them both visibly shift; once again she belonged at the table. The lie was an easy one, as Ann Arbor was only an hour's drive from Grosse Pointe, and she'd visited the campus many times with her parents when she was little: returning for football games and alumni events. Laila very well might have gone there herself, had things been different.

"Wow, good for you," Kim said.

Fortunately, neither girl asked Laila any more questions about herself. They were both eager to share their knowledge of the city with her and to tell her all about their dreadfully dull lives. Laila listened raptly, for this was key to getting people on your side, and she *did* want them to be on her side. She couldn't imagine what they thought she would do with their collective wisdom about the subway (never again!) and dealing with a half dozen roommates in their railroad flats.

It was only when Daphne mentioned the Hamptons that Laila perked up. The twins, she knew, decamped to the Hamptons each summer. Perhaps she'd underestimated Daphne.

"Where is your place out there?" Laila asked. The Greek fries she'd ordered with her sandwich were salty and delicious, and she found herself devouring them. No matter, she could always pull a Nora and have champagne and cucumber slices for dinner.

"We did a share in East."

"How many people?" asked Kim.

Daphne rolled her eyes. "Eighteen. Next year I'm only doing one if everyone has a bed."

"I don't know why you bother with it," Kim said.

"I don't know how you stay in the city all summer!" Daphne said. "Just wait," she said to Laila, "the city in the summer is *so* disgusting. It's humid and smelly and totally dead. Everyone who can leave does."

"Will you still be in New York then, do you think?" Kim asked Laila.

"Oh yeah," Laila said. "I'm here to stay."

✢

It wasn't until several weeks in that Laila's work life took a turn for the interesting. "Laila, can you come here for a moment?" Liberty called to the auxiliary office where they had set her up, though she often worked in Lib's office with her if she wasn't taking calls. She would, in these moments, surreptitiously study her cousin, watching her elegant economy of movement. Laila enjoyed being in quiet, companionable proximity to her; more and more, she envied the twins their fortune of having her as a sister. She exuded grace: so tall and slender that she often appeared to be made chiefly of lovely angles, like a fashion sketch.

Laila popped her head into Liberty's office. "Hey, Lib."

"How's your day, honey?"

"Oh fine, just, you know, breaking hearts, crushing dreams," Laila said, referring to the never-ending task of combing through the "slush" pile. At first this name had struck Laila as odd, but after two weeks delving into the watery grubbiness of unsolicited submissions, the term seemed apt.

Liberty gave her a wan smile. "You get used to it. Writing rejections used to keep me up at night; I was afraid I was accidentally going to pass over the next John Kennedy Toole and send someone over the edge."

Laila nodded, though she didn't know who her cousin was talking about. She'd learned she could bluff with Liberty, who tended to give people the benefit of the doubt.

"I have a big favor to ask you. Tom Porter just called last-minute to say that he's in the neighborhood and he's dropping by the office."

Tom Porter was a youngish (Laila learned that this included anyone under the age of forty in the publishing business) writer who had the rare distinction of being both a critical and commercial success. He was Liberty's prize client. Laila had seen photos of him in the press files that Liberty had her organizing; he was reasonably good-looking in a bookish way, with big, expressive eyes, a full head of wavy hair, and a magnanimous smile.

"Doesn't Tom live nearby?" Meaning he was always in the neighborhood.

"Yes," Liberty said, rolling her eyes. "The problem is Gerard encourages all the authors to stop by anytime to chat."

"Probably because he doesn't actually do any of the work around here," Laila said, laughing. Gerard Mills was a bloviating old boy, loud and crass, with seemingly little sense that his leering habit of complimenting his female employees' looks was embarrassingly retro at best. He was a solid forty pounds overweight and wore a black toupee that strained the limits of credulity, even from a distance. No powerful woman would have gotten away with such a slovenly appearance, but it didn't seem to hurt Gerard, who'd been responsible for the careers of dozens of bestselling authors. He was a kingmaker: no one cared about his hair.

Liberty gave her a quick smile, and Laila panicked that she'd spoken out of turn.

"Authors can be a bit like jealous boyfriends; you can never allude to the fact that there is more than one of them in your life. Normally I wouldn't mind, but, and this *cannot* leave this office, Anton Bjornberg is considering switching agents; I have a lunch meeting with him."

"Oh my gosh, how exciting! Where are you meeting him?" She hadn't read Bjornberg's books—for God's sake, they were each a thousand pages at least—but he was sexy in an overserious Swedish way, and he was, confusingly, a very big deal in publishing.

Liberty scrunched her nose. "At his town house. It's a little unusual, but he insisted, for discretion. So anyway, you don't mind having a drink with Tom?"

"A drink?" Laila said, leaning over to peer at the antique banjo clock affixed to Liberty's wall. "It's barely one thirty!"

"It's publishing. Anyway, he's a sweetheart. You'll like him, I promise."

"Of course!" Afternoon cocktails with famous authors was much more what she'd had in mind for herself with this gig. There came a faint rapping on the door frame, and Laila turned around to see the author himself—taller than she'd imagined, wearing a tweed coat—standing in the doorway.

"Tom!" Liberty said, coming out from behind her desk to greet him. "It's so good to see you. I want you to meet my darling cousin and new intern, Laila. She's just moved from the Midwest."

"It's a pleasure," he said, "I love it there." Laila noticed with satisfaction that his eyes bounced off her nervously, as though he were trying not to stare at her.

"Good Lord, why?" she blurted.

To her immense relief, he laughed and shrugged. "Nice people. Good bookstores."

"It's so funny that you're here," Liberty interjected, "because I was just telling Laila about you this morning and saying that she should meet you, and here you are." This benign untruth practically made Tom blush and stare at the floor. Laila was transfixed; how did such a shy, pliable creature exist in this hard city? "Would you mind spending some time with her this afternoon? I want her to learn everything she can about the business, and you've got such a good perspective."

"Of course!" he said, so quickly it made Laila smile.

"I would join you, but I have a late lunch meeting, and I think it would be impossible to reschedule at this point."

"It's not a problem at all; I really just stopped by to say hello. Laila, shall we?"

Laila beamed at him and went to fetch her coat: a brand-new Burberry trench with navy piping.

"It's so lovely out," he said once they were together on the street—indeed, it had warmed up since that morning; she hardly needed her coat. "Would you want to go and grab a glass of rosé on a terrace somewhere? I know a good spot close by. Unless you'd prefer coffee. Or tea."

He was babbling. How charming. Tom had been short-listed for a Pulitzer Prize for his last novel, but that didn't make him any less nervous around a pretty girl.

"Rosé sounds delightful."

They took a table outside a quiet Gramercy café and, after a moment's deliberation, ordered a bottle to share. It was a perfect October afternoon; there was no better time to be in New York, Tom said, no better time to be alive.

"I have a confession," Laila said when the waiter had filled their glasses and nestled the wine bottle in the ice bucket nearby. "I knew of you even before the agency. I read all of your books back in Michigan. I'm only sorry I didn't know I would be meeting you today; I would have brought my copy of *Perjury* to the office so I could have you sign it. Oh, listen to me! How embarrassing!" Laila felt herself flush with the sip of wine and realized that this would have the effect of making her appear to be blushing. She had a copy of *Perjury*—Tom's most recent novel—that much was true. Liberty had given it to her, along with a stack of recent books by other clients of hers. It was sitting on Laila's nightstand, unopened.

"I haven't had such a good compliment in years," Tom said. Laila knew from his eyes, shining and earnest, that he was being truthful. "And where in Michigan are you from? They have an excellent writing program at the university there, did you know? I've been there on several occasions to speak."

Laila nodded enthusiastically and said she had once imagined she might go there herself—she wasn't a writer, obviously, but she just loved books so much. She quickly mentioned Grosse Pointe, and then deftly turned the subject back to Tom before he might ask her more. For the remainder of the afternoon, Tom basked in Laila's many questions about his life as a writer, where his ideas came from, what his process was, which writers inspired him. She just had so much to learn from him, she said, she hoped that he didn't mind how interested she was. And what should she read? Other than his books. She was sorry, she was gushing.

And poor Tom was done for.

8

"TELL ME you're still coming to Soho House tomorrow," Reece said. Liberty, who had just taken a delicate bite of her sashimi, smiled and nodded.

"Good, I know it's not your favorite. But I figured we'd ease Cameron back in."

Liberty shrugged. She didn't like anywhere as scene-y and exclusive as Soho House was, but it wasn't the worst of the worst. And she was always happy to be spending time with Reece. Once the two had practically lived at each other's apartments, but their jobs had grown too demanding to spend that much time socializing. "How long was he in London for again? It seems like he's been gone forever."

"Two years. And the bastard didn't even come home for a visit. If I hadn't been able to convince work I needed to go on a scouting trip, I wouldn't have seen him at all. Of course, my mom and dad flew out there, like, every two weeks; couldn't stand not seeing their baby boy."

Reece's older brother, Cameron, had been living in the family's town house in Notting Hill, working at the Michaels Steel Company's London office for the past two years. Of course, Reece could have gone over any time, but between her busy job and the fashion line she was working on—an absolute secret to all but

Liberty and Reece's younger coworker and collaborator, Cece, she barely had time for anything else. Liberty had known Reece since they were kids. Their bond had cemented as teenagers at Spence, and as adults, their relationship—best friends in the truest sense—had become something rarer still. Reece was Liberty's one real confidante and often the only one she felt knew her at all.

"Are you excited to have him back?" Liberty asked.

"The return of the prodigal son." Reece rolled her eyes. "But yeah. I think London has been good for him."

Cameron was five years older than Reece and Liberty and loomed large in the latter's childhood memories. Their father had been an Olympic skier, and their mother was a Connecticut socialite and an avid tennis player. Both Reece and Cameron were gifted athletes; Reece played volleyball for Northwestern and Cameron had rowed crew all the way through prep school and then at Harvard. Both were regal and imposing—Reece stood at nearly six feet and her brother six foot five—towering over crowds like a pair of Norse gods.

"Speaking of long-lost family members, how are things going with Laila?"

It was Friday, and Liberty had stepped away from the office for her weekly lunch with Reece. She felt a little guilty for leaving Laila behind instead of inviting her, but she cherished this alone time with her friend. Besides, Liberty held on to the hope that Laila might discover something in the agency's never-ending submission pile. After nearly ten years working with books, there was still no greater pleasure for Liberty than this. She, of course, got plenty of referrals from industry friends and school acquaintances; she'd even had an e-mail from a Spence parent that morning— *Bradford is working on the most marvelous fantasy series, we really feel it could be the next Harry Potter!*—but the projects Liberty treasured were the diamonds in the rough that she'd discovered herself, those that she'd read the opening pages of with hope and delight blooming in her chest: undiscovered talent.

"She's doing well, full of enthusiasm. It's sweet to see her so excited about being in New York."

"So crazy, the way you two reconnected. And she was married to a doctor in Michigan before this, right?"

"A dentist." Liberty took a sip of her Perrier.

"A dentist! How do you even meet someone who's a dentist? Was she his patient?"

"Well, I'm pretty certain that dentists date and go to bars like everyone else," Liberty said, "but actually, she worked for him."

Reece looked at her blankly.

"She was a hygienist."

"Shut. Up." Reece slapped the side of her thigh and let out a laugh that caused some heads to turn in their direction. There was a bigness to Reece—her stature, her laugh, her personality—that she pulled off with a grace few women could achieve. Her brother had it too, but no one minded men taking up space. "A dental hygienist? Are you sure you guys are related?"

"Don't be a snob, Reece."

"I'm not!"

Liberty made a face at her.

"Okay, I definitely am. I'm sorry. But you have to admit, the idea of *your* cousin being, like, a dental hygienist slash suburban housewife is pretty wild. It's like . . . Lawrence in a parallel universe."

"But she isn't those things anymore. Now she's an intern at a literary agency in Manhattan. Come on, you know *you* hate it when people define you by your circumstances."

"Right. God. She must have culture shock. Her side of the family must be really different." Liberty had shared with Reece what she knew about Laila's parents—the mysterious rift—but of course, there was not much to tell.

"They were, I gather." Normally, Liberty loved Reece's bluntness, found it refreshing. But she felt protective of her cousin. She could see Laila straining so hard for her approval, for her family's acceptance. New York seemed to leave her dazzled but a little terrified.

"Does she talk about them?"

Liberty shook her head. "I've asked, but she doesn't say much. Her father died when she was ten. She didn't even know we existed before her mom died two years ago."

"And you don't know why?" Reece popped a delicate piece of California roll in her mouth. The Michaels family was tight-knit and cheerful. Low-drama.

"All I know is her dad had a falling-out with my grandfather and my dad. I've never been able to pry out anything more."

"Sad. Well, she's lucky to have you. How do the twins feel about her being here?"

"Nora is delirious. It's like she ordered up a ready-made best friend."

"Oh, Nora."

"I know." Nora was so dear but so hopeless; no chance of survival outside her own cosseted and circumscribed world. Being neither especially beautiful nor academically inclined, nor gifted at sports, she hadn't been popular at Spence where naturally no one was impressed by the fact of the family's wealth. Mostly girls cozied up to her to get close to Leo, and when they were unsuccessful—or worse, when they succeeded and then were promptly abandoned—they lost interest in Nora swiftly and brutally. Laila's appearance in their lives had given Nora the longed-for opportunity to have someone to dazzle, someone who wouldn't abandon her on a whim. Liberty thought this was good for her sister.

"Well, the whole crew will be there tomorrow night, right?" Reece asked.

"Yes! It will be fun."

"It's such a thrill when I can get you to leave your apartment these days."

Liberty rolled her eyes. "I enjoy keeping my own company; nothing wrong with that." She found that most days, she'd had enough of other people by the time she got home to the solitude of her East Village apartment.

"I'm excited to get to know Laila," Reece said, scooping the last bite of her seaweed salad between her chopsticks.

"Do *not* tease her about being a dental hygienist."

"I would never."

Liberty made an incredulous face.

"I won't! I promise," she said, holding her hand in the air as if to say, *Scout's honor*. "By the way, Cameron asked about you."

"He did?" Liberty felt a trip wire of excitement. This was not the adult Liberty reacting but the buried teenage Liberty—the Liberty before—for whom Cameron seemed both as desirable and unattainable as a movie star. The Cameron of her teenage imagination had been an amalgam of facts—his sports victories, the pretty girls he'd dated, the funny thing he'd said the other day, the daring pranks that had made him a legend at Collegiate—which could be collected and parsed from his similarly worshipful sister and Liberty's own fleeting observations of him: that he drank red Gatorade after crew practice, he listened to N.W.A, and he had several volumes of Keats in his bedroom. She'd of course met him again in adulthood but had never spent enough time with him to replace or even interfere with the impressions of her teenage years, already burrowed so deeply in her psyche.

"*Excuse me*, are you blushing?"

"No!" But she was; she could feel her stomach flipping. She hadn't felt this way in such a long time that she'd forgotten it was even possible. Liberty didn't date much—and when she'd had boyfriends over the past several years, they were chosen in a cool and intellectual sort of way. Her last serious relationship, with a PhD candidate from NYU, had ended nearly two years ago, and she had not gone on more than a handful of dates with any one person since then.

"Anyway, he did; he said he was looking forward to seeing you 'all grown up'—his words, not mine. Because, ew."

"Well. I'm looking forward to seeing him too."

"Oh, *are* you?" Reece said teasingly.

"Oh, not like that. He . . . isn't my type." This was true and not true. Of course, Reece had been her coconspirator in worshipping Cameron in their youth, but that was a very long time ago. They were grown women now—both thirty-two years old.

"I would love for you to elucidate what your type actually *is*."

"I don't know. Smart, serious."

"And my brother isn't?"

"No, he *is*. But he's too good-looking." She wanted to say too sexy, too hot, too out of my league. A dozen teenage clichés bombarded her at once.

"That is not a thing." Reece smiled and pointed a chopstick at her.

Reece's dating habits were the opposite of Liberty's: she was always seeing someone. Models, actors, Wall Street guys, artists, bartenders—the only thing these romances had in common was they ran hot and burned out fast. Which was, by all appearances, how Reece preferred it.

"Remember when we were kids, we used to talk about how you could marry Cameron and then we'd get to be sisters?" Liberty was mortified that her friend remembered all of this.

"Yeah, and I'm pretty sure my reaction was *ew, boys*, so I don't think that's entirely germane."

"Presumably you no longer think boys are gross, or maybe you do! Is that why you don't date more, babe, because boys are gross?"

"Be honest, though, aren't they?" Liberty rolled her eyes. "Are you saying you *want* me to date Cameron?"

"Gah, of course not. I just want you to date someone. You know Petra asked me if you were a lesbian once?"

"She didn't."

"I couldn't tell if she was relieved or disappointed when I told her you weren't."

Petra was obsessed with her daughters' marrying. But after the six months they didn't speak, she never pressed Liberty about that or anything else. It had broken her heart, the thought of losing her daughter.

"I do date. I mean I will, but work right now . . ."

"Work always!"

"You're one to talk!" Liberty smiled at her friend. "And I'm proud of you for it. Why shouldn't we be focused on our careers right now?"

"Because we're over thirty," Reece said. "Even I'm going to have to get serious sometime soon."

"Ugh, you sound like my mother. After all this progress, men still get the hero's journey, while we're left with the marriage plot? What bullshit."

"Well, *plus ça change*, I guess," Reece shrugged. "I just don't want to wake up and find that it's too late. You know? I want to give Elin and Thatcher some grandbabies someday. All of that. God help me."

Liberty knew, for who didn't fear that? A part of her could imagine being happy in her solitude. She could work and read and travel alone. It could be a lovely life, in a way. Her brother and sister would have children; she'd be their fascinating auntie. But then, there was the desire she'd felt assaulting her with more frequency lately, the stirring at the sight of a toddler with his father or the scent of a baby's head. Unsettling, but gratifying, to be reminded that she was still so human.

9

LAILA WAS overjoyed about going to Soho House. An entire episode of *Sex and the City* had revolved around its exclusivity. Like many young women of her generation, this show was how she'd known New York before she'd *known* New York. It was a dated but precise version of the city. Of course, she knew better than to mention the connection, but she could hardly contain her excitement as she and Nora got ready that evening. They'd gone on yet another shopping excursion that afternoon, for which Nora had once again picked up the bill. Whatever discomfort Laila had felt the first time her cousin had taken her on one of her Bergdorf sprees had dissipated. After all, it wasn't precisely *Nora's* money she was spending—Nora had casually mentioned the trust fund they'd all come into upon their twenty-first birthdays—it was *Lawrence* money, and Laila was a Lawrence. Only an accident of fate had separated her from the fortune with which she was now being reunited. She was careful to express none of this to her cousins, of course; she recognized that, for the moment, she still lived at the mercy of their whims.

Just that weekend, Nora had lain in Laila's bed with her and said "I just love you staying here." Laila had replied that she loved it too. "Don't ever leave; we'll make up the guest room just as you like it, and you can just stay forever." Laila didn't think she'd stay, but the offer of a permanent situation was still an immense relief. She had only a few thousand dollars to her name. When she'd been married to Nathan, it was she who handled the family finances. For two years she'd diligently skimmed a small amount for herself. Never enough that he would notice but just enough to get her here. It would barely be enough to cover first and last month's rent anywhere she'd be willing to live.

"Laila, you're wearing the black Hervé Léger tonight, right?" Nora called out from the bathroom, where she was flat ironing her blond locks into glossy submission.

"I think so."

"Okay, I'll wear my pink Narciso Rodriguez." Nora flounced into the closet, where Laila was surveying her options for shoes.

"That one is superhot on you." Laila smiled with approval.

"Yeah?"

Laila was distracted by the buzz of her cell phone. She read the text message that had come in and smiled.

"What?" Nora's eyes lit up. "Tell me!"

"I just got a text from that author I had drinks with the other day, from Liberty's office?"

"Tom Porter?"

"Yes!" Laila was a little surprised her cousin remembered; you never did know what would stick in her head. "He asked if he could take me to dinner some night," she said, "'if he may be so bold,' that's what he said! How cute is that?"

"Adorable. Are you going to go?"

"I don't know." Laila's mind was firing in multiple directions doing the math of such a proposition: Liberty might be annoyed, but Tom was definitely a catch. Was he the best Laila could do, though? She'd just gotten here. What Petra had said at Bergdorf's stayed with her; Laila was keenly aware that there was only a small window where she would be still young enough to have so many options. She saw before her a narrowing tunnel. It was eerie how Petra's words echoed her own mother's—Betsy's spirit manifesting in this unlikely host. *The most important decision you'll ever make.* She'd already gotten it wrong once.

Leo appeared and leaned on the door frame with a dramatic sigh, shirtless and in tattered sweatpants, cradling a tumbler of scotch. "Do we really have to go to Soho House tonight? That place is so tired."

Laila felt a flash of indignation at the way Leo had of making all that she was so thrilled by—the nightclubs and restaurants and the very city itself—seem utterly passé. He was forever talking about moving to Berlin or Costa Rica. He wore his jaded attitude the way Nora wore her Louboutins, the flashing signal of her privilege, dear to her though they made her miserable.

"Yes, we do. Jesus, get dressed, would you? At least you get to see your girlfriend," Nora said, riffling through a series of clutch purses.

"Girlfriend?"

Leo smiled at her and clutched his heart staggering forward. "Reece Michaels."

Nora laughed and rolled her eyes.

"Liberty's best friend?" Laila asked. She leaned close to the mirror to fix a smudge in her eye makeup, using her pinky nail to avoid disrupting the whole look.

"Queen of my heart, goddess of my soul."

"You only want her because you can't have her," Nora said.

"Lies!"

"You'd drive each other crazy; you're practically the same person," Nora said.

"A match made in heaven."

"You're too young for her. Besides which, you don't date your best friend's brother."

"Reece, really?" Laila asked.

They both looked at her as though a little surprised that she'd venture an opinion. Laila had the distinct impression that she was welcome with the twins as long as she remained in her place. There was a mysterious hierarchy that seemed vital to the twins' understanding of their world and the social order that it revolved around. Laila didn't know where she would eventually settle in it; at the moment her newness gave her novelty, but that couldn't last, nor did Laila always wish to be the adorable rube.

"Well, you've met her," Nora said. Laila shrugged. Laila had spoken to her briefly several times when she'd come by the office to have lunch with Liberty. She found her to be a little bit loud, and Jesus, so tall. The way she carried herself made Laila think she'd be arrogant. Besides, she wasn't even *that* pretty; she was good-looking in a well-bred kind of way, but the way she acted, you'd think she looked like Liberty.

"If she only knew how I could love her," Leo said wistfully.

"So what are we celebrating tonight?" Laila asked, eager to change the subject.

"Her brother, Cameron, has just come back from two years in London," Nora explained. Laila smiled. A male Reece? That could only be insufferable.

"Oops," Nora said, glancing at her phone, "car's here. Leo!"

"I'm going! Five minutes."

Laila felt a thrill run up her spine as they ascended the elevator to Soho House. She tugged nervously at the hem of her dress, though painted on as it was, it was not going anywhere. She followed her cousins through to the back room, pausing as they said brief hellos to the people they knew. The room had a dark and cozy feel with large leather chairs and an intricate ceiling of stamped metal tiles. The curtains were pulled back on the window to reveal an expansive view of the glittering city below. Laila felt all eyes clinging to her: with interest, with lust, was there a tiny hint of malice? Was it envy that she felt landing on her skin like a frost? This thrilled her most of all.

She spotted Cameron first, from across the room. He was impossible to miss, even from a distance, and she could see the resemblance to his sister. He was very tall and blond and could have been mistaken for the actor Alexander Skarsgård at a glance. He was wearing a dark, well-cut suit. Laila felt a wave of lust radiate from the pit of her stomach, out through her limbs. He glanced her way and smiled as the twins pulled her along in the direction of the group. Nora greeted him with a hug, and Leo gave him a hearty handshake.

"Welcome back, my friend!"

Reece and Liberty stood up from the couch where they'd been sitting. It was Liberty who introduced Laila. Charmingly, Cameron leaned in to kiss Laila's cheek, which made Reece laugh mirthlessly. "Jesus, Brother, you'd think you've been in Spain. Kissing strangers. Quite Continental."

He turned to her with an indulgent smile, and Laila was sorry to have his attention diverted. It felt as though a cloud had crossed over the sun.

"Well, Laila is not a stranger, though," he said, smiling back at her as they all took their seats, "she's practically family."

Laila subtly edged her chair closer to his as she arranged herself in it, taking care to position herself at what she felt was her most flattering angle: shoulders back, legs twisted around each other.

She noted that he was drinking something dark on the rocks: scotch? She caught sight of a gleaming cufflink as he reached for his glass and took a sip.

"So, how are you enjoying New York?" he asked her.

"Oh, I love it! I don't ever want to leave. Although London sounds marvelous." She didn't know where she'd pulled that word from. She was loath to admit that she'd only ever been abroad once, to Mexico with a boyfriend. She hoped he wouldn't ask about this, and he didn't.

"London can be dreary, but I do love the history there. It has quite a different soul than New York. And it was wonderful to be in Europe and able to go visit all of my favorite spots on a whim."

"Which are?"

"Paris, Burgundy, Majorca, Prague. Too many to list."

"I'd love to go," she said, meaning: *To one of them, to all of them, especially with you.* He smiled as though trying to size her up.

Nora grabbed her arm and handed her a cocktail in a champagne glass. "What is this?"

"A French 75."

Laila took a sip. It was crisp and deadly delicious. Before she knew it, the slender flute was empty, and another appeared.

The group eventually moved on to dinner at Scarpetta, where they shared heaping plates of meats, cheese, olives, and some of the best pasta Laila had ever tasted—though she found she could barely eat in Cameron's presence. They went on for drinks at La Esquina. It was Laila's first time there, and she was utterly confused as they walked through a kitchen then descended into the cavernlike basement, lit with candelabras, where beautiful people sipped mojitos in the corners.

Laila's memory of the night was hazy after that, but they had gone to a nightclub, she couldn't recall which one. Liberty had bowed out, of course, but Reece had stayed on to enjoy herself, playfully fending off Leo in a dance the two seemed to have perfected over the years. They'd run into a girl called Cece, who worked with Reece in fashion PR; she and Laila hit it off and at one point did tequila shots together. Cameron definitely seemed interested, and Laila couldn't believe her good fortune. The only problem was Nora, who didn't seem to enjoy having Laila pay so much attention to someone else, and she alternately hung off her arm or fumed nearby.

The next morning, Laila had the kind of hangover that meant giving in to the lure of the breakfast sandwiches from the deli on the corner and otherwise moving as little as possible. Fortunately Nora was in a similar state, and the two curled up in her enormous cotton-candy-pink damask all day, binge-watching *Gossip Girl* reruns and eating junk food. Laila felt a triumph as she had flashes of standing next to Cameron, of his leaning over her to hear her, her touching his arm, and then at the end of the night slipping him her phone number on a cocktail napkin, as though they were in an old movie. She was certain he would call or text her. Most likely later today. She felt the acute freedom of having unbound herself from Nathan fully, her relief long having eclipsed any sliver of guilt she might have felt at having abandoned him for no reason that he could discern. Honestly, what had he expected? He'd proposed to her the day after her mother died—*I'll be your family now, Laila, be my wife*—he must have known she didn't truly want to marry him. She felt decades older than Nora, knowing all the small ways you could die a little each day with the wrong person. But that was all the past, and it couldn't touch her.

10

For a time, Reece had worried that her brother would not come home, or that if he did, he would not be the same. And so, in her haze the next morning—God, she could not drink like she could when she was in her twenties—her overwhelming sense had been one of relief. Her brother was back and seemed good as new.

Something had happened before he left. He'd been dating a girl—no one Reece had met, but Cameron had been with her for several months, which for him seemed promising—and then suddenly he was not. Then he'd gone to London, and though the two events were so obviously connected, he would not explain how. It made her wonder if her brother—the inveterate playboy—had had his heart broken. If so, she was sorry for him, but also took this as a good sign, that he might someday meet someone and have a family. She didn't want her brother turning into one of those awful old, wealthy bachelors who continued to date women in their twenties as they steadily marched toward their dotage.

Reece was finally roused from her bed late morning by her Jack Russell terrier, Rocket, who'd had enough of trying to cajole her out of bed and had resorted to a high-pitched bark that Reece knew her West Village neighbors would *not* appreciate. During the workweek Reece hired a dog walker to come twice during the day: once to jog with Rocket, once to take him to the Union Square dog run, attempting to exhaust the indefatigable mutt, who showed no signs of mellowing with age. On weekends Reece herself took him on marathon adventures, and he evidently wasn't letting her off the hook today, hangover or no.

Cloisters? she'd texted Liberty that morning.

This had long been a favorite spot of Liberty's, and her friend knew that she could always be persuaded to take the long ride on the 1 train to reach it for a few hours of sanctuary. On a crisp and sunny fall day like this, it was one of the most beautiful, and certainly the most serene, places in the city.

I'm out with FIT squad. Meet at 11?

Of course, Liberty was out working with her favorite charity, Literacy in Motion, that morning; it had been her ostensible reason for going home early the night before. She was part of the organization's Family Involvement Team and spent her Saturday mornings talking to parents, reading to their kids, and signing families up for library cards in the far reaches of the Bronx and Brooklyn. As far as Reece could tell, no one she met through the organization had any idea who Liberty's family was, and this was the way she wanted it. She said her work with them wasn't just altruism: she loved it; it gave her a chance to step outside herself; it was selfish, really. Reece told her that was a rather adorable version of being selfish. But she saw that for her friend, there was something cleansing about getting outside her own world on a regular basis, almost baptismal. She was always happiest right after she'd been with them, cheerful and lighthearted as she was this morning.

As soon as they walked into the cool stone foyer of the building, past the faded tapestries, and through to the quiet gardens, all the city seemed to have faded away.

"Ugh," Reece said as they stepped out into the sunshine, "I feel like shit. I should have gone home when you did last night, Grandma; you look fresh as a daisy."

"Hey! I stayed out until midnight. I partied."

Reece laughed. "Did you have fun? It was a good night."

"I did have fun." Reece thought she caught a secret smile float across her friend's lips, but it was gone before she could ask about it.

"Cameron is in good form. Seems pleased to be back from London," Reece said.

"He does, it seems like he's happy to be home. So, listen, did you get a chance to chat with Laila at all last night?"

Reece was startled by the abrupt subject change, though she sensed that for some reason her friend was very concerned about whether the two got along.

"Only a little. To be honest, she seemed much more interested in my brother."

Liberty smiled. "Oh, she's harmless."

"I don't know about that. She was practically in his lap." Reece might not have mentioned it if Liberty had not broached the subject of her cousin first, but she'd felt wary of the girl. There was something about her that didn't sit well with Reece, though maybe it had only been her instinctive response to a woman going after her brother. Though she knew she had no reason to be protective of him, it didn't stop her from feeling it.

"Well, I'm sure Cameron can handle a pretty girl flirting with him."

"He'd never go for her," Reece added. She was reassuring herself as much as anything.

"Why do you say that? She's beautiful, smart. Too young for him, but when has that ever mattered?"

"Come on, Liberty, you know why."

Liberty looked at her friend expectantly. Rocket strained at his leash in the direction of a particularly massive crow that was hopping along, looking unconcerned about the dog's interest, the two being approximately the same size.

"He's just picky," Reece said. "He's got taste, it's one thing I can say for my brother."

"Cut her a break. Why do you dislike her?"

"I don't! And anyway, Liberty, it's not on you. I guess I just find her a little . . . tacky."

"She's brand new to the city. She'll calm down. Not everyone grew up around all of this."

"Oh, not the speech," Reece said with a smile.

By this she meant Liberty's somewhat frequent screeds about their privilege relative to nearly everyone else on the planet. Truthfully, Reece loved her friend's sharp eye toward the real world; it kept her honest, and she treasured Liberty's good heart, her sense of justice. Reece and Liberty had helped each other become who they were in the world. Reece gave Liberty courage; Liberty brought Reece down to earth. They shared a desire to create something tangible of their own, rather than to simply add some extra layers to the wealth they'd been born with—or worse, run in circles around it while contributing nothing at all. The Michaelses' family fortune went back to the robber baron era, and there'd been too many in the family who'd been content to simply leech it away.

"No speech." Liberty adjusted her black peacoat and rearranged her red scarf to cover her collarbone, which had gooseflesh from the wind. "I suppose I just want you to like Laila. She's important to me."

"Then I adore her," Reece said, taking her friend's arm in her own, "as long as she stays away from my brother."

⤜⤛

Later, after they parted ways and Liberty went home to fetch a pile of manuscripts and hole up in the nearby café where she so often spent a portion of her Saturdays, she thought about her darling friend.

Liberty often felt she'd only survived Spence because of Reece. The two had known each other since they were kids but only became friends in the middle school at Spence when Liberty had a run-in with one of the nastiest girls in their class. Olivia Fowler was one of those dreadful blue bloods whose relatives had been born into wealth so far back that there existed not even the memory of struggle in any living family member. And for reasons unknown to the latter, Olivia *despised* Liberty. At thirteen Liberty had all the makings of her coming beauty—even in her gawky adolescence, the resemblance to Petra was undeniable—but she was of no interest to the boys at Collegiate, their brother school, and she was far too studious and unsporty to be of interest to the girls in her class. Olivia, on the other hand, was not only the first in their class to develop spectacular breasts, but said rack did not at all hold back her career as a tennis champion. Between her money and background, and the ease with which cruelty came to her, she was a natural queen bee. What Liberty had done to attract her ire was simply not to care about her, not to try to curry her favor as every other girl in their class seemed beholden to do—every other girl but Reece, that is, but Reece was untouchable for her own reasons. For one thing, she was one of the best athletes in the school—one of the youngest on the varsity volleyball team and already its star—and then there was her family's wealth, which went back far enough to have no trace of vulgarity or newness; and, of course, her gorgeous brother, whom everyone knew doted on her. It all added up to a preternatural confidence for a thirteen-year-old girl.

But with Liberty, Olivia smelled blood. She made up a rumor, the variety of which only the lurid imagination of a devious teenager could come up with: that Liberty had promised and delivered blow jobs to the entire lacrosse team of Collegiate should they beat their rival, Trinity. The proliferation of this piece of gossip by Liberty's classmates, though dubious even on a logistical level, had everything to do with the desire to keep Olivia's malicious attentions running in any direction other than their own.

School became a nightmare for Liberty, who had no one to ask for help. She was too ashamed to tell her parents, and the teachers at Spence seemed at least as terrified of Olivia as the students. The rumor had been circulating for a solid month—a lifetime—when Olivia piled on an additional rumor, this time that Liberty was having sex with the coach: a rotund, married man of forty.

"I heard she's going to let him put it in the back door if they win the championship this season," Olivia said to her ladies-in-waiting one day as Liberty passed by them in the dining hall, using a stage whisper loud enough for all to hear. Liberty, who had remained mostly stoic in the face of her tormentor until that moment, felt hot tears rising. Then Reece's voice cut through the whispers and tittering from a neighboring table.

"Olivia, will you kindly shut the fuck up? You made this all up and you know it."

Liberty froze. Everyone seemed to be holding their breath; who had dared defend her? But of course it was Reece. Up until now, the rumor had not seemed to register on her radar, but her dislike of Olivia was well-known. If Olivia was the meanest—and conversely, most popular—girl in the class, Reece remained the most intimidating. For one thing, she was inches taller than everyone else in their grade and carried herself like an Amazon warrior goddess.

"Girls," Olivia said, regaining her composure, "did you hear that? I think it was the call of a lesbian Sasquatch."

With that Reece pushed her chair back and strode to where Olivia sat. The laughter of Olivia's minions abruptly stopped, and a look of panic flashed across their faces. Reece stood calmly next to where Olivia sat, ignoring her for a long moment. A hush fell over the dining hall: Was she going to hit her?

Olivia rolled her eyes. "*What*, Reece?"

Reece smiled and crouched to whisper something in Olivia's ear. The blood drained from the girl's face, and she only recovered herself when Reece had returned to her seat, shrugging and smiling when her own cohort asked her what she'd said. Olivia struggled to regain her composure and rolled her eyes with forced indifference.

"Liberty," Olivia said now, all sweetness, "you know this was all just a joke, right?"

"I guess," she said unsteadily. "I mean no, not really. I know it's not true, but I don't get why you think it's funny."

Again, an eye roll. "Ugh, that's the point. Because it's so clearly not true. Like, it's satire? Jesus, like, of course, you're *obviously* a virgin."

At that moment a bread roll came flying from Reece's direction and smacked into the side of Olivia's head—leaving crumbs in her shiny dark hair. Now the crowd, having felt the subtle shift of power, laughed openly. Olivia shook out her hair and leveled a glare at Reece, who glared right back.

"The point is, I made it up. It was just a joke. You forgive me, right, sweetie?"

Not wanting to provoke any further drama, Liberty nodded. The next day, Reece had asked her to sit with her group at lunch, and the friendship had been cemented. Only later did she ask what Reece had whispered in her nemesis's ear.

"I just reminded her that my brother would do anything for me, and if she didn't want rumors about *her* spread to every hot prep in town, she'd better can it."

"What can I get you, miss?" The waiter in his little half apron materialized at Liberty's side.

"Oh, just a cappuccino, please."

"Regular or soy milk?"

"Just regular, please."

"Whole milk or skim?"

"Whole, please."

"Any sugar? Splenda? Stevia?"

All of the options he'd just offered to bring for her cappuccino were tucked in a tidy Lucite box in the middle of each of the little bistro tables in the coffee shop. It was at this point Liberty realized that the waiter knew who she was and was trying to draw out their interaction. She'd forget for whole stretches of time that her family was famous.

"Nope," she said with a patient smile. "Just plain, thanks so much."

"You got it," he said. She couldn't be annoyed when the interaction was obviously making his afternoon. As long as he didn't start taking cell phone photos of her while she worked.

"You look *fabulous*, by the way," he said as he sallied off to the espresso machine.

Her notoriety—for you couldn't call something like that fame, could you?—was another thing she had uncomfortably inherited, another thing she and Reece shared. It wasn't as though anyone knew who either of them was outside Manhattan, but here their families were covered in tabloids like Page Six and on gossip sites like Gawker and Guest of a Guest consistently. Her father's three marriages and estranged family members had not helped matters, nor had her grandfather's elderly playboy antics. Liberty tolerated the media interest insofar as it could be very helpful in getting coverage for her clients, a daunting task for all but her most well-known authors, but in general she found the whole thing tiresome. Reece was less ambivalent about it, in part because the press had a tendency to describe her using a bucket of adjectives that she knew to be euphemisms for *fat*: *zaftig*, *statuesque* (which she was), *curvy* (which she wasn't, exactly). Fortunately Reece's self-esteem was in no real danger; her parents had seen to that. She'd always been delightedly encouraged to be exactly who she was.

Liberty had loved spending time with the Michaelses growing up. Reece's mom, Elin, was a formidable and prominent socialite who seemed to forever be cracking the whip on the other ladies who lunched but perhaps didn't take the causes as seriously.

"If you're going to do that kind of thing," Reece would say, with the clear distinction that she had no intention of becoming a lady who luncheoned, "at least she does it right." Her committed charity work didn't leave Elin any less time for fretting and managing her kids' lives, however; she even cooked dinner herself many nights. She drove Reece a little crazy, but Liberty was envious. Their father, Thatcher, whom Liberty found mortifyingly handsome, was tall and jocular in his Barbour jackets and seemed like he'd never had a bad day in his life. Liberty never turned down an invitation to Reece's house, and it was only partly because her brother would be there on the rare occasions that he wasn't out with a girl or his friends. He would say, "Hey, kiddo," to Liberty and ruffle her hair, and she would feel the warmth radiating there for hours after.

It wasn't that Liberty's own parents didn't love her—but they were nothing like the Michaelses. Her father was a workaholic in the mold of his own father, forever reaching in vain for the untouchable bar that Frederick had set. And Petra, while utterly devoted to her family, was maternal in a rather unsmiling Russian way that seemed to revolve around giving instructions.

It was Liberty's grandfather who doted on her, who fussed over her, but he was too involved in his own affairs (both literal and figurative) to be a consistent presence. Rather, he would show up in a whirlwind of affection, adventures, and presents, and then be gone for months afterward. It was he who first stoked Liberty's twin indulgences: vintage jewelry and rare books. When she'd turned eleven, he'd gifted her with her first piece from Fred Leighton—his preferred jeweler, though he also frequented Christie's—a whimsical nineteenth-century charm bracelet featuring tiny animals with rubies and emeralds as eyes. It was an outrageous gift for a child but one she'd adored beyond reason and still frequently wore. Frederick had come from nothing; this was a fact he alternately felt righteous about and ashamed of. It was America—everyone was from somewhere else—but it was the East Coast, and people, especially Frederick's contemporaries, still cared about lineage. He could not buy himself a different history, but he could acquire it through objects. Newness became anathema to him.

Things began to change for Liberty the year she turned fourteen. That was the year she molted her chick feathers. Her cheekbones began to emerge from the roundness of her baby face, and her thin limbs acquired a coltish elegance. She suddenly noticed that people looked at her differently when she walked down the street. Sometimes when she was out to eat with Reece or with her parents, men in restaurants would blatantly adjust their chairs to get a better look at her.

It wasn't until she started modeling that the tabloids became interested in her—particularly because she was her mother's daughter and doppelgänger. She was leaving the Lawrences' penthouse to meet Reece for a movie one day after school when her mother was in the midst of a photo shoot for *Elle Decor.* The magazine was doing a story on each of the Lawrence homes: the penthouse and the East Hampton property, both of which had been masterfully appointed by the same up-and-coming decorator whom Petra, along with a dozen other women on the Upper East Side, claimed to have discovered. Liberty had gone to the sitting room to take a look at the shoot and give her mother a quick wave to let her know she was out the door. When she saw her daughter, Petra asked to take five.

"Mom, it's fine, I'm on my way out."

"Nonsense, darling." She gestured to an assistant, who appeared at her side with a glass of Perrier.

Petra asked what her plans were for the afternoon, and as Mother spoke with Daughter, the latter became aware of the subtle click of the photographer's camera, which perhaps only registered to Petra as so much ambient noise after her many years in front of cameras. After a moment, Liberty turned to him with a questioning look, but he didn't stop taking pictures. "Petra, your daughter is stunning," he said, a disembodied voice from behind his lens. Petra straightened and looked Liberty over, as if only now realizing how beautiful her daughter had become. She smiled.

Liberty blushed and made her excuses. But it was too late. The candid image of mother and daughter in a quotidian conversation revealed a well-preserved, fortyish Petra standing with a mirror image of her younger self. And Liberty's fate was sealed.

11

CAMERON DID not call Laila after the party at Soho House. As the following day went by, and she and Nora went about their weekend routine of brunch and shopping, Laila became increasingly aware of her phone: a silent and lifeless thing in her pocket. Perhaps he was playing it cool for a couple of days; men didn't usually show such restraint around her, but Cameron was a different species, a man who could have anything he wanted. She used brunch as an opportunity to grill Nora about him, via a subtler inroad of questions about Reece.

"Oh, I love Reece," Nora said, when she broached the subject. "Isn't she the sweetest?"

They were at a corner table of one of the busy West Village bistros they always went to for brunch. Laila's head was swimming a little from drinking a mimosa on an empty stomach. She wished Nora would make up her mind and either get the brioche French toast she actually wanted or decide to be "good" and go with the egg-white omelet.

Laila did not, in fact, find Reece to be the sweetest. She remembered the look on her face as they'd been introduced. Imperious. "I don't think she likes me."

"Oh, no, I doubt that's true," Nora said. "Just a few more

minutes," she pleaded to the bored waitress who hovered next to their table. "Ugh, I just can't decide!"

"Just get the French toast." Laila tried to hide her irritation as the waitress receded into the crowd. "I'll have some."

"Okay!" Nora closed her menu at last, though who knew when the waitress would return now. Laila's stomach growled. "Anyway, Reece just takes a minute to warm up."

"Hmmm." Laila had seen this with most of her cousins' friends, who were not exactly welcoming to outsiders. She'd met various members of the twins' circle; she had naively thought that because she now dressed as they did, lived where they lived, and was a blood relative of two of their own that they'd be accepting. But after a few cursory questions, they ignored her entirely. "Her brother seems nice," she ventured.

"Ugh, isn't he so hot?"

Laila shrugged.

"Oh, shut up, I saw you."

Though Nora smiled, there was an edge to her voice. Had Laila overstepped by flirting with Cameron? But he'd flirted with *her*. What were the rules? A moment later, the waitress rescued them from their awkward silence by swooping in with another round of drinks, and they at last gave her their order.

"So, do you think you want to become a literary agent like Liberty?" Nora asked, gracefully changing the subject.

Laila shrugged. Liberty's job was respectable—though she worked much too hard—but to be one of the assistants toiling away? She'd watched Daphne and Kim eating their sad little lunches at their desks. They were so bright-eyed and determined; they thought they could be Liberty someday. Was Laila the only one who saw that they could not? Because Liberty did not exactly need the money, she chose only projects she adored and then poured her whole heart into them, ensuring that they would meet their full potential, whatever that may be. Her instincts—unclouded by the desire to chase either trends or cash—were razor sharp, and others could not help but respond to her authentic love of her work, to be infected by her enthusiasm. It was a rich woman's paradox: she didn't need the money, so she didn't chase it and was therefore followed by it everywhere. If there was anything Laila wished to learn from her cousin, it was *this*, her ability to move through the world uncompromised. She was envious that Liberty had something she loved so much: a guiding star.

"I don't know—some of it is pretty dull. Reece's job seems like more fun, actually." Laila had to begrudgingly admire her cousin's friend, who was glamorous and well connected. Her job seemed to consist of going to parties and hanging out with varying classifications of celebrities.

"Maybe she would hire you," Nora mused.

"Maybe." Laila wondered why the sudden interest in her finding a job.

"Or I guess you could go back to your old job. Plenty of dentists in the city. I love mine; maybe he's looking for someone."

Laila was mortified by the suggestion. The scraping, the picking, the rinse-and-spit, the scrubs with little animals on them; none of this fit with her new life. She wished that her cousins didn't know a single detail of it, though of course they hardly knew much of what there was to know. And thank God they'd never actually met Betsy.

"No, not that. That was just . . . it was practical."

"Yay! The food is here." Why this sudden focus on work when

just the other day Nora had been complaining about Laila's abandoning her to go to the office on a day she was feeling blue?

"Well, you'll find something," Nora said with a smile. "I'm just going to be so busy for the next few months with my new cochair."

"Operation Smile? That's so exciting!" Laila had not yet heard the download from the luncheon; she only knew that Nora had been incensed when she realized that her table was miles from Lydia Hearst, who had ostensibly invited her. But perhaps things had progressed.

"No," Nora said, making a face as though Laila had just asked her something absurd. "Dark Dining! We're going to have this fabulous dinner, and everyone is going to wear blindfolds, well, not everyone, some people will get these special glaucoma glasses. It helps the blind!"

"Oh, well, that sounds great too," Laila said. She found it hard to keep track of Nora's efforts at branding herself as a socialite, or a *philanthropist* as she insisted on calling it. It seemed to consist of going to very boring dinners in very expensive gowns and being photographed. Laila had not yet been invited to any of these events, which she was secretly relieved by; they seemed rather out of her league, and furthermore, deeply silly.

On the way back to the apartment, Laila's spirits were temporarily buoyed when she noticed that she had several new text messages on her phone. Her heart lurched at the thought that one would be from Cameron. But alas, the messages were not from him. One was from Cece, Reece's junior coworker whom she'd bonded with, inviting her to a party that Tuesday night. The other was another message from Tom Porter making an attempt to solidify plans. There was a reading he thought she might be interested in the following week at the KGB Bar; would she like to go? Perhaps have dinner after?

Laila quickly accepted both invitations. She could not count on her cousins alone: if she was to embrace this new life and truly leave behind the old one, she needed to let her roots deepen; she needed something to hold her here. She needed Frederick. She'd asked Liberty about meeting him, but he seemed to still be perpetually traveling despite being in his nineties.

"But he does know about me?" Laila had asked her cousin, trying not to sound pleading. "I mean, he knows we've reconnected?"

"Yes, of course, I've told him all about you." This she said smiling, taking Laila's hand reassuringly.

"But he doesn't want to meet me?" her voice sounded small.

"He *will*, Laila. It's hard for him. You know he had this falling-out with your father—God knows why—and he died before they could ever make amends. It's been hard on my dad too, I know. But once he meets you, he'll love you like we all do."

Of course, Laila did know why Frederick had fallen out with Gregory. It was there in the notes and mementos that her mother had kept for all of those years. She hoped never to have to so much as mention their existence. Bringing out these sad little keepsakes would be, in its own way, mortifying. She hoped that with a little time, all of the family's doors would open for her. But it didn't mean she wouldn't break them down if she needed to.

◦◦◦

Cameron Michaels had owned two pieces of real estate in Manhattan: a small one-bedroom in the Financial District around the corner from his office that resembled a hotel room—this was where he worked out in the building's well-appointed fitness center, came from the office for a quick shower before client dinners, and sometimes slept during the workweek—but his *home* was a town house on West Eighth Street, all three floors of it. He was elated to be back in New York; to be able to enjoy it. London had been fine, suitably far away to let the girl fade from memory, so that he could return fully restored to himself. He had a number of friends already living there for various reasons, and he'd had a pleasant enough time with them, enjoying Shoreditch House and the proximity of Saint Tropez and Paris; he'd packed in weekend jaunts and treated the whole thing as his own little European tour. But he'd missed his home.

"You know," he said to his younger sister now, as they lounged side by side in the Adirondack chairs on his back terrace, "I think I might renovate the kitchen this winter."

"Oh? Because you do so much cooking in there?"

"No, but if I'm ever going to have a family, I need a better kitchen, more counter space. Maybe a breakfast bar."

"Excuse me?" Reece nearly spat out her beer, her sunglasses sliding off her face as she sat upright. Her brother was only thirty-six; she was shocked that the idea of a family had even crossed his mind.

"What's wrong with a breakfast bar?"

She gave him a look.

"You're so shocked I want a family? I don't mean tomorrow, but you know, someday." Cameron was somewhere between annoyed and amused at his sister's reaction, though he knew he'd earned it. He'd cut a wide swath through their friends and acquaintances both here and in London. He'd always tried to be kind to these women, or so went the story he told himself. He always *meant* well. And there seemed to be a limitless supply of enthusiastic partners, making the very idea of finding the right woman all the more elusive. Perversely, he envied his friends who were less good-looking, less charming, but found themselves happily coupled because a woman truly willing to love them had come along; simplicity was its own kind of privilege. But he had returned to the city with renewed determination. A good woman would set him to right, as his father had said many times when talking about his own bachelor days and how meeting Elin had flipped a switch in him. Cameron knew he was often attracted to women who brought out the worst in him: wild, destructive women who took him to the edge of himself. But too many of these pairings had ended in catastrophe. They were behind him now.

"Ah, I see," Reece said, settling back into her chair. "So in, like, the next ten or fifteen years or so."

"No," he said laughing. "More like two to three. I think you're confusing my timeline with yours."

"Ha! I'll have to get my shit together sooner than that, brother. I am, in fact, a woman, remember?"

"A woman who could have any man she wants. And he'd be a lucky bastard too."

"Eh," Reece said noncommittally. Cameron worried that his sister emulated him too much in her dating life. Unfair as it was, she was right that she couldn't get away with it for as long as he could. The world would wait forever for a wealthy bachelor to decide he wanted to settle down. Reece was beautiful but intimidating too, and thirty-two now. Her options would become limited as the years passed in a way that his would not. And he saw how she defined herself by her single status: it wouldn't be easy to let go of that independence, though he suspected she'd want to someday. He dreaded to think of her with someone who did not deserve her; the very notion sent a bolt of fury through him.

They sat in companionable silence for a moment while Cameron tried to determine how to broach the topic of Liberty, who'd been on his mind every moment since the previous weekend. He was glad to be with his sister; he felt as though he was stepping back into his old life fully revived.

"So what do you think of the new Lawrence?" Reece asked.

Cameron was dismayed that she was bringing up the sexy cousin. She'd come on to him full force that night. Ordinarily, he might have gone for it. He got the sense that, had he wanted to, he could have had her right there in the bathroom of the nightclub; could have pushed her up against a wall like some degenerate cheating on his wife with a desperate diner waitress. The idea of such seediness thrilled him—in his overly polished life, these fantasies added a touch of the exotic. But Laila was not just a hot stranger; she was Liberty's cousin. So when she pressed up against him, grinding her pelvis against his in the hallway of the club, barely obscured from the rest of their group, he'd gently separated from her and diverted her attention by telling her that he'd love to see her again sometime; in his lust-spiked panic he'd said something abominably cheesy like "show you around town" and asked for her phone number. Like any good huntress, she'd diverted her attention to the long game once she'd seen it was a possibility.

He'd known he wouldn't call her, of course, and he hoped she wouldn't be too hurt. That could backfire if she was important to Liberty.

"She seems sweet. The poor thing has been through a lot, I gather."

Reece sighed. "So everyone keeps reminding me. I just . . . there's something about her that puts me off. You know? She gets my hackles up for some reason."

"Stand down, little sis. She's twenty-five; she's a kid."

"She just seems . . . climb-y."

"Well, she's new here. We've never had to go through that. It's lonely living in a new place. I went through it in London."

This wasn't completely true; he'd slipped into London with ease the way that any of their cohort did when on a stint in the European capitals. But he'd ached for New York too. Cameron had considered it his exile, and his relief at its being over was acute.

"Okay, okay. Let's talk about something else."

"Liberty is doing well in her work, it seems," he started awkwardly. His memory of seeing her for the first time in several years was vivid and it rose up in him now, catching in his throat. She'd been wearing a simple black dress that hung on her elegantly; she'd drunk little and left early, sometime after dinner. She had sharpened into a beauty that was reminiscent of her mother, Petra, but somehow less ostentatious too, and all the more enthralling.

"That girl is kicking ass," Reece said. "I'm so proud."

He was a little surprised that his sister didn't immediately see through him. But how could she understand the different light in which Liberty suddenly appeared to him, when he'd never shown interest in her before? Of course he'd noticed she was beautiful, but now he could sense some depth, some fragility that stirred him even if he didn't know its source. Had she changed, or had Cameron's senses refined themselves at last? Was it simply growing up that had finally revealed her to him?

"She's looks so much like Petra, but I daresay she's even more beautiful."

Now Reece turned slowly sideways in her chair, pushing her sunglasses atop her head to look her brother in the eye.

"What?" he said, though of course he knew. He squirmed under his sister's gaze.

"Cameron, *no.*"

"No *what?*"

"Liberty. No."

"What do you mean, 'no'? Why ever not? I would have thought you'd be happy."

"That you're going to try to break my best friend's heart? If she'll let you, which no one is saying that she will."

Cameron crossed his muscular arms firmly over his chest. Secretly, he was pleased at his sister's resistance. He was always in search of a challenge to rise to. "That is really unfair, Reece, and hurtful. What makes you so sure I'd break her heart?"

This she answered with a simple incredulous glare.

"Haven't I just been telling you that I'm ready for a change?" He wanted to explain, as he mounted his defense, how he had forsaken Laila offering herself on a platter. But he sensed that this would not help matters. Reece had always had a fiery streak—as a teenager, she'd been in a constant battle of wills with their mother, who had always been indulgent of Cameron. But it wasn't often that she'd openly questioned her brother. She'd worshipped him as a kid, as had all of her friends, including Liberty. And now, while his back was turned, it seemed his little sister had come into her own.

"Give me a chance here, Reece. Don't you want me to be happy?"

"Listen," she said after a long pause, "if you're going to pursue Liberty, I can't stop you. But what I ask is that you're *sure* that she's who you want to be with before you do. Why don't you spend some time getting to know her again? You've been gone for years."

"So, what . . . be her friend?"

"Why not? If you can't be her friend first, then you don't mean her well. Cameron, listen to me: if you make an honest go of it, and things don't work out, okay. But I swear, if you go into this all cavalier and hurt her, I will never forgive you for it. I'm serious."

The bar raised, the prize made more valuable, Cameron felt himself being galvanized. "I think you're not giving Liberty nearly enough credit, let alone your poor brother, who I had no idea you had such a low opinion of, thanks very much."

She let out a long sigh, reaching out to put her hand on her brother's arm. "Just do this for me. Cameron: get to know her again first. It will be best for you too, and I love you both too much to see either of you hurt."

Cameron did not now confess his fear, for he knew Reece wouldn't tolerate it. What if he spent all this time with Liberty, fell madly in love with her—which he, in that moment, felt a deep certainty that he would do—and she wanted nothing to do with him romantically? What then? He was unaccustomed to failure, romantic or otherwise, and the possibility of it loomed larger in this case. He'd missed out on the thousand tiny rejections his peers had experienced, those disappointments that made the possibility of out-and-out heartbreak more palatable, less daunting. Cameron had everything except resilience. He'd never needed it.

"Okay. I'll do as you ask. Only because I love you so much."

She rolled her eyes and smiled at him.

"And because I need to set a good example. So that you, dear sister, might be encouraged to someday take some worthy man as your husband."

"Shut up." She laughed, taking a last sip of her beer as the sun dipped behind the trees.

❦

The Wednesday after the Soho House party, Laila came into Liberty's office to confess that she had a date with Tom Porter the next evening. She'd worn her mother's pendant for the first time since arriving in New York, hoping it would bring her luck.

It was a busy day in the office; Liberty had two books at auction, one with a debut novelist who tended toward the hysterical. Every time the phone rang she jumped—would it be one of the editors with deal news or the author again, wanting to know if she could make just one more *tiny* change to the manuscript? And still, she'd noticed the pendant right away.

"What is that necklace? It's gorgeous!"

"Oh, this." Laila's fingertips went reflexively to the smooth, cold lacquer of the pendant. "It was my mother's."

"It's stunning. May I see it?" Liberty asked.

Laila was surprised but handed it over, and slid into the small leather armchair that faced Liberty's desk. Her older cousin didn't seem nearly as into fashion as her younger brother and sister, and she dressed plainly for work—pencil skirts for meetings, dark jeans otherwise. But now that she thought about it, Laila *had* seen her with some unusually lovely bracelets and earrings on occasion.

Liberty held the pendant in her palm, mesmerized. "Do you know where your mother got this?"

Laila shrugged and shook her head. The piece definitely stuck out among her mother's belongings, and she'd worn the necklace often, but she'd never told Laila where it had come from.

"It looks nineteenth century to me," Liberty said, peering at it. "You should have it appraised," she added, handing it back to Laila, who secured it once again around her neck.

"Wow, I had no idea," Laila said. The necklace felt different on her skin now. She'd always found it beautiful but had no idea it might also be valuable. "I didn't realize you knew so much about jewelry."

"Vintage jewelry is my guilty pleasure. My . . . *our* grandfather is a collector, you know? One of Fred Leighton's best customers."

Laila felt her eyes go wide, and she quickly smiled to disguise it. Frederick. Of course.

"So anyway, sweets, what's up?"

Laila regained her composure. Suddenly the pendant felt like a talisman, a weapon, even, and she let it embolden her. She told Liberty about her date with Tom. She'd meant to ask her permission, but now she asked instead simply for her blessing.

"Laila, isn't he a bit old for you?" Liberty said, leaning back in her chair, looking dismayed.

"Not really, no. He's younger than my ex."

"Well, I mean you're both adults, obviously." Sort of, she thought. Liberty was disappointed in Tom; the twenty-five-year-old intern? Forget that Laila was her cousin; Tom was becoming a cliché. She'd known him for years and had helped launched his career. She remembered him sweet and dorky and giddy over his first successes. As for Laila, she didn't seem to understand that this was unprofessional. But then, she had *married* her former boss.

"Come on, Liberty. He seems so wonderful."

Just at that moment, Kim appeared at her doorway, gingerly opening the door, aware that she was interrupting.

"Hi, Kim, what do you need?" It seemed she was destined to have nothing but distractions today.

"I'm so sorry to interrupt you guys. But Cameron Michaels

is in the lobby. Does he have a meeting? I didn't see him in the books; did I make a mistake?"

Liberty was taken aback, though pleasantly this time. What was Cameron doing here?

"No, he must just be swinging by. Go ahead and bring him up." Kim nodded and hurried off, her relief that she hadn't mucked up the schedule palpable. She supported several of the agents in the office, and though Liberty was always kind to her, the other two could be terrors. One of them, Maryanne, could be heard bellowing her name down the hall throughout the day.

"Sweets, can we talk about this a bit later?" Liberty said now to Laila.

"Sure," Laila said. "It's not that big a deal. I mean, listen, maybe he just wants to be friends, so maybe it's not even a thing."

Liberty looked up at her cousin, confused by how her entire demeanor seemed to have changed in an instant. A moment before, she'd seemed insistent about going out with Tom. And of course he didn't just want to be friends; was she that naive? Before she could make sense of it, Cameron appeared in the doorway.

"Good afternoon, ladies," Cameron said, delivered by Kim who was nearly losing her composure in his presence. He was wearing a handsome suit that was expertly tailored to his frame, which appeared nearly as athletic as it had in his youth.

Liberty got up from her chair and, infuriatingly, found her legs felt weak beneath her. Seeing Cameron, she seemed to lose all the years that separated her from her teenage self. There she was once again, sitting in the Michaelses' vast, sparkling kitchen, watching him raid the fridge after his afternoon crew training, his every pore gleaming with good health. The sensory memories of the long-buried—but apparently still-living—crush bombarded her.

"Cameron," she said now as he moved through her small office toward her, his long legs gliding across it in a single step. He kissed her on the cheek. "What brings you here?"

"Oh, hello, Laila," he said, as though he'd just noticed her there, and perhaps he had.

"Hi, Cam," Laila purred. Oh dear, Liberty thought, maybe Reece was right about Laila's being into Cameron. She couldn't keep track. But every woman reacted like that to him, didn't they? Kim's concentration would probably be shot for the rest of the day.

"I was hoping to take you to lunch," Cameron said, turning back to Liberty. "I was seeing a client in the area."

"Oh," Liberty said, stepping back behind her desk to peruse her calendar. "I would love to, but I'm afraid I have a lunch with an author I'm courting today. She's that research scientist at NYU who wrote the big article on autism in the *New York Times* last week; everyone in town is after her." She realized that she was giving Cameron far more information than he needed. What did she want him to know, exactly? That she was important enough to land a lunch with such a coveted potential client? Or simply that the person she was having lunch with was a woman?

"That's too bad. Not about the potential client, of course; that's fantastic. Look at you." He sparkled at her, and Liberty felt her spine straighten, felt herself standing to attention. "I would have called first, but if you can believe it, I don't have your cell."

Liberty smiled. Of course, Cameron easily could have gotten her number from Reece or found the agency's number online. He'd wanted to see her.

"Well, here," she said, passing him one of her client business cards, which included every possible way to reach her. "For next time." Oh, let there be a next time, she thought.

"Okay," he said, looking at the card. "Well, I'd better be on my way and let you ladies get back to work. Lovely to see you both."

"So . . . Cameron, huh?" Laila said after he'd left.

"Is an old friend," she said to Laila, her tone rather stern, "and that is all."

"Okay, okay," Laila said, putting her hands up.

The two lingered there in a stilted silence for a moment as Liberty riffled through a small stack of papers on her desk. She looked up at Laila, not certain why she was still sitting there. Liberty's own thoughts had been scattered—for the happiest of reasons—by Cameron's unannounced visit.

"I just . . . ," Laila said. "The thing with Tom."

"Oh, right." So we were back to that again? "Listen, honey, do what you like, but proceed with caution, okay? It's just a bit delicate."

"Okay!" Laila said regaining her cheer. "You got it."

⁊⸱

The next morning, Liberty woke feeling as though she were at the bottom of a well. She had felt the black dogs—Churchill's metaphor, which she found so apt—nipping at her heels all throughout the day before but had gone to her regular measures to try to curb them: white tea and no wine; a long yoga class to stop her thoughts from ricocheting in her brain. She'd been distracted by Cameron's visit and her lunch with the potential new client, which had gone exceptionally well. The client, Victoria Forrester, had seemed to take to Liberty right away. Liberty knew she was the only female agent courting Victoria, but she didn't know whether this would help or hurt her cause until she'd met her. In the first few minutes of their lunch, she'd known it would be a plus: Victoria was an obvious girl's girl, with her hug upon meeting her and her "call me Vickie." This certainly meant that she preferred doing business with other women, as Liberty did; this had been true since her modeling days, where men were unavoidable. It wasn't like she was never hassled now, but it was mostly women who worked in her industry. She'd cut one male client loose the previous year when his marriage started falling apart and he took to leaving Liberty long, late-night voice mails declaring his love. Liberty had been mortified for him, and baffled. What had she done to make him think she might want to hear these things? Intellectually, she knew that it likely had nothing to do with her, that this was simply him unleashing his tortured ardor on the nearest woman. But it tapped into a deeper shame that could not be so easily reasoned with: the dark suspicion that the way men behaved around her was *her* fault.

Liberty's cat—Catniss Everdeen, drunkenly and shrewdly named in her kitten-hood by Reece for the literary heroine of the moment—jumped up on Liberty's bed, climbed directly onto her chest, and nuzzled her face. Catniss was a highly empathetic cat and could always seem to sense it when Liberty's black moods hit her.

"Good kitty," Liberty said absently, scratching behind her ears as the cat began to purr loudly. Liberty's limbs were heavy as she dragged herself out of bed and made her way to her small kitchen. Even scooping the beans into the grinder for her French press felt like a substantial effort. She mentally ran through her schedule for the morning; could she afford to stay home? Fortunately, Gerard was usually too busy lunching with all his old-man publishing cronies to much care or notice when she worked from home. She had three new books from clients that she could stay home and read, though that was ordinarily work she did on the weekends. But it was a risk to go into the office like this—feeling as she did, that she was made of glass. The wrong look from a colleague or a too-brusque e-mail from an editor could send her death-spiraling, even just an errant memory that surfaced and flooded her with shame.

She'd only had a panic attack in the office once, two years ago. She'd curled up in the space beneath her desk at once, praying no one would find her and hoping she wouldn't pass out from the shallow breaths she was taking: these fears only made her worse. She stayed down there for who knows how long. When the panic had exhausted itself, she left the building and hailed a cab home immediately, emailing the office later to tell them she had food poisoning.

Plenty of New Yorkers wore their neuroses like medals—traded names of therapists as though they were hairdressers, compared meds, and even casually topped each other off if need be—but this was not Liberty's style. Her armor to the outside world was her very pulled-togetherness. Only Reece knew of her terrors and her insomnia, ameliorated only somewhat by the Lexapro, the Xanax, and the Klonopin for sleepless nights that could otherwise trigger a whole week of imbalance. And only Reece knew what had happened to her, where the trouble had truly begun.

Once she had her coffee, she returned to bed and curled herself around her cat who was purring loudly. "Catniss, can you get me my laptop? No? Okay, I'll just e-mail work from my phone, then." Even opening her e-mail felt exhausting.

Seeing Cameron the day before had been a happy thing, but she wondered if it also had triggered something. Having Cameron back in her life, it returned her to her younger self, the self that was still untouched, uncorrupted, innocent, and hopeful.

He'd been at college by the time she was in the thick of her modeling career, which had begun at fourteen and that she'd left the moment she'd gone to Columbia. She ought to have stopped when she was sixteen, after what happened. Even though she'd hired a much more protective team and had never been through anything similar after the disastrous lingerie shoot, she feared that her additional two years in front of the camera had somehow compounded the damage; that what was broken in her when she was sixteen had never properly set. She should never have started modeling in the first place, but the force of her mother's excitement and pride—both of which felt so much like love, and not the cold, authoritarian kind she'd become accustomed to from Petra—had been too compelling for her. And it offered a chance to feel beautiful, to *be* beautiful, which was appealing to any fourteen-year-old girl.

Until James Marsh. He was the biggest name that Liberty had ever been photographed by. The girls in her agency, including Tasha, an eighteen-year-old from the Czech Republic who'd been modeling since she was thirteen and was slated to do the shoot with Liberty, had said that he was "weird" but "fun," and that, regardless, it was worth it.

On set, he'd told them to call him Uncle Jimmy. His assistants had all been young, cool twentysomethings who looked like art school grads—or, more accurately, like the actresses hired to play them in a movie—and they were sisterly and warm with Liberty and Tasha. They had made it feel so natural, so expected, that they would strip down to their underwear (*Here!* Jimmy said, *I'll get naked too!*), that they would kiss each other (*Weren't they friends?*), that Jimmy would join them. It was an experience so surreal that Liberty left her body as though in a dream; there was no anchor to the real world within this studio. All she saw were smiling faces around her, encouraging her; everywhere she looked, there were subtle reminders that if she said no, she'd be letting them all down. They couldn't have known that she'd never so much as kissed a boy before. James Marsh, with his thick handlebar mustache and his thinning hair, was not whom she had pictured as her first.

After, Tasha had seemed more or less unconcerned with what had happened. Liberty wondered if she was overreacting. Then the panic attacks had started. . . .

Liberty's phone buzzed.

Hey you! Nice to see you if only briefly yesterday. There is an event at the 92nd Street Y tomorrow that I was thinking of going to. Margaret Atwood. Any interest?

Liberty felt her heart lift a little. Had he pumped Reece for information? How would he have known this was one of her favorite authors? Nothing she knew about Cameron led her to think that he was that interested in literature. But it had been a long time since she'd seen him, and perhaps London had left him with new interests; or perhaps he was feigning interest to be able to spend time with her. Either option thrilled her.

Liberty knew it was magical thinking to imagine that giving her teenage self the thing she wanted most—the highest prize, her best friend's dreamy older brother—could erase what had been done to her; a thing she intellectually knew she could not take the blame for but nonetheless on some bodily, cellular level, she had, and forever would. Still she found herself craving that feeling of being near Cameron, the heady mix of nostalgia and desire burning, even after all these years. He felt both exciting and safe, and where else would she possibly find that?

12

LAILA WAS shocked that Tom Porter didn't have more money. What did *bestselling* even mean if not that the author was wealthy? They'd been dating for nearly a month now, and she'd spent as much time at his apartment as she could bear. It was a small, dark one-bedroom with evidence of his scruffy bachelorhood in every corner: from the aging black leather couch to the mismatched silverware to the plain blue coverlet on his bed with its paucity of decent pillows. True, it was in a choice neighborhood, Gramercy Park, conveniently nearby Liberty's office. Tom would often beg Laila to come over for "lunch," which naturally meant midday sex.

Gramercy was the shabby apartment's saving grace. One of the things Laila had learned in her time in New York was that neighborhood was everything: even odd, little apartments like Tom's could be worth an absolute fortune if they were in the right location. So perhaps he *could* do better but just didn't, out of that particularly male laziness that allows them to live in squalor even when they don't need to. Perhaps what Tom actually lacked was taste and style. Well, those things Laila could bring him. They could move together toward being the kind of New Yorkers who would fit right in with the Lawrences. Tom brought the intellectual gravitas, and Laila had beauty and youth, a currency accepted everywhere.

One night in early November, as Laila was getting ready for a date with Tom, she solicited Nora's opinion about which boots she ought to wear with her sweater dress. Nora collapsed on the chaise to examine the options, all of which she had purchased for her cousin. Laila felt the knowledge of this draped over the two of them like a veil. It occurred to her—and not for the first time—that perhaps these trips to Bergdorf's were not completely without obligation on Laila's part.

"You're seeing Tom *again* tonight?" Nora said, raking her hand through her blond hair, which fanned out beneath her on the chaise.

"He *is* my boyfriend." Laila smiled at the word. She had always preferred being paired; when she was not, she felt the negative space radiating next to her like a phantom limb. Her mother had been the same in her youth: a steady boyfriend since the time she was fourteen right up until the day she met Gregory Lawrence when she was an undergrad at the University of Michigan and had deposited all her dreams upon him. Before Betsy had realized that she'd never be able to convince him to return to the life she coveted in New York—the very reason she'd fallen for him in the first place—she'd had Laila and sealed her future. It left Laila nearly breathless how close she had come to living out the same fate: trapped under the intractable weight of marriage, eventual motherhood, and a mortgage. But she'd been braver.

"You don't love me anymore," Nora huffed accusingly. "You never spend time with me. It's always Tom or that girl Cece." She nearly spat the latter's name. Laila had originally hoped the three of them could all be friends, but though neither would say so directly, Laila intuited that Nora thought Cece was too common to bother with, and Cece found Nora snobbish and bizarre—and,

Laila suspected, a little bit stupid. Ever since Nora's little speech about Laila's getting a job, she'd been on high alert, though her cousin had not mentioned it again. She suspected that keeping her on her toes in this way might have been exactly the intention.

"That's not true," Laila said. She sat next to Nora on the chaise and reached for her hand. "You're my sister now."

"Everyone abandons me!" Nora said so dramatically that Laila had to close her eyes so that she would not roll them.

"Why don't you come with us?"

"And be the third wheel? No, thank you. Anyway, all Tom does is talk about books I haven't read and gossip about writers I don't know of and would probably be bored to death by if I did." That was true enough.

"I could see if he has a friend he could bring. Or you could finally call Poor Larry back," Laila said, smiling at her cousin. Larry, the clothing magnate Oxana had set her up with, was always Poor Larry: Larry who had taken Nora out to one dinner and fallen in love with her, Larry with his lisp and his bad hair and his buckets and buckets of money. "We could double; it would be fun! Oh, let's."

Nora didn't disguise what she thought of that idea. "Just stay home with me," she said, giving her face over to a full pout.

"If you really need me to, I will. It's just that I hate to cancel on Tom at the last minute. But I can tell him I'm not feeling well. He'll understand."

The two had done this dance a half dozen times before. As long as Laila showed an earnest willingness to throw over anyone for Nora, she would usually be given a reprieve.

"Oh, just go," Nora said with a sigh.

Laila curled forward and put her head in Nora's lap. "I just can't wait for tomorrow!" she said, trying to turn her cousin's mind to something other than her disappointment. The next night all of them—Leo, Nora, and Liberty, along with Tom and Laila—were going to a party at Capitale, a benefit for a charity called Earth Love.

"Yes, that will be fun."

"I almost wish I could stay home tonight just so we could plan our outfits!" Laila was aware that she was laying it on a little thick now.

"Oh, go," Nora said, at last cracking a smile. "Poor Tom."

❧

"Dear God," Tom had said when he came into the monstrous pink bathroom the next evening to find Laila there, still only halfway through her preparations, though they were running late for dinner, "what are you wearing?" She'd told him they could go to dinner before the benefit but that she had to get ready with Nora; it was their tradition!

She had on a sparkling green bustier that presented her spectacular cleavage in all of its glory. Her legs, sheathed in sheer stockings, were covered by a wispy skirt made of pieces of tulle and feathers. She'd been sitting in the living room with curlers in her hair for the previous hour: it was now teased back away from her face, and she was securing it with jeweled hairpins and yet more feathers. Nora and Leo had delighted in helping her. They thought the whole idea was hilarious and loved the idea of their cousin's becoming a downtown eccentric.

Her date looked her polar opposite. Tom's wardrobe suited him well enough—a collection of shirts and blazers in conservative colors from Thomas Pink and Hugo Boss, which he wore with dark jeans or trousers—but it was decidedly dull and made

him look older than his thirty-seven years. He was less than enthused about going to the party in the first place, and now there
was the fresh hell of his much younger girlfriend dressed like a
circus performer.

"Do you like it?" Laila trilled. "I'm the Green Fairy!"

Tom looked perplexed. In the vivid light of the bathroom, Tom
suddenly appeared pale and tired. Laila pushed the thought away:
he was only *acting* like a grumpy old man; he wasn't actually one.

"Is it a costume party?"

"It's a *theme* party. Green!"

"Couldn't you have just worn a green dress? How about the
one with the spaghetti straps? I love you in that dress," he said
hopefully.

"What fun would that be? Anyway, I spent all day on this
outfit. I thought you would appreciate it! The Green Fairy was a
muse, and you're always saying that I'm your muse."

"Well, Green Fairy really just means absinthe, which obviously
the bohemians associated with the muse, but . . ." At this Laila
gave him such a look that he trailed off. "It's just a little much,
is all."

"That's the point, Captain Pedantic," Laila said, getting irri-
tated. She turned back to the mirror and started vigorously apply-
ing a shimmering topcoat of powder to her face.

"Oh, Tom!" Nora chimed in now. "Don't be such a wet blanket! She looks spectacular."

"Don't be mad at me," he said, coming up behind her and
putting his arms around her waist. "You look amazing, I wasn't
trying to be critical."

"She'll be the talk of the party," Leo said with a canny smile.

"It's not that," Tom stammered, clearly feeling like the maligned adult in a room full of children. Laila had known he'd hate her outfit, as it was so important to him to be taken *seriously*. It added to her fun to see how far she could push him.

"You just think I'm ridiculous." She affected a moody pout.

"Laila, you know that's not true," he said.

"Well, it doesn't always feel that way," she said, frowning. She affixed a pair of giant black-and-green false eyelashes to her eyelids and turned around, her fairy drag now complete. "I feel like you don't take me seriously."

She brushed by him in a cloud of perfumed glitter and slipped into a sparkling pair of green four-inch heels; she'd already owned these and had imagined the outfit around them.

"But I do!" he protested.

Laila imagined he was more used to academic types: mousy women who carried canvas bags from the Strand in lieu of purses. These women populated the endless readings Tom took her to.

"Maybe I should just change; this was a silly idea."

This was met with vehement protests from the twins.

"No, no. You *do* look spectacular. What do I know?" Tom pleaded.

"Let's just go to dinner," she said as though her mood had now been ruined. She whispered to the twins as they left that she wished she was going to dinner with them instead.

"At least we're eating on the Lower East Side," Tom said as he helped her into the cab. "Your outfit probably won't even stand out."

She gave him a weak smile.

⤎⤏

Laila pouted through dinner, pushing her salmon tartare around and woundedly sipping her Pinot Gris. She'd really thought dating someone like Tom would be more fun, that he'd have more imagination. But she brightened immediately when they arrived at Capitale, the magnificent venue where the party was being held. She'd never actually been inside, but it seemed like the kind of place where Caligula might have thrown a party if he'd lived in present-day Manhattan. There was a lot of fanfare at the doorway, and clusters of glittering people crowded the red carpet and the tall step-and-repeat banner that featured the Earth Love logo.

"Jesus Christ," Tom said, his voice full of dread. But Laila felt a charge run up her spine.

It was an hour into the party when Laila crossed paths with Simon Beauchamp for the first time. Tom was deep in conversation with Liberty, who looked nearly as relieved to be talking to him as he was to her. Laila knew that her cousin had been going to parties like this since she was a teenager and found them utterly boring; she showed up and was polite, and that was all. Unable to bear their shoptalk any longer, Laila had gone off to look for the twins and avail herself of the gloriously well-appointed open bar—they were serving Veuve Clicquot, her newly discovered favorite—and get away from Tom, who was dampening her spirits just by existing that evening.

"Dear God," said a man approaching Laila at the bar. She immediately recognized him as the party's billionaire British philanthropist host, Simon Beauchamp. He was tall with thick, gray hair that surrounded his face in tight curls, "I must have had too much to drink already. I am hallucinating a beautiful green fairy. You had better cut me off, Frank." The bartender smiled at him, pouring the cocktail he'd been shaking into a delicate frosted martini glass.

"Unless you're seeing more than one of her, I think you're

safe," the bartender replied. "She appears to be real. Another glass of champagne, Green Fairy?"

"Yes, please," Laila said coyly, batting her heavy false lashes at him.

"She speaks!" Simon said, closing the gap between them effortlessly, like a shark. "Does she also have a name?"

He was at least fifty, but he was surprisingly alluring. He radiated power.

"Laila Lawrence," she said, giving him her hand, which he kissed—to her delight.

"Lawrence? As in Ben and Petra Lawrence?" he said, showing his age by the Lawrences his mind immediately pulled up.

"My aunt and uncle."

"Are you having fun, my dear? I would daresay so, judging by your outfit."

"Oh, this?" she asked, running her fingers through the feathers of her skirt. "I just love getting dressed up. When you think about it, as a woman, I'm practically in costume half the time anyway. I put on a fancy dress and high heels and makeup, and spend an hour on my hair. What is that if not a costume?"

He laughed and tapped a finger against the rim of his martini glass, as though he couldn't decide whether she was joking or in earnest.

"I'm sure you look just as beautiful without all the makeup."

"You've never seen me first thing in the morning."

"Chance would be a fine thing."

She blushed.

"So you're an aspiring actress? Model?"

"Actually, I work with my cousin Liberty at a literary agency." She smiled. She knew that literary work functioned as a sort of class shorthand, that people would automatically assume she'd been to an Ivy League school and a prep school before that. They would assume that she was a proper Lawrence.

"Ah yes, I know of your cousin as well, of course. Good for you. She's a smarty, that one. You'll learn a lot from her." Laila could see the admiration in his eyes. Just then, someone Simon knew tapped him on the shoulder and diverted him.

"Excuse me, Ms. Lawrence. Enjoy yourself tonight."

He smiled, and that was it. Laila stood there for a moment more, drinking champagne and feeling deflated. A billionaire had been flirting with her; it must count for something somehow. A check mark on some version of Becoming a New Yorker bingo?

She saw him only once more that night. He came to wish her goodnight when he was making his rounds to leave the party and slipped her a cocktail napkin with his phone number printed in his neat script. Well, there, she thought. She had no idea what she'd do with it but was delighted nonetheless.

~∽~

Everything that Laila had known about the Lawrence family prior to her parents' death had come from her mother's rare revelations over the years. When she was young, they lived in a lovely four-bedroom colonial a few blocks away from the lake-shore that seemed, in Laila's youth, to circumscribe her mother's entire existence. Betsy had grown up in a different part of town, one of three children of a single mother. A life in Grosse Pointe, Laila imagined, might have been more than enough for her had she never met Gregory Lawrence, never gone to New York after graduation, never seen what else was out there. Her reminiscences would always begin the same way: "Laila, did I ever tell you about when we lived in New York?" Normally this was after two or three glasses of the Chardonnay that was always on hand in their fridge. Betsy would be cooking, waiting for Gregory who was always later returning from work than he said he'd be. He might have left his father behind in New York—but he could not leave his inherited obsession with work. Laila would be sitting at the kitchen table doing her homework.

As her memories of the couple's two years there grew more remote, they seemed to become only more potent in Betsy's imagination: the vivid juxtaposition of the crime-ridden lower part of the city with the gleaming Upper East Side where the Lawrences lived. Ben had already left his second wife for Petra: "She was so classy," Betsy would say when she treated Laila to these little trips down memory lane. "So elegant. It's a whole different way of living there. None of the ladies did any of their own cooking or cleaning; we would go to these huge houses in the Hamptons." Nary a mention of Liberty, whom she must have met. Why not tell Laila about her? Did she imagine she was somehow protecting her?

These conversations would always stop abruptly when the great clattering of the garage door signaled Gregory's return home.

Laila wondered what her mother would think of Tom. Betsy had told her not to settle for Nathan—which was probably half the reason she'd married him right after her death, just to spite her. When they had first begun dating Betsy had said, "Nathan is a lovely man, but with your looks, you could do better."

Betsy often spoke this way of Laila's looks, as though they were a thing separate from her entirely, something that Betsy had handed down to her and that she now had a responsibility to use properly. The irony that Betsy had ruined her own looks seemed not to occur to her. Though she loomed for Laila as a cautionary tale.

After her father's death, Laila and her mother had managed, though in retrospect, Laila wasn't sure how, since her mother never really worked. She would have ideas for oddball moneymaking ventures—selling makeup or knives—and constantly spoke of getting her real-estate license, an idea that never materialized. These ideas were as ephemeral as the diets Betsy was forever pledging to go on. Laila suspected that her mother had fallen a little in love with the idea of being an impoverished widow, whittling away at what her husband had left behind, until it was tapped out. The result was that there wasn't a dime left for Laila when she died. Nor had she been groomed to be self-sufficient, in the modern sense. She'd only been taught an outmoded version of womanhood—one in which her survival depended on her being what others wanted her to be. Laila had become a skilled chameleon, and her repertoire of roles was quite impressive—temptress, good girl, caretaker, ingénue—but these transmogrifications had taken so much effort, there wasn't much energy left for constructing an identity of her own.

Laila knew how false it was, that beloved American ideal that true reinvention was always possible. She'd seen her mother lose not only her will but her opportunities. She'd once been beautiful, she'd had cards, but she'd played them wrong, and her sad end was the result. But Betsy had left one parting gift—the letters. Whether this was intentional or not, Laila would never know, but she liked to believe it was. Whatever the case, Laila would not let her chances pass her by.

13

"SO IS it Aspen with the parents for Thanksgiving?" Liberty asked Reece, taking care not to trip over Rocket's leash as he sprang in front of her in pursuit of some irresistible scent at the base of a tree.

"Nah, I'm going to skip it." Reece pulled the collar of her coat tighter with her free hand, covering the tiny patch on her collarbone not protected from the November wind by her scarf.

"Really? No skiing this year?"

"If I go up, I won't get any chance to work on the collection before the end of the year."

"Wow." Liberty was impressed with her friend's sacrifice; she knew she loved trips to Aspen. She would always come back blissed-out from the adrenaline rush of the skiing—or maybe it was the sedative effects of drinking whiskey in the hot tub with some sexy ski instructor.

"Well, come have Thanksgiving with us in Tuxedo; you can't work the *whole* time."

Reece smiled at her. "Can you take on Cameron too? He was going to spend it at home this year as well. And this one," she said, calling Rocket back from where he was staring down a German shepherd approximately five times his size.

"There's *always* room for Rocket." Liberty knelt down to

scratch him behind his ears, his eyes narrowing in ecstasy. "And Cameron too, of course. You know my parents: the more the merrier on holidays."

Ben and Petra had a habit of packing the vast Tuxedo Park mansion with a wide array of friends and acquaintances. The house belonged to Frederick, but he was rarely in it and insisted that his son go there frequently to make sure the place was ship-shape and also to keep an eye on Birdie, who lived nearby. Liberty suspected that their holiday overkill was to distract the father from who was missing—who now, would always be missing—his only brother.

"Well, if you're sure, then we'd love to."

"Of course I'm sure."

In the two months since they'd reunited, Cameron and Liberty had seen each other nearly once a week, or as often as their busy schedules allowed. At first Liberty had thought he was asking her out, and this had filled her with a heady mix of anxiety and desire. She had never been comfortable on dates and generally avoided them. But thus far, Cameron had done nothing more intimate than hug her and kiss her cheek at the beginning and end of every outing. True, he paid for everything, but this was in Cameron's nature: he wouldn't let *any* woman pick up a check; it was an old-fashioned kind of politeness that Liberty felt intellectually ambivalent about but appreciated in practice. So, what they had begun was a friendship, which was both a relief and an immeasurable disappointment. That lack of overt romantic intention had, however, allowed her to settle a little more fully into her adult self with him. He seemed impressed with all she'd accomplished, with her passion for her work. And he had grown too, of course, from a cocky youth to a man to be reckoned with.

"You have to be nice to Laila, though," Liberty said, getting back to her feet as the trio forged on out onto the wide stone walkways that lined the shore of Battery Park. It was only 5:00 p.m., but the street lamps were already coming to life, and the sun would soon be gone. The choppy, slate-gray surf crashed against the breakers.

"I *am* nice to Laila," Reece said, ignoring her friend's incredulous look. "Well, I'm not mean to her, anyway." Things between the two women had not improved. They were polite to each other, but a current of hostility ran between them that Liberty could not decipher.

"Yes, but she feels it nonetheless. She is always asking me why you don't like her."

"Okay, well, I will make a genuine effort."

"Anyway, there will be a lot of us there. It will be the usual intimate dinner for thirty-five or so."

"Can't wait," Reece said.

❧

The Thanksgivings of Laila's childhood memories were as different from the Lawrences' catered, cosmopolitan affairs as one might imagine. They were spent with Laila's mother's side, which included her grandmother as well as her two aunts, two uncles, and a mess of cousins Laila had very little interest in. Betsy was the baby of the family, and her older sisters, Jennifer and Lisa, had both become devout Christians as adults and used the holiday season as an excuse to initiate long-winded premeal prayers and numerous invitations to church activities.

The New York Lawrences' Thanksgiving dinner, by contrast, was a coveted invite. Petra made no pretentions about cooking herself, and every year there was a lavish spread of decadent holiday food: the truffled mashed potatoes and the tiny Gruyère mac-and-cheese bites the chef served as appetizers were legendary. The guests brought expensive bottles of wine and cognac to drink by the fire.

As Tom and Laila drove north toward Tuxedo Park in the Prius that he'd had borrowed from a friend, he could barely contain his excitement.

"I'm so looking forward to meeting your aunt and uncle," he said. "I've known Liberty for years, but I've never met them."

"Well, they're my family," Laila said with a smile. She disliked the way he still spoke of her aunt and uncle as though they belonged to Liberty, as though Tom himself still belonged to her cousin, when he was *her* boyfriend. "So of course you should get to know them."

He smiled at her, oblivious, and reached over to squeeze her knee.

"What is their house in Tuxedo Park like?" he asked.

Laila gazed out at the illuminated title of the tunnel walls. She felt uneasy leaving Manhattan, as though once gone, she might not be allowed back in. "Oh, it's gorgeous, enormous. But you'll see," she said. She didn't want to admit to Tom that she had yet to be invited out to the family's country house. She'd seen pictures; the landscape was lush, and the stone behemoth sat high upon a hill with a clear view of Tuxedo Lake. She had no doubt Tom would be blown away, as she would certainly be herself.

She hadn't yet decided whether she would marry Tom. Not that he had asked her, but instinctively, she knew that this option was on the table. If she were to give herself over to the relationship with Tom entirely, he would happily have her. She could tell he was tired of being single, of the hassle of caring for himself without a woman's devotion. He'd asked her to move in with him, but she was undecided about that as well. He broached the topic now, in a roundabout way, by asking her how things stood with her and Nora.

"Oh, things are okay. The maddening thing is that she won't talk about the fact that she's pissed, but then she does all these passive-aggressive things like telling the maid to skip my room or ordering in from Balthazar and only getting enough for her and Leo."

Tom laughed. "The struggle is real."

"I know." Laila smiled self-consciously. "But it's more what she means by it."

"Which is?"

"That my welcome is wearing thin. I mean, was I never supposed to have my own life here? Only be there for her?"

"Good thing someone *else* is rolling out the welcome mat for you, then."

She smiled at Tom indulgently, put her hand on his knee, and casually let her fingers brush the inside of his thigh. "And you're so sweet. But I wonder if I shouldn't just get my own place for a while."

Laila was bluffing, since of course this would mean getting a job, which she didn't intend to do just yet, if ever. And the money she'd come with wouldn't last her. Since Nora had gone cold on her, she'd already blown through a shocking amount of it on clothes and eating out with Cece. Thank goodness when they went to nightclubs, someone else always seemed to be picking up the tab. "That's what Wall Street guys are for," Cece said, referring to the young bankers who paid a grand for a bottle of vodka to be able to sit at the banquet tables of these nightclubs and have lovely women—at least half of them models too young to legally be standing there—surround them and drink their overpriced Grey Goose. Cece's lifestyle was like an elaborate sleight of hand: beautiful clothes that she had her pick of from the office; myriad connections that opened mysterious doors and made bar tabs disappear. She was young, beautiful, and cunning, and the perks seemed endless.

"Well, whatever you do, I'll support you."

By the time they were driving through Paramus, a light snow had begun to fall.

"Wow, it's early for snow," Tom said.

"Will we make it out there okay?" Snow was yet another thing that reminded Laila of her former home. Her anxiety ratcheted up with the sudden thought that Tom was secretly driving her back to her old life; that at the other end of the drive, instead of the Lawrences—the family with whom she belonged—Laila would be delivered back to Nathan, back to her past. She suddenly, irrationally, imagined a conspiracy between the two men; could see them shaking hands on the doorstep of Nathan's Victorian on Waterloo Street. "Thanks for bringing her back, man." "Oh, my pleasure; all just a big misunderstanding, you know?"

The image was so vivid that when Tom said, "We'll be fine; it's barely sticking," Laila imagined that his soft brown eyes had a traitorous gleam. She took several deep breaths to bring herself back to reality.

"Remember we have to pick up Birdie," she said when she'd regained herself, when Nathan's face had faded into the background once again. "Wow," Tom said as they drove through the majestic stone gates that led to Tuxedo Park. They'd been tasked with picking up Ben and Gregory's sister, Elizabeth—"Birdie"—to bring her to the party. She didn't live far from her brother's house, but she didn't drive, which seemed unimaginable to Laila considering how far out in the suburbs she was.

"Oh, I'm just the madwoman on the bicycle in all weather!" she'd said in her cheerful boom when Laila had asked her about this. She'd only met Birdie once. She'd come into the city earlier that fall and insisted on taking Laila and the twins to dim sum at a place she claimed to know well in Chinatown. She attempted to chat with the waitstaff in Cantonese, but they didn't appear to understand a word.

Laila felt a strange relief wash over her as her aunt's lawn came into view—it was *impossible* to miss, even with the snow blanketing the rest of the street in anonymity—for it grounded her back in this life, the other one hurtling into the distance far behind her. Birdie's lawn was covered with dozens of plastic pink flamingos, which looked all the more incongruous with little piles of snow accumulating on their heads.

"Are those . . . lawn ornaments?" Tom said, choosing what seemed like a rather charitable term for the cheap plastic birds.

"Oh yes, this is the place. Nora and Leo told me all about it."

"So I gather she's a bit of an eccentric?" Tom's smile was wide. Being a writer, he loved strange people.

"I don't think the flamingos are the half of it."

They parked in the empty driveway and made their way toward the blazing lights of the house. *I am with my boyfriend who is a famous novelist, and I am spending Thanksgiving with my family who live in New York. And I live in New York, and I work for a literary agency and can get into any nightclub I want. I have a billionaire's number in my phone.* As she formed the words in her head, they felt true and not true.

Birdie answered the door wearing her nightgown; over it was a blue-and-yellow fur coat. She immediately threw her arms around Laila and squeezed her hard.

"Oh, *Laila*! You're here. And you must be Tom! Oh, you're a hundred times more handsome than in your author photo, and anyway I always thought you were one of the better-looking authors. . . ."

She bustled the two of them inside, talking nonstop, her words running together.

"I was just thinking about getting a fire going, and now I think I definitely will."

"Aunt Birdie, I think we'd better get a move on; it's . . ." Laila looked to the wall in search of a clock but utterly lost her train of thought as she took in her surroundings. It was exactly as strange as Nora and Leo had described: vulgar and magnificent all at once. She reached out to touch the vintage carousel horse that took up the middle of the entryway, mesmerized by its be-jeweled eye.

"I call that one Arabella," Birdie said shyly, like a little girl showing a grown-up her treasured doll.

"It suits her," Tom said, smiling. "This house is amazing!"

Birdie herself was just as beguiling and grotesque as her house: her hair a mess of springy curls, her long fingernails a livid red, her makeup like something a showgirl might have accidentally slept in. One of her fake eyelashes drooped from her eyelid.

"She's my favorite," Birdie said, beckoning them into the kitchen.

"She" was by no means the only horse; there was a smaller one in the kitchen and at least one more that Laila could see on the porch.

"Tea or wine?" Birdie asked.

"Auntie, we're supposed to be there in an hour, and you're not yet . . . ," Laila began. She wanted to say that her aunt wasn't ready to go yet, though it suddenly occurred to her that perhaps this *was* what she meant to wear to the family Thanksgiving.

"Wine for me, please," Tom said, unhelpfully.

Birdie floated to the kitchen and took down a bottle of wine from a high shelf. "Oh, pooh, Thanksgiving. But must we? It will be so dull. We could stay here and say there was car trouble." She speedily filled three glasses and beckoned them to sit. Tom and Laila settled themselves on a bright green sofa while Birdie perched herself on a love seat shaped like a giant pair of lips.

"Aunt B., this is my first Thanksgiving with all the family," Laila said softly.

"Oh," she said, her free hand flying to her cheek, "you poor thing! How could I not have thought of that? I'm such an old flibbertigibbet." She set her glass down and leaned over to Laila, taking her face in both of her hands. "My darling girl, of course we will go to Thanksgiving!"

Her aunt Birdie seemed to feel her own unique strain of guilt about not having known Laila growing up. She'd never had any falling-out with Laila's father; it was only that she was utterly dependent on her own father and her eldest brother and therefore was compelled to side with them in the feud. "But you were always in my heart," she said to Laila again and again. Laila accepted her torrents of love gracefully but truthfully didn't care much one way or the other. Different as their circumstances and personalities were, Birdie reminded her of her mother. Both were women who seemed lost in the world of adults, unable to properly fend for themselves, and both were strangled by loneliness; in

Betsy it had calcified into bitterness, and in Birdie it radiated off her in desperate waves ensnaring anyone who came close. Betsy and Birdie were names for little girls; Laila would have reverted to the more dignified Elizabeth decades ago.

Once they finished their wine, Birdie roused herself to give them a tour of the house and get herself ready to go to dinner— she seemed to have realized only belatedly that she was in her nightdress. All the while, she regaled them with a steady stream of stories, her voice taking on a Doppler effect as she moved in and out of rooms, never pausing. She told them of her younger days in New York when she was a dancer in a burlesque troupe and once went on a date with John Voight "before they holed me up way out here in the country," she said. It seemed just as likely that the stories were true as that they were made up. Tom was devouring them; would Birdie now be a character in his next novel? She would surely love that. Laila had the feeling that their visit was the most exciting thing to happen to her in quite some time.

By the time they arrived at the Lawrences, they were only a merciful twenty minutes later than they'd planned, which felt like a miracle considering how many outfits Birdie had tried on before at last deciding on a flapper-style green silk dress, which she wore over tights with silver Mary Janes. She looked no less ridiculous when she walked out the door than she had upon their arrival—the fur coat remained—but certainly more purposeful. Tom couldn't disguise his delight.

A valet who looked all of thirteen met them in the turnaround of the vast driveway and drove off to park the Prius somewhere below where the stately Tudor sat high atop its hill. Laila and Tom followed Birdie as she walked through the foyer, as though it were as much her house as anyone's. And perhaps it was: the three siblings were tributaries off the same ocean of wealth; did any one part matter more than the others? In the house's grand living room, the party was in full swing. There was soft jazz music playing and tasteful, shimmering decorations hanging from the ceiling. Like tiny, elegant swords of Damocles. As they entered the main room, an autumnal smell of cloves and cinnamon hung in the air, as though someone—certainly not Petra—had been cooking spiced breads and mulled wine all day long.

Ben and Petra were absorbed in conversation with a younger couple, and Laila had a moment to watch them before they noticed her and Tom approaching (Birdie had been distracted by a painter she claimed to know on their way in). Tom went to get drinks, and Laila stood absorbing the lively party around her. Petra stood regally next to her husband as if she were a slender Amazon guarding her camp. Laila thought again of her own mother on Thanksgiving, lumbering around the kitchen with Laila's other aunties bustling in her wake, instructing her in their grating way at every turn: Did she know that she really ought to use more cream in the mashed potatoes? Those green beans were looking a little limp, and how many glasses of wine had Betsy had already, for heaven's sake? Laila did not exactly miss her parents; she did not long to be able to talk to them or put her arms around them. She did not, as Cece described about her own father, think of things she wished to tell them only to realize, crushingly, that she could not. What she felt was some primal disconnect: the only two people to have witnessed Laila's childhood were now gone, and all of the tertiary connections had been shaken off. She had not liked her aunties while her parents were alive, so why would she spend time with them once they were gone? They reached out frequently, cloyingly, for the two years she'd remained in Michigan, but after she'd left for New York, they seemed content to leave her be. Which was fine by Laila.

"Laila, my darling," Petra said, spotting her. Her elegant aunt closed the distance between them in several long strides and put her arms around Laila.

"Thank you for bringing Birdie. Where is Tom?"

"He's getting us drinks. This is a beautiful party, Aunt Petra."

Her uncle Ben looked over and gave her a smile but held up a finger as if to say that he could not just yet excuse himself from his conversation. Ben had proven thus far unreachable, though whether this had anything to do with Laila was unclear. He was forever absorbed by his phone and the consistent, apparently urgent stream of calls, e-mails, and other information that came through it. Laila didn't know if she—the only daughter of his only brother—evoked any emotional response in him whatsoever but certainly none showed.

"Let's go find your cousins; they're back here somewhere." Petra took Laila's arm. "You must forgive your uncle," she said quietly to her as they made their way to the back of the house. The expansive windows looked over the rolling green hills behind them, now doubly picturesque covered with snow: the sun had just gone down, giving the landscape a lovely crepuscular glow. "Seeing you reminds him of what he's lost."

She nodded. "But I'm still here." Laila had only meant this in the literal sense, but she could see that her words moved her aunt.

"He'll get better. He has to find a way to forgive himself for never making peace with Gregory. He does not like to admit it when he's wrong."

Laila nodded and took her aunt's arm affectionately as they walked. She wasn't sure if Petra was only trying to make Laila feel better, if she was projecting the way she thought Ben *ought* to feel about Laila, or—a third, more hopeful possibility—that she was right, that Ben had regrets he would in time process, allowing him to be open to the possibility of a relationship with her. Laila found regret to be the most useless of emotions; it kept one tethered to the past when the future was the only possible direction. She tried to devote all of her energy to moving herself forward. Onward ever; backward never.

They came upon Liberty and Reece perched on one of the long cushy benches that bordered the windows. Reece caught Laila's eye, and under her gaze, Laila felt as if her dress constricted, felt herself become someone unsightly. But to her surprise, Reece smiled at her and came to kiss her cheek.

"Happy Thanksgiving," she said, enveloping Laila in her robust, blond warmth.

"You too, Reece. Lots to be grateful for this year."

"I agree."

Liberty smiled at them, clearly pleased to see them both making an effort. Then a different, yet more luminous smile crossed Liberty's face, and Laila turned to see who had inspired it. For a moment she doubted her vision: Cameron and Tom, carrying drinks and laughing chummily with each other, were making their way toward them. Laila felt a pang looking at the two men side by side. Cameron towered over Tom, who was a couple of inches shy of six feet. And Tom's nebbishy handsomeness was obliterated next to Cameron's golden-boy radiance. Tom was barely older than Cameron, but damned if he didn't look a decade north of him in that moment.

"Look who I found!" Tom was jovial, oblivious to Laila's uncharitable thoughts.

"You made it!" Reece said, hugging her brother.

"Hi, Cam," Liberty said next. Laila watched as they locked in on each other and exchanged a cheek kiss, their eyes full of some unspoken thing. Liberty would still only admit to a friendship, and indeed, Laila believed that nothing romantic—well, nothing *sexual*—had happened between them, but she knew how much time they had been spending together: going to lunches and dinners and the opera, giving Liberty a chance to wear some of the showier estate pieces she'd collected over the years, even on a drive upstate in a vintage car that Cameron borrowed from his auto club to see foliage. The silver topless heritage Aston Martin was glamorous but had jostled the two of them all the way back; instead of ruining the trip, it seemed to have made for a delightful in-joke. Why it was worth it to Cam to do all of this when he could have any woman with a quarter of the effort, Laila couldn't fathom.

"And Laila!" he said, with empty cheerfulness and a too-brief cheek kiss, "how nice to see you." It was as though her presence here was a surprise instead of his.

"Are your parents here as well?" Laila asked, turning to Reece. She hadn't meant it to sound so much like an accusation—the appearance of the Michaels siblings wasn't something Laila was prepared for. "Do the families always spend holidays together?"

"Oh, no, our parents are in Aspen skiing themselves into oblivion. We usually go along, but with work this year, I couldn't get away," Reece said. Cameron nodded, though Laila wondered if skipping out on the family trip had been little more than an excuse to come be by his beloved for the holiday.

"I'm going to leave you kids and see where my husband has gone off to," Petra said. She beamed at Liberty and Cameron; there was no wondering what she thought of the match.

"God, Lib, your mom looks amazing," Reece said when Petra was out of earshot. "Is she bathing in the blood of virgins or what?"

"If they offered it at J Sisters, she might."

"Beauty is only fleeting for some," Cameron said, giving Liberty a look that made it clear he was not only talking about Petra. "So, Tom," he said, clapping the shorter man on the shoulder in a way that made Tom light up, "tell us about the new book. Are you going on tour this time?"

And off Tom went into a spiel Laila had heard a hundred times already. How quickly his work—something everyone seemed so impressed with—had come to bore her. There was, she had been distressed to discover, nothing all too glamorous about being a writer. It was not different from any other job, except she knew now from all the time she spent at his apartment that Tom often wore sweatpants while he did it, which Laila felt a man should never do, at least not if there was any danger a woman might see.

Eventually everyone took their seats around a long mahogany dining table. Laila felt her mantra of the night repeating itself in her head: *I am a Lawrence and I belong here.* The group was an eclectic mix: musicians, fellow former models, and several designers, one of whom was seated next to Reece. Even sitting, the man was half her size but had a bright, warm smile. He was handsome and compact with dark features and an accent Laila could not quite place: Spanish, maybe? At any rate, Reece seemed enthralled with him and was asking him dozens of questions about his work, which he seemed happy to answer. Her uncle sat at the far end of the table, taciturn as ever. Were these all Petra's friends? Laila surmised that he was one of those men who mostly let his wife run his social life on his behalf. Laila was between Tom and Leo, the latter showing off for the former by talking about all the books he'd read in the last year. Leo played the part of being a writer himself when it suited him, and Tom, who *hated* this behavior, was acting like Leo was a colleague. Nora attempted to sit on the other side of her brother, but her mother shooed her into a different seat, exclaiming, "Nora, you cannot sit on the corner!" She'd rolled her eyes and smiled at her brother, saying, "Lest I remain unmarried forever!" Leo laughed and explained to Laila and Tom that this was a Russian superstition. The food was exquisite. In lieu of turkey—an impractical measure considering the thirty-odd guests, they were served Cornish game hens with truffled mashed potatoes and the most delicately fried brussels sprouts. A half-dozen former models took one glorious bite of each.

After dinner, the party carried on.

"Good thing everyone is spending the night," Liberty said to Laila, settling into the couch next to her. "Otherwise they'd all float home."

Laila leaned into her cousin's shoulder. Reece was still wrapped up in conversation with her dinner companion, who Liberty explained was Francisco Costa, a name Laila was too embarrassed to admit meant nothing to her.

"Are you having fun?" Liberty asked.

"It's amazing. I've never seen anything like it, if you want to know the truth."

Her cousin laughed, "My mom does go all out. It must be hard, though," Liberty said, reaching her arm around Laila. "You must miss your family."

A thousand things went through Laila's mind. Her family. *Her* family.

"Of course, *we're* your family too," Liberty added, hurriedly.

"What were your parents' Thanksgivings like? Unless you don't want to talk about it."

"No, I like talking about them." It wasn't true; Laila wasn't sure why she'd said it. "Imagine the polar opposite of this, throw in a couple of fat midwestern women and a golden retriever making laps around the dinner table, and you're just about there."

Liberty smiled. "I always kind of fantasized about having holidays like that."

"You must be kidding."

"No! It sounds like a John Hughes movie. You know, we've never had a holiday meal that's been just family?" Was it true, Laila wondered, that we were all doomed to long for what we didn't have: that those with everything could wish as ardently for the simplicity of having less as the reverse?

"And that's a bad thing?"

"All this food and a bunch of aging models to push it around their plates." Liberty sighed. It was interesting to Laila how Liberty seemed to not think of herself as a model, yet she'd been one and still resembled one. In New York, it seemed that "model" was less a profession and more an ethnicity.

"We never had friends at our family holidays," Laila said. "Except one year when my dad's golf buddy was going through a divorce."

Her father had always had friends in that particularly male way: friends from college who lasted no matter how little he had in common with them. Then there were the golf buddies who more or less encompassed everyone he'd met in his postcollege adult life. Laila's mother, on the other hand, never really had friends. She only had her sisters whom she spent time with but did not particularly seem to like. Laila had once asked her about it after noticing that her friends' mothers spent more time with "the girls" drinking wine and going to book club meetings. Her mother had shrugged and smiled. "I've never been much of a girl's girl. Women . . . you have to understand they tear each other down."

"Tom and Cameron sure hit it off," Liberty said now as she watched the two men talking spiritedly by the fireplace. Cameron stood with a glass of whiskey in one hand and the other on his hip, as if he were posing for a Brooks Brothers catalog. Tom was talking about something using both of his hands; the more Cameron laughed, the more animated Tom became. Laila thought she could see tiny flecks of spit coming from his mouth. She was repulsed.

"Yeah, I had no idea Cameron was so interested in Tom's work."

"You know, I wouldn't have thought so either. He was a total jock when we were growing up. But he reads all the time now, and we've gone to a bunch of events at the 92nd Street Y."

"I guess people surprise you. Now, if Tom turns out to secretly be a jock, we'll really be blown away."

Liberty gave a little laugh. "Oh, poor Tom! Though he certainly has a little spring in his step since he met you."

"Do you think so?"

Liberty raised an eyebrow at Laila. "I've known Tom for years; this is the happiest I've ever seen him."

Laila was pleased. This was how she wanted it.

"And you're happy with him?" Liberty asked. She pivoted her body to look her cousin in the eye.

"Of course. Tom is kind. And so smart, so accomplished."

Liberty's eyes narrowed a fraction.

"It's early still, right? We've only been seeing each other a few months," Laila said, feeling a wave of her cousin's incredulousness.

"Of course."

Laila excused herself to use the bathroom only to find it occupied; after waiting a few minutes, she got impatient and ventured deeper into the house to find another option. One of the caterers directed her to the back of the house; she thanked him and took a glass of wine from his tray. She needed to take the edge off. Liberty had unnerved her. Laila had the sense that she saw not only the version of her that was sitting there—the present, polished Laila—but the shadows of all her previous selves that she carried with her. Laila longed to be close to her cousin, but she also feared it. She was apprehensive of being truly seen. Laila imagined that if they'd known her mother, her cousins wouldn't have accepted her the way they had.

The hunt for another bathroom had taken her down a long corridor and into a part of the house far from the crowd, which she could only hear faint echoes of. After using the bathroom, she retreated a bit farther into the house. She stopped cold when she heard her uncle's voice—which boomed despite the fact that he seemed to be straining to keep it down—and halted outside the study door from which it emanated.

"I'm not keeping you from doing anything. For God's sake, she's *here*, isn't she?"

Laila heard her aunt give an exasperated sigh in return.

"You've barely interacted with her," she said, "the poor child. Do you think she doesn't notice? It's bad enough that she grew up with *nothing*, and of course you won't even consider making up for that, will you?"

Laila had never heard Petra upset; her accent grew more pronounced with her distress.

"You don't understand what it's like for me," Ben said, "she *ruined* him, Petra. If it wasn't for her . . ."

"Betsy ruined him, *not* Laila," Petra said firmly. "Would you like to be held responsible for everything *your* father has done?"

"She looks exactly the same," Ben said, with something like wonderment in his voice. "You must see it. Every time she walks in, my heart stops. I think it's her."

"Oh, Ben, you're being ridiculous. And you call me superstitious. She's no older than the twins, and she's an orphan."

"You and the kids do whatever you like. But if you think *Frederick* is going to want to see her, you're dreaming."

"Well, *he* liked her mother just fine. That's the root of this whole problem, in case you've forgotten."

"For God's sake, let's not do this during the holidays. *Please.* I'm going back to the party."

So. Laila had not imagined his iciness, then. She slipped off down the hallway before she could be seen, escaping into a large, glass-ceilinged room that felt like the perfect place to collect herself. She imagined that it would be filled with sunlight during the day, but now it opened to a bright, clear, starry sky. She lay back on the cushioned bench that hugged one of the walls: a reading nook that she could imagine Liberty loving. She wondered if this room had been made for her, if it was one of her favorite parts of the house. As she lay there, she absorbed the conversation she'd just overheard. Ben and Petra had known about the affair, even if her cousins still did not. But even if Ben proved intransigent, it must mean something that she had Petra on her side. Time, she just had to give it time.

"Hiding?"

She sat up with a start to find Cameron standing in the doorway smiling at her.

"I was just getting a little overwhelmed," she said, smoothing her dress. As soon as she spoke, she realized she was tipsy. "This is my first holiday with . . . everyone." Her heart was still racing after what she'd heard.

He nodded, looking down into his glass and swirling the ice cubes—immaculate squares—thoughtfully.

"Are your family's holidays like this?" Laila asked. Perhaps this was yet another New York thing she didn't understand.

"Ours? No. We usually have a few extras, but nothing like this. There's a who's who of the nineties back there."

He was like a movie star; he had an otherworldly sheen to him, something too precious to really exist.

"So, how you doing, kid?" He looked briefly behind him down the hallway—why?—as he came to sit beside her, put a brotherly hand on her shoulder. "Adjusting to New York life?"

Suddenly it was as though that first night they'd met—when lust had seemed to hang heavy in the air between them—had never happened.

She wound her crossed legs tighter and crossed her free arm underneath the hand that held her glass. She shrugged.

"I love it here, but . . ." She felt a sudden urge to confess to Cameron what she'd just overheard, but no. "I don't fit in," she said carefully. "You know, everyone is so glamorous and beautiful, and it's like they all know some . . ." She tried to put her finger on it. "Secret code?"

"Come on," Cameron said, "you're beautiful. You know that."

He said it in a friendly way. But as Laila turned her head

toward him, she could smell him: something spicy and musky mixed with the whiskey he was drinking. She felt her limbs loosen.

"Do you really think so?" she was fishing, hoping. Her free arm came loose from her chest.

"Of course! Are you kidding? You're a knockout."

Her fingers moved swiftly to the inside of Cameron's thigh, and her lips reached up to the skin below his ear.

Then everything happened in quick succession: Cameron was on his feet, and a split second later Liberty had appeared in the doorway.

"Hey, you," she said and then, surprised, "Laila!"

"Hey, Lib." Laila sipped her remaining wine to hide whatever her face might otherwise reveal.

"You found my very favorite spot in the house. My reading nook! I used to hole up here for hours when I was a teenager." Liberty was babbling strangely, acting as though *she* had been caught out in something rather than Laila.

"It seems perfect for that. I was just getting a moment by myself. It's been quite a night."

The situation suddenly became clear to all of them: Laila had been sitting alone, interrupted by Cameron, who'd come to meet Liberty. Why? The two spent half of their time together, despite claiming that they were just friends. Perhaps tonight had been the moment for some sort of declaration. Good, Laila thought, at the idea that she'd forestalled it.

"Shall we go back to the party, then?" Laila asked. "I ought to find Tom. Though I'm sure he's more concerned with where his new best friend, Cameron, has gone." Laila knew that Tom had been scrawny and nerdy as a teenager, and she imagined that tonight was his chance to feel equal to the popular jock who'd tormented him in prep school. Pulitzer or no, Laila thought, Tom would never be Cameron's equal. He wasn't born for it.

"That's a solid man you've got there," Cameron said, again the brotherly hand clapped on her shoulder. "I like him."

"Tom is my favorite client," Liberty said, "but don't tell any of the others I said that."

Their cheerful bantering was a thin covering. Did they think they were fooling her? Laila wondered.

That night in bed, on sheets with a thread count so high they seemed to melt beneath Laila's skin, Tom reached for her as soon as the lights were off—always with the lights off, for Tom—and she batted his hand away. "Not here," she said harshly, "it's my family's house."

~§~

The next morning, Reece was awake before anyone else had emerged from their beds; Rocket bound out of the room behind her, ready to take on the day as ever. She made coffee—she'd stayed at the Tuxedo Park house dozens of times and knew where everything was—and installed herself at the granite countertop with her sketchbook full of tear sheets and notes. She lost track of time as she worked steadily for over an hour. Morning was her favorite time of day; it belonged to her in a way the rest of the day did not. She knew that she could technically quit her job and do only this. All she had to do was tell her parents about her and Cece's plan for the line. But she feared their overbearing enthusiasm. Her mom would start calling every person she knew with influence in fashion, and her father would start buying things—it didn't matter what, the latest design software, a plush workspace—and she would have all the time in the world to launch the line. And none of it would belong to her anymore. This was not a thing she could express to anyone other than Liberty—well-meaning, meddlesome, rich parents were the most privileged problem a person could have, but they were still a problem.

"What are you working on?" Leo asked as he came into the kitchen, stretching his arms over his head so that a flash of his taught stomach was revealed for a too-brief moment. On impulse Reece shut her notebook. Rocket got up from his dog bed and did an excited lap around Leo's feet. Leo knelt down to scratch his ears, and the dog let out a comic groan of ecstasy.

"Oh, just some ideas for work. My mind is always buzzing in the morning."

"Mine too," he said. "I thought I'd make some headway on the book. I promised my agent I'd get him some pages by the end of the long weekend."

Ah yes, the book, Reece thought. Leo and his agent had originally sold it as *The Man About Town's Guide to New York*, and it was meant to be a collection of his existing columns fleshed out with some context and some additional lifestyle tips, whatever that meant. The reason the book had sold, Reece imagined, was the fantasy that being Leo Lawrence was something one could learn. But as the project carried on—or stalled out, more accurately—Leo began to entertain delusions that it could be something more substantive. He'd begun to talk about Jack Kerouac, Tom Wolfe, and Charles Bukowski. What these literary titans had to do with Leo's admittedly spot-on recommendations for where to buy suits (Duncan Quinn) and how to approach a woman who was out of your league (have your friend show interest in her friend, be polite but a little standoffish, and for God's sake, you fool, don't even *think* about negging her)—well, that was anyone's guess. But this moving target of a subject matter kept him from having to do any of the work.

"So that's why you're up," Reece said. "I confess, I'm surprised to see you awake."

"Oh, Reece," he said, sliding into the stool next to her, his elbow on the counter and his chin on his hand, "there is so much about me that would surprise you."

They had always done this, since Leo was a teenager mooning after her. Reece knew two things: that she'd never actually date Leo and that she would be sad the day he fell in love with someone else.

"And how is the book coming along?"

"Oh, I have a fantastic new idea for it," he said, "I want to go deeper into my philosophies about life, you know? Not just rehash my columns. I am thinking of calling the new iteration *Manifesto of a Modern Gentleman*. What do you think?"

"Catchy title," she said with what she hoped was an encouraging smile. Although she thought white men might, at the moment, rather want to avoid using the word *manifesto*.

"It's so beautiful outside," she said. The sun was just coming up, and the sky was, for the moment, clear. The snow that covered the ground and blanketed the trees glowed, and the heavy icicles that hung from the eaves glinted.

"We should go for a walk!" Leo said, sitting up in excitement.

"I didn't bring clothes for it," Reece said.

"You can borrow some of my mom's; I bet they'll fit."

"It might have to be your dad's stuff." Reece laughed. "But I'm willing to try."

Leo and Reece went to the vast closet where the family kept

all manner of outdoor equipment for the weekends they spent at the house. The two pawed through great heaps of parkas and skis and scarves.

"Ah!" Leo said, pulling a snowshoe from the pile, "I have an even better idea! Let's go snowshoeing. There are trails in the woods. It will be beautiful."

"I'm up for that," Reece said, "I could use the exercise." Even one day off her exercise routine left Reece a little jittery. The Michaelses were the kind of clan who'd grown up going on family runs, bike rides, and hikes: all despite their city life. In their family dogma, there was little that a vigorous workout could not cure.

"Fantastic," he said, giving her a thousand-watt smile.

They left a note on the kitchen table and made their way out behind the house. For a while they trudged forth in companionable silence. Clouds had rolled in, but rays of sun still peeked through the gray, illuminating patches of snow falling through the bare branches of the towering oaks.

"God, it feels good to be outside," Leo said. "Being in nature: if there was ever a reason to leave New York, that would be it."

"Can you even imagine leaving, though?"

Leo shrugged. "You know I have a brother who lives in Alaska? Well, a half brother, Beau."

"Liberty's talked about him a little, but I've never met him."

"That's because he won't come to New York."

"Won't come at *all*?"

Leo shook his head. "He doesn't speak to our dad. He blames him for what happened to his mom."

Reece knew this much: that his mother, Patricia, a once-prominent socialite, had killed herself sometime in the two years after Ben left her for Petra. The boy, who was then living with her, had been the one to find her. She'd taken pills and was found dead on the bathroom floor. Beau was eleven years old. He had left for the remote town of Banff the moment he'd finished prep school and turned eighteen.

"Do you guys keep in touch with him at all?"

"Only Liberty." He took large, deliberate steps as the trail widened and the snow became deeper. "He has a soft spot for her since they were closer in age, and she got to know him before he left. He could give a shit about Nora and me."

Reece could understand Leo's bitterness, but Beau had been through something that neither of them could imagine. As had Laila, as had Reece's Cece, who'd lost her father when she was twelve. Nothing had touched Reece in that way, and despite all that swirled beneath the polished surface of the Lawrence family, Leo and Nora had been sheltered from it. They'd never known any of the deceased. And they didn't know the half of what their older sister had been through.

"Families are complicated." Reece shook her head.

"It must be nice having Cameron back," Leo said. "He seems different than I remember. But I guess I haven't seen him much since I was younger."

"Different how?" Reece asked, but she thought she knew what Leo meant. Her brother had grown up, and she was proud of him. He had, at least as far as Reece knew, shaken the desperate trail of girls that had seemed to cling to him throughout his teens and twenties. The girls, if memory served, were mostly desperate because he'd made them so, promising things he no longer wished to deliver once the moment had passed. There was at least one pregnancy that Reece had known about, as it had happened in the days of the landline, when a call could be intercepted by one's little sister, and a

distraught lover could spill one's secrets. There was a termination—
Reece knew this too—and her brother had declined to accompany
the girl. He'd paid for it, he said in his own defense. Not as dearly
as the girl, Reece imagined. She wished she'd never known about it.

"I don't know, I just like him better. Don't take that the wrong
way. Can we stop for a minute?" Leo asked as they reached an
overturned log in a small clearing that opened from the trail.
Nearby, a stream burbled beneath a thin coating of ice.

"Sure." Reece smiled. Leo was wearing out, but Reece was just
getting in her groove, despite this being her first time in snow-
shoes. Rocket sprang up and sat proprietarily between the two of
them. Leo removed his bulky gloves to pull a flask from the inside
pocket of his coat. "Want some?"

"It's ten in the morning, not even."

"And?" That killer smile. "It's a holiday!"

"Yeah, okay." Reece sipped without asking what it was, and a
gratifyingly smooth whiskey hit her lips when she tipped the flask
back. They settled into a comfortable quiet, the hush of the snow
swallowing the sounds of the forest. The snow had begun falling
lightly again, and the flakes were catching in the tufts of Leo's
thick hair that stuck out from beneath his cap.

"Speaking of Cameron . . ."

"Yes?"

"And my sister?"

"Nora?" Reece cocked her head. Leo gave her an incredulous
look, and she laughed. "Cameron and Liberty are friends."

"Oh, that's adorable."

"Well, they're not dating, are they?"

"Actually, I believe they are—all the boring parts, anyway.
They're not fucking, maybe."

"Ew, Leo. Your sister. My *brother.*"

"What? We're all just animals." He gave her a sly smile. Just once, if they could be assured there would be no consequences—which there would be, there *always* would be—but just once, in a perfect moral vacuum they would. They'd never speak of it again.

"Yes, well, I have given my brother marching orders *not* to act like an animal if he wants me to keep speaking to him." She hadn't meant to tell Leo that. The woods made confessions feel safe somehow.

"Ah. I see."

Leo smiled to himself.

"What?"

"You're a good friend, Reece." With this he kissed her on the cheek and was on his feet. They made their way back toward the house, the snow growing heavier beneath their feet.

14

"YOU HANG out with Laila a lot, right?"

Reece was sitting on the sturdy table of the atelier.

"I do," Cece said. "How come?" Cece was at the tiny sink in the corner. The two of them had been working on the new designs for hours; Cece had just been pouring two paper cups full of the Reserva Añeja Rum she kept stashed in the cabinet. She only drank rum when she was working. She'd told Reece that she remembered her father, an architect, drank it sometimes when he was up late at his drafting table. She'd been too young to share it with him, but he'd let her try a sip now and then when she was eleven, the year before he died. It was a mark of how close she felt to Reece that she was willing to include her in the tradition; Cece kept things like this close to the vest. They'd worked together ever since Cece graduated from Parsons and Reece had snapped her up to be her assistant. And for two years they'd been working in secret on their clothing line.

Reece let out a long sigh. She and Cece's personal relationship had long been intertwined with their working one, but still it felt petty to talk to her about this. But Reece was hungry for insight into Laila, to put a name to the discomfort she felt in the girl's presence, to know if it was simply her own bias curdling into a kind of paranoia. She'd tried her best over Thanksgiving, but there was something about her. It was subtle—a too-loud laugh; a calculating gleam in her eyes when she looked at her cousins—it wouldn't let Reece go.

"I just . . . you don't think there's something off about her?"

Cece frowned thoughtfully. "I don't think so, but I mean, we're not *that* close. We party together, we get along. We have a lot in common in some ways."

"You and Laila have a lot in common?" Reece asked skeptically, finishing her rum and holding out her cup for Cece to refill it. In her mind Cece and Laila were about as opposite as two twenty-five-year-olds could be. Cece's parents had immigrated to New York from the Dominican Republic the year before Cece was born, and her father had died when she was twelve. Her mom was a nurse, and they'd struggled to make ends meet. Her mother, whom Reece knew well at this point, was outrageously proud of her only daughter for graduating from Parsons with honors and for her fancy job. Whereas Laila's primary achievement seemed to be the way she'd enmeshed herself into her cousins' lives.

Cece shrugged. "We both lost our dads young, and she knows what it feels like to be an outsider here. That's huge; that's hard."

"You're not an outsider!" Reece said. "You grew up in New York."

Cece smiled. "There are many New Yorks; you know this."

"Well, sure, but I just don't think of *you* as an outsider. Period."

Their relationship was like this—mostly Reece played big sister, but every once in a while, it flipped. "I know you don't, Mama. But just because *you're* not the problem doesn't mean that there isn't a problem."

And of course, when she bothered to think about it, she saw it, the bifurcated Cece—the real and complex woman she knew and the one whose voice and manner subtly adjusted when she was around the girls from work—sliding unnoticed into their overwhelmingly white, upper-middle-class world. She'd started going by Cece because, as she'd once confessed, she could not stand the sound of her name being mispronounced *See-lia* instead of *Sey-lia* as it was meant to be. It made her feel like a fraud every time, she told Reece.

"Maybe she gets nervous around you. It's intimidating, Manhattan, even just coming from the outer boroughs."

"Do *you* think I'm intimidating?" Reece said.

"You don't intimidate *me*, girl, please. But you know, you wanted to like me. I don't get the sense you *want* to like Laila."

Reece knew Cece was right. And now she was faced with the fact that she might feel a ripple of distaste for Laila for the worst possible reason: class.

15

LIBERTY KNEW that she and Cameron could not go on forever pretending they were only friends. Over Thanksgiving, he'd asked if there was someplace they could talk privately, and she'd told him of her favorite spot in the house. The sunroom where her reading nook was, where she had spent so many hours of her childhood weekends kept safe from the world with her Jane Austen and Sandra Cisneros and Margaret Atwood: her literary godmothers. But when she'd arrived there at the appointed moment, Cameron was there but not alone: Laila had been sitting there too, drinking wine. She could not have known they were planning to meet there. But how had she found her way to this most sacred spot of Liberty's? So the conversation they were meant to have remained unspoken, and Liberty feared he might now decide against saying whatever it was he'd meant to tell her. It was by such small accidents that life unfolded, in the end.

The first Monday of December, she was his date to a charity cocktail party that someone from work was hosting, and she hoped that he would tell her then; that the moment hadn't passed. It didn't feel out of the question; there seemed to be a struggle going on just beneath the surface of him. He was still trying to decide about her, she thought. So much so that she wondered if there was someone else. She'd resigned herself to being his friend, if that was all he meant to offer her.

But the night had felt different right away. After the charity event, they went to Lavagna, a tiny, romantic Italian restaurant in the East Village where the owner kept a gleaming red Ducati parked on the sidewalk outside.

"I'd like to get one of those."

"Don't," Liberty said, "I really prefer you alive."

"I'm so glad to hear that," and with this he'd taken her hand, curling his fingers around hers on the tabletop. The owner came over to say hello, and Cameron greeted him warmly, introducing Liberty as the most beautiful and brilliant woman in New York. It was cheesy, but who cared?

The only discordant moment had happened when the waiter had forgotten to put Cameron's dressing on the side and he'd snapped at him, rolling his eyes when the man apologetically scurried away to have the salad replaced. But the irritation seemed to pass as quickly as it had come, and he was back in good spirits—leaving, she presumed from the waiter's smile as they left, his usual hefty tip.

That night at her door, which had become a place of swift hugs and the occasional deliberate cheek kiss, she sensed that he'd either say something now, or he never would.

"Thank you for dinner," she said softly, her shoulders rounding as though her body was submitting before him.

"Of course," he said with a smile. He had a palm on the door frame so that he was leaning slightly over her from his great height. "Of course," he said again. He looked her straight in the eyes to say the things that, suddenly, did not need saying. Instead, he kissed her.

Liberty felt her body shift forward into his and then go slack as he engulfed her in his arms. He pressed her back up against the heavy door to the apartment. His kiss released in her a thousand things, and she felt them all at once, picked up by the wave of them and carried to its dizzying crest. It was joy because he wanted her, and lust and longing because she wanted him; it was decades of wanting him. She felt him hard against her thigh, and the wave went higher, and then suddenly a new variety of thoughts came skittering in. She felt a cold panic gripping her, pulling her down. A tide of unwelcome memories of other lips and other hands. He felt her tense. Pulled back an inch.

"What is it?"

His face was so close to hers, and she felt the warmth of his breath. She wanted to be in the moment but was instead spiraling away from it. She dug into the cloth of his shirt, trying to anchor herself there, but it was hopeless.

She said something a second later; she couldn't remember what. Not that it mattered: What could she say to excuse the way she practically dove into her apartment and closed the door in his face? He'd called her name once and then she'd heard a deep sigh and his footsteps walking away. She felt the waves of panic coming up from her stomach, and she let herself slide down to the floor. Her desire for Cameron—the potent mix of both present and remembered feelings—had lowered her defenses, and now she was collapsing in on herself. Her mind looped: You stupid girl, you ruin everything, no one could love you, how could they love you, you broken, hopeless, silly thing. She knew what was happening, but the fat yellow pills in the drawer in her bathroom felt a hundred miles from where she sat, her knees curled to her chest. Her breathing got shallower, and her thoughts grew indistinct, simply circling like the whir and thump of an old washing machine.

Catniss came in from the bedroom and nudged at Liberty's tightly crossed arms until she let her cat crawl into her lap.

"Good kitty," Liberty said, her tears falling into the soft fur. She sat there for she didn't know how long, until the panic had exhausted itself. Then she took a whole pill—not the half that she was instructed—and fell into a deep and cloudy sleep.

❧

What could he have done differently? Goddamn it! What did this woman want from him? It couldn't be too soon; he'd waited months to even so much as kiss her. And then she'd slammed the door in his face. Such a thing had never happened to him. He was confused, and his ego—felled and wounded—clung heavily to him like a soldier he was dragging from battle. And why, really, should he even bother with all this? Men like him had the advantage. Liberty was over thirty; certainly plenty of men still wanted her now, but it wouldn't be so for long. Whereas his advantages over the opposite sex would only increase from here. Why was he obsessing over this one girl in a city of millions just as beautiful (and younger, with more years of beauty before them), just as smart, just as accomplished? He could go and find one this very night if he wanted! He made his way past Butter—an overpriced, mediocre restaurant with a well-known nightclub below it—and decided he would prove it to himself. His ego perked, straightened itself, and still clung to Cameron's back but at least began to carry some of its own weight.

❧

Laila had been there with Cece for nearly two hours. They'd begun their night with two rounds of tequila shots at the bar.

"Fuck!" Laila said when she looked at the eighty-dollar bar tab. "Let's not pay for any more of our own drinks tonight. Deal?"

"Deal."

"Thank you for coming out with me tonight. I really needed it," Laila said to Cece, whom she'd called only hours before and who helpfully knew all of the Monday-night doormen at Butter.

"Yeah, sorry to hear about Nora."

Nora had suddenly, capriciously, insisted that she needed her guest room back. She said a prep-school friend of hers—a dear friend, the variety of which Laila didn't think Nora actually had—would be coming to stay with her for a few weeks. The idea that such a person would have no other options, if she did in fact exist in the first place, was ludicrous. Nora segued into a speech that, you know, Laila couldn't just *live here rent-free* forever, and oh, of course she knew that she didn't intend to. But now, if she could be out in a week or so, that would be wonderful. Laila had failed to register the signs of her cousin's increasing unhappiness with their arrangement. It would seem that she wanted Laila there only if she could have her all to herself.

"What about Liberty?" Cece asked now. Though she was being sympathetic, Laila knew it would not extend too far. In many ways, it was Cece Laila admired most—she'd *earned* her place in life, unlike Laila's cousins. And Cece held herself with a steady grace that said she deserved to be there. It was natural that she and Nora repelled each other—Nora didn't believe status could be earned; she believed it ran in one's blood. She wasn't shy about sharing her disdain, referring to Cece as Laila's "little Mexican friend" on more than one occasion.

Laila shook her head at her friend's suggestion. Working with Liberty was one thing, but living with her would be different. She knew Liberty would take her in, but she also sensed she wouldn't appreciate having her in her space. Liberty was intensely private. So this left Laila in a bind.

"I would say you could crash with me," Cece said. "But I have two roommates, and our couch is a love seat." Cece lived on the far Upper West Side, right on the border of Harlem. Cece herself didn't seem to spend much time there; it was more of a place to shower and sleep, to store one's clothes. Life in New York was not a life of the home, except for the very rich. Laila wondered for a moment whether this should be her New York life instead of this facsimile of her cousins' lives she was trying for. But strangely, Cece's life—her perpetual single-dom, her career ambition, her flinty independence—seemed even more out of reach.

"I think I'll probably just move in with Tom," Laila said now, casually. "He's been on me about it anyway."

"Whoa! That's kind of a big deal, though, right?" Cece said. Laila knew turning to a man would have been the last solution on her friend's list.

The crowd around them had begun to thicken. They'd gotten there early—even with Cece's connections, the door could be brutal. It was a quarter past eleven now, and people who didn't have to be concerned with such things were filtering in. Laila felt a flash of recognition as a tall, boney blonde with impossibly shiny hair floated by her. For a moment she thought it was someone she knew, but then she realized that she knew her indeed—from the Victoria's Secret catalog.

"Yeah," Laila said, "I guess? I don't know. I love Tom."

The words were wooden on her tongue. *I love Tom. Love Tom. Tom.*

"Yeah, but . . ." Cece saw someone she knew, smiled, and held up a finger to say they'd be over in a minute. "That's a huge step in a relationship."

"I mean, I don't know if I'd move in with him permanently. Just until I figure something else out. I don't know." Nothing had to be permanent, Laila knew. You could walk away from anything. No bond could imprison you unless you let it.

"Hey," Cece said, putting her hand up, "no judgment. You do what you've gotta do."

They joined Cece's friends, who were mercifully generous with their bottle of Grey Goose. Laila drank hers on the rocks, no sugary mixer. Something Tom had said to her the other night was echoing in her mind: *I love that you have curves; so many New York girls just starve them right off.* How could he have thought this was a compliment? Laila knew she needed to appear to take it as one, but now it was haunting her. Twenty-five and curvy. In New York. Her window ever narrowing. Her mother's voice echoed in her ears. Soon Laila was drunk, and the thoughts were floating away. Who cared about Tom? Look at her, look at her life! And Cece was her own friend, not out of pity, not out of obligation. And the city was theirs.

⁓∾⁓

It was close to midnight when Cameron arrived. He'd texted his friend Jeremy, a banker, who'd said he'd be out that night. And of course he was here: there was nothing much else to do on a Monday night. He walked down into the strange room that was like a luminous, abandoned subway tunnel.

He sat, Jeremy clapping him on the back and reaching for a glass.

"The girls are drinking vodka, but I got a bottle of Johnnie

Walker Blue for the gents," he said proudly, clumsily pouring Cameron a too-full tumbler. Cameron vastly preferred Macallan but smiled gamely. Jeremy introduced him to the three model-looking girls at their table—Marcie? Mikela? Monica? He'd not heard the names the first time, and he'd never need to know them, so who cared?—then he saw her. The room was small, and she'd locked in on him already a moment earlier, flitting her eyes away so as to let him think he'd seen her first and decide what to do about it. And now he saw her, like a chimera, like a harbinger of doom.

He groaned softly. Of all the nights.

"Dude, your face. What?" Jeremy laughed; beneath it was desperation. He looked up to Cameron, wanted him to approve of the scotch he'd chosen, the girls he'd collected for his table. He wanted him to have fun.

"Oh, it's just . . . Liberty's cousin is here."

Jeremy turned around unsubtly and looked in Laila's direction; Laila laughed into her hand, gave them a little wave. Mercifully, she stayed put.

"She's hot," Jeremy said. An assessment.

"I'm aware."

"Invite her over," Jeremy said. Laila was short, a little heavier than he'd normally look at; a size 4 at least. But hey, whatever floated Cameron's boat.

"Nah," he said, "I'll go say hi later. She's kind of a climber."

Jeremy shuddered, thinking his friend had said "clinger," as in stage five. As in a woman who showed any desire to be attached to someone and therefore must be avoided at all costs.

After an hour, Cameron was drunk and having fun. He'd even stopped checking his phone to see if there was a message from

Liberty. There was none, there would not be, for Liberty had fallen into a shattered and medicated sleep. She would never be in a place like this, Cameron thought, because she was dull. Dull. Dull. Dull. He was rich, he was the best-looking man he knew, and he was still young. Fuck Liberty. He could have anyone. He would have everyone.

⁓ঽৄৄ৽⁓

Laila watched Cameron rise toward waking, then mumble, re-adjust, and bury himself back into a fitful, boozy sleep. It was nearly eight, and she was supposed to be at the agency at nine, but being on time was the last thing on her mind. When she was certain he was asleep once again, she crept out of bed to explore. If he asked, she could say she'd gone in search of a glass of water.

The town house was three stories, with Cameron's bedroom on the top floor opening up onto its own small terrace. The middle floor was an entertainment room full of sleek electronics with plugs that disappeared discreetly into the walls and floor. There were an additional two rooms here: one a guest bedroom, one an office, a bathroom between them with an elegant claw-foot tub.

The bottom floor was a large open kitchen with gleaming marble countertops, an attached dining room, and French doors that opened onto a secluded, enclosed patio. Laila flashed to an image of herself carrying a tray of drinks out to waiting friends on a summer afternoon. Perfection.

She thought of Tom's Gramercy apartment with its terrible carpet in the sitting room (why had he not had it torn up yet?), the decades-old grime that had buried itself between the tiles in the shower, the dust that collected on all the piles of books and papers—dust that was dislodged by Tom's occasional attempts at tidying but not actually dealt with. (And why didn't he hire a maid? Surely he could afford it.) Cameron had twice as many books lining the walls in beautifully built-in shelves, and seemingly not a speck of dust. As Laila made her way toward the glass-paned French doors that opened out onto the patio, she shook off the memories of the other man, who was of course not a memory at all but very much a presence. Were she to check her phone at that moment, she would see she had five text messages and two voice mails from Tom trying to determine her whereabouts. This was not because he was alarmed at not being able to get ahold of her but was simply their usual pattern. He could not go more than a few waking hours without reaching out to her, and she routinely took her time replying. Of course it made him want her more, and of course she played this hand. The weak winter sunshine filtered into the frost-covered courtyard, making it sparkle. Laila felt the rightness of it settle on her: this was where she was meant to go next.

≈

When Cameron woke in bed, he felt a momentary panic that he would not be alone. When he looked to his side and saw no one, he let out a deep sigh of relief. He felt as though all the water had been leached from his body; he could feel his brain contracting, his organs shifting and twisting, his skin parched and tight, his whole body in a rage at him for poisoning it. Why had he drunk so *much*? But of course he knew why. Liberty had rejected him. The prince had deigned to love, and his love had been denied. And then Laila. Oh God, had he? She was not here, so perhaps he had not. Perhaps the sweaty memories of his hand in her flaming hair, of his tongue tracing the inside of her thigh, had all been dreamed?

He had especially vivid dreams sometimes, so it could be. And she was not here. She was not here. He looked at his bedside alarm clock: eight fifteen. He would be late to work. No one would care.

Presently he heard soft footsteps on the narrow staircase and sat up straight. She appeared on the landing of the wide-open space, wearing the collared shirt he'd discarded on the floor the night before. She was tiny, and it went practically to her knees. With her makeup worn away by sleep and sex, she looked like a little girl standing there holding her glass of water. She seemed surprised to find him awake.

"I hope it's okay," she said, curling the fingers of her free hand around the cuff of the shirt, "I was dying of thirst."

"It's fine," he said, leaning forward with his elbows on his knees, his hands covering his face to hide his annoyance that she was here. He detested waking up with a stranger in his bed. There were plenty of night visitors, but he was diligent about getting them to leave before the morning. Of course, Laila was not a stranger; so much the worse. When he pulled his head up, she'd walked to the edge of the bed and, tossing her mussed hair over her shoulder, teased at the top button of the shirt. She wanted more of him. Cameron felt an unexpected stab of pity for her. He would have to tread carefully.

"I would love to," he said, taking her hand. "You are so supremely hot. But I am going to be late as it is."

She sat down next to him and stuck her bottom lip out. "We could be quick. . . ."

He felt himself recoil not at the idea of having sex with Laila again—this idea stirred him more than he would have liked—but at something dark and desperate that lashed across Laila's green eyes.

"Listen," he said, ignoring the come-on. Now he knew he must be tender with her, must get her on his side. "Last night was sublime. But . . ." No sooner was that word out of his mouth than Laila's entire demeanor shifted, a strange and chilling smile coming onto her lips.

"Liberty," she said, spat really, as though the tumble of consonants that was her cousin's name bruised her tongue.

"Yes," Cameron said. So at least they were on the same page.

"But I've been led to believe—by *both* of you now—that there is nothing romantic going on. So . . . what's the issue?"

"It's complicated." The very last thing Cameron wanted to do was discuss his relationship—fragile, uncertain thing that it was—with this woman who, he now saw without question, presented a threat. For in the light of day, he wanted nothing more than Liberty. She was so beautiful, so intelligent, so pristine. He would see her as soon as possible and find a way to get them past the previous night.

"Anyway, I'd imagine you'd want to be discreet as well. You know I have the utmost respect for Tom; he is a brilliant man."

He, thought Laila bitterly, is a brilliant man who managed to have an oddly feminine and pudgy physique despite his skinniness. He was a man whose freezer was crammed with sad Stouffer's meals for one. But for now, Laila needed him, so she smiled and agreed with Cameron. "I love Tom. And it was never a question of me being discreet. I love Liberty too, you know. I would never do anything to hurt her. If I'd known that you were involved, I never would have . . ."

And with this she had the ammunition. She could feign innocence. It was all Cameron could do not to throw himself at her mercy, but he knew that would only weaken his position. "So we're agreed," he said, standing up, leaning down to kiss her forehead. "I've got to be off, but make yourself comfortable." *Comfortable*, not *at home*, anything but that. "The door will lock behind you."

He disappeared into the vast white tile of the bathroom. Laila heard the click of the lock and heard the shower come on. She hurried out, not wanting to be there when he emerged. She needed to regroup.

∼⚮∽

Liberty awoke feeling shaky. As she walked gingerly around her apartment on Bambi legs, she debated not going to the office. But yes, she would; solitude was not the answer for today, distraction was. If she stayed here, the memory of the kiss, of her slamming the door in Cameron's face and crumpling against it, would loop endlessly in her mind. The walls would close in on her. She needed the armor of her competence today, the anchoring force of her work.

It was a busy morning, so busy she only tangentially noticed how sulky Laila was.

"Do you want to have a drink downstairs after work today?" she said to her as she sat desultory in her tiny side office, sorting the piles of mail. It was *shocking* how many people sent the agency their full, weighty manuscripts—sometimes bound with makeshift cover designs on the front—despite the explicit directions on the website not to do so. These hopefuls seemed under the wrongheaded impression that making their work physically harder to dispose of might make it harder to disregard. Laila perked up at the invitation. "Sure!"

"Great," Liberty, said. It was a tonic to be needed by Laila. "Thanks for taking the mail pile. I know it's not the most fun."

"Oh, to the contrary." Laila smiled. "At least five writers this morning have promised they have the next *Da Vinci Code* for us, so we're all going to be very rich, very soon."

"No next Harry Potters this morning?"

"Not yet, but I'm barely a third of the way in."

Liberty laughed. "Well, keep fighting the good fight in there."

Liberty was working through lunch, picking at a rather uninspiring salad that Kim had fetched for her from the deli below, when the girl arrived at her door carrying a bouquet of purple and white dahlias.

"These came for you." Kim smiled.

A great warmth came over Liberty. She feared checking the card, in case she was wrong—though she knew she wasn't. She recalled the slow, silly back-and-forth they'd had not long ago.

I want to know everything about you—all the details.

Such as?

Favorite color?

Purple.

Favorite ice-cream flavor?

Mint chocolate chip.

Classic. Favorite flower?

Dahlias.

And these were perfect, with their short stems in a square vase. The card was perfect too, simple, saying *I'm thinking of you . . . —C.*

So, her little freak-out had not ruined everything? Deep down, she knew that if it had, he would not be the man for her. She knew that she needed someone who could see all of her—who would not simply be looking for her competent, organized, undemanding proxy—but she kept hoping perhaps she could simply cure herself of the maladies before anyone saw them.

❧

Laila had seen the flowers, floating to Liberty's office in Kim's hands. They could have been from anyone; it wasn't unusual for Liberty to get flowers from a grateful client for whom she'd landed a deal. But as Laila peered around Liberty's door and caught the look on her face, she had no doubt whom they were from.

"Lovely flowers," she said with a careful smile.

Liberty looked up at her with watery eyes.

"Are you all right?"

"I'm . . . they're from Cameron."

Even though she already knew, it stung. She was gripped by a visceral memory of his broad shoulders vast above her as he moved inside her. "They're *gorgeous*," Laila said, her voice too loud, and Liberty laughed.

"Aren't they?"

After work they headed to a nearby dimly lit bar with the curious name of Dear Irving. Laila pressed her about Cameron.

"So, not to *pry*, but I thought things weren't romantic between you and Cameron."

Laila knew it was her moment to ask; Liberty was practically bursting to talk about it.

"Well, they aren't. I mean, I don't know what they are. He kissed me last night." It was as though the words came out before she could stop them. She'd never looked so girlish.

"And?" Laila plastered an interested smile on her face to disguise her dismay at the fact that she'd been the night's consolation prize. Even more surprising was the flash of guilt that struck her. Had she unwittingly betrayed her cousin? Or had it not been unwitting at all?

"Well, that's the problem, I kind of slammed the door in his face. Oh, Laila, it's a mess, to be honest."

"Why did you send him away if you have feelings for him? Poor Cameron!"

"It's a little more complicated than that. I don't do well with relationships sometimes."

Laila examined her cousin; she'd never seen her like this: nervous, hopeful, vulnerable.

"Why's that?" she asked gently.

"I don't know. Maybe I'm just afraid of losing my independence." Her smile said otherwise, and suddenly Laila saw something she'd never noticed about her cousin: what appeared to be self-containment was actually a deep sadness. Something had happened to her. In many ways she was the opposite of her siblings, those two spoiled, emotionally weightless beings.

"Well, with the right man," Laila said, "you won't have to."

"Anyway. I can't believe he sent me flowers. And my favorite ones."

"He wanted to make it up to you," Laila said.

Liberty looked at her strangely for a moment, and Laila panicked.

"I mean, he must have known you were upset last night."

She nodded. Laila was reassured that only she could see what tainted the expensive blooms, their stems elegantly coiled to suit their geometric vase: guilt. Laila deftly changed the subject.

"So, what do you hear from our grandfather, anything?" She could not bring herself to refer to him—this shadowy man who seemed so likely to reject her—by her cousins' familiar moniker, Opa. She wasn't entirely certain what he was to her, but he certainly wasn't anything so sweet as her opa.

"Oh," Liberty said. "Yes, I meant to update you. So, Opa met a woman, in Switzerland."

"A woman? He's in his nineties, isn't he?"

"Yes, though it seems not to have slowed him down much." Liberty smiled affectionately. "So now he's found some hot-to-trot young girlfriend, not even seventy!"

"A baby!" Laila said. Her mother, of course, would have only been fifty were she still alive.

"Indeed." Liberty rolled her eyes. "They're traveling for a bit, he *hates* New York in the winter, but he'll be back in the spring, I promise. I know you're anxious to meet him, and I've told him all about you!"

Laila nodded, trying to appear encouraged, though Liberty seemed to be assiduously avoiding any mention of what Frederick actually thought about Laila's reappearance.

"Can I ask you something?"

"Of course!" Liberty said, nodding at the waiter who was gesturing to them about bringing another round. "Anything."

"I know you don't know much for certain, but what do *you* think happened between my father and Frederick?"

Liberty took a deep breath, as though considering the matter anew. "Well, it's hard because after your dad died, it was totally off-limits to talk about it. Very healthy, I know. But I guess I always assumed that Opa was really hurt that your father moved your family back to Michigan, and it just . . . escalated from there. Then your father died, and there was no chance to reconcile. I don't know. Opa has a good heart, but he is *so* stubborn. And I guess you really don't become who he is without that quality, you know? He's an immigrant; he grew up with nothing. I guess I always gathered that he felt betrayed by Gregory in some way, by his leaving New York. Maybe it felt like a rejection of what he'd built here. I think he always hoped to have both of his sons running his business someday."

Laila nodded. This was an interesting take. Evidently Liberty did not suspect the truth.

"What is he like?" she asked. "As a grandfather, I mean."

Now Liberty's face softened, as it was clear she adored the old man. "Honestly? He's the best. I think it was easier for him to be loving as a grandfather than as a father, having that remove. My siblings are so much younger than me, and my parents were always so busy when I was growing up—my childhood was actually kind of lonely. If you want to know the truth, most of my best memories from growing up are with him."

"Well," Laila said, smiling at the waiter as he set their next round of drinks down, "I can't wait to meet him when he comes home in the spring."

⁓⁓

That night when she got home, Tom was absorbed in some research for his book, and Laila took the opportunity to pull out the soft leather case she'd brought with her from Michigan that contained her mother's little collection of scandalous mementos from Frederick. Since her conversation with Liberty about the lacquer bird pendant that had been her mother's, she'd had it appraised. It was indeed a nineteenth-century estate piece, one worth approximately $20,000, and she'd kept it buried in the drawer of the nightstand next to her side of Tom's bed, terrified of losing her only item of value. There was no wondering how her mother had come to acquire something so expensive—she'd complained many times that her husband was a cheap gift giver, so it certainly hadn't come from her father. Frederick. She knew of his love for this kind of jewelry. *Something with a history, something with a soul,* Liberty had said in a rapturous little soliloquy about her and her grandfather's shared love for estate jewelry when Laila had asked about the funny little charm bracelet with the jewel-eyed animals that Liberty often wore.

As Laila considered the objects together, she began to see her mother's affair in a new light. If Betsy had kept the pendant through many lean years rather than selling it, she must have loved the old man. And as this realization settled on Laila, so too did an entirely different explanation for why her mother had saved these tokens yet never gone to the Lawrence family with her story. With growing horror, she thought of her mother's constant—though wholly ineffective—mission of personal improvement: the self-help books, the diets that seemed only to make her grow heavier. Betsy hadn't played her hand with the Lawrences because she had foolishly held on to the hope of an outcome far more appealing than subterfuge: that she could restore her former beauty and win Frederick Lawrence back. Her mother hadn't wanted blackmail. She'd wanted belonging.

16

FOR TOM Porter, Laila Lawrence was a breath of fresh air. He'd had an early marriage to a poetess he'd met in his graduate program in Mississippi. On the lush campus, thick with green, glistening with the humid southern afternoons, their love had seemed perfectly of a place. They would sit together under the magnolia trees while she composed sonnets. Everything had been sublime and protected—they'd been married on campus; he was twenty-seven, she twenty-five. Once they moved to New York, however, the poetess's charm had quickly tarnished. She'd accused Tom of selling out the moment he signed the deal for his first novel a year after landing in the city, a place that pulsed with money and ambition. They divorced after two years: the poetess moved back to Oklahoma from whence she came.

Since his divorce, nearly a decade before, Tom had dated a steady stream of women who'd terrified him. Being from Boston, Tom thought he knew big-city denizens, but New York women were polished and fierce as warriors. They sized you up and spit you out. Men were always being told that they had the advantage numbers-wise in New York, but Tom felt made small by these women: so stylish, so aggressive, the masculine ethos of the city having seeped into their blood and made them a mutated form of the feminine. Amazon goddesses; Wonder Women all. Even his beautiful agent, on whom he'd at first nursed a debilitating crush, was alarmingly self-contained. He could never see her needing anyone, much less a man.

But Laila . . . sweet Laila. He'd known from the first time he'd seen her in Liberty's office, her lovely shy smile, her open expression, that she was purity and goodness. She was what his mother, a feisty, unbreakable Jewish widow who now lived with her best friend, would have called a "nice" girl. Leave the fact that she was not Jewish. She took care of Tom and did things no other woman he'd been with since his divorce had done: baked him muffins and rubbed his feet and listened to his stories about his work—fully and intently—without needing to immediately counter with stories of her own. She luxuriated in being a woman; there seemed no danger of her absorbing the masculine affect of the city. True, she was divorced—some awful dentist she'd worked for who'd taken advantage of her grief and then *cheated* on her—but an orphan. Her sadness rallied the strongest side of Tom: here was a woman who *needed* him, openly and ardently, something no other woman he'd met in the city would ever confess to. Tom knew it was hopelessly retro, but he loved that Laila did not seem terribly attached to her career—such as it was—and when he spoke of wanting children, a dreamy, faraway look would come over Laila's face, a look he interpreted to mean that she too was longing for babies. And she wouldn't need to work; Tom could support their little family, not in the city, of course—he wasn't a *billionaire*, for God's sake—but in a nice suburb in New Jersey or Westchester. Tom's backlist was selling well, and he had a new book due in the spring, one he was secretly certain would be his ticket to the next level: it might be made into a movie, not simply optioned into obscurity as three of the others had. When Laila at last agreed to move in with him, he took this as a definitive step in this direction, and his own dreams of the future obscured his vision of the woman now under his roof. He made the fatal flaw too many male novelists are allowed: he assumed that he knew what women wanted.

But alas, ever so slightly at first and then all at once, she'd begun to slip away. She'd been spending too much time with her friend Cece, for one thing—a girl Tom could form no reasonable objection to, except that she was tough in a way that made her seem vaguely imperious; he of all people would be mortified to ever admit that he preferred women he didn't feel were as smart as he was. And for another thing, Laila's head was being turned by the glamour of the city. Where at first she'd been filled with wonder when Tom took her to Michael's or to a reading at KGB, it soon became clear that she preferred the glittering nightclubs and fashion launches her cousins frequented: places packed with models and hedge-fund managers and downtown dilettantes, not a serious intellectual for miles. He wanted reassurance that he was all Laila needed, but when she came home announcing that she would be taking a trip to Mustique with "friends"—including Simon Beauchamp, a rich playboy so notorious even Tom had heard of him—he realized he had been sorely mistaken. Laila had not come to New York to rub Tom's feet and bake him muffins. Up, up, up she went.

❧

"I don't know why you're throwing a hissy fit about this. I'm just taking a little vacation; am I not allowed?" Laila wasn't naive. She knew that Tom would be livid about her going away with another man. But she had found herself in a bind. She had realized with a jolt several weeks back that she was tired of Tom. She had undergone that subtle but definitive transformation in which the idiosyncrasies of one's lover go from endearing to grotesque: his habit of humming open-mouthed, the way in which he rubbed his hands together before sitting at his computer to write in the morning, offering up a cheesy platitude as though it were an invocation, sayings such as "The early bird gets the worm!" or "Another day, another dollar!" Suddenly it was with her again: *no, no, no.* This was not right, this was not her life.

The allure of his fame had long since worn off. It wasn't even a proper kind of fame. No one recognized him on the street; it didn't have any noticeable effect on people whatsoever, unless they were at some literary event, stuffed to the gills with nerdy young strivers and crusty old people who were deeply impressed with each other, drinking until they fell over while eating decidedly mediocre food. The girls from the teen soaps whom Leo was always dating had more cachet. But she couldn't very well just *dump* Tom; Liberty would be pissed, especially after she'd warned her about this exact thing.

Tom had seemed to barely notice the erosion of Laila's feelings for him. In their early, heady days, they'd discussed getting married, and he still referenced it—much to Laila's bemusement. So when Simon the Billionaire (she couldn't help but think of it all together that way, as though he were a superhero, which in the modern world he sort of was) had asked her to come to Mustique with him, it presented an obvious out.

"You're going to a private island with some rich old man you just met!" Tom screeched at her. He'd been writing in his pajama pants all day—a habit Laila detested—and she wondered if he'd even so much as brushed his teeth. When he got going, he told her, he sometimes went manic—forgetting personal care and feeding—he said this as though it were a thrilling altered state, but she found it more slovenly than inspiring. He had definitely not showered by the time Laila had arrived home that chilly March day, unwound her long scarf, placed her slouchy wool hat on the counter, and announced that she was taking a little vacation, leaving tomorrow for five days in Mustique.

"It's not a *private* island; it's semiprivate, and there's a whole group of us going. It's not as though it's a *romantic* trip. Simon is just a friend."

"Oh yes? And then why wasn't I, *your live-in boyfriend*, invited?"

Laila pondered the phrase for a moment: *live-in* had such a dull domestic quality to it, like live-in maid, live-in au pair.

"Well, I'm a guest myself. I couldn't very well go asking for a plus-one! I didn't even think you'd want to go; you're on a roll, as you keep reminding me. You've barely left the apartment in a week! Besides, you don't know anyone."

"Neither do you! You just met Simon. And you're insane if you think he wants to be your *friend*."

"I met him last fall, at the Earth Love party, six months ago at least," she said, as though this were the point. Simon Beauchamp was a known womanizer whose name had spent plenty of time in the tabloids next to those of supermodels and actresses. Laila understood the appeal; his power was dazzling—it went beyond his money, though he nonetheless wouldn't have retained it if the money disappeared.

"I know two of the other women going." She was lying, of course.

"Laila, I'm not comfortable with it." He said this as though it were the final word on the subject.

"Well, I'm sorry to hear that. You should work on your trust issues."

He looked at her, and she saw a flash of rage in his eyes.

"Laila," he said carefully, "you're not going."

On the one hand, it was the most forceful she'd ever seen Tom, and she had to confess that this was something of a turn-on. And yet, the audacity of him to think he could just *tell* her what she would and would not do! He'd suddenly come full circle to remind her of her ex-husband, Nathan: *You can't just leave! What kind of woman are you?* With the memory fueling her, she swept up onto her high horse.

"Tom, I am going. If you don't trust me enough to *allow* it, then we've got bigger problems."

And then she'd done it: opened the conversation she'd known would let her break free of Tom. It unfolded late into the night as they talked around and around it. By the time they finally fell into bed spent and exhausted, he was both begging her to reconsider and had become thoroughly convinced that the breakup had been his doing.

⤚৯৶⤙

Laila had run into Simon the previous week while she was out with Cece. Tom, holed up with his writing, could barely be bothered to take Laila out to dinner once in a while, let alone out dancing at a nightclub. She and Simon had merely chatted the night she saw him at Beatrice Inn, and that might have been it if she hadn't gotten a call from him the following Tuesday.

"Listen, darling," he said right away when Laila answered her phone, "if you have plans for the rest of the week, cancel them and come to Mustique with us. It's going to be loads of fun."

Blood rushed to her head. Mustique: an überposh island in the Caribbean, one of the most exclusive vacation spots in the world. It made Saint Bart's look like a Sandals—or so she'd overheard one of Leo and Nora's socialite friends say. She was ever attentive to details like this, convinced they were the key. At this point it was late March, and winter was clinging to the city, making a tropical getaway that much more appealing. Laila was used to hard winters but not the way they played out in New York. In the Midwest, you simply threw on your giant parka and headed from one heated space to another, via your heated car. If you were an outdoorsy type—which Laila was not—you could do any number of winter activities. In New York, the city seemed to be at war with winter from the moment it set in. The snow would blanket the streets, making everything peaceful for a too-brief moment, before the irrepressible mechanics of the city would begin churning beneath it once more, tracking dirt and salt into the pristine snow and piling it in great filthy drifts along the sidewalks. Now that Laila lived with Tom, she no longer had access to the car and driver that took the twins everywhere they needed to go. Tom, to Laila's horror, mostly took the subway when he had occasion to leave the small radius of his neighborhood, which contained his apartment, the several restaurants he frequented, and the offices of Gerard Mills. Otherwise he walked, and so, now, did Laila.

"Oh, I really couldn't," Laila said to Simon when he'd asked. "I'm so busy this week, and it's not much notice for work." She did not mention Tom, of course.

Despite her protests, he carried on, talking about Alumbrera, the five-thousand-square-foot villa they'd be renting out for the week. Laila's head began to spin as he described the vast outdoor spaces, the picnics they would have on nearby Macaroni Beach—

It's one of the most beautiful beaches in the world, did you know that? When he told her there would be a private chef on hand, she agreed as if that detail had finally convinced her, though she'd more or less been mentally packing her bags ever since he mentioned the word *Mustique.*

She told Liberty she was going away with a few friends for the rest of the week; sorry for the late request; did she mind?

"Well . . . I wish you'd given me more notice. But if you can take a few manuscripts with you to read, I guess it's okay. Is Tom going with you?"

"Oh, no, he has to stay in town. He's been working so hard on the new book. Honestly, he barely has time for me these days!" Laila said the last part with a forced cheerfulness. Perhaps she could come back to this reasoning when Liberty found out about their breakup.

"Well, I'm sorry to hear he's being a crappy boyfriend, though of course, I'm always glad when he's working," she said, smiling. "Who are you going with?"

"Some girls I know through Cece. I think Cece is going to try to come, but she wasn't sure she could get away."

"Okay, well, be safe, and I'll see you Monday."

She remembered Liberty's words as she tried to calm her frayed nerves that night and get some sleep. "Be safe": a simple enough platitude to offer someone heading out on a trip, and yet Laila knew that playing it safe was the last thing she could afford to do in her situation. What she needed was to be bold.

17

THE DAY Laila was slated to leave for Mustique, Tom slept in long past his usual hour, and Laila crept around as quietly as possible in hopes of absconding downstairs to the airy hipster coffee shop below Tom's apartment to wait for Simon, who was picking her up later that afternoon. But he woke just as she was doing a last inventory of her things. She'd overpacked, taking with her most of the things she really cared about with the understanding that, in the worst case scenario, they might not be here for her to collect upon her return.

Tom emerged from the bedroom in his boxers, bleary-eyed, his skin crepey and worn. He'd never looked older to Laila. She felt the thrilling lure of freedom just on the other side of the door.

"I didn't want to wake you," she said, trying to make her voice kind. "I know you have a deadline coming."

"How can I even think about my deadline?" he asked, his voice going up several octaves. He really ought to have put some clothes on—or at least a robe—if he was going to get hysterical, Laila thought. His knees were knobby and red, and a soft paunch clung to his lower abdomen. The effect was unsightly.

She let out a deep sigh, trying not to let her contempt show. "I don't want to miss my flight; we'll talk about it when I get back, okay?" There was a lie in every part of this sentence. Simon wasn't picking her up for hours, and there was no missing her flight to worry about. They were flying private. As far as discussing things when she returned—if she could help it, this was the last Laila would ever see of Tom.

Tom's eyes darted to her many suitcases. "Are you moving there? Jesus, you said you'd be gone for five days!"

"I will," she said as though speaking to a child on the verge of a tantrum. "But I just didn't know what to pack. You know me, I like to have options." She smiled and immediately knew it had been the wrong turn to invoke even the slightest bit of sentimentality. His face crumpled, and he closed the space between them in a few quick strides. All at once he was sobbing on her shoulder.

"Don't go."

She tried to laugh lightheartedly, but it was tinged with cruelty. She needed to get out of there. "It's not such a big deal. I'll be back in a few days, okay? I just think we need to go to our corners for a little bit."

Suddenly he turned angry again. "And your 'corner' is a private island with a billionaire. Very convenient."

"I'm not having this discussion again," she said, pulling away from him and straightening her spine to make the most of her five feet and two inches. With that, she turned on her heel and left the apartment: unwieldy with all her luggage but determined in her stride.

In the café, she collected her thoughts. She envisioned Tom receding into the distance, though she knew he was only several floors above her, pacing the apartment, panicking and plotting on how to mend what was broken between them. Poor man, he had no idea what the real problem even was.

Frederick would be back from Europe soon after Laila got

back from Mustique, and if she could only meet him—and wouldn't he *have* to meet her once he was back in the city?—then she wouldn't have to worry about depending on anyone else ever again. She couldn't imagine that the old man would want anyone else in the family to know what Laila had discovered.

In the meantime, while she navigated this delicate family drama, a billionaire friend could only be an asset. And Laila was convinced she could make him her friend. Liberty seemed to be able to do this so well—make men she wasn't sleeping with care a great deal about her—why couldn't Laila?

Simon pulled up an hour later in the sleek black Rolls-Royce he'd told her to watch for. His driver hoisted Laila's many bags—which she would not see again until they arrived at the villa—into the vast trunk and ushered Laila into the back seat with Simon, who had not emerged and was still ensconced in the car speaking to someone in German on a cell phone. He smiled tightly at her but did not break from his conversation as she settled in next to him and the car pulled away from the curb. He put his hand possessively on her thigh, and Laila felt very small suddenly. She moved her gaze nervously between Simon and the window. Simon looked much older than he had upon their first two meetings; indeed, she had looked him up, and he was fifty-three—more than twice her age. In the dim light of the two evenings she'd spent with him, she had not noticed the jowly neck or the preponderance of pink scalp that was visible beneath his thinning hair. As his phone conversation grew more heated, he moved his hand up Laila's thigh. She had worn a jersey dress with a sweater for comfort and suddenly regretted it as his hand—which, gnarled with hair on the knuckles and brown age spots, belied his age perhaps more than any other part of him—continued its steady progress toward her crotch.

As they sped toward New Jersey, Laila began to panic. Simon's voice over the phone sounded angry, but she couldn't tell if this was only because of the language. At last he hung up. "Pardon the phone call, darling. Bloody Germans. All ready for the island adventure, then?"

"Yes, I'm so excited." She pivoted her body to face him and tried to delicately maneuver out of his grasp, but he held fast.

"Wait until you see the place. One of the grandest on the island, I assure you."

Laila nodded and smiled, feeling manic with dread. She thought of ways to put herself on equal footing with Simon, but the reality of her error in judgment was deepening by the minute. He was a billionaire, and she was no one. Beauty and youth were nothing compared to the power of that much money. How much stronger would her position be if she had her own fortune? But she did, or she would, she reminded herself—it simply wasn't at her disposal right then.

When they boarded Simon's plane, Laila was momentarily distracted by the opulence of the Gulfstream. There were eight seats of buttery tan leather and a small sitting room toward the back of the plane where the two other couples lounged with glasses of champagne.

The other two men looked a bit younger than Simon; the one named Alex was handsome and incredibly fit and tanned, and the other was a slightly paunchy man named Bert. Their companions looked to be in their midthirties, but it was hard to tell with Manhattanites—both women (whose names Laila immediately forgot) had those severely arched eyebrows that come from too much Botox. They gave her frozen smiles.

"Nice of you to join us, old boy," Alex said good-naturedly, standing and giving Simon a handshake and a hearty clap on his shoulder.

"Sorry to keep you," he said breezily. "Downside of flying Air Simon, I'm afraid. Subject to my schedules and whims."

"Oh, I think we'll live," Alex said. "And who might this lovely young woman be?"

"Laila Lawrence," she said, hoping that her name, at least, would mean something to this group, but no one seemed to care. Once they were in the air, the women chattered idly about luncheons and spas and housekeepers they'd had to fire; the men discussed business and sports. Laila was utterly marooned and buried herself in her book. She'd packed *One Hundred Years of Solitude* for its seriousness and its lush cover, which led her to believe it might double as a beach read. She hoped someone would notice what she was reading, ask her about it, and be impressed by it. Instead, she felt she'd been absorbed by the succulent leather and had become utterly invisible.

When they arrived at the tiny airport—a short landing strip that seemed to materialize only as they were coming in for a landing—Laila saw that it was little more than a hut. There were two members of the house's staff waiting with a tray of drinks. Both were short, lovely, round women with brilliant white smiles that Laila found comforting.

They rode the short distance to the house in two little vehicles called mules, bumping up dirt roads and hugging corners, the lush vegetation skimming their shoulders. There were virtually no cars on the island—with the exception of a service vehicle or two—and everyone traveled to and fro in these souped-up golf carts.

The house was so majestic a property that it seemed laughable to call it a house at all. It sat high upon a hill, and all of the main rooms, including the larger bedrooms, had retractable walls that could be rolled up, exposing the spaces to the mild tropical air and magnificent view of the green slopes that rolled down to the sparkling blue ocean—an unobstructed paradise.

The group took a tour around the grounds. Laila—whose awe was becoming more akin to disbelief by the moment—turned her camera to video mode and started recording; she got no cell service, but fortunately all the other features of her phone still worked. One of the women rolled her eyes. "She's like a Japanese tourist," she said in a loud whisper as they headed back into the house. Laila ignored her. She was giddy at the thought of recounting all of these details to Cece, perhaps even Nora if the wind blew her way again.

They made their way back to the main house, where they ate a light meal of sandwiches and salads that the chef had prepared for them, and got settled into their rooms. Simon made a show of hefting Laila's largest and most overstuffed bag down the hallway himself, dismissing the staff member, who looked distressed as he watched the middle-aged guest grunt as he slung the bag over his shoulder, declaring it "light as a feather."

"Here we are," Simon said as they entered the room. There was a giant bed with a mosquito net over it and a pristine white bedspread. The walls were rolled up to reveal green vistas of the forest below and a vast expanse of ocean in all directions. Simon handed her a rum punch that must have been delivered by a staff member who had subsequently disappeared into thin air. It looked gratifyingly cold and delicious. She took a big sip.

"Careful there, my darling! They make that with Sunset Very Strong Rum, eighty-four proof. It will knock you flat."

She smiled but considered polishing the rest off in one gulp when she noticed that Simon's bags had already been placed in the corner.

"Your bedroom is amazing. So where am I staying?" she asked.

He laughed, and she smiled back nervously.

"You'll go in the staff quarters if you're naughty," he said, stepping closer and putting his arms around her waist. "Here if you're *very* naughty."

He kissed her, and Laila felt herself recoil. She hoped he didn't notice. Her head spun from his words and from the rum sloshing around in her empty stomach.

"But, um . . ."

He stepped back and looked at her curiously.

"Yes?"

"We're staying together?"

"Of course we're staying together." His voice was on the edge of anger, perilous and tight.

"Well, we haven't known each other that long. I just thought . . ."

"You thought?" Now his voice took on a hint of dark amusement, even more menacing.

"Never mind," she said, kissing him lightly on the lips. She couldn't think of a halfway delicate way out of this situation, so she stalled. "You know, I'm absolutely *exhausted*," she said. "I didn't sleep well last night; I might get ready for bed soon."

"Get comfortable, and we'll have a drink on the balcony," he said.

Well, Laila thought, a drink could only help.

She changed into a nightgown and silk robe, the kind of thing she wore to bed when she was with a man. Just because she didn't want to sleep with Simon didn't mean she didn't want to impress him. A staff member appeared with a bottle of champagne. She was disappointed not to see more of the rum punch; as promised, it had gone straight to her head, and if she had another, she might just pass out—which would temporarily solve her problem.

"You know, Laila," Simon said, gazing out into the blazing Mustique sunset, "everything I have, I built. I came from nothing; grew up in a council flat. Housing projects, you call them here."

She wished he might just let her quietly enjoy the view. "You must have worked very hard."

He looked at her keenly for a long moment as though trying to determine something.

"Ruthlessly," he said, "that's the secret. And you know, that night I met you, I thought, Ah, one of mine."

"Me?" Laila sputtered. Her heart fluttered. She nearly choked on her champagne.

"Oh yes. My darling, you don't think I haven't done my research. I know you didn't grow up in New York with your cousins. Grew up middle-class and falling in Michigan; orphaned, poor thing. And divorced at such a tender age."

Her heart ricocheted around her rib cage. What did he mean by bringing all of this up?

"And?" she said, unable to disguise her bitterness.

"Relax, my darling. It's a compliment. You're like me. You'll do what you must to seek higher ground."

"I just wanted to be with my family," she said.

"Well, family matters most of all, doesn't it?" The way he said this sent Laila back into a deepening spiral, thinking of poor, bewildered, loyal, ridiculous Nathan. About her own family and their seeming ambivalence to her very existence.

As she finished her second glass of champagne, Laila felt something looking at Simon—not attraction, which she'd half hoped might emerge—but the flicker of recognition. If only she could cultivate his friendship, perhaps they were kindred spirits after all. She could certainly learn from someone who'd accomplished all that he had; who'd begun his life as an outsider.

"Ready for bed?" he asked at last.

Laila drew a breath of relief. "Yes." She needed to sleep off this surreal turn of events.

"Let me just go wash up," Simon said.

Simon headed for the bathroom, and Laila dove beneath the bedcovers. By the time Simon reemerged, smelling of cloying aftershave, she was doing an excellent impression of being asleep.

"Laila, my darling," he said, curling himself around her, the coarse hair of his chest scratching against her back, "wakey-wakey."

She let out a sleepy sigh and kept her eyes glued shut. Simon's hands continued to creep over her, pushing her flimsy nightgown up over her hips. He jostled his arms around her, pinching her nipples from behind. Laila felt herself go rigid. She could feel Simon's erection, which protruded from his shorts. He pulled her underwear down to her midthighs, and she felt his hands, thick and dumb like the hands of a large teenager, prodding between her legs, trying to produce some response. Laila tried to imagine he was someone else, calling back those raw flashes of her night with Cameron months before.

"You are clean, I presume?" he asked, his breath cloying and warm on her ear, "and on the pill?"

She could not find a voice to speak and instead simply nodded.

"Good, good," he said, stroking her hair and then taking

a fistful of it in his hand, bending her neck forward painfully. Laila felt a shiver of revulsion as she heard him spit into his free hand—having quickly grown weary of trying to produce the genuine effect in her—and massaged it impatiently between her legs, guiding himself roughly inside her, letting out a mortifying "Ohhhhh" as he did so. He pushed her onto her stomach, one hand planted beside her, the other still tangled in her hair, pushing her face against the pillow beneath it. Laila called upon all the force of imagination to think of someone else inside her—with the softness of his protruding belly pressed against her back, it was impossible to conjure up Cameron with his lean, muscled chest and torso, but even Tom would do for now. She would have given anything in that moment for Tom; Tom who loved her and cherished her and always put her first, in lovemaking and elsewhere. For whatever else Tom had lacked in the bedroom, he was masterful and enthusiastic with his tongue, spending however long was needed between Laila's legs to make her respond. Tom who loved the taste and smell of her. Tom whom she had traded—ruthlessly—to be here with this ogre on this painfully beautiful island.

Those moments seemed a suspended hell in which time ceased to exist, then at last Simon pulled out of her with a strangled "Ugnnnhhhhh," and she felt the hot ooze of semen spreading between her back and his torso as he collapsed, his unwieldy frame nearly crushing the breath out of her delicate one. At last he kissed her shoulder and removed himself to rinse off. Laila remained still, feeling the wetness on her back cool, gluing her silky gown to her skin.

Simon returned from the bathroom several moments later and lay down without a word, disinterested in the woman beside him now that he'd had her. At last Laila swung her legs out of the bed, shaky upon them, pain radiating between them.

The bathroom of their suite was a thing to behold: with a massive stone shower separated from the night by only a curtain, pull it back and you were suddenly in the open air. The bathroom faced the opposite direction from Macaroni Beach, so there was no one to see you other than the occasional passing yacht. The showerhead was so massive that it felt like standing beneath a waterfall. Laila turned it on and climbed in with her nightgown on. It was ruined anyway; how could she ever wear it after this? As the water rushed over her, she slowly let herself collapse to the shower's smooth tile floor. The pain of where he'd been inside her radiated, nearly consumed her; her body unwilling to consent to what it had been offered up for. She felt a deep and rancorous humiliation at being a woman at all. She caught her breath—only then realizing that she'd been crying—and looked out onto the calm ocean and had the wild thought that she could just escape into the jungle beneath the villa, hide here forever. After all, going back to New York was going to be a debacle. She couldn't go back to Tom, not after she'd left with Simon. Laila's foremost skill seemed to be burning bridges so thoroughly that there would be no hope of return—perhaps this was her way of daring herself to keep going. Onward ever. She closed her eyes and let the water stream over her face. She would go back to New York, connect with Frederick, reveal what she knew. Never be dependent on a man again. Or on anyone. At last her fingers and toes had pruned, and there was nothing left to wash from herself. She discarded her ruined nightgown and put on her matching silk robe, which was still pristine. She curled herself on the bed as far as she could possibly get from Simon, who snored intermittently throughout the night. She fell into a fitful sleep, and when she woke, she was mercifully alone. She looked around for a clock, but there seemed to be none in the entirety of the house, and she could not remember where she'd left her phone. It wasn't as though she particularly wanted to see Simon that morning, but it still did not feel good to wake up alone. She put one of the house bathrobes on over her slinky one and made her way down the hallway.

The other guests were just finishing breakfast and looked up at her, startled. Everyone else was fully dressed: the men in light pants and linen shirts, the women in billowing white bathing-suit cover-ups.

"There you are!" Simon said.

"Good morning," she said sheepishly. She found she didn't want to go any nearer to Simon, that she might be sick if she was close enough to smell him.

"Please sit down, miss," one of the servers clearing plates said to her. "What would you like for breakfast?"

Laila let him usher her into a chair next to Simon and looked at him helplessly.

"Egg-white omelet?" he suggested. She nodded gratefully.

Simon pulled his chair closer as the others drifted away from the table with what seemed likely to be their second or third mimosas held aloft.

"Did you sleep well, darling? Thought I'd better leave you to it."

Laila smiled and nodded, gulping the mimosa that had been placed in front of her. By the time she'd had two, she began to feel better. She could almost forget the heavy thud of Simon's body collapsing onto her own. Almost.

That morning they buzzed around the island in their mules. All but Simon were on their first visit to Mustique, and he clearly relished being able to show the place off. The villas were like miniature kingdoms unto themselves, houses with thousands of square feet, containing commercial kitchens, numerous pools, and waterfalls, some with their own private golf courses. Even in her cousins' rarefied world, Laila had never seen anything like it. The jungle that spread between the estates was lush, and along the pristine beaches were piled dozens of pink conch shells.

Later, Laila went to Macaroni Beach with the two other women while the men left to play golf. The beach was like nothing Laila had ever seen: pure white sand, imposing green cliffs rising on either side, topaz waves crashing gently while the world's most privileged children ran in and out of them. The women were relaxed and becoming a bit nicer, especially when Laila effusively complimented them on their bikini bodies and insisted on getting some snaps of all of them. By the midafternoon, she'd nearly forgotten the events of the previous evening. She took a video of herself walking along the beach, holding the camera at an expertly crafted angle. She needed something to document this, to make it look as though it had all been a beautiful walk on the beach.

That night the group ate dinner at the massive table on the house's outdoor patio. Simon's pale skin was sunburned, and he'd had a bad round of golf that afternoon, which was making him surly. His attitude cast a shadow on the group, and from the way the other men appeared to be working overtime to cheer him up, Laila understood that she was not the only one whose way was being paid by the billionaire. Everyone seemed relieved by the time they piled in their mules to head down to Basil's Bar.

"So," Simon began as he drove the mule too fast down the narrow road, "did you enjoy yourself today?"

"I did," Laila said, gripping her seat. It was the first time she'd been alone with Simon since the night before, and her heart was fluttering in her chest. She was not sure how she could spend the night with him again.

"Bloody right," he said, his posh facade slipping for a moment, a sliver of his East End origins coming through. "This is one of the most exclusive islands in the world. Do you know how few people get to come here?"

"I do; I mean, yes. It's really special. It was amazing of you to bring me here, I'm so grateful." What could she say? She wanted to *be here*, of course, but with someone, anyone, else. She missed her cousins. She missed Tom. She fantasized about Cameron, who could easily afford to bring Liberty here.

"Well, at least you appreciate it," he grumbled. Laila wondered if somehow her fellow stowaways had failed to show sufficient gratitude by beating him at golf. "So goddamn tired of these people." This he said to no one, to the night air.

Basil's looked like any other beachside tiki bar until you noticed the extraordinarily well-heeled clientele of minor European royalty, movie stars, and Manhattan socialites inside. The bar had a thatched roof and was open air; between the band's songs, you could hear the waves crashing just outside.

They filed into a booth and ordered champagne, which Simon drank glumly. The others seemed unable to resist the cheerful lure of the place.

"Who is that?" Laila asked one of the other men in their

group, Alex, who sat in the booth beside her. She pointed at an older man who seemed about eight feet tall and was dominating the dance floor. He looked like a cross between Morgan Freeman and Sidney Poitier, his graying hair a shock against his ebony skin. He wore a dashiki and the serious expression of someone who's seen everything twice.

"Don't you know?" Alex said, teasing her. Everyone was at least a little drunk by that point. "That's Basil, the king of Mustique. He owns this joint and half of the village. He's the most famous person on the island," he continued, clearly de-lighted to be in the know. "The legend goes that Colin Tennant found him by the side of the road in Saint Vincent after he was injured in a motorbike accident. Gave him a job as a bartender at Cotton House. The rest is history." Colin Tennant was the eccentric British founder of the island, and Cotton House was one of only two tiny, exclusive hotels on the island. At that moment, Basil noticed the pair looking at him and walked over to their table.

"Young lady," he said, holding out his hand to escort her to the dance floor. He told her that the way she danced reminded him of Princess Margaret when she was young, that she'd been a close friend of his. Laila was suddenly on top of the world or rather, at the white-hot center of it. She handed her phone to Alex to get him to take some video of them dancing. She imagined telling her cousin, *Nora, look, it was so amazing. Nora, look. I belong.*

Once freed from her shackles at Simon's side, Laila had no wish to return.

She pulled up a seat at the bar where she could watch the reg-gae band playing on a small stage in the middle of the floor. There was a very drunk man harassing one of the steel-drum players, seemingly trying to convince him to let him join them onstage. He was middle-aged with a face that must have once been handsome and a chin-length mane of salt-and-pepper hair. He looked as though he might have been tumbling around in the ocean for a while before washing up onshore.

"What is that guy doing?" Laila said to the woman sitting next to her at the bar.

"Oh God," she replied. "He's been bothering everyone on the island. German media mogul, just lost his company, or at least that's what I heard. He must be on some kind of bender. We saw him drinking an entire bottle of wine by himself this morning at breakfast." The two women watched, enthralled, as he gave up on the drummer and began dancing awkwardly.

Not five minutes later, the German had cornered Laila by the bar and introduced himself to her breasts. Laila saw a young, cool-looking girl standing by the bar alone, shining like a beacon. She excused herself from the German with a brief, "Sorry, I just see my friend over there."

"Don't leave," he ordered. "Where are you going?" If he'd been able to figure out how to take a step in her direction, he surely would have followed her.

"Hi," she said to the girl. "I'm Laila."

"Persephone." She smiled serenely and offered her hand. She had on a filmy white dress that hung loosely off her sculpted shoulders, and her hair was done up in elaborate braids.

"What a fantastic name."

"Thanks," she said, "I was born in Eugene, Oregon. Hippie parents."

"Oregon? Wow, you're a long way from home. Who are you here with?"

"I live here," she said, taking a sip of her caipirinha. "I'm a yoga instructor. I teach group classes at Macaroni Beach four mornings a week. I do privates as well; great way to see all the villas."

Laila was relieved to have someone to talk to, and found herself fascinated by Persephone; she'd traveled all over South America and Europe teaching yoga, sometimes living in hostels for months at a time. Laila's eyes brightened as she talked about teaching on the Amalfi Coast two summers before, and she wondered how often anyone here asked about her life at all. Laila found herself pouring out the whole story of how she'd come here and was now, it would seem, trapped under the thumb of the lecherous and grouchy Simon.

A gorgeous young man with blue eyes and a deep tan emerged from the crowd and kissed Persephone's cheeks.

"All right, Perse?"

"Hi, Chad," she said. "This is my new friend, Laila. We have to save her from the awful Brit she came here with."

Chad leaned over and kissed her cheeks. He smelled like the ocean: salty and vast.

"Bloody Brits on this island; that'll teach you," he said, putting his arm around her. "Good thing you've found us now."

He was Australian, and he taught surfing and kiteboarding to the bored-looking offspring of the wealthy island guests who would otherwise be left to wreak havoc. Laila had seen a boy who couldn't have been more than twelve drinking a beer and driving his parents' mule just that afternoon.

Drinking, laughing, and dancing with Chad and Persephone, it occurred to Laila how much they had in common: they were the young and beautiful people rich people paid to keep around; rich men, mostly, for weren't many of the wives on this island just like the three of them in that way? It was only the degrees of freedom that differed. Chad and Persephone were just doing jobs, which they clocked in and out of and from which they maintained their dignity, but still got to live in this miraculous place.

Chad leaned down and whispered something in Laila's ear, pulling her close.

"I couldn't hear you." Laila leaned up to his ear, her lips almost grazing it.

"You're gorgeous," he said again louder, nearly shouting it with a big, bright smile. Laila felt the jealousy of the wives radiating in her direction, and out of the corner of her eyes, she could see Simon glowering at her from the booth.

"Can we get out of here?" Laila said to both now, suddenly desperate to be away from the place.

"Let's take her to our beach, Perse," Chad said.

As the three of them walked down the dirt road by the harbor, they came upon the fishing village, which looked as though it might have been hastily erected that afternoon or else had been there for a thousand years. The men sat around on the beach out-side their huts drinking rum in the moonlight, which bounced off the calm seas for miles.

"This might sound totally obtuse, but it's strange to me that anyone lives on this island," Laila said. "The whole place seems like a hotel."

"They were here first," Chad said, gesturing to the rows of crooked shacks on the small beach.

"Amazing," Laila said, and just then she caught eyes with one of the fishermen who looked back at her impassively. She felt an unexpected flash of kinship. They'd been forced to the edges of what was rightfully theirs and were now dependent on the goodwill of those who had taken it. Just as she depended on her cousins.

They took Chad's mule careening through the foliage to a secluded beach. As they rode through the trees and spilled onto the moonlit sand, Laila felt the relief of putting distance between her and Simon; somewhere on the periphery of her thoughts, she knew she would pay for what she was doing now, but she pushed this from her mind.

And who could think of anything negative as they drank rum punch in the moonlight and watched the glowing jellyfish phosphorescent beneath the waves? Chad and Persephone seemed so happy, so light in spirit—Laila wondered if she could just abandon the mess she'd made in New York and set herself free. She liked yoga; how much would it really take to be an instructor? Did she even *want* the life her cousins had?

She pulled out her phone and took some video of them dancing in the waves. Persephone snapped a picture of Chad holding Laila in his arms as she pretended to swoon in the style of a romance novel cover.

They settled onto some blankets to look at the stars.

"Here," Persephone said, passing her a bottle of rum punch.

"I probably shouldn't." She knew she'd already drunk too much champagne at the bar.

"Mandatory, love," Chad said, leaning over to give her a lingering kiss on the mouth.

She giggled and took the bottle from Persephone.

"You guys seem really happy here."

"How could we not be?" Persephone asked. "Look at this place."

"I love New York, but sometimes I think that if I find my way in, I'll never find my way out." She knew she was barely making sense. She hadn't told them about her family, only that she lived in New York and worked for a literary agency.

"There's always a way out," Chad said, squeezing her hand.

⁓

Laila woke up to the blazing sun on her face, sand sticking to her burning skin, her head throbbing like she'd been hit with a two-by-four. She propped herself up gingerly on her hands. Her ruined dress was splayed around her legs, and her gold sandals had been placed next to her. She was alone.

She rummaged in her purse for her phone. What time was it? Where was she? Her phone was dead.

She looked behind her, but there was no sign of anyone. All that remained were the tire tracks of the mule leading back into the forest.

Was this a prank?

"Persephone? Chad?" Her only answer was the sound of a large manicou scurrying through the woods.

She got to her feet. Her head was throbbing and spinning. Her mouth was parched. Her heart pounded as her circumstances dawned on her. She was alone on a beach, though she had no idea which one. She remembered the mule making its way through the trees, off any number of paths. Was this a hidden beach? Why would they leave her here? What had she done to them? She dragged herself under the trees and pulled her knees up to her chest. She fought back tears; she couldn't afford to dehydrate herself any further. She strained to remember what had happened the night before, but only shreds remained. She recalled kissing Chad, kissing Persephone, and then . . . had the two of them argued?

She tried to steady her shaking body and tumbling mind. She reminded herself that this island had to be one of the safest places in the world to be lost. All she had to do was find someone, *anyone*, and she'd be fine. One option would be to follow the coastline, which would at least keep her from getting lost. But the terrain between beaches was rocky, and there might be parts she couldn't get across. She'd also be completely exposed to the sun, and her fair skin would surely fry. The other option was to follow the mule tracks back through the forest and hope they led her to a road. The thought of becoming lost in the woods was terrifying, but it seemed like the better option given the certainty that she would end up with a blistering sunburn otherwise. She felt as if she were in a Grimms' fairy tale. The thought was unexpectedly galvanizing: yes, she thought, a heroine facing peril.

She put her useless gold sandals back on her feet and began following the tire tracks.

The calm of the forest began to seem menacing, and she longed for any sign of another person. Surely Simon would send someone to look for her. Wouldn't he? If not him, then others in the house. Wouldn't they?

She hit her exposed toe on a branch and it started bleeding. Her feet were soft from regular pedicures, not suited for trekking across terrain any more challenging than a dance floor. *Why* had her new friends abandoned her like that? Had she been drugged, or did she simply have too much rum? Perhaps their relationship with one another was more complicated than the easy friendship it had appeared to be. The last thing she remembered was lying on the beach with them feeling happy and adored.

At last she came to a road. Between her hangover, the accompanying dehydration, and her walk in the woods, her head spun and her legs quivered beneath her. She sat at the side of the road and waited for someone to pass by.

A couple staying at one of the nearby villas found her sometime later. She wept with relief at the sight of them. The woman fell upon her with concern.

"Oh my goodness," she said, "what happened to you? Should we go to the police?"

"No, no," Laila said, "just back to the villa where I'm staying. I'm sure they're worried."

The husband seemed more concerned about missing his tee time than about seeing Laila safely home. "The head of the bank is going to be there, Geneva."

"*Mark*," the wife said, "this is more important; golf can wait."

Laila had the feeling this was the kind of fight that carried on in different iterations over decades; it had the cadence of a well-rehearsed bit. As absurd as it was, the thought made her feel lonely. She didn't even have anyone to bicker with—she was ever the disposable member of the family.

The couple left her at the foot of the walkway to the door of Alumbrera. She thanked them and hurried to the door. She knocked and was greeted by the butler, "Hello, Ms. Lawrence."

"Well, you're in a state," Simon said, thundering forth. "What on earth did you do?"

"They left me," she said stunned. Something caught her eye in the corner of the foyer: her bags, packed. Her sun hat sat gingerly atop her luggage.

"Your boyfriend? Oh, what a shame."

Laila saw a smile flash across the lips of the butler as he handed her a glass of water with a thin slice of cucumber at the bottom. What betrayal! She saw in a sudden moment what she was to the staff: just another spoiled, hysterical white girl. On the way to the villa, she'd built up a considerable head of rage about being abandoned, and now she unleashed the torrent of it, insisting to Simon that they go to the police, or to whatever equivalent existed there, about Persephone and Chad.

"Did they steal something from you?"

"No, but they . . . I think they drugged me!"

"With Sunset rum?"

She screwed her eyes shut to hold back the tears of frustration.

"It sounds to me like you got shite-faced and passed out on the beach. Hardly anyone's fault but your own."

"That is *not* what happened. I don't drink like that; not ever!"

"I'm not going to get two poor kids fired because you decided to go get drunk on a beach. Your entitlement is appalling."

Laila didn't argue. She was too defeated. She barely heard him as Simon told her that he'd booked her a flight back to New York for the following day.

"And until then?" she said, looking again to her bags. He clearly meant not to spend another minute with her, which was fine by Laila.

He shrugged. "Why don't you stay with your new friends?" And with that he turned and went back to where the rest of the group had convened on the patio.

"Come on, miss," the butler said gently, "I can take you wherever you need to go."

Laila let him lead her out of the house, bewildered.

"Is there a hotel or . . . ?"

"I will take you to the Firefly; my friend Phillipe, he will look after you."

Upon arriving at the B&B that was nestled in the lush hillside above Britannia Bay, Laila was momentarily distracted from her plight by the sheer beauty of the place. The bar, which also functioned as the reception, opened out onto the sparkling bay. The series of infinity pools built into the hillside gave the place the look of an organic island paradise.

To Laila's relief, the Firefly did have a room for the night. To her horror, the price was $1,500. By the time she'd made this alarming discovery, Alumbrera's butler was long gone, and the bartender, Phillipe, though kind, was not in a position to give her a free room. He offered to call down to Cotton House, the only other hotel on the island, to see if they had a room available. All they had was something called the Residence, which was over $3,000 a night.

Laila spent the night in the most beautiful hotel room she'd ever seen, weeping.

The next morning she left the island on a tiny plane to Barbados, where she waited for several hours in the hot, dingy airport until her flight for New York departed. Even with her small size, she felt claustrophobic in the middle seat in coach. She felt certain that Simon had purposefully gotten her a middle seat. At least he had paid for the ticket back. She had gone on this trip to start anew; to break with Tom and make some powerful new friends. Instead, she had burned bridges, humiliated herself, and drained a good chunk of the last of her savings. Fifteen hundred dollars. It was far more than most people's rent in the rest of the country. Enough money for an entire vacation to someplace else. Or it was a shopping trip of Nora's at Bergdorf's—on a light day. Or it was a night in a hotel room on one of the most exclusive islands in the world. Dinner for two at Per Se. Money was meaningless without context. Laila was meant to be in a position where this amount was a frippery, a night on the town. Her determination steeled: she would confront Frederick Lawrence, who would have returned at last from Europe. She would appeal to him as his granddaughter first, but if necessary, she would threaten to expose him; she knew he must care that his past with her mother remain hidden. No one would have gone to all this trouble to keep a secret if it didn't matter. She'd be reasonable, so long as she was given what her cousins had been—the trusts, the property—she wouldn't even broach the question of paternity.

When at last her plane touched down in New York, she started her phone up again. As it returned to life, Laila was flooded with messages from her cousins. Something had happened. Her heart racing, she played one of the five voice mails Nora had left her.

There was urgent news of Frederick Lawrence.

18

NORA HEARD the woman who'd stayed over with Leo murmur a good-bye to him and creep out the front door, not noticing that Nora was burning a hole in her from behind where she stood in the kitchen with a French press.

"Nora?" Leo called out, his voice sounding small, hopeful but uncertain it would find his sister.

"Yes, my love?"

"Can you bring me one of my kombuchas?"

"Be right there."

She carried the French press and two mugs, tucking the chilly bottle of kombucha carefully under her arm. She found her brother in bed and crawled over to him, curling herself in the decorative chenille throw on top of the duvet, not wanting to get under the covers, thinking about what was probably lurking there after his night with the woman, who even from behind Nora could tell was too old for him. The room still had the faint odor of sex; her brother's familiar smell mixed up with some overtly feminine one. Nora's nostrils curled from the assault of a stranger's scent.

Leo put a lackluster arm around her and stroked her hair.

"I take it that *wasn't* Amanda who just left." Amanda was a gorgeous, prominent fashion editor Leo had met a month ago and fixated on ever since. She was in her midthirties, married with two children.

Leo shook his head, staring wistfully at the ceiling. "The woman who left wasn't half of an Amanda."

"I don't know why you do this," Nora said, and they both knew what she meant. He would fall in love with women he could never have—mostly married but sometimes otherwise unattainable; once it was a lesbian cellist from the Metropolitan Opera—and then proceed to sleep with other women who were not them, ones he could have and therefore did not want; all of it a masochistic cycle. "You think it will make you feel better, but it always makes you feel worse. Who was she?"

He shrugged. "I met her at Gold Bar last night. It was awful when she left this morning," he said. "She looked so hopeful, and she was lingering, so I asked for her number." His voice sounded strained and wretched. "But I know that I'll never call her. I'm always letting people down."

"No, Leo," she said, reaching out a hand and placing it on his chest. "What can she really expect? She came home with you from a nightclub. It's not a commitment; if she has expectations, it's her own stupid fault."

"How can I judge anyone? I'm in love with a married woman!" Though Leo's description of his inappropriate and fleeting infatuations as love might appear frivolous, he felt them deeply. We all need our agonies in order to be happy, and how else was someone as privileged, as beautiful, and as beloved as Leo to find them except where he could manufacture an unrequited passion? The heart doesn't only want what it wants, it wants *to* want, craves desire itself, a state that can only exist in the moments before it's fulfilled. Leo reached over and pulled his glass pipe from the drawer of his bedside table, packed it with weed, and lit it in one fluid, practiced motion.

"It's different," Nora said, taking a toke and lying back.

"She could be a wonderful girl; what if she's right for me? What if *she* would actually make me happy?"

"Who?"

"Gold Bar girl."

"You don't remember her name?" Nora asked gently. It was bleak, this kind of coupling.

"Not just now, but she wrote it down . . . I think."

"So call her."

"I could," he said, his voice brightening for a moment, then fading. "But I won't. I want to. I want to want to."

Nora sighed; she understood. The twins wanted for nothing and therefore wanted everything.

"Do you ever think it would be better?" Nora asked. They often did this to each other: expected the one to pick up a thought the other was having without saying it aloud. Many times it worked, but Leo was too distracted this morning to hear his sister's thoughts.

"Hmm?" He passed her the pipe, and she took a deep inhale.

"If we could just live normal lives? No fortune, no famous parents, no famous us," she said, her words chasing the fragrant smoke.

Leo flipped on his side and looked at her, grinning, the weed settling in on both of them.

"Tell me about this other life."

"I live in Westchester, in one of those big houses with the stone foyers, with a fountain in the back, maybe even a little swimming pool. I have a husband named . . ." She bit her lip and thought about it. "Brad. He's a doctor!"

"What does he specialize in?" Leo asked, smiling.

"He's a pediatrician! He works hard but still makes plenty of time for us. And he adores you, and me, of course, and our children, and our dog, Gunner."

"What kind of dog is Gunner?"

"A golden retriever," she said, "and we have two children, a boy and a girl."

"Sounds idyllic. And what am I up to?"

"You still live in New York, but you gave up all the money, so you live way out in Brooklyn with a painter. And you love her, and you write your books, and they're the toast of the town. And everyone recognizes that you're brilliant, and no one ever says it's because you had this or that help from Mom and Dad, because we aren't us, and everything we have is ours."

"Brooklyn and Westchester are too far apart," he said, "I don't know if I like that part of the story."

"We have lots of room for guests; you and Shelby spend most of your weekends with Brad and me."

They went on like this for a while, getting more and more inventive with the details, talking about Shelby's vegetarian cooking and Brad's cashmere sweaters. They had only the faintest idea of how people without their means lived in New York—and they couldn't bring themselves to conjure lives of anything approaching actual struggle—so what emerged was a rather more cinematic version than a realistic one, with Leo living in a vast loft space with fascinating, artsy, ethnic neighbors, and Nora baking cookies in a kitchen from the set of a Nancy Meyers film. Eventually a silence settled over both of them, and Nora thought her brother might have drifted off to sleep until he said, "You know it's never going to be like that, though, don't you?"

Nora let out a long sigh and felt it all slip away: Brad in his sweaters and the green-eyed children, Gunner and the pancakes on Sunday mornings. She felt a great hole suddenly. She turned and scooted backward into her brother's arms, the little spoon.

"I know," she said. "As long as we're together, I guess I don't care what happens."

"We will be," he said. And then he did fall asleep.

~ک~

They were woken later by their sister calling their names from Leo's foyer. They came down the stairs to find her looking frantic, her green eyes red-rimmed.

"Why are the two of you not answering your phones?"

"We were taking a nap," Nora said, coming closer to her sister, tentatively, alarmed by the urgent tone of her voice.

"What happened?" Leo asked.

Liberty took a deep, steely breath. "Opa. He's had an aneurysm."

"What? When?" Nora said.

"On the plane on his way back from Europe."

"Is he dead?" Leo and Nora asked practically in stereo.

"No," Liberty said, "the doctors are taking him in for surgery. But . . ." Her voice faltered, and tears streamed down her cheeks. Her siblings closed around her, and the three of them held fast to each other.

"What do we do now?" Leo asked.

"We have to tell Laila," Nora said.

"She doesn't even know him," Leo scoffed.

"And now she might never!" Nora howled. "Oh, it's too awful."

"Laila is still on Mustique," Liberty said.

They looked at the itinerary she'd sent them and called Alumbrera, only to be told that Ms. Lawrence had left them. They at last were able to get Simon on the line; he curtly passed them along to his personal assistant, who had arranged Laila's flight details and whom, fortunately, they were able to reach right away. Meanwhile, Nora left frantic voice mails on Laila's cell, as though calling again and again would get her through.

A plan was hatched that they should all gather at the Lawrence penthouse uptown. They left Laila a message telling her they'd send a car to the airport to bring her straight there.

Their father's face was ashen when they arrived at the penthouse, and Birdie was pacing, dramatically ringing her hands. By the time Laila at last arrived, she'd worn a path in circles around the apartment and was sitting drinking a martini and being comforted by Petra. Nora flew to her cousin and wrapped her arms around her. "We're so glad you're home."

Laila felt shaky, unable to make sense of the events of the past several days of her life. Her skin was painted with a fierce sunburn in the patches her sunscreen had missed.

"How was your trip?" Liberty's voice was neutral; did she not know about Tom yet?

"It was kind of a disaster," she said softly.

"Oh no!" Nora said. "Darling, tell us everything!" In her grief, Nora seemed to have forgotten that she was mad at Laila. All the better; Laila didn't have many options other than to move back in with her at this point.

"It doesn't matter right now. I'm just glad I was able to get home to be with you guys." Nora ate this up. But Birdie had barely heard her.

"All these months he's been gone to Europe doing God knows what. Doesn't even bother to come home for the holidays. Off with *God* knows who, who we'll now have to deal with." In all of the drama, they'd forgotten the new girlfriend, whom they now feared would emerge like a vulture at his bedside. She never did come, but the way they discussed her that night made plain to Laila the numerous women Frederick had courted in the decades since his wife's death; had her mother not been his own son's wife, she would have simply been another unremarkable one of many.

∼ৎ৯∼

A half hour later, Cameron and Reece showed up, brandishing large bags from Citarella.

"You're too sweet," Liberty said, her relief at the sight of the siblings palpable. "You didn't need to do that."

"You have to eat," Reece said. "I'm so sorry about your opa," she added softly, "I guess I'd always thought of him as invincible."

Liberty smiled wanly. "Me too."

Laila watched as Cameron put his arm around her cousin, enfolding her as though beneath a massive wing. Flashes of the dreadful Simon grunting behind her, his gnarled hand in her hair, came back and sent a wave of repulsion through her. She was certain no one would ever treat her treasured cousin the way Simon had treated her, or the way their own grandfather had treated her. Disposable.

That night, while they waited to hear from the doctors, the family sat with one another in disquieting limbo, as though they themselves hovered between life and death. It felt blasphemous to stray too far from the subject of Frederick himself, and so his son and daughter started telling stories about him from their childhood. Laila noticed how carefully they avoided mention of her own father, and she wondered if Ben and Petra had not just known about her mother and Frederick but perhaps had even helped orchestrate Betsy's removal from New York. Still, Laila knew to stay quiet for the moment. To bring the letters up directly to Frederick—the culpable party—that was one thing, but to bring it up to anyone else in the family would make her seem like a threat. It would appear as though she had come here intending to blackmail them, when she'd only ever considered it as a last resort. Mentioning it now would get her shut out, make her a person to be dealt with rather than a person to be welcomed into the fold. Laila was, as ever, on her own with no protector. But her aunt, she reminded herself, and Liberty would help. And perhaps it would even be easier with Frederick gone.

❧

After steadily consuming scotch for an hour or so, Cameron at last got up to relieve himself. Of course he loved Liberty and wanted to be there for her in her time of need, but the quiet waiting and consoling of this vigil were deeply uncomfortable for him. He wanted to *do* something, to fix things for her and be adored in return. He relished the feeling of being needed by her, but she so often seemed utterly independent. And there were still walls he had yet to breach, he knew. He had complained to his sister about this, and she'd told him to be patient. Now at last her walls were lowered, but what could he do? *Wait with her*, Reece had said. Simply wait, as he had waited to kiss her, as he waited longer yet to seduce her, as he would wait longer still to begin to push her boundaries in the way that would truly satisfy him. He'd casually mentioned the idea of bondage once, but she'd thought he was kidding. The guest bathroom of the Lawrences' penthouse was down a long hallway, and he felt his head swim a bit as he made his way toward it. He could only hope the waiting would soften Liberty around her hard, controlled edges.

He washed his hands and regarded himself in the mirror. A good man, he thought, I will be a good man for her. Cameron wanted to believe that underneath it all, he was the best of men, the man his parents seemed to believe he was. Liberty too, now.

When he opened the bathroom door, Laila seemed to materialize whole from the gloom of the hallway, aglow in her unseasonably light dress; her aunt had given her a cashmere wrap, but she had left that behind on the couch. Her nose and the tops of her shoulders were freckled and peeled from the sun, making her look girlish and vulnerable.

"Cameron, I need to talk to you," she said.

"About what?" Cameron asked in a hissed whisper. He towered over her, long arms crossed over his broad chest.

"I . . ." She paused and made a step toward him. "Ever since we were together, I can't stop thinking about you."

"We cannot talk about this here. Especially not tonight."

"Cameron," she said, reaching out and placing her hand on his chest, "please."

He pulled her into the bathroom, knowing it would at least be soundproof.

"What, Laila? You have five minutes to say what you need to say. I thought we had agreed that we'd never mention it to anyone?"

"I haven't! I won't. I don't even really want to talk. I just want *you*."

And then Cameron felt it, the thing unfurling deep in his belly, clawing its way toward the surface, and before he knew what he was doing, his hand was around Laila's delicate throat and he had slammed her head up against the wall, between two vintage

Viennese prints that decorated the interior wall of the bathroom.

With his free hand he reached between her legs, felt the wetness there.

"Oh, you *like* this?" He pressed hard against her throat with one hand, pushed his fingers into her with the other. She let out a thick, strangled gasp that he recognized as one of enjoyment. Her eyes were flashing but not with fear. Or indeed with fear, but with something else too: bliss. The ecstasy of fear. He felt suddenly as though she saw him in a way he was unused to being seen. He maneuvered his thumb, still moving his fingers inside her, still gripping her throat—suddenly as intent on bringing her pleasure as he was on bringing her pain. He felt her yielding to him, pliant as a rag doll, until she came hard on his hand, and he was forced to release her throat in order to cover her mouth. He turned to wash the slickness from his hands. She crumpled to the floor and stayed there. He found he was afraid to look at her, and when he at last did, he saw why. Her hair was rumpled, her limbs loosened like an abandoned marionette's, but her eyes were victorious.

⁓⁓⁓

The next day, Frederick came out of surgery, and though he had reportedly regained consciousness for a brief moment, he'd lost it again by the time the Lawrences arrived en masse at the hospital. Laila's first and last vision of her grandfather was of a piqued, pale old man with tubes emerging from his every orifice. There he was: originator of the fortune, seducer of innumerable women; the man whose decisions had misdirected her entire life. She had so frequently fantasized about brandishing the secret letters before him: proof of his wrongdoing, proof of what he had cost them all. But now it seemed she would never get the chance.

19

A WEEK AFTER her grandfather's death, Liberty returned to work. Reece had called her that morning to check on her.

"Are you sure you're ready?"

"Honestly, I'll go crazy if I spend another day at home watching Lifetime. I need my work." Liberty leaned against the counter, lightheaded. She knew she needed to eat more but had no appetite.

"Okay, well, do you want to meet up after? For, like, tea or something?"

Liberty laughed. "By tea, I assume you mean cocktails."

Reece was relieved to hear her friend's laughter. "For some reason I felt like that would be insensitive."

"Please; my opa would want it that way."

"He would." Reece smiled. Given Liberty's status as favored granddaughter and Reece's as her best friend, she had always bathed in his good graces.

"Let's go to Trapdoor. It will be quiet on a Monday," Liberty said.

"*Yes*, we can stare at Bartender Sean. How could that not make you feel better?"

Bartender Sean—never just Sean—was a source of some fascination for them. He worked in the outrageously hip bar below Liberty's apartment, and they would often go down there to drink martinis and ogle him.

"God, he really is painfully hot," Reece whispered to Liberty as they settled into seats at the end of the bar later that evening. He had dark blond hair that brushed the tops of his shoulders, light blue eyes, and a smile that hit you like a punch in the stomach—partly because he didn't use it much. He seemed to have mastered a sort of glowering half smile that he used with most customers. It wasn't impolite, but it made you long for the real thing.

"Right?" Liberty caught his eye as he finished with the two women at the other end of the bar whose tongues were practically wagging. "The first time I saw him here, I thought, He looks like every bad decision I'll never let myself make."

"There's still time," Reece said. "Gah! Don't tell Cam I said that." Liberty stifled a giggle as Sean appeared before them.

"What can I get you? I bet I can guess," he said, approaching and flashing his real smile at Liberty.

"I'm so predictable. Honey, you want the same?" She asked Reece, meaning the lychee martinis that she always ordered at Trapdoor.

"Two, please," Reece said.

"You got it, gorgeous." His voice was deep and smooth, he threw Reece a wink.

"Don't," Liberty said.

"Don't what?" Reece feigned an innocent smile, which Liberty met with incredulity. "Fine. Why not?"

"Because you'll dump him after five minutes, and we won't be able to come here anymore. Can nothing be sacred?"

"Okay," Reece said, putting up her hands, "but if he ever tells us he's quitting, I'm getting his number."

Liberty laughed, and the sound was a delight to Reece.

"Oh god," she said, "I'm so happy to see you. I needed to feel normal today."

Bartender Sean returned with their drinks, distracting them for a moment.

"How are you doing with everything?" Reece asked when he was again out of earshot.

Liberty shrugged. "I know it shouldn't be shocking; he was ninety-three. But still, I guess I'd come to think of him as eternal."

"Yeah."

Liberty opened her mouth as if to speak and then deliberately shut it, lifting her glass to her lips instead.

"What were you going to say?" Reece pressed.

Liberty looked at her and took a deep breath. "He left me everything."

Reece's jaw dropped open.

"He left you . . . everything, like, *everything*?"

"More or less. I mean, the twins still have their trusts, there are provisions for Birdie, my dad got the business . . . but other than that, yeah."

"God." Reece knew it would be too gauche to ask the dollar amount, but it was in the hundreds of millions, no question. "Did you know?"

"Of course not! I would have talked him out of it."

"You would have tried," Reece said. As the shock wore off, she realized how unsurprising this turn of events actually was. It made perfect sense: Frederick loved his family, but he'd only ever really *approved* of Liberty. And this gave him the added bonus of getting to die knowing he'd leave drama in his wake. He would have been delighted by that. He was a bold man, a troublemaker to his dying day and, apparently, after it.

"The irony," Liberty said. "You know, I'm the last person who wanted it."

This, Reece thought, Frederick had undoubtedly known, and it certainly contributed to the appeal of leaving it all to her. "So what are you going to do?"

"I have an idea," Liberty said with a smile. "You know how I love the Literacy in Motion folks. . . ."

"Right," Reece said.

Liberty smiled. She took a sip of her drink and left it at that.

"What, *all* of it?"

"Why not? I don't need it; my family doesn't need it. I loved my opa, but I don't want this money; it isn't mine. And I look at what having all of this has done to my siblings, and honestly, even my father probably would have been better off without so much. Then there's Birdie, who, much as I adore her, has not exactly been the most productive member of society."

Reece cringed. "Yeah, point taken."

"And obviously all of them still have plenty of money from the trusts and the company and whatnot. But as for the rest of it? I think it's time for the next generation to hit the reset button. And so maybe I don't give all of it to the one organization, but think of everything I could do with it! I could start a scholarship fund, even build a school with a trust this size."

Reece nodded and took a moment to absorb what her friend was saying. Of course she saw her point, but to *talk* about giving away the family fortune was one thing. To actually part with it all was another.

"Well, damn, girl," Reece said with a smile. "My brother is a lucky man; I hope he knows that."

Back at the twins' apartment, Laila and her cousins sat around the fireplace of Leo's penthouse. Overnight, the twins had gone from superrich to merely wealthy, and they were not handling it well.

"How could he do this? It's just . . . so *unfair*! What have we ever done to deserve this?"

Laila smiled inwardly at the unintended truth of her cousin's words: nothing, they'd done nothing to deserve all they had, several million each in a trust and their extraordinary apartments that were technically family-owned but which they lived in rent-free.

"He always liked Liberty best," Leo said glumly.

"Oh," Nora said getting to her feet. She was wearing her long silk dressing gown, and her breasts jostled underneath it, threatening to burst free. "Well, doesn't *everyone* like Liberty best? Isn't that her whole raison d'être?"

"Maybe she'll share," Laila ventured. It had been on her mind since the decision was announced. She had been thinking constantly about what to do next. She could go to Liberty and reveal what she knew, not with the intent to blackmail her—the longer Laila was in New York, the more unsavory this option had begun to seem—but simply to make her understand how Laila had been cheated, that she hadn't had the same opportunities as her cousins and this was why. She would have hoped to quietly reconcile with their grandfather, without ever spoiling Liberty's image of him, but that was no longer an option. His will had specified Liberty, not simply grandchildren. There was no way around it.

"She thinks we should all be *working*," Leo spat as if the very word hurt to say.

"But you *do* work! Your column and the book . . . how will you be able to write if you have to get some awful regular job?

And I'll have to give up my charity work . . . I was this close to getting a seat on the World Wildlife Fund's Jungle Boogie Gala committee!" At this, an idea seemed to dawn on her. "Maybe if we start a charity, then she'll contribute," Nora said.

"Wouldn't you have to then use that money on other people?" Laila asked gently.

"But at least then we could throw a gala every year, invite all of our friends," Nora was nearly in tears by now, "if we even *have* any friends by then!"

Laila saw it fully then: how her cousins' lives had been built around the expectation that they would inherit the vast fortune of their grandfather. And for perhaps the first time, she pitied them.

❧

On Monday, Laila stopped by Liberty's office to ask if she wanted to have lunch. Though the outcome had been disastrous, the timing of Frederick's death was serendipitous in that it made Liberty more willing to overlook the fact that Laila had broken the heart of her prized client. Tom had initially called Liberty bemoaning his fight and the resulting breakup with Laila, but with the death of Frederick—something about which everyone in New York had swiftly heard—he'd been forced to let it go, at least where Liberty was concerned.

It was a blustery mid-April day, and with the patio closed, Laila and Liberty were given a mercifully quiet corner table at Posto. Laila was tempted to order a glass of wine to calm her nerves but feared it would somehow undermine what she was about to say. The mementos—including the necklace—burned in their leather pouch, nestled in the bottom of Laila's oversize handbag.

"I just still can't believe I'll never get to meet him," Laila said.

Liberty nodded sympathetically and reached over to squeeze her cousin's hand.

"I know. You would have liked him, I think. He was a true character."

"I think . . . I wanted to . . . ," Laila began, and then it all felt too abrupt.

"Go on," Liberty said, for every millimeter of Laila's face said she had something to say. Laila changed her mind and reached into her bag to pull out the leather pouch, unzipping it and drawing out the enamel pendant with its delicate, jewel-eyed swallows.

"Remember you told me you thought I should have this appraised? Well, I did. . . ." Laila handed over the necklace as though it contained everything her cousin needed to know, which in its way, it did.

Liberty gazed at the intricate pendant and found she was moved by its beauty. It was very much the kind of piece she had always loved. Though she wasn't sure what her cousin was getting at.

"And?" she asked.

"You were right," Laila said. "Nineteenth century; you've got a good eye. The jeweler I took it to said she thought it probably came from Fred Leighton, and it's worth about twenty thousand dollars."

Liberty looked up at her cousin slowly, her eyes wide.

"So . . . your father also had a thing for vintage jewelry?" she tried, her voice sounding small.

Laila shook her head, and Liberty nodded, taking it in. Laila knew then that she understood.

"Oh, Laila," she finally said. "Frederick and your mother? That's why your parents left?"

"It would appear so," she said. With this, Laila pulled the papers of all their varying sizes, the cards from floral arrangements, the hotel stationery worn soft with age. "I found these when I was going through my mother's things. I would have told you about it, but I wanted to talk to Frederick, to our grandfather, before I said anything to anyone else."

Liberty's face fell as she examined the papers. "Oh God, the Carlyle."

Laila raised her eyebrows.

Liberty gave her a squeamish smile. "Yeah, let's just say they knew him there. He was a man of routine."

Laila nodded. For a moment Liberty grew quiet, and Laila feared she was angry at her for keeping the letters a secret, or worse, might revert to denial about the scandal they revealed.

"Oh, honey." Liberty put the letters gingerly on her own lap and reached across the table once more. "God, you should have told me sooner. You must have been so angry with him."

Laila shrugged. "I was ashamed . . . and my *mother*. I wanted to give him a chance to explain; that's why I didn't say anything until now. . . ." Real tears bloomed in Laila's eyes now. "I feel like he took away the opportunity to be a part of this family." And the money, she thought, all of it kept from her.

Liberty looked down at the table, absorbing Laila's words. "Sweetie, I don't know what to say other than that we're all here for you now. Whew." There were tears in Liberty's eyes as well. "This is a lot to take in."

"I know," Laila said, squeezing her cousin's hands, "but you understand why I didn't tell you sooner? I just, I knew you were so close with him."

"I know, honey, but you could have told me. I just want you

to know that you don't have to carry everything alone like that. Frederick was a complicated man. A bit more complicated than I realized, as it turns out. But I want you to know," she looked into Laila's eyes earnestly, "that we *are* your family, and I'm so sorry it took your mother's death to bring us back together, but we can't change the past, can we? I'm just so glad you're in our lives now."

Laila smiled at her, trying not to let her desperation seep through. She knew better than to directly ask Liberty about the money. It wasn't how this was done.

"How is it being back with Leo and Nora? How are they doing?"

Laila suspected Liberty knew that the twins were not taking the news of the inheritance terribly well.

"They're hanging in there," Laila said. "Trying to figure out how to scrape by on their trust funds."

To Laila's relief, Liberty laughed and rolled her eyes.

"Those two. Between you and me, I can see why Opa didn't want to give them any more money to fritter away. I'm kind of hoping that this will shake them up a bit, help them get motivated. They need to be more resilient. Like you," she said, smiling.

"Well, I see where you're coming from." Did Liberty think it was *better* to be raised with nothing? Could she really be that naive? "But I shouldn't criticize them, really; it's so sweet how they've taken me in and everything. I really should get my own place soon, though. I need to start living a real life here. Truly get settled."

At this, Liberty smiled approvingly.

"I'd been meaning to talk to you about that, actually."

Laila's heart jumped to her throat: Had it all been easier than she'd imagined? But of course, Liberty had always been the cousin who truly cared about her, who'd come all that way to find her. It made sense that she wasn't sharing the money with the twins; they'd had everything. But especially in the light of what she'd revealed, she'd want to help her, wouldn't she?

"Daphne is leaving to go to graduate school," Liberty continued, "and I could speak to Gerard about hiring you to replace her. I'm sure he'd agree; he always prefers to hire from within."

It took a moment for Laila's head to clear, to understand what she was being offered: a job. She felt like she'd been punched in the stomach but smiled sweetly. An internship was one thing; she could pretty much come and go as she pleased. But the agents' assistants worked long hours and read manuscripts on the weekends. It was a real, all-consuming job. Being a star agent like Liberty was one thing: she had power and prestige. But an assistant? This was something else entirely.

"I've been thinking of going back to school, actually . . . ," Laila said.

"Really? Well, of course, we'll cover it if you do. There's no reason you couldn't do both! The New School has an amazing program."

"Oh wow, that's really sweet of you. I'm just . . . can I think about it?" Laila asked.

"Sure," Liberty said, looking a little taken aback at Laila's lack of enthusiasm. "But not for too long; we've got a stack of résumés a mile high."

Laila knew that there were girls who would kill for a job like the one Liberty was offering her—and her education paid for to boot—but she cringed to think of them, living in apartments out in the far reaches of Bed-Stuy and Queens, crammed on top of each other, standing in line for rush tickets to a Broadway show when their college friends came to visit. Laila had just come back from Mustique, for God's sake! Maybe there was a time when the life Liberty was offering her would have been enough. But she knew that now it would not be. Having been given carte blanche at Bergdorf's, living with the twins in their penthouse, having the worst vacation of her life in the most beautiful place she'd ever seen, she could not go live on the other side of the city, the striving, clawing side that she could see glimpses of everywhere when she looked closely enough: the wearied faces of people coming in and out of Manhattan. The doormen and security guards and bodega workers who lived God knew where. If the money was not to come from Liberty, she had to find another way.

⤫

The inheritance would take time wending its way through the legal system, and so, by the time the following week rolled around, it had mostly faded from Leo's and Nora's minds. They'd always had money; they'd never even had to think of it in any concrete terms. The idea of worrying over it was so foreign to them that they could not keep the notion in their heads. They'd convinced themselves that it would all work out, that Liberty would take care of them. It had always been her they'd gone to with their problems; why would her having the money instead of Opa or their parents change anything? No, it would be better! They knew nothing, of course, of Liberty's real intentions for the fortune.

By the following Thursday, Nora was instead completely consumed with an event that she and Laila were attending. Since Frederick's death, Laila had been reinstated in the penthouse as though she'd never left. There was a party for the relaunch of the *New York Spectacle*, affectionately nicknamed the *Spec*: an ailing paper past its prime that had just been purchased by twenty-five-year-old wunderkind Blake Katz, a real-estate scion whose father had served time for money laundering and yet still managed to be obscenely rich.

Laila sat on the chaise in Nora's closet, wearing a silk robe and drinking a glass of champagne as her cousin fretted over what to wear. She'd bought three new dresses from Bergdorf's that afternoon—the inheritance imbroglio hadn't slowed down her shopping—and suddenly she hated them all.

"How can I have all these clothes, and nothing to wear?" She howled, pacing an angry lap around the closet. She wore a flesh-colored pair of Spanx and a nude strapless bra, giving her the sexless appearance of a Barbie doll.

"I love the Michael Kors," Laila ventured.

"Ugh, it makes me look old!"

"What about the Jason Wu?"

"Don't get me started. Why did you let me buy something with a peplum, Laila? It totally emphasizes my gut," she said, slapping her flat stomach.

"You're being crazy! Come here, sit down. Have a drink."

Nora relented and took a seat on the edge of the chaise, Laila handed her a glass of champagne, and she sipped with a quiet sigh as though imbibing something medicinal.

"What's going on with you?"

"It's Blake," Nora said, looking at Laila helplessly.

"The newspaper guy?"

Nora nodded. "He went to school with Leo. We've known him forever."

Of course they had; another member of their set, as the twins referred to their social circle. As though it were a matching collection, one that presumably ought to be kept together and remain unsullied by the presence of outsiders.

"And?"

Nora let out a beleaguered sigh. "And I am completely, madly in love with him. Always have been. He always has a girlfriend, but he *just* broke up with someone, so he's finally single for a minute."

"Oh! And what," Laila said, grinning, "tonight's the big night?"

"Only if I can find something to wear; I can't go out like this!"

"You could throw some heels on, your chrome hearts necklace; it'd be a look." Laila was enjoying being back with her cousins more than she'd expected to. It was a relief to be back in Nora's paradise of delusion.

Nora laughed. "I'm serious; help me!"

"Let me think." Laila got up and circled the room. A form-fitting, strapless, red silk Betsey Johnson dress with a sweetheart neckline caught her eye. It was the only dress she'd seen Nora wear more than once. "This," Laila said, pulling it out decisively.

"I've had that dress forever," Nora said dismissively.

"But you love it," Laila ventured. "You feel like yourself in it."

Nora's eyes softened, as though this were the first time in her life she'd been truly understood.

"You're right!" she said. "I really do. Oh, thank you!"

Several thousand dollars of new dresses lay crumpled at her feet as Nora wiggled into her old faithful. In this dress, from a distance, Nora was knockout: a Jessica Rabbit facsimile. It wasn't until you saw her up close that the slightly plastic wrongness of her features presented themselves, that you realized her eyes were just a bit too closely set together to be beautiful.

"See?" Laila said. "Gorgeous!"

"Oh, hurray! Put your dress on; let's go hang out with Leo until it's time to leave."

As they made their way to the bookcase door, they could hear the sounds of Leo playing a Billy Joel song. He sat on the piano bench in his sweatpants, a painfully skinny and dressed-up brunette glued to his side. She looked up, startled, when Nora and Laila entered the room—she doubtlessly didn't know of the secret door and it would have seemed to her as though they'd materialized out of thin air.

"Hi, sis, Laila," he said. Still playing, still gazing down at his fingers, he sang out a couple of lines:

If you said good-bye to me tonight
There would still be music left to write
What else could I do
I'm so inspired by you
That hasn't happened for the longest time

His voice was surprisingly sweet, and the girl was mesmerized. He let his fingers trail cacophonously across the keyboard and abandoned his station, standing up to greet them.

"How was your day, Leo?" Nora stepped forward and put her hand on his forearm a little possessively. She shot a sideways glance at the girl sitting on the piano bench but didn't acknowledge her.

"It was good!" Leo ran his fingers through his hair. "I got through my second chapter! Alyssa came over to keep me company while I worked."

Laila thought the girl did not look dressed for hanging around with Leo while he allegedly wrote his book. Spending time with

Tom and at the agency for more than six months had shown her the essential truth: that Leo would never finish this or any other book. He simply did not have it in him.

"You girls look nice," he said, taking them in, "where are you off to?"

"The relaunch party for the *Spec*."

"Oh, good old Blakey," Leo said.

"Anyway, why aren't you coming?"

"Ugh, media parties. Tell him congrats for me, though! I'll take him out for a scotch soon."

"An awfully big deal, him taking on a whole newspaper," Nora said.

"You say that like he's stepping up to rule a small European country," Laila said. She kept her voice light, but she found it wearisome how these Manhattan kids congratulated each other so much for winning a hundred-yard dash they'd begun at the ninety-yard line. If she had $100 million or so at her disposal, she might buy a newspaper too.

"Only slightly more dysfunctional," Leo said. The brunette laughed, and they all startled a little, having nearly forgotten she was there. "Anyway," Leo continued, "if anyone can make it work, Blake can. He always worked so hard in school; God knows why, he didn't need to."

Then as if by some telepathy, he and Nora sequestered themselves a foot away, talking in hushed tones. They did this every once in a while: pulled away in some secret twin tête-à-tête, regardless of who else was in the room. According to Liberty, they'd done it constantly when they were kids. It appeared as though Leo was comforting his sister, perhaps giving her a pep talk. Laila pulled out her phone and busied herself with it, the better to not have to acknowledge the girl at the piano; she knew from experience she'd never see her again.

～∿～

The party was the half-glamorous, half-frumpy mix that media parties always are. In a reverse of the usual equation, the less pulled-together someone looked, the more likely they were to be important. Laila therefore suspected every middle-aged man in grubby tweeds of having won a Pulitzer. The opportunities were both endless and obscured. She barely knew where to begin.

Nora was warming up, flirting with guys she and Leo had gone to school with and lobbing empty and effusive compliments at the women she knew. Suddenly she whipped around and steered Laila toward the bar, saying, "Oh God! Come on, quick."

"What?"

"I don't want to get cornered by Imogen. She's *so* dull, and for God's sake, she's got Zander Plus-one with her. Ugh, so desperate."

Laila examined the fortyish woman and her handsome date who, though she had her arm in his, seemed to be looking anywhere but at her.

"He's kind of hot, to be honest. Why do you call him Zander Plus-one?"

"Yeah, he *allegedly* used to model, which he'll tell you in the first five minutes he meets you if you let him. Anyway, he's, like, everywhere, but never as an invited guest, only as someone's plus-one."

"Oh." Laila wondered if Nora heard the words coming out of her own mouth sometimes. For wasn't Laila her perpetual plus-one? "I'll be back," said Laila, just as Nora spotted someone she *did* want to talk to. She waved her cousin off.

꡾

Laila kept an eye out for the man of the hour as she crossed the floor looking for another waiter with a tray of champagne, or better yet, the bar. She was suitably intrigued by this Blake guy given Nora's adoration, though if he'd gone to school with the twins, he would almost certainly dismiss her for being from the Midwest—meaning she would loathe him. Plus, he was only twenty-five! Men that age didn't know their ass from their elbow. Too many men her own age—especially within this crowd— were childlike in their innocence, regardless of how debauched their lifestyles might be. So many of them hadn't suffered a true loss, had never peeked over the abyss, had never taken one solitary step in life without a hundred layers of safety nets beneath them.

Laila wandered the room solo, unable to get out of her own head and enjoy the party as she wished to, preoccupied by her own lack of a safety net. Her funds were running dangerously low. Even without having to pay rent, spending money in Manhattan was as easy and invisible as breathing. She'd played her trump card, and so far it had yielded nothing. Of course, her cousin had offered her a job; there was that. Laila had done a little digging and discovered that assistants at the agency started at $35,000 a year, and worse yet, that this was slightly higher than the industry standard. Thirty-five thousand dollars wouldn't get her much in Michigan, but in Manhattan it was a like a kick in the shin. She'd learned that there were two kinds of assistants in publishing: the variety who ran to fetch coffee for their boss in their dainty Repetto flats, a Goyard tote stuffed with bound galleys bouncing off their shoulder, those girls whose parents paid their rent for a nice little one-bedroom somewhere "safe" like the Upper East Side or the West Village; their salary was spent on cocktails and hair care. Then there were the Kims of the industry: smart and scrappy without an ounce of style, toting manuscripts with them on the long train ride to their far-flung neighborhood in Queens—for even most of Brooklyn was now out of reach, barring Bed-Stuy and Bushwick. Laila knew Liberty admired the industry's scrappers, and truthfully, Laila did too. She did not, however, want to become one. She knew that if she took that job and accepted that lifestyle, the world of her cousins would slip forever from her reach.

All of these thoughts weighed heavily on her that night. No one at the party seemed to be paying much attention to her, nor was she enthused about mingling. She wasn't interested in most of the men she saw. There was a *type* of man that moved to New York to pursue his fortune, and Laila was sick of them, their striving and arrogance, their neuroses, their fussy clothes and effeminate tendency to be familiar with handbag brands and to judge you accordingly; and this party was full of them. Or at least half-full. And the other half? Grubby tweeds. Laila had the unwelcome thought that she really longed for a man like Cameron; the memory of their last encounter suddenly went through her like an electrical charge. How lucky Liberty was to have him; where did someone find another like him? She felt certain she could not chance another tryst with him—though this knowledge did nothing but stoke her desire.

Truthfully, young and handsome and rich was not terribly easy to come by—the repugnant Simon was more of a common model of billionaire. Was it so terrible to admit that you wanted someone to take care of you? Everyone talked about independence as though it was the highest virtue, but Laila had had plenty of looking out for herself.

"Oops, I'm sorry," an older man she had just collided with apologized, though she was fairly certain it was her fault that they'd run into each other.

"No, *I'm* sorry," she said, putting her hand on his arm. He had snow-white hair that was thick and tousled, wire-rimmed glasses, and warm brown eyes. She recognized him. He was Sam Green, the longtime editor of the *Spec*. She'd done her homework earlier in the day.

"Are you enjoying the party?" he asked.

"So far," she said. "I just arrived."

"You look like someone who has just arrived." She wasn't sure whether to be insulted or not. Was he calling her an arriviste? But his eyes were kind; perhaps she was simply being defensive.

"Sam!" a voice bellowed. "I've been looking for you."

A tall, young man leaned in to shake his hand and clap him on the shoulder.

"Blake," Sam said. Laila noted that he looked genuinely pleased to see him. "I was just about to introduce myself to this beautiful young lady, so naturally you would appear."

Blake laughed, revealing an impressive row of gleaming white teeth. He had light brown eyes and olive skin. Laila found herself utterly distracted by the sharpness of his jaw. He looked her in the eye only briefly, but it practically rendered her speechless.

"I do have excellent timing," he said. "I'm Blake Katz."

"Laila Lawrence."

"Lawrence?" Sam said. "Ah."

"The midwestern branch," she added.

"Midwest values meet New York glamour," Blake said with a

flourish, as though bestowing her with her own headline, "who could beat that?"

"So, Sam," Laila said, trying her best not to be dazzled by Blake, "I should confess that I'm a fan of your work. Big changes at the *Spec*, with the new boss and all." She flicked her eyes over to Blake. She'd spent her day reading pieces from the paper's online archives. It appeared to be an august publication; what the young millionaire might want with it was still a bit of a mystery.

"It's in good hands," he said, looking warmly at the younger man. Who, to Laila's complete surprise, blushed.

"You're just saying that," he said. "I could only hope to live up to what you've built there."

"I never just say anything. The paper needed new blood."

And a massive infusion of cash, Laila thought. Still, she hadn't expected Blake to seem so guileless and sincere; they were difficult qualities to fake.

~§~

Unsurprisingly, Blake was pulled away moments later; it was his party, after all. Laila talked to Sam Green for a while longer before he was monopolized by a blowhard op-ed columnist with no interest in her, and she was slowly frozen out of the conversation.

Laila drank too much that night, unsettled by her run-in with Blake and how generally out of place she felt at the party, especially after Nora's comments. Was she a Laila Plus-one, herself? Nothing more than a hanger-on? At one point she saw Blake in the corner talking to Nora and another girl she didn't recognize. She tried to feel glad for Nora, but she felt something slipping through her hands, something she was desperate to grasp.

ல்‌

"We cannot do this again."

These were his first words upon waking. He hadn't even looked over at her, or he would have realized she was still half-asleep, face buried in the pillow, her petite frame curled in on itself as it always did when she slept. He stared directly at the ceiling.

"Mmmm?" She stirred, raised her head.

"I'm serious," Cameron said as though she were arguing with him. "We have to stop. *You* have to stop. What were you thinking, coming here last night?"

His regret was looking for a place to put itself, and it landed squarely on Laila. Even as he closed his eyes, he could feel her there, pulsating next to him, a demon of his psyche, materialized.

"What were *you* thinking, letting me in, then, if you feel that way?" Laila peeled her head heavily off the pillow, propping herself on her elbows to look at him.

"What if Liberty had been here?"

"She told me she was staying in."

"What if she'd been lying?"

At this, Laila laughed. "Liberty doesn't lie. She isn't like us, Cameron."

The night before, he'd answered the door only after she'd buzzed several times. He'd been asleep, exhausted from an eighteen-hour day at the office. Laila had appeared at his door like a hallucination. She was drunk enough to be bold, not drunk enough to be easily swayed or dealt with. He'd argued with her at first, trying to put her in a car home, but she'd come in, bolted the door behind her, and peeled her dress off. She told him she'd been thinking about him all night, slipping her hand between her legs. That had been it for him. He'd roughly removed her bra and panties, ripping the delicate lace on the latter. She'd tried to kiss him, but he'd deflected it and sunk his teeth into her shoulder. Then she'd been on the stairs, propped on her elbow and knees, opened wide before him. Cameron, much like Laila's cousins, had never wanted for anything, and so the desire that filled this void was for something no man could have, two opposing things at once: Laila *and* Liberty. He was fooling himself, however, if he thought that merely having each of these women would satisfy him. For he wanted to be both the man who could have anything he wanted *and* the man who had the character to resist temptation. His was a void that would devour countless mistresses, one no amount of sex or other indulgence could sate.

"There is no 'us,'" Cameron said now.

"If you say so. I think you should just admit that you're bored with her. She's too conventional for you."

He stared at Laila. She appeared to be alarmingly calm this morning: poised, triumphant, her big eyes shining out from that deceptively innocent-looking, little fox face of hers. She was so unlike the woman he loved—and he did love Liberty, he did—were they really related?

"And," she continued, somehow finding her way to a moral high ground, "you really *ought* to let her go. Liberty deserves better than someone who cheats on her."

"Laila," he pulled himself from the bed and put on the sweatpants that were crumpled on the floor, "this cannot happen again. It's not worth it. I have something real with Liberty; she's the kind of woman I could marry. And you . . . well you're . . ." he let the thought trail off.

She was quiet and curled her head to her knees; he'd hurt her, which he'd intended to do, but he suddenly saw the danger in it. She could ruin things for him faster than any other person.

"Laila," he said, coming back beside her on the bed, "we have fun; you're an incredibly sexy girl. But if Liberty ever found out . . ."

"What, you think *I'm* going to tell her? I have as much to lose as you do. More! My family . . ."

"There you have it, all the more reason to stop this nonsense."

Cameron wondered why he was making this so hard for himself. There was a city full of anonymous young beauties at his disposal for those moments when the existential dread brought on by the thought of being tethered to one woman overwhelmed him. Certain friends of his had even turned to prostitutes once they were married: fewer complications; less chance of the girl's getting attached and losing her mind, causing trouble. But Cameron didn't want to be like them—weak, gluttonous. And of course, if his parents ever found out he'd been seeing prostitutes, they'd be apoplectic; that was a PR nightmare waiting to happen.

"But that's just it," Laila said, calm now, resigned, responding as though she could hear his thoughts. "The fact that *both* of us have so much to lose is what makes it ideal. It's mutual assured destruction. I know you'd never tell, and I'd be a thousand times worse off if this got out. I don't have any other family; at least your parents and sister would still love you." She did not add the obvious, which was that he was a rich man many times over.

She suddenly looked much older than her twenty-five years— something about her eyes in the dim morning light that crept through the curtains. He felt a stirring of renewed desire; there was something dark at the core of this girl. He didn't need to know about its origins, but there was a mix of fear and anger and desperation in her that made her wild. Poor Tom Porter; no wonder she'd destroyed him. He'd reached out to Cameron after their breakup—having felt, the latter supposed, that they'd formed a real bond over the holidays—and the two had met up for a drink where the poor sad sack had spoken of nothing else. He pitied Tom, for Tom was piteous in the wake of his heartbreak, but seeing this wreckage deepened what so intrigued Cameron about Laila. Here was a drug that could ruin a man.

"Mutual assured destruction." He laughed. "Bleak, but I suppose that's one way of looking at it."

It was an elegant line of thinking, he had to admit. For what he wanted was, of course, everything: the thrill of the possibility of being caught and a way to reassure himself that he was invulnerable to it.

"Think about it," she said, smiling. Moments later, she was dressed, kissing him on the cheek, and gliding out the door like the devil called back to hell.

⤚❦⤙

Laila walked in the door to Nora's penthouse quietly, hoping her cousin would still be sleeping. She carried her heels in her hand and was naked beneath her dress. In the morning light, she saw that her lingerie had been ripped to shreds, so she abandoned it, presumably to be discovered by a curious maid. She found Nora in the kitchen frantically stirring pancake batter, singing along to a Katy Perry song that was blaring.

"Good morning," Laila said sheepishly.

"Oh, good *morning*," Nora said, "you look like a lady with a story to tell." Her cousin was distressingly cheerful, manic even.

Laila forced herself to laugh. "Not much of one, I'm afraid.

245

Some random from the party. We went out drinking after; terrible idea. Made out and passed out. I snuck out this morning before he woke up."

"Oh, you bad girl." Nora's laugh was shrill. Her eyes were sparkling. With what? Cocaine? She knew the twins indulged occasionally but also that Nora—like all of them, it seemed—had a bevy of prescription drugs in her medicine cabinet, so really, it could be anything.

"And what's going on here this morning?" Laila asked carefully.

"Pancakes," Nora declared. Laila noticed now that her cousin was drinking a mimosa.

"Do you have friends coming over?" This would be a surprise, that Nora had friends.

"No," Nora said. "Just felt like making them. But now you're here!" She put down her batter and poured a second mimosa for Laila, who sat down reluctantly, plastering a smile on her face. She wanted more than anything to go and sleep off her night, let the dust settle, and process her conversation with Cameron. In the moment, she felt as though she'd played her cards adroitly; Cameron was besieged by a Madonna-whore complex. The more she played the whore, the more he would need her, for Liberty was his obvious Madonna. Cameron was an outrageously wealthy man: a life could be made as his mistress. And then, perhaps, she could keep her family too. She'd never have to threaten them with blackmail in order to survive. Otherwise her options seemed to be ever narrowing to this one unappealing prospect.

As she sat there, she heard her phone buzzing with a text message. She looked at it discreetly, hoping it was from Cameron.

Hi Laila. I hope that you don't mind that I got your number from

Leo. I was pulled away before I could ask you about writing something for the Spec. Can I call you sometime?—Blake

Laila's mind flashed back to her brief interaction with the handsome young scion the previous night, how he'd stared at her in that familiar way. She'd been thinking about Cameron that night, the plan to show up at his door already forming in her mind, so she hadn't noticed. She'd taken his attentiveness to be nothing more than the natural charm of a man in his position.

Can you call me at noon? she replied.

"Who are you texting with over there?" Nora's voice sounded almost as if she knew it was Blake—although she couldn't have.

"Oh, just the guy from last night," Laila said. Her phone trilled a response, and her hungover mind contracted with happiness. *I'll call you at noon.*

"Are you going to see him again? Who is he?" Nora's voice had the edge of an interrogator.

Laila shrugged. "Maybe? I don't know."

"Men!" Nora spat, angrily flitting around the kitchen and placing a pile of pancakes before Laila.

"Yeah?" Laila was so thrilled about the texts from Blake that she dug into the pancakes, not minding the carbs, the fat from the butter, the sugar in the syrup. "Bad night?" she ventured.

"Just . . . disappointing," Nora said, settling in next to Laila with a stack of pancakes of her own.

"What happened?" Laila did not especially want to sit there and listen to Nora's litany of top-shelf first-world problems, but it was her obligation as their semipermanent houseguest.

"I got myself all worked up to see Blake, and he barely noticed me! He talked to me for, like, five minutes," Nora said.

"Well, it was his party. Maybe he was just distracted?" Laila ventured. Not too distracted to notice *her*, she noted with a flush of pride.

"I asked him if he wanted to catch up later," Nora said sulkily, "but he blew me off. Said he'd love to, but he's just *so* busy with the newspaper."

"I'm sorry, honey," Laila said. "But you want to be with someone who really wants to be with you. You shouldn't waste your time worrying about anyone else."

"Someone who really wants to be with me. And who would that be?" Nora said wistfully.

"What about Larry? You know he's crazy about you! Maybe you should give him a shot."

Nora rolled her eyes at the mention of her most ardent suitor, whom she had deigned to see only once or twice since meeting him. Yet he, for whatever reason, had hung in there. He *adored* Nora, and her ambivalence only served to increase his slavish devotion.

"You think *Larry* is the best I can do?"

"Of course not." Laila knew she needed to tread carefully, though she saw it would be helpful to encourage the idea of him. "I just think an older man might be more apt to really see everything you have to offer. To appreciate how sophisticated you are."

"Maybe," said Nora, depositing a bite of pancakes in her mouth. "Maybe."

⤙⤚

Blake called Laila at noon on the dot.

"Laila, I hope this isn't out of order to call you like this. I know we only spoke briefly last night."

He was like something out of an old-fashioned movie. It

amazed her. When she'd finally managed to break free of Nora, Laila had spent an hour frantically Googling him before their call. His father, it appeared, was a wealthy but especially unsavory character: a developer who'd briefly been jailed for a heady mix of high-class crimes including blackmail, witness tampering, and illegal political contributions. Blake seemed to have kept his nose excessively clean, perhaps in reaction, and had made a number of successful real-estate investments while an undergrad at Harvard. Impressively, he appeared to have paid the rumored $10 million for the *Spec* out of his own funds.

"Of course not," she said. "I was sorry we couldn't talk longer."

"The life of a literary agent. Very glamorous," he said. His voice was playful without sounding like he was making fun of her. "So yes, I asked around."

"Ha!" she said. "If you only knew. Glamorous is the last thing it is." She decided not to mention that she was only an intern. "Nice stalking, though."

He laughed. "Now that I'm a newspaperman, I have to get in the habit of doing my research. Though I'd prefer to get my information straight from the real Laila, if I should be so lucky."

A wild thought danced through her mind that she was going to fall in love with this man. Perhaps she already loved him. During the hour of skimming interviews with and countless photos on Patrick McMullan, a vision of a life with him had sunk its roots into her mind. However privileged he was, he was clearly also very bright and was serious, like Liberty. She'd read that he'd been the one to start up his family charity foundation. Here was someone whose love could, in all ways, elevate her.

"Speaking of which," he continued, "I'd really like to see you again. I'm headed to my place in Montauk for the weekend;

could you meet me for a late lunch before I take off? I know it's last-minute."

"Sure, I think that could work. April is a bit early in the season for Montauk, isn't it?"

"I like getting out there when the place isn't full of awful summer people, when it's quiet and cloudy, and I have the waves all to myself."

"Surfing? *Brrrr!*"

He laughed a warm, hearty laugh that she felt settling on her like a cozy blanket.

"Well, I do wear a wetsuit. Balthazar at two?"

"Yes."

❧

Two hours later, Laila put on a cream-colored eyelet DVF dress, threw her trench over it to protect her from the spring rain, and headed to the nearby bistro. Balthazar seemed like a place where they would run into someone Blake knew. She couldn't decide whether or not she hoped that they would. On the one hand, she couldn't pretend that she wouldn't love to be seen with Blake Katz. On the other, she wanted to spend some uninterrupted time getting to know him. And then there was the issue of Nora—but she didn't want to think of her just now. She was sick of her life being circumscribed by the twins, though she didn't want and couldn't afford to lose them.

❧

Blake stood when he saw her coming through the door. He was dressed casually in smart jeans and a light sweater. She leaned over to kiss his cheek when she reached the table; he looked and smelled absurdly clean, as though his whole being was spotless, including his soul.

"You look gorgeous," Blake said, "thanks for coming to meet me."

"I was happy to hear from you," she said. "A little surprised, though."

"That just shows that you don't know me yet," Blake said, settling back into his seat, his words becoming half lost in the din of the restaurant. "I don't let good things pass me by."

"You mean like the *Spec*?"

"I see what others can't sometimes," he said with a broad smile.

"What makes you so sure I'm a good thing?" She delicately unfolded her napkin on her lap.

He shrugged.

"Well, for one thing, you're Leo's cousin, and Leo is good people despite some of his . . ."

"Eccentricities?"

"Ha-ha, exactly. Honestly, I can just tell. Call it my sixth sense."

She laughed. If it hadn't been delivered so earnestly, she would have thought it was a line. But Blake seemed sincere; a rare quality anywhere but even more so in cynical, sarcastic New York.

"Your sixth sense?" she asked. "You see good people?"

She blanched; was that a stupid joke? She realized she was nervous. To have woken up next to Cameron and be sitting here now with Blake gave her whiplash. But if Cameron wanted his chance to be made good by someone better than himself, could she not want the same? If she was to be Cameron's secret, hidden whore, could he not be hers as well?

"It's something I've had to develop, being my father's son," he said. "My dad has it too. He taught me tricks."

"Oh? Care to share your secrets?"

"So," he said, leaning forward, hands on the table, "you have to study someone's face. But you have to do it without them seeing you, because if they do, you won't be able to tell anything. You want to catch them at rest, in between conversations, in a lull. There's always a moment when the mask comes off, and you see the person underneath," he said, brushing her chin with his thumb. "Like when I saw you that night at the party."

"We talked for five minutes."

He shook his head. "It was later. I saw you standing by yourself at the edge of the room. Maybe you were searching for someone; I don't know. But you were kind of smiling to yourself, and I thought, Look at her; she's in awe. There's this miraculous moment where someone's childhood self kind of filters through the cracks."

Laila was stunned. Being seen through the cracks in her facade was the thing she feared most and, consequently, exactly what she longed for.

"Oh God," he said, leaning back and raking his hand through his hair, "have I just completely creeped you out?"

"No!" she said. "No, not at all." Impulsively, she reached out and grabbed his hand across the table. He seemed reassured.

"Phew!" he said, his face brightening into a charming smile that crinkled his eyes. "Truthfully, it was the same with Sam Green the first time I met him; he still owns a minority stake in the *Spec*, and I would never replace him as editor in chief. I guess I knew right away that I wanted to have him as a mentor."

"What's he like? I only met him briefly at the party, but he seemed lovely."

"He's amazing." Blake's eyes lit up with admiration. "I mean,

I'm sure I don't have to tell you that most men his age would not be excited about the idea of a twenty-five-year-old investor stepping in to save the day, but he took me under his wing. I grew up with the *Spec*; that's why when I heard about its financial troubles, I had to step in. New York is, like . . ." Blake gestured as though trying to pull the words out of the air. "It can seem like it's all about money, but without its cultural institutions, it's nothing! No one would *want* to live here."

"You sound like Leo." Laila smiled, thinking about her cousin's rants about investment bankers and traders, his slavish little fan base who tripped over themselves to share their liquor with him when they saw him in a nightclub.

"Well, Leo knows of what he speaks. It's different growing up here, you know?"

"Yes," Laila said. "Well, I mean no, I don't *know*. My childhood was nothing like all of your's."

"Tell me," he said, "tell me everything."

Much to Laila's surprise, she did just that. While she omitted the tawdry portions—the affair, naturally; no reason to share the unsavory details with someone she'd just met—she embellished nothing. She told him how disappointed she was to have never met her grandfather after coming so close. He was a good listener, unusually so for a man, and drew her out.

When the bill appeared and Blake swiftly produced his credit card, Laila's stomach sank. Their time was almost up.

"I have a crazy idea," Blake said as the waiter walked away. "Come to Montauk with me for the weekend."

Without hesitating, she said yes. Somehow her hangover seemed to have dissipated. Next thing she knew, she was racing home to the twins' apartment to pack a bag. Suddenly, she froze in the middle of the room, remembering the last time she'd accepted an invitation for last-minute travel. But this felt different on every level. This felt like nothing less than the universe delivering her in a new direction.

"Hey, what are you doing?"

Laila had been so lost in her thoughts about her new paramour that she had failed to notice that Nora had appeared in the doorway of the guest room.

"Oh, um . . . packing."

"Packing? Where are you going?"

Laila needed a story, but no obvious lie appeared. Instead she let a big smile take over her face, and she let her very real excitement about the turn of events surface. She didn't need to hide what she was doing, after all, only with whom.

"Okay, promise you won't tell?"

Nothing thrilled Nora more than a secret.

"Of course! Oh my gosh, *what*?" Nora whirled into Laila's room and sat on her bed, hands clasped around one another.

"Well . . . it's the guy from last night. I just had lunch with him, and he wants me to go away with him for the weekend to the Hamptons. I know it's impulsive, but I like him so much, Nora!"

"Oooohhh! Not another crusty billionaire, though, babe, not a good look."

"No! God, never again. He's our age. And so dreamy."

"Oh my God, who *is he*?"

"Oh, you don't know him." Laila wished she could tell her.

"Well, what's his name, anyway?"

"Jake." The name was out of Laila's mouth before she could think of anything better. But of course, Nora had no reason to suspect the connection, and so it triggered nothing.

Just then, mercifully, Laila's phone beeped with a text message. "Oh, honey, that's him! I have to go, but I promise to tell you all about it when I get home, okay?"

Nora cheerfully sent her off, blissfully unaware that the man she'd spent hours crying over that very morning was the very one spiriting Laila eastward.

~∾~

During the long car ride to Montauk—that once-sleepy town on the farthest edge of Long Island—Laila quickly began to feel like she'd known Blake for years.

As he drove, he told her about his family—and there was much to tell. His father's legal imbroglios, it turned out, barely held a candle to his personal ones. Blake had a half sister from his father's previous marriage, his only sibling, and she'd been in and out of rehab for years. Blake's theory was that she'd never recovered from her father leaving their family for another woman—not Blake's mother, blessedly—that it had done indelible damage. He respected his father and still loved him, but their relationship was strained. It had become Blake's mission to live his life entirely in opposition to the example that was set for him.

Laila listened intently, for she knew that such an outpouring might not happen again for some time. In the very beginning, some men tell you everything you need to know about who they are, what they want, if you're able to read between the lines a little. It's so easy, after all, to unburden oneself to a beautiful, patiently listening stranger. But then once the stakes were raised, once you were no longer a blank slate, the dam would close.

~∾~

They stopped in a tiny, ruinously expensive grocery store to pick up provisions. The domesticity of the errand made Laila's heart ache. Rather than imagining their wedding—a moment of triumph her mind might have otherwise skipped forward to—she pictured the marriage itself. As she watched Blake chat with the grizzled man behind the fish counter, she imagined them in ten years, toddlers in tow. In thirty, on their own again, making their way through this same little grocery store, laughing at how quickly the years had gone by.

By the time they reached the house, it felt to Laila like they'd known each other forever. She looked at her phone and realized she had a text from Nora: *Let me know you got there safe! Xoxo*

She returned the text and smiled to herself. A loose end tied for now. She would not allow a whisper of guilt to take hold; Blake was a single man.

The house was a spectacular, modern, beachside mansion of cool gray stone and steel angles.

"It's my family's house," Blake hastily explained, "though I'm the only one who comes out here much. Since the whole prison debacle, my dad prefers to summer in the Riviera. Too much scrutiny here."

Laila smiled; Blake might feel like a kindred spirit, but he still used *summer* as a verb.

"Let me show you the beach side," he said, taking her hand. He'd kept his hands to himself up to that point, though she wished he wouldn't.

The back deck was a sleek stone patio with a covered swimming pool, beyond which was a tall sand dune dotted with a small fence poking through the sparse seagrass. And beyond that, the silvery ocean, churning beneath the cloudy sky. Laila felt herself being absorbed into a new identity, one completely separate from her cousins. Perhaps they were meant to be a bridge, and Blake was her destination.

She finally turned to Blake, taking his face in her hands and kissing him.

The weather was overcast and cool that weekend, and Laila was grateful to spend the time inside curled up with Blake.

"I want you to know," he said as they snuggled on the couch after dinner that first night, "that I don't expect anything from you."

She looked at him, confused.

"I mean," he said, putting his hand on her knee, "there are plenty of bedrooms in the house. I would never be so presumptuous as to ask you to . . . you know," he said.

Blake's confidence had finally faltered; the self-assured golden boy was practically blushing. It made Laila insane with want. She swung her leg over him and pulled herself onto his lap. Her skirt came up, and she saw that there was a bruise on her thigh from the night before. For a moment she feared that her body radiated with the memory of Cameron, that there would be other signs she couldn't obscure. But he didn't appear to notice anything.

"Oh God," he said.

She pressed into him and could feel him getting hard underneath her. In one motion, he stood and picked her up. She thought there was no way they would make it all the way to the bedroom like that, with her wrapped around him, but he was surprisingly strong.

"Are you going to keep carrying me like this?"

"A tiny thing like you? Please."

He laid her down on the bed and stared down at her.

"God," he said, "you're so beautiful."

She reached up and gently pulled him toward her, tugging his shirt over his neck and throwing it to the side. Blake appeared slender in his clothes but was surprisingly chiseled underneath, which thrilled her to no end: with the exception of Cameron, she'd become accustomed to the slight paunch of her older lovers.

When they were both down to their underwear, Blake hesitated once more.

"Are you sure?"

Laila resisted her immediate urge to tell him to fuck her, fearing that it would shock him. If she was with Cameron she could say it, though she wouldn't have to, he'd have already stripped her down and begun commanding her. She would have begun the encounter on her knees.

"Please," she said instead, "I want you so much."

He needed no further encouragement. He kissed the length of her torso and buried his head between her legs.

Normally, she disliked the vulnerability of having new men go down on her. She always feared that she'd be just the wrong side of her last Brazilian, feared how she may smell or taste. But Blake's tongue was on her most delicate skin before she could protest— and then protesting was the last thing she wanted to do. She entwined her fingers in his silky hair and lost herself in the sensations.

Despite his initial caution, once released, Blake was fearsome in bed. Laila finally saw the man who had taken over a newspaper at the tender age of twenty-five, the man who took what he wanted. He gripped her hair as he slid himself inside of her, dug his fingers into the flesh of her hips as he pulled her on top of him, gently but firmly turned her over and told her he wanted to have her every way.

Afterward, she curled herself in his arms, with his strong chest pressed against her back, and fell into a deep sleep of exhaustion and wonder.

The next morning he got up early to surf, kissing her forehead before he left. She drifted back off to sleep and woke a couple of hours later to the sounds of his making breakfast.

"Oh my God," he said when Laila emerged in his sweater, "seeing you in my clothes is so hot. Come here."

She kissed him.

"My dream girl," he said.

With those words, the real Blake came into view. He was a romantic. During the car ride, he'd also talked about his grandparents—how they'd been married for sixty years, how his grandfather had known his wife was the one the moment he laid eyes on her. And Laila suspected then that nothing about this weekend trip had been as spontaneous as it appeared. Perhaps Blake believed she was the one from the moment he'd seen *her*. What he thought he'd seen, exactly, she wasn't certain, but there would be time to determine it, to become it.

"Don't say that," she said, looking coyly away from him, as though overwhelmed by her own feelings.

"Why?"

"Because I'm already falling for you," she whispered. And perhaps it was even true.

"Well, that makes two of us." His hands were inside the sweater on her bare skin.

"Do you mean that?"

"Laila," he said seriously, sitting on a nearby stool and taking both her hands in his, "I know we haven't known each other long, so you'll have to take my word for it. I know there are a lot of guys who will say whatever, but I'm not one of them. I take this stuff seriously. I'm no player, I'm a one-woman man."

She wanted to laugh; she was almost in disbelief over his earnestness. She felt herself struggling with her own skepticism. Who didn't want to believe that they were good? That they could be loved? But she knew she didn't have the luxury of simply being credulous. That was reserved for those who needed from their partner only love itself.

"I'm glad to hear that. I am a one-man woman," she said. I will be, she thought, exactly what you want.

"Good," he said, kissing her, "because I can't handle cheating. I don't want to compete with anyone else."

She knew he meant it. Cheating, for him, meant ruined lives. And suddenly, being faithful felt possible to Laila. Suddenly, she couldn't fathom wanting anyone but him. She felt the emergence of a soul already half-saved from a day in Blake's company. Was this what Cameron loved so much about Liberty? Did she purify him? Make it feel possible to be someone better?

❧

The sun finally appeared later that day, and they made the most of their afternoon at the beach: sprawling on an enormous over-size fluffy towel, naming the cloud shapes ("That one looks like a camel." "That one looks like Donald Trump.") between make-out sessions. On the way home, they stopped for an early dinner in one of the tiny seaside towns that dotted the route between Montauk and Manhattan; they ate in a charming, quiet, little diner that was sparsely populated in its off-season slumber. When they finally neared the city, it was late Sunday night.

"I can take you home," he had said as they approached the

Queensboro Bridge, Manhattan coming swiftly toward them, ready to swallow them. "Or you can stay with me tonight," he continued when she didn't answer right away.

"Okay." She knew she should probably go home, have a good night's sleep, give him some space, let a vacuum open to let the longing in. The strategic part of her said this was right. And yet . . .

"I just have to get up superearly tomorrow."

"Do you not want me to stay?" Just like that, she was thrown. An early-morning wake up? Was this a brush-off? Was he the kind of man for whom a fling had to be romantic to be satisfying? Was that the extent of it? Leo was like this: there were torrents of love for the woman in his crosshairs; passionate obsession. But once he'd had her? On he went. It wasn't that his affections weren't real to him in the moment that he felt them, but his infatuations were like all-consuming yet swift-moving viruses: out of his system before any permanent damage was done.

"Hey," Blake said, reaching out to put his hand on her knee, "of course I do. I just didn't want to wake you up so early. But of course I want you to stay."

❧

Blake held her sweetly that night but was all business the next morning, taking a phone call the minute he emerged from the covers and barely breaking his stride to kiss her good-bye.

Laila hurriedly got into a cab outside his Upper East Side town house before the tears pricking her eyes spilled over. The street felt too bright that morning. She croaked out the address of the twins' town house then immediately started crying. She felt a little horrified at the sobs that burst forth, but she was relieved that she'd been able to hold them back until then. For some reason she couldn't quite put her finger on, she was terrified that she would never see Blake again. She felt waves of vulnerability washing over her. If he blew her off, if she'd been wrong about how she fit into his romantic paradigm, then she might have just played her last card. She knew that if Nora found out, she'd never forgive her. She was exhausted from all of it.

"Ah, don' cry," the cabdriver said. "It will be all right; don' worry."

She sniffled, caught off guard by the cabbie's deep, soothing voice. She looked at his license, which featured him smiling, his brilliant white teeth against dark skin. He was from Lagos; this detail struck her as romantic, though she couldn't say why.

"Thank you," she said. "I'm sorry."

"Don' be sorry," he said with a light laugh, "people, they cry in my cab all the time." He shrugged. "All the time."

"Maybe they can tell that you'll be kind."

He laughed softly, "Maybe so. You crying over love, pretty girl?"

"Maybe so." She herself had to laugh. For it wasn't just the thought of her plans going awry that had upset her. Her whole year in New York had been a high-wire act; she was used to it. And somehow, here in this cab with Isaac from Lagos, she was able to let it out. Blake felt different. "How could you tell?"

"That is the usual reason," he said. "Everyone back home say, *Ah, Isaac, people in New York, they so haad*, but I say no. People in New York always weepin' over love."

Love, Laila knew, should not even be making the list of her worries at the moment. Love, she thought, is for the rich and foolish. And yet.

20

THAT EVENING, a convergence of feelings descended on Laila: anxiety, but determination too. She went to meet Cece at Rose Bar and arrived before her, which would normally send her scuttling off to wait out of sight until her well-connected friend arrived. Instead she gave the doorman, a handsome bearded gent in an expensive suit whose gaze was soaked with ennui, her ID and a self-assured smile, and he let her right in. Not even a question of the list. Was this the secret? Act like you belonged and suddenly you did? Soon Cece joined her, and they were absorbed into the warm glow of the amber-hued, rococo-style cocktail lounge, removed from the humid April drizzle outside.

"Sorry, I have to check this," Laila said as she pulled her buzzing phone from her handbag, "I told Liberty I'd keep an eye on my phone; she's got this auction going, and she's super anxious about it." This much was true, though of course she was hoping it *wasn't* Liberty.

"No worries, girl; do your thing." Cece did a quick scan of the crowd before turning to her own phone to scroll through messages.

Laila looked down at her phone:

Beautiful Laila, you made my weekend. I cannot wait to see you again. I have back-to-back meetings the next few days but I'll call you as soon as I come up for air. Until then, I hope that thinking of me is making you smile even a little. It's making me smile like a fool.

She beamed and stared at the screen.

"Not Liberty, I take it," Cece said when she caught the look on her friend's face.

She knew she should be more careful, but now the whole story of her weekend in Montauk came burbling forth.

"Cece, I honestly think he might be the one."

"The *one*? Wow, who are you right now?" Cece laughed. "But okay, if he is, I'm happy for you. He's a catch—not my type, too clean-cut—but he's definitely hot."

Of course, Laila told herself she did not mean *the one* the way other women did. What she meant was that Blake was the answer, or at least that he could be. Reconnecting with her family had not gone as she'd hoped. Now she would have to get where she wanted to be via the oldest trick in the book: marriage. With Blake she could be so much more than she could ever be alone. She could see herself like Petra, only with perhaps a more loving marriage. Her focus would be on throwing beautiful parties and on looking beautiful herself each day: on surrounding herself and Blake with only the best things. She was certain a man like Blake would want children, and she felt under the right circumstances that mother-hood was something she could abide and perhaps even enjoy. After all, they'd be able to afford nannies. As long as she was not forced to change diapers and drive carpools, she felt she could love a couple of little ones. Perhaps it would be the opportunity to be the mother she did not have herself.

"I know, I fully sound like *that* girl right now," Laila said. At that moment a waitress arrived with two glasses of champagne.

"Excuse me, ladies," she said, setting the glasses down next to their still-half-full cocktails. "From the gentlemen at the bar," she added, quickly gliding away as though she couldn't be bothered to explain any further. Laila and Cece glanced over, and there were at least three twosomes of men, all looking in their direction. They raised their glasses and nodded in the general direction of the men, neither of them interested in engaging with anyone they saw there.

"Did that ever happen to you?" Laila asked, returning to their conversation.

"What, like, love at first sight?" Cece asked, smiling.

"No. Or, I mean, I guess? I don't know. Where you just . . ." Laila put her hands up in frustration, lost for what she was trying to express. But Cece nodded.

"Yeah," she said, with a sad smile, "I felt that way with Steven."

"Gah, Steven who we hate?" Laila had heard all about Steven: the one serious boyfriend Cece had had that she knew of. He'd cheated on her with one of her roommates. Cece and Laila had seen him out one night at Marquee with some clients. They'd amused themselves by hiding in the corner of the bar and sending the girliest drinks they could think of to his table: he was the sort of master-of-the-universe type who would be embarrassed by a daiquiri—complete with an umbrella that the bartender had managed to find—showing up unbidden. Both the bartender and the bottle-service girl who'd ferried the drinks were on Cece's side once they heard the backstory, and insisted to Steven that he'd ordered them. Not that anyone who worked in that place needed any more of a reason to hate investment bankers.

"We didn't always hate him, though," Cece said now.

"Well, naturally."

"Yeah, at first," Cece said, "he just seemed like a dreamboat. He was so interested in my career; he seemed like he really believed in me. It was so different than all these dudes that just want arm candy. I was," she shook her head and sighed, "a goner from the word *go*."

"Excuse me, ladies?"

Laila and Cece had been so absorbed in their conversation that they hadn't noticed the pair approaching—Italian suits, glinting cufflinks, bankers almost certainly—and now they were trapped. They looked up warily. This was, of course, a routine they'd seen before. Send the drinks first, ensuring if not a warm welcome, at least an obligatory one.

"Enjoying the champagne?"

"Yes," Cece said, raising her glass. "Uh, thank you. That was . . . nice of you."

"I just have to ask," said the other, stepping forward to peer at Cece, "where are you from?"

Laila could see Cece stifling an eye roll. "I grew up in the Bronx."

"No, but, like, where are you *from*?" he said.

"You're asking about my ethnicity?"

"Yeah!" he said, oblivious to her tone. "You're just so . . . exotic-looking."

"My parents are Dominican," Cece said flatly. "Thanks so much for asking."

"Gorgeous," exclaimed the other, equally tone-deaf.

"Where are you from?" Laila asked sweetly.

"Upper East Side," said the first, "and my boy Brad here is from Boston. Have you met Brad?"

"I met Chad here at Harvard," Brad said. "Have you met Chad?"

"Harvard, huh?" Cece said. "Humph, never heard of it!"

"So, Upper East Side and Boston. Brookline, maybe?" Laila continued.

He touched his nose like, *You got it*. And they both nodded smugly.

"So, they don't teach you any manners there, or what?"

"Oh, Laila," Cece said, "don't be harsh! Maybe they've just never seen a brown person before."

With that Brad and Chad got the message. They turned on their heels, muttering under their breath, "Bitches." And, "Not even that hot."

"Okay," Laila said, downing the rest of her cocktail and turning to the hard-earned glass of champagne. "Brad and Chad, is that even real?"

"That could *only* be real," Cece said. "So, the moral of the story?"

"Guys are douchebags?"

"Ye-ah. But if you find a diamond among the douchebags, give him a shot."

"Cece," Laila said, "that's the most romantic thing I've ever heard you say."

⁓

Blake's message buoyed Laila temporarily until, for no good reason, she slipped back into a funk and by the following evening, she had convinced herself that she'd never see him again. She reasoned with herself that if he was in fact ghosting her, at least it would save her any accompanying Nora drama. There were always other men, thousands of them teeming through the streets of the city; they couldn't all be Chads and Brads. But something about

Blake had sunk its hooks into Laila. The effort of trying not to think about him wore her out. And so it went until three days later, he called.

"I wish I had the whole weekend free to spend in bed with you," he said, "but I have a couple of boring dinners with potential advertisers for the paper that I need to woo."

"Oh well, I know it's a crucial time for you with the business." Laila thought she might pass out from disappointment.

"It is," he said, "which is why it would be so amazing to have my favorite beautiful, brilliant sidekick with me. What do you say? It would really help me out."

She swooned. He saw them just as she did: more powerful together.

Laila spent the next two weeks at his side: going to parties where you tripped over celebrities and supermodels, eating at restaurants so new and hot even the twins hadn't heard of them, and attending parties and fund-raisers shored up by money new and old, held everywhere from burned-out loft spaces in Dumbo to the National Arts Club.

As it happened, Blake's social circle did not cross over with the twins' as much as Laila had feared. Blake had left behind much of the prep school circle the twins still spent their time with, especially all the young dilettantes Leo favored. Nora, in the meantime, was busy with her new boyfriend, Larry. Nora had at last grown lonely enough to give in to Larry's affections. He sent her flowers every week. He brought her a bracelet from Tiffany on their third date: a silver cuff of interwoven olive leaves that Nora now wore nearly every day. He showered her not only with gifts but with effusive compliments: being near the two of them (he would always come to the door to fetch Nora for their dates) was nauseating, for it meant listening to Larry gush about how unbelievably beautiful Nora was. Larry himself was homely, albeit in a rather endearing way with a large, goofy smile and bushy, expressive eyebrows. He did have the benefit of being tall, which always made men seem a bit less ridiculous than they might otherwise.

Nora was happy, and Laila was glad. If she was engulfed by a new love, then perhaps she would forgive Laila for Blake. And it would be such a relief to leave that bridge intact.

∽✦∽

After two weeks of nonstop togetherness, Blake left for a series of meetings in London, where several of the paper's other investors lived—leaving Laila feeling distracted and unmoored. She was no romantic, but she felt a certain *rightness* when she was with him: she would look at him—so handsome, so well dressed, so *innocent*—and feel a calm settle on her that she was in exactly the place she should be. Was this what others meant when they said they were in love? For Laila realized that though she'd spoken the words numerous times—what else was there to do once a man said it to you?—the voice, *No, no, no,* had always been there, and eventually it screamed loud enough to untether her. But with Blake this voice was nowhere to be found.

It did not help that given the time difference and how busy he was in London, Blake was only able to send her the occasional e-mail, and she felt the loss of his physical presence keenly: his voice, his hands, the comfort of him inside her.

One night she sat at home attempting to read: her idea of what the kind of girlfriend she wanted to be would do while her boyfriend was traveling. She'd pictured herself thusly that day: soup from the deli taken to go, one glass of wine from the bottle of sauvignon blanc Nora had opened the night before, and then a couple of hours redoubling her efforts to love the literature that she was always claiming to adore. She was several chapters into *East of Eden*, and my God, it was slow. Liberty's mind must be equipped with some preternatural patience to love these sorts of books. Before long, Laila was itching not to be sitting there alone. Nora's side of the penthouse was empty, and who knew if Leo was home. Laila couldn't fathom how to be by herself here, how to be still. The chaos of the city pulsed just beyond the walls; how could she resist it?

After an hour and the first two glasses of the sav blanc, she gave in and called Cece, who was at a regular haunt of hers on the Lower East Side. She knew she'd been neglecting her friend a bit since she'd met Blake and was relieved that she seemed not to bear her any grudge. They made their way through their usual series of bars on the Lower East Side until they ended up, somewhere after midnight, at the Box—a trendy, vaudeville-style club on Chrystie Street. Laila had heard of it, but this was her first time inside.

"My God," she said to Cece, as they stepped into the jewel-box theater that looked straight out of the nineteenth century, "this place is amazing."

"Yeah, it's a cool aesthetic. You have to be in the right mood for it, though," Cece said enigmatically.

Laila was too stimulated to play it cool and couldn't help but scan the tables along the walls. The Gatsbyesque atmosphere had the usual bankers and glittering beauties, the recognizable faces of a model or actor popping out at her every so often.

"Oh God," Laila said to Cece, turning abruptly.

"What?" she said, letting Laila adjust their course.

"It's Simon, that billionaire guy."

"Ruh-roh, the one from Mustique?" Cece asked, her voice light. But then she hadn't seen the look Simon had just given Laila; he'd spotted her first, and so when her eyes fell on him, his face was already fixed in a hideous glare. He seemed every inch the kind of man that would hold a grudge.

"Cece, maybe we should go somewhere else," Laila said. Cece was distracted, on the lookout for the friends they were supposed to be meeting.

"Don't be silly. He doesn't own the nightclub, does he?"

Laila stopped short. He'd mentioned something about investing in nightclubs, but did he say which?

"Well, I don't think so. Maybe, though."

She laughed as if Laila was talking nonsense. They'd both already had plenty to drink. "He's not going to do anything. Come on!"

Laila was several more drinks in when her phone trilled a message. She attempted to be discreet as she looked at it so as not to offend the men they had joined at a table near the stage of the ornate theater, and also because cell phones were technically not allowed inside.

Where are you? I want you.

The message was from Cameron. Laila nearly laughed at the audacity of his message. *Of course* he wanted her now. Now that Laila was otherwise occupied with a new man in her life, it would follow that he would suddenly find her irresistible.

The friend of Cece's who had invited them to their table was a photographer, devastatingly handsome. From the look on Cece's face, as they talked with their heads together, Laila suspected that she would go home with him, maybe not for the first time. The two other men at the table had been polite enough when introduced but were now ignoring Laila. She knew it should mean nothing to her that they had their attentions so clearly tuned to the gorgeous teenage-looking models floating by, and yet it did. New York was a place where one didn't have to look far to feel diminished, to be made invisible.

I'm at the Box, she texted back, *catching a show. Anyway you can't have me. So there.*

This was perfect, she thought, for she had Blake now and could simply reject Cameron; she would have this final word, this upper hand. And still, what was that stirring? That twitch at the center of her. Maybe she shouldn't have left the penthouse. But here she was: already a little drunk, her senses submerged in this flashy, nightmarish, beautiful room. No one was paying attention to her, so no one noticed that her champagne glass was empty. She was seated on the outside of the booth and reached over to grab the bottle out of the ice bucket and refilled her own. The other men got up from the table—a hunting party of two—and Cece and her friend were making out. Laila quickly drank her glass then refilled it again. The lights went down, and a tall, shirtless man with a tattooed and chiseled torso appeared onstage. He wore heavy makeup, and his bleached blond hair was spiked into devil horns. "Welcome to the Box! Theater of oddities and delights!"

It was somewhere soon thereafter that Laila lost the thread. The rest of the night came back to her only in flashes the next day. Cameron had appeared and sat beside her in the booth. Something bloomed inside her at his presence. He had chased her down; he was with her *in public*. Blake was not there to want her, and this had left a void, a need in Laila to be wanted by someone. After that, she only absorbed pieces of the show: flashes of naked bodies; the midget; the fat woman. There were contortionists and a scantily clad acrobat dangling above them. And all the while, Cameron was pouring her more champagne and keeping a steady hand between her legs. Only one moment was crystal clear: as she shook from an impending orgasm, he pinched the inside of her thigh and leaned over to whisper, "I own you, do not forget that." They'd eventually decamped to a dark corner by the bathrooms on the lower floor, where Cameron pinned Laila up against a wall. Then, having gotten what he came for, he'd left. It was all too easy the next day to pretend that none of it had really happened. But, of course, it had.

❧

Several days later when Blake at last returned, Laila made the trip out to surprise him at JFK. She spotted him before he saw her. He was wearing a tight gray T-shirt and had a smart Tumi carry-on slung over his broad shoulders. She'd been about to stand on tiptoes and wave frantically at him so that he'd see her, but she held back for a minute, suddenly awed by the sight of him. He didn't look like he could possibly be there to meet her, like he could be her *real* boyfriend; he looked like the television actor hired to play him. He walked right by her, and she momentarily worried that he *wasn't* actually there to see her; that she was going to watch him get enveloped in the arms of some other woman.

"Blake!" she shouted. He turned at the sound of his name and glanced over his shoulder, his face lighting up when he saw her.

"Laila! You're here!" He pulled her into his arms, lifting her off her feet exactly the way she'd dreamed he would.

"Since when do New Yorkers pick each other up at the airport?"

"I decided to make an exception," she said, almost unable to breathe as the smell of him washed over her. She suddenly wondered if she'd overshot by coming all the way out here. But no, he looked so happy to see her that she knew it had been the right thing to do.

In the cab on the way back to the city, she sat nestled against him; it was like some long-held but unspoken dream had materialized beside her. Unwelcome thoughts of Cameron suddenly bombarded her. Blake was drawn to the part of Laila that was good, but perhaps she needed Cameron in order to be that good woman; perhaps her demons needed someone else to absorb them. Could this be what they were to each other? A receptacle for each other's worst selves so they could be otherwise loving and loyal to their better halves? There was a twisted logic to it that held. Perhaps rather than betraying Liberty, she was protecting her from the side of Cameron that she undoubtedly didn't want to see. For if she wanted to see it, she would have: after all, *Laila* had seen it right away, could see it flashing in his eyes as he looked her over that first night; something there that couldn't be hidden by any amount of gloss and polish, and Cameron had plenty of both. And Cameron had seen her too, beneath the naive midwestern veneer. And what a thrill it was to be seen, to be recognized by your same animal.

Perhaps, it occurred to her, there was no natural end to this quartet: perhaps they were four legs of a table. But even in that moment, cuddled next to her better half, Laila knew she was fooling herself. It was all too beautiful to last.

21

SEXY NEW COUPLE
HITS MONTAUK HOT SPOT

Saturday, June 1st

Blake Katz was seen at Surf Lodge Friday night with **Laila Lawrence**. "The two have been quietly dating for some time. They're crazy about each other," a source close to the couple tells us. The gorgeous redhead originally hails from Michigan and is the granddaughter of real estate mogul Frederick Lawrence. They reportedly spent the weekend in Katz's $5.7-million beachside home.

~∾~

"This is a disaster," Laila said to Blake the next morning as she read the article aloud to him at the breakfast nook in Montauk.

"Wow," he said, biting into an apple, having just returned from a few hours of early-morning surfing, "I didn't think you'd be so shy about being in the press! You're so cute!"

Cece had texted her that morning: *Girl, check Page Six, you're famous* ☺

"It's not that," Laila said, "ugh, I should have told you this before." He looked at her questioningly. Laila let out a deep sigh. "Nora has—had, anyway—a huge crush on you. So I kinda haven't told her we're dating."

"Where does she think you've been spending all your time lately?" He looked amused.

"Well, she knows I'm seeing someone. I told her I had a new guy named . . . Jake."

"*Jake*, huh? Sneaky." His eyes sparkled with laughter, and for a moment, his levity calmed her. If he wasn't taking it seriously, perhaps there was nothing to be concerned about. But Blake didn't know Nora like she did.

"Don't laugh! I'm worried. I don't want her to hate me."

"Come here," he said, pulling Laila up out of her chair and into his arms. "Don't worry. We'll figure it out. And doesn't Nora have a boyfriend?"

"Larry."

"Larry! Well, I'm sure she's over her crush. Why don't you just talk it out when you get home?"

"Blake, you don't understand. This is bad. What if she kicks me out?"

"I think you're overreacting." Laila was not so sure. "But if she does, you'll come live with me."

"Blake, stop."

"I'm serious, how great would that be? Anyway, just talk to her; it's not as though she and I have a history. How mad could she possibly be?"

❧

When Laila returned to the city, Nora was not at the penthouse.

Hey! Want to grab dinner tonight? Maybe order in?

Laila's cheerful text received no reply, the first harbinger of her cousin's fury. Nora always carried her phone with her, always looked at it, and always responded immediately—her hunger for connection forever churning.

And so Laila was forced to pace the floors of the penthouse waiting for her cousin's return. The air-conditioning was frigid, and Laila alternated between the living room and the patio, unable to get comfortable, waiting and wondering. She resisted the urge to text her cousin again, attempting to calmly maintain her vigil. At last, around nine o'clock, Nora appeared.

"Hey, honey!" Laila said, pretending to ignore the cloud of foreboding that seemed to waft around her cousin as she entered the room. "There you are! How was your weekend? Did you and Larry have fun in East?" Larry owned a house in East Hampton with a swimming pool and tennis courts.

Nora didn't look at her but instead smiled menacingly in the direction of the floor.

"I had a lovely weekend, thanks so much for asking. And you? How was *your* weekend? With, oh, what was his name? Jake, is it?"

Laila's stomach turned. Of course she'd read it: gossip traveled like a lit fuse in New York—and Nora never missed an update. And of course she was furious.

"Nora. I'm sorry about that. I just didn't want you to be mad."

At this, Nora laughed mirthlessly. She came to sit on the couch adjacent to where Laila was and yet somehow still a thousand miles from her. "So, naturally, creating a fake boyfriend was the way to go."

"I figured that there was no point in telling you unless we got serious." Laila's head spun; there must be a way out of this. She was used to being able to outmaneuver her cousin, but she'd mulled it over all day, and a foolproof angle had not presented itself. She could say she knew her cousin would be upset if she'd told her, but that would be admitting she'd knowingly done something to hurt her. She could say she'd just been trying to keep a vulnerable new relationship private, but Nora didn't believe in privacy—especially not from one another. There was also no satisfying answer as to why Laila's new love had to be, in a city of thousands of eligible men, one Nora adored. Or at least that's how she would see it.

"And? Are you?"

Laila looked at her for a moment.

"Serious? Are the two of you serious?"

And then it came to her. Nora was a romantic; perhaps this was the angle, the path to her cousin's forgiveness.

"Oh, Nora, we are. I've never felt this way about anyone! I think he could be the one, I really do."

To Laila's horror, Nora's look became icier still. Normally Nora's reactions were histrionic; this chilly calm was alarming. "I'm so glad for you. Now you can stop pretending to care about me."

"Nora, how can you say that? I love you, you know that!"

"You know, I really thought," Nora said, standing now and picking up her bag to take it to her room, moving such that Laila had to follow her to continue to hear what she was saying, "that if we were generous with you, if I just really tried to love you, that you could get over your jealousy of me, of all of us. I thought if we welcomed you with open arms, you would flourish. But the fact that you had to go after the *one* person you knew I wanted the most, and then lie to me about it straight to my face . . . it's just *beyond*, Laila. Leo was right; you're just in it for yourself."

Laila felt her knees go weak beneath her. This was so much

worse than she'd even anticipated; the whole thing felt so terribly final. "Leo thinks that?"

Now her cousin looked back over her shoulder to where Laila stood nearly trembling in the door frame. "Oh, Laila, *everyone* thinks that."

～✤～

She didn't tell Laila to move out; she didn't need to. Laila steered clear of Nora for the remainder of the evening, and once she had left the next morning, she hurriedly packed everything she'd come with. She would have liked to leave every shred of clothing that Nora had ever bought for her, but the sad truth was she'd scarcely have a single thing to wear if she'd done so. The few clothes she'd brought with her from Michigan had long since been discarded.

She showed up in Blake's lobby later that day with two huge suitcases. She charmed his doorman, who knew her by then, into letting her up and waited anxiously by the door for Blake to get home. She ran the ideal scenario in her mind over and over to steel her nerves—she pictured him picking her up and swinging her around, carrying her off to the bedroom they would now share, and making love to her in his sweet and comforting way. The reality was somewhat less picture perfect.

At first he'd been simply surprised to find her there. But then, as he'd taken in the luggage that sat piled at her feet, the confusion had coalesced into outright bewilderment.

"Laila, when I said you could move in here, I meant we could, you know, discuss that as a next step if things got bad with your cousins. . . ." He trailed off, rubbing the back of his head with his palm and seeming to look anywhere but at her.

It settled in on Laila how desperate the move had been, and

she knew better than anyone that moves born of desperation were always the wrong ones. You had to behave as though your options were infinite even as they dwindled.

"I don't know what I was thinking," she said, her voice quavering, "I'm an idiot. I'll get a hotel." And at this, a sob escaped her. She found in that moment that she was wracked by a genuine and horrible fear that she'd be left with no one. She had only a couple hundred dollars to her name after blowing the bulk of her reserves on the beautiful hotel room on Mustique. There was the pendant, which she had worn today, as this felt like the safest thing to do in transit. But she'd have to sell it: the one possession that connected her to her mother.

"Laila, come here," Blake said, reaching for her where she stood with all of her worldly belongings at her feet. The smell of him was comforting despite the circumstances.

"I was taken by surprise," Blake said, "don't hold that against me."

"I get it; you said it offhand, and I took it seriously. God, you must think I'm crazy." She pulled back and looked at him, her eyes wide and wet, hoping he saw something worth saving.

"Laila, it was *my* idea that you move in here. I simply didn't realize that you were going to do it quite this fast. I'm happy that you did, but you have to give me a minute here."

"I don't think Nora is ever going to speak to me again," Laila said. As the words left her mouth, she wondered if they were true. She saw now how easy it would be for her cousins to shut her out as easily as they welcomed her in. Her attempts to secure herself a more permanent place at their table had failed utterly.

"I'm sure it's not so dire," Blake said. "We'll talk to Liberty. She'll help. Now, let's get you settled in."

22

"MAYBE WE should just stay here all summer," Liberty said, luxuriating in the pleasant June sun that was streaming onto Cameron's lush patio.

"You won't say that once you see the place in Sag," Cameron said, handing her one of the mojitos he'd just made, bending over to kiss her before taking his place in the Adirondack chair next to her.

"God, this is perfect," she said, taking a sip, "and yes about that." She turned and beamed at him. "Why all the secrecy? What have you got up your sleeve?"

"Oh no, not telling. The look on your face when you see it is *my* part of the gift."

She reached out to squeeze his hand. Throughout the months of their relationship, he'd seemed extraordinarily good at giving her exactly the right thing: closeness when she'd needed it, space when she began to feel the vulnerability of that closeness too sharply. He seemed to understand her as a real and complete person in a way that no other man had been able to do. Certainly her lifelong friendship with his sister—with whom he'd become increasingly close since returning from London—was partly responsible for this, but Liberty felt seen in a new and thrilling way. In a practical sense, she found the idea of two people being made for one another ridiculous, but she nonetheless began to feel this sentiment in her bones.

There were small moments of dissonance, of course—but these were inevitable between any couple, weren't they? Not that they didn't occasionally tug at the edges of Liberty's happiness. When Liberty had first seen Cameron's town house, she'd been immediately thrilled by the sight of the walls of built-in book-shelves and had gone to examine them close-up while Cameron went to fetch a bottle of wine. The books were an odd mix—clas-sic novels, ancient-looking reference titles, a book labeled *Volume Two of the Complete History of Haberdashery*—and when he re-turned, she asked about them.

"Quite an eclectic library you've got here," she said.

"Oh, those? My decorator bought them by the yard; they're just for show."

He said it casually, but somehow, their presence felt obscene to Liberty. She didn't, in general, care overly much about decor, but if she and Cameron were ever to live together, these false idols would have to go. She sometimes found herself lying in his bed at night thinking about them. She kept this to herself, naturally; she knew she was being weird.

The other moment that had lodged in her mind but that she compelled herself to look away from had happened when they'd been getting ready for bed one evening after eating a particularly rich meal with two other couples at Le Bernadin. While brushing her teeth, Liberty had inadvertently passed gas. She'd laughed about it, but Cameron had seemed mortified for both of them and a little disgusted. But this was just how men were, she told herself; they had to accept you as human a little at a time.

"You know *I* don't mind staying in the city," she said. "But it'll be nice to get some fresh air." Liberty loved the summer months when the city cleared out on weekends—releasing her from the constant feeling that spending her weekends with a book made her boring. Reece often stayed in town now too, meaning Liberty wasn't alone. Reece had once loved the Hamptons but was growing tired of it. She complained that the party circuit there was somehow more concentrated with douchebags than in Manhattan. "It feels like I run into every last person I don't want to see when I'm there," Reece said after being at the family's estate in South for Memorial Day.

"You're going to love it," Cameron said, "I've never been so sure of anything."

Blake's apartment was sharp and modern, immaculate at all times. It was very much a contrast to the twins' place, which managed to become a mess between regular visits from the housekeeper, who they then complained about, as though she ought to be taking preventative measures as well as cleaning up after them.

It felt to Laila like she was living in a hotel at first, but soon she began to see it as her home. They spent most weekends in Montauk, and one chilly evening in late June they lay curled up by the fire, drinking an especially nice bottle of wine to celebrate their three-month anniversary.

"I have something for you," Blake said, dislodging himself from her side.

"We said no gifts!" Laila said, delighted that he'd disregarded this.

He shrugged and smiled enigmatically. He went to the

kitchen, and she watched him through a dreamy haze of alcohol and warmth thinking simply: the man of my dreams. He returned and held forth a box that Laila immediately recognized as Cartier red. She had a visceral reaction to being presented with jewelry by Blake that was so intense it screamed in her brain: *Yes, yes, a thousand times yes!* before she could take the time to register the size and shape of the box, clear indications. And so, horribly, her first feeling upon discovering the iconic golden LOVE bracelet within was disappointment.

"Do you like it?" Blake asked worriedly, having perhaps caught the flash—however brief it had been—of letdown that had crossed her face when she'd opened the box and not found a ring.

"*Of course!* Like it? I love it, pardon the pun!" she said, flinging her arms around him on the couch, the box still clutched in her palm. "It's the best gift I've ever been given!"

This much was true. Her ex-husband and former boyfriends had all had simpler tastes; this bracelet was easily more expensive than her old engagement ring—which she'd been nonetheless compelled to return, as it was a family heirloom.

"Good," he said, "it's not too much?"

"No! I'm just overwhelmed. And *delighted.*"

It could never be too much from Blake. It could never be enough.

≈

Cameron had hatched his plan for his perfect summer with Liberty after seeing the well-loved copy of *East of Eden*, which appeared to have a permanent place on Liberty's bedside table. The other novels—some of them in manuscript or bound-galley format—rotated at a brisk pace, but the thick paperback tome remained. She had several other copies, including a rare first edition, lined up in a row on her bookshelf. She could never resist, she explained, buying a copy when she saw a different edition than those she already owned.

He remembered a Harvard friend—a blond kid from Texas—telling him that his aunt had been married to John Steinbeck, and that his home in Sag Harbor remained in their family. Cameron had rented it for the month. It was one of two rather large surprises he had planned for Liberty this weekend. All she knew was that they were going out east. He was admittedly a little nervous, which was terrifically unlike him, and as they neared the exit to Sag Harbor, he caught himself rambling.

"And where will the twins be this summer? They're welcome to stay with us, obviously. Though I'll warn you, it's a bit close quarters." Cameron's was an empty offer; he could barely imagine Liberty's ridiculous little sister with her piles upon piles of luggage put up in the funny little bunkhouse.

Liberty smiled. "I'm not sure about Leo. Nora's new beau has a place in East, maybe? I can't remember. Did I tell you she's on the outs with Laila again?" Liberty smiled and rolled her eyes. Thank goodness, she seemed not to get too involved in the little dramas of her younger siblings. To hear her say Laila's name made his stomach churn. He'd had moments of weakness: all part of the process, he'd told himself, of expelling his last demons as he moved ever closer to his beloved. Never again.

"Oh goodness, what now?" Cameron said. Whether his great effort to sound casual showed outwardly, he didn't know.

"This boy Laila's seeing. Honestly, I don't know the details; I try not to indulge Nora too much with this kind of thing. Once she starts making herself the victim, it's a whole downward spiral.

At any rate, Laila might be better off. I don't think the twins are a very good influence on her."

"Why do you say that?"

Liberty sighed. "Well, I practically offered Laila a job at the agency on a platter, but she didn't seem very enthused. Maybe she just wants to do something different, but I worry that she's caught the twins' allergy to employment."

Cameron smiled.

"I just don't want her to get lost here—in New York, I mean. She means well," Liberty said, "but she's naive."

It occurred to Cameron that perhaps he knew Laila better than Liberty did.

As they turned off Mill Road onto Noyac Bay Avenue, Liberty was mercifully distracted as it began to dawn on her where they were headed.

"My God," Liberty said as they pulled up in the drive. "It can't be."

She recognized it immediately, as he hoped she would. The cottage, on a property that jutted out in a cove of Noyac Bay, was a funky little place. Cameron preferred something grander, with a bit more light, something a little closer to town or with a proper beachfront. But this wasn't about what he wanted—or rather, it was about what he wanted most of all.

"Look!" Liberty said as they made their way through the kitchen. "Here's where he marked the heights of all the guests that came through; here's Charley!" The eponymous dog of memoir fame. The backyard brought yet more delights, with its quirky, kidney-shaped swimming pool and the little writing cottage at the edge of the property.

"Cameron," she said, turning to him, "how did you do this?"

Had she ever been more beautiful than she was in that moment? There was a slight breeze coming off of the quiet little bay, and it lifted her hair off her shoulders, which were covered in a little spray of freckles from the sun. He'd never seen her look less guarded, more open. He saw it then: it could all be enough if he had her.

"I'd do anything for you," he said, taking her face in his hands, "that's all you need to know. Now go get settled in, I have some things to take care of."

~~~

So it was there on that mildly humid evening, just as the sun was going down, that Cameron dropped to his knee in the tiny writing cottage—which he had decked out with candles—and presented Liberty with an art deco ruby-and-diamond estate ring from Fred Leighton that had been burning a hole in his pocket all afternoon. He could not have orchestrated the moment any better, with the last remnants of a glorious sunset hanging over the water and fireflies flitting through the tall grass at the edge of the lawn.

Of course she said yes. What more could she ever have wanted?

23

W HEN LIBERTY arrived at the office on Monday, the ruby caught Laila's attention before she could say a word. Liberty was normally in the office long before Laila arrived between nine thirty and ten, so her late arrival alone was notable. Laila had waited far too long to make a decision about throwing her hat in for the assistant's job, and they'd hired a girl from the endless pool of Ivy League graduates who'd streamed through the offices, one after the other, gushing about the agency's client list. As it did not make sense to keep Laila on forever as an intern, Liberty had given her a job as a reader, paid by the hour. She seemed a little stung that Laila hadn't wanted the job, but she'd been happy enough to keep her around.

"Excuse me," Laila said, stopping her cousin in her tracks as she swanned in with a soft *Good morning*. "What is *this*?" she said, grabbing Liberty's left hand and pulling it in for examination.

"Cameron proposed," she said quietly, as though telling a secret; if she hoped to keep this from anyone for long, she was dreaming. It was only a matter of time before the tabloids were all over it.

"I can see that." Laila felt the great swell of a thousand conflicting emotions, all of which she bundled and disguised as joy. "Eeeee! I can't believe it!" She threw her arms around her. "Tell me everything!"

Liberty shushed her cheerfully, and Laila followed her into her office to hear the story of the weekend, the proposal, the engagement party planning that Cameron's overjoyed parents already had well under way.

"I wish they would give us a bit more time to have it just to ourselves, to be honest," Liberty confessed. But Laila could barely keep her mind on the conversation at hand: she'd still been seeing Cameron occasionally, but he'd become unpredictable. He'd seem to be pulling away and then become doubly insistent that he see her. For her part, she would consider cutting him off—she had even more to lose now—but then in the moment, she'd find herself unable. In the most romantic light, she thought perhaps her and Cameron's could be a great, clandestine love affair: that they could protect Liberty and Blake from the parts of themselves that those two innocent souls would have preferred never to see without ever involving anyone outside the family, anyone who didn't love them. But she also knew that there was nothing like love between her and Cameron, though what bound them had its own visceral pull.

⁓⁓

Reece was also thrilled by the news—and not a little bit surprised. Her brother, married! To her best friend! And he wasn't yet forty. She'd known for some time that he was serious about Liberty, but marriage was something else altogether.

Their mother, Elin, had settled on the family compound in South Hampton for the couple's engagement party. The place was curiously named Lily Pond, though there was none of either of these things on the property—evidently there had at some point been a duck pond, which had been done away with when the tennis courts were put in a decade before—but the name lived on. It was undeniably a beautiful place, with acres of lush greenery and walking paths connecting the four guest cottages, the tennis courts, the two swimming pools, and the stables. There was a pristine beachfront where guests often took picnics out to the cabanas. The decor was all aimed at giving the effect of lightness, of cheer and innocence, of pure Waspy sensibility. It was laid-back only in the most cultivated way. One expected to come around the corner to find Martha Stewart in the midst of a craft project, or for Ina Garten to show up at the back door with dinner. Both had, incidentally, been guests at Lily Pond at one point or another.

The morning of the party, Reece was summoned to Elin's bedroom. Thatcher was already on the golf course with Cameron and a horde of his Harvard rowing buddies. Her mother was trying to choose among a pile of brand-new dresses she'd had sent over from Ted Baker.

"Oh, good, you're up!" Elin said when Reece padded in with a giant mug of coffee.

"You say that like it's noon." It was not yet 8:00 a.m., and frankly, Reece could have used another hour of sleep. She'd been spending late nights in the atelier working on her line with Cece. Reece had no desire to be in her midtwenties again, but she had to confess she envied the way her younger friend was able to let her work consume her without a care in the world. When she was Cece's age, not a single one of her friends was even in a long-term relationship.

"Well, there's so much to do today!" Elin said as Reece folded herself into the plush white armchair in the corner of the room, "but I can't even focus on the rest of the preparations until I know what I'm wearing." Elin's wardrobe was elegant and exact. Her clothes were feminine and classic: Max Mara, Carolina Herrera, Escada—Ralph Lauren and Michael Kors for a more sporting look. No matter what, Elin always looked pulled together, which made everyone think the best of not only her, but of Thatcher and their children as well: What could ever go wrong under the watch of a woman like that?

"I have it narrowed down: this one," she said, holding up a floral tea-length dress, "or this one," now a teal eyelet sheath dress with a narrow belt around the waist.

"The second one," Reece said decisively. "How many people are coming tonight?"

"We have one hundred and fifty RSVPs," Elin said matter-of-factly, "though you know people *always* show up with extras, especially out here. Someone always has a houseguest who just couldn't possibly fend for themselves for an evening. But what matters is Liberty and Cameron, *obviously*."

Reece knew her friend would not actually enjoy a party in her honor, especially one of that size. She could barely be persuaded to do more than a quiet dinner out for her birthday every year.

"You're quiet this morning, my dear," her mother said when Reece did little more than nod and smile. "What's on your mind?"

She couldn't very well tell her mother that Liberty wouldn't like the party. How strange that Elin would now be her best friend's mother-in-law. Strange, though of course wonderful too, that they would all be a family.

"I'm just a little overwhelmed by all of this. Liberty and Cameron . . . it's just weird."

"It's *weird*?"

"You know what I mean."

"I don't. I would think you'd be elated."

How could Reece explain? Of course she was happy about Liberty and Cameron; there were echoes of the sisterhood of her teenage fantasy. But she was also unsettled, and she couldn't say why. It seemed her brother's affections were a great tide that had lifted Liberty and carried her along. Whether getting married so soon was what Liberty truly wanted and needed, whether she was even ready for this next step, seemed another thing entirely. From the outside, there could be no more perfect match than these two, but one didn't live life from the outside in.

"It just seems fast to be getting married, I guess. Don't you think?"

"Well," Elin huffed, "when you know, you know. And I imagine they'll want to start trying for kids right away. Neither of them is getting any younger."

"Thanks, Mom."

"Oh, sweetheart, you know what I mean. The two of them were meant for each other; *I* could always see it. It just took your brother a little longer to sow his wild oats than one might have hoped."

Reece understood then: Elin not only supported the proposal, she had helped engineer it. Of course her brother hadn't come up with that perfect ring on his own. Left to his own devices, he might have gotten her some giant cliché rock from Tiffany that she would have loathed. But Elin was a woman of details; she would have noticed the stunning vintage jewelry Liberty wore on more formal occasions and would have recognized that that funny little charm bracelet she treasured was actually a valuable estate piece.

"You think they'll be happy together? I love them both so much, you know that."

Now her mother came and knelt down where Reece was sitting.

"I really do, honey," she said, taking her hand, "I know it in my bones."

Privately, Reece considered Elin the smarter of her two parents by a wide margin. She was wise, and though she didn't know everything about Liberty, she had known her a long time. And no one was closer to her brother. Reece felt herself being drawn into her mother's certainty about the match.

∽❧∼

Cameron and Liberty were staying in one of the more secluded guest cottages that featured a small porch looking out onto the ocean. Liberty woke early that morning and curled up in a thick robe with coffee and the novel she was reading. From here, with the grand estate far in the background and no other sign of civilization along the secluded stretch of beach, Liberty could fantasize that she was in some nothing little town on the Atlantic. This was what you paid for in New York: space, peace, the ability to create the illusion of isolation while actually being mere paces from the white-hot center of it all. Liberty was desperate to spend some time alone before the engagement party—for which they were to arrive at the main house no later than six. But before that, Elin had planned a rather full day for her, Liberty, and Petra, who would be arriving with Ben and Birdie that morning: brunch with Reece (thank goodness) and then a preliminary meeting with the house manager about the possibility of having the wedding onsite. No pressure! Just a thought.

Liberty wasn't the kind of woman who'd devoted a lot of time to envisioning her wedding in advance of having one to plan. But when it had crossed her mind—as it inevitably did during the parade of weddings that consumes one's early thirties—she'd envisioned something small and simple. A tiny ceremony with her and her beloved plus a few close friends—somewhere out in nature, the woods, or a lush field—and a beautiful, bountiful dinner, passing hearty dishes along one big table. She understood that with the Michaels family, this sort of wedding would not be an option. But she wasn't so attached to that, was she? She didn't really care that much about the wedding itself, did she? Marrying Cameron was the main thing; as long as that happened, she didn't mind all the fuss. She ardently shoved down the thought that perhaps life with Cameron might follow in much the same line as the wedding preparations were headed: that she might be expected to trade her lifestyle—circumscribed and deliberate—to be by Cameron's side at business dinners, parties, and the innumerable charity events that Elin hosted. Well, they'd compromise, wouldn't they? Introverts and extroverts got married all the time, didn't they? And compromise was how every marriage worked out . . . wasn't it?

⁓

"What if," Birdie began, bringing an immediate smile to Reece's face and weariness to Elin's, "Cameron came in on a white horse? Oh, wouldn't that be divine?"

"It's an idea," Elin smiled flatly. Petra closed her eyes, and Liberty smiled at her aunt.

The house manager nodded cheerfully. "We'll add it to the list!"

"You know they do that in India," she said, pronouncing it *Injia*, as though she'd morphed into a British colonialist. "Indian weddings are so stunning! So colorful! Liberty, wouldn't that be wonderful? Oh, how breathtaking you'd look in a red sari! And the henna: it's magnificent, really."

Liberty took her aunt's arm. "I've never been to an Indian

wedding. But it sounds amazing. Tell me, Birdie, when did you attend one?" And with this she had her aunt off on a story from her past: some boyfriend long ago who she claimed was related to a maharaja.

Elin smiled at her daughter-in-law-to-be. How deftly she'd handled the outrageously tacky suggestion that they appropriate an entire culture's wedding traditions. She was a quiet young woman, Liberty, but smart, poised, and so good for her son. She would be such an asset to him and to the family. Elin moved over next to Petra, as they made their way toward the beach.

"I'm so glad you're here," she said to Petra. "What an incredible time this will be for us all."

Petra smiled at her, a still-dazzling effect. "I'm overjoyed for Liberty. I've been hoping she would find the one, and look, there he is, right under her nose. Between you and me, I'd begun to worry, but you know how it is with these children; you can't tell them anything!"

"Indeed," Elin said. Liberty and Petra looked so similar, and despite their many differences, Elin could see where Liberty had come by her self-contained grace; so unlike that other silly little flip of a daughter and her equally ludicrous though dashingly handsome twin. "Sometimes I think Reece may never come to her senses." She whispered this, leaning into Petra's shoulder, to avoid being heard by her daughter.

"What have these girls got against marriage?" Petra said. "I'll never understand it. I know that some of it, for me, is cultural, of course."

"I am equally as baffled, though Reece tells me she just can't find anyone worth the trouble."

"Then she needs to look harder," Petra said. "Reece is beautiful, and good men have always been hard to come by. You must be deliberate."

"Well, that's certainly true," Elin said. She hazarded a glance at her daughter, walking ahead of them, flanking Birdie, and looking wholly entertained by whatever the old bat was going on about. She hoped her daughter would find love, but in truth, Elin had never worried about Reece. It was always her other child who'd been the source of tumult. Cameron had kept her up nights and at times brought excruciating tension to her own marriage. But that was all in the past now.

～⁕～

For his part, Cameron was thrilled about the giant party his parents were throwing in their honor, as well as the idea of an all-out extravaganza on the day itself. What was the point of a wedding if it wasn't going to be a proper party? Though, of course, none of the wedding *planning* was expected to be his domain, and he spent the day playing golf at Shinnecock Hills with his father and his Harvard buddies. That evening as he and his new fiancée got ready for the party, he was dashing in a dove-gray suit and as cheerful as Liberty had ever seen him.

"I'm so excited for you to finally meet all of my friends from school!" Cameron boomed as Liberty put the final touches on her makeup. She had realized between lunch and that evening that the beachy sundress she'd been thinking of would not be up to snuff for the party Elin had planned. Fortunately, she'd packed a cream Zac Posen maxi dress that looked a lot more formal. Reece had assured her this option would work.

"You look gorgeous," Cameron said as she joined him in the small foyer of the guesthouse. "Wait until they see you."

Though Cameron and Liberty had occasionally run into friends and acquaintances while they were out and about together in New York, they had spent most of their time one-on-one. Group outings and double dates had just seemed beside the point; they were so wrapped up with one another. Liberty, for her part, did not have so many close friends she felt the need to introduce to a fiancé. Namely, there was Reece.

"Will we get along, do you think?" Liberty said as much to herself as to Cameron.

"Are you kidding? They'll love you."

In truth, Liberty wasn't so worried about their liking her, but rather the opposite. The prep-school-turned-Ivy-League sons and daughters of fortune were a crowd she knew well and, for the most part, had assiduously avoided. But perhaps Cameron's friends would be different; if he loved them, perhaps she could as well.

The few minutes that comprised the walk to the main house were the last peaceful ones of the night. The moment Liberty appeared on the grand back patio where the alfresco engagement party was being held, she was shanghaied by Elin who had *oh* so many people she wanted to introduce her to. Liberty heard her and Cameron's much-abbreviated love story told over and over again. There was nary a mention of Liberty's career, her life's work; really, she barely appeared in these conversations. But right, of course it was about *them* not *her* that evening, and Elin was just excited.

At least the Lawrences were there as well. Petra mingled enthusiastically with Ben in tow: both were beaming. In fact, it occurred to Liberty that she'd not seen her father looking so happy in a very long time. Birdie was in a black Roberto Cavalli gown with an orange flame pattern licking up from the hem that she'd purchased for the occasion. It was breathtakingly inappropriate both for the venue and for a woman her age—but everyone at the party adored her, for every family was allowed one Birdie. Nora was busy ordering Larry around, lately her favorite pastime, and Leo seemed content to let Elin's female friends make fools of themselves by flirting with him.

Cameron spent most of the evening surrounded by a deep circle of his rowing buddies. At some point he stole his bride-to-be away from his mother in order to introduce Liberty to the pack of aging but still strapping jocks before their wives and girlfriends carried her off. The men clapped Cameron on the back and told him he was a lucky bastard.

"Your and Cameron's love story is just *so* cute," one of the women—also recently engaged and therefore consumed with wedding giddiness—said to Liberty when they were sufficiently far from the menfolk. Was her name Kate? Kit? Kat? Something. "I mean, David and I just met through friends at a benefit. Boring!"

Liberty had come to understand that her "love story" with Cameron was that he had always adored her but had waited until he knew he could be the man she needed before making his move. Of course, as she saw it, she had been the one with the early crush. Then they'd formed a friendship that had become something more. But she supposed everyone's love story was glossed with a convenient layer of fiction at some point. Real love was complicated. Love did not make for tidy anecdotes. There was a *Times* reporter there that evening, and Liberty knew which version was likely to end up in print.

"Cameron's such a catch," a horsey blonde named Lauren said. "I guess now we know why he never settled down." Her voice sounded a little bitter. If the couples were correct in Liberty's head, she was married to one of Cameron's Wall Street buddies, who was tall and muscular but with a rather unfortunate face that featured an odd, crooked nose and eyes a bit too close together. Jesus, Liberty thought, where was Reece?

"Because he was already in love with Liberty!" Kit, Kat, Kate chimed in, clasping her hands to her heart and sending the row of Hermès bangles on her wrist clattering.

"Yes, well," Liberty said, "we've known each other a long time. But we were friends first; I think that's important."

"When's the date? You'll get married here? Such a good choice; it's so gross when people choose a 'venue.' Like, do you want to have your *wedding* someplace other people have had theirs? Not special. It'd be like wearing a used wedding gown. Bad karma. I learned so much about that in my Buddhist retreat this spring; it was so life changing."

"Oh, we don't have a date yet. We're not in that much of a hurry," Liberty said. They'd spoken vaguely of next summer, though having spent the day with Elin, she felt certain she would push for spring at least.

"You need to lock down your date!" a third girl chimed in. They stood around Liberty in a circle, and suddenly she felt as though she were surrounded by wolves. "You don't want the good vendors to book up. And you have to get on Maurizio's calendar early."

"Maurizio?"

"The only wedding planner you should use in the Hamptons! I can put in a call, but I don't know. It just depends."

The conversation went on like this, and Liberty found, to her relief, that it was better if she mostly smiled and nodded. She found after twenty minutes or so she was even picking up their cadence: *totally, ohmigod, thank you so much! Super excited.*

Fantasies of elopement played wildly in her mind as she counted the minutes to the party's end.

～♈～

Laila wore the LOVE bracelet that night, but it suddenly felt insubstantial on her wrist. The day she'd received it, she felt it said to the world: *I am loved*, but now she silently heard those words followed by: *but not enough*. For a girlfriend, even a live-in one, was a disposable thing, she knew. A fiancée, a wife, was so much less so. There were legal ties and of course, perhaps even more crucial, financial ones. They were in the Montauk house that weekend, and as they prepared to head out to Lily Pond, Laila felt a flash of desperation to stay put.

"I'm happy for your cousin," Blake said as he fastened his cufflinks, "I always liked her."

Laila felt a sudden paranoid flash: *Liked her?* But no, of course Blake meant nothing by that. He was as straightlaced as a choirboy. He paid parking tickets immediately, probably didn't have so much as a late library book in his past.

"I am too. I'm nervous about tonight, though."

"Why, because of Nora? She'll get over it," Blake said, taking her shoulders in his hands in his fatherly way. "Just give it time."

Laila was not so certain that she would. She hadn't spoken to her since she'd moved out. Tonight at Liberty's engagement party would be the first time they'd seen each other in weeks.

"I hope you're right." Laila was surprised by the fact that she actually missed Nora. She was a silly creature, but Laila had grown accustomed to her warmth, her company.

But if she had to choose between Blake and Nora, she knew she'd chosen right. Laila had been living with Blake for nearly a month by then, and thus far it was going as smoothly as she could have hoped. He had come home from a long day at work earlier that week, sexy as anything in his sharp suit, and looked a little bemused as he took in the colorful throws and pillows that Laila had added to his pristine white couch.

"You don't like them."

"It's just different," he said, "but no, I do like them. I want you to feel at home here; I want you to *be* at home here."

Yet she could feel his discomfort. Of course, he had never lived with a woman before. And she had never dated a man her own age before. Suddenly, the difference between him and her former boyfriends was showing. An older man had spent more time with himself, become more set in his ways and less anxious about letting both his flaws and his needs show through. Her former lovers were so predictable; but she realized Blake could not himself predict how he would react to all things, so how, then, could Laila anticipate it? Nathan and Tom had been so comfortingly *obvious* that it hadn't been hard to keep them happy, at least for as long as Laila was interested in doing so. She'd so easily convinced them that her own happiness was to be found in theirs; therefore they didn't see it when she'd grown restless and were blindsided by her departure.

And there were many more wonderful moments with Blake than awkward ones, with ecstatic sex in all parts of the apartment, including the balcony that faced onto the Hudson. They cooked meals together in his kitchen—both of them novices who laughed over their mishaps—and in those moments watching him carefully sautéing mushrooms, Laila felt certain of all of the choices that had led her here.

When they slept side by side at night, she could feel herself cleaving to him, as if she were trying to keep him from escaping. The feeling unsettled her. In her last few relationships, she'd been the younger, sexier one, and in that she'd had the upper hand. She'd never been with someone so many other people wanted. He seemed blissfully unaware of just how many women would kill to be on his arm, but Laila saw them: they were everywhere, from female acquaintances of his to the girl at Bergdorf's who sold him his suits to the waitress at the diner below his apartment. She knew what she had.

Something else lurked in the dark corner of her mind. Every so often it would skitter out from the shadows, and she would wake up in a cold sweat. Cameron. At times, she could almost convince herself that these interludes had not even happened at all; that they had simply been vivid dreams. But tonight, they would all be in the same room for the first time.

"Are you . . . ?" Blake began when Laila walked out of the master bathroom of the Montauk house dressed for the evening. He caught his words before they could leave his mouth, something he occasionally did that drove Laila crazy; she'd rather just know what the second half of the original sentence had been.

"Am I what?" She found she was immediately on the defensive, as she knew what he was reacting to. She had brought two options for the evening: a sweet Marc Jacobs floral-patterned dress and the one she'd chosen, a bright blue Hervé Léger with a plunging back.

"Your dress. I mean, you look gorgeous, but . . ."

She cocked her head at him, daring him to continue. "The invite said cocktail attire. This is a cocktail dress."

He cleared his throat and appeared to be weighing his options. What he could not have known was that every other suitable dress

Laila owned, including the Marc Jacobs, had been purchased for her by Nora. The dress she'd chosen was one she'd picked up during a trip to Century 21—the lower Manhattan discount luxury mall—with Cece. She'd ferreted out this find and had been saving it for she knew not what. She knew that people would think it was too sexy for the occasion, but she'd rather have Cameron's friends think she was a slut than give Nora the satisfaction of seeing her in a dress she'd bought for her. It was the kind of thing that Nora would certainly remember.

"Your pashmina," Blake said, "you should bring it. It can get chilly on the water."

⤳⦿⤳

The night had been going exceptionally well. Cameron's friends' wives could be bitches, but they clearly adored Liberty. He loved that she was not some social butterfly everyone in his circle already knew. Many of his friends had even previously dated each other's eventual wives; their romantic lives a tedious game of musical chairs that ended in marriage once their families grew impatient. But Liberty was his special secret, and she'd never looked more radiant. Each time he looked at her, standing surrounded by the other women, he cataloged the ways in which she outshined them. Her elegant style; her beautiful features that required only the tiniest touch of makeup. Her shy smile; her soft laugh. And of course, she was smarter than all of them put together. He loved that about her; it reflected well upon him. His father had always adored his smart wife—and he clearly approved of the match. He even admired her ambition, though Liberty eventually was going to have to ease up on the job a bit. Liberty was quite attached to her career, but a woman's perspective changed when she got married. He'd seen it with his friends.

The only threat to his happiness that night had materialized in the form of Laila, who—though she came on the arm of another man—was looking every bit the mistress. What was she thinking wearing that *dress*? What was her angle? He'd hoped that given her falling-out with Nora, and by association, Leo, that she wouldn't show up, but of course she had. Maddeningly, Liberty hadn't distanced herself, and even appeared to be trying to smooth things over between Laila and the twins.

He knew Blake Katz only a little, but he couldn't imagine he was serious about Laila. But then, he was young; he didn't need to be serious about anyone.

"Jesus Christ," his friend Mike said when he caught sight of her coming through the door, "that's the cousin?"

"Yes," Cameron said tersely; he could not be seen to have any opinion on Laila whatsoever.

"Fuck me," said another friend, Baron, "and I mean that literally."

"Don't be a pig, Baron; she's Liberty's family."

"I'm pretty sure that's the reaction she was going for in that dress."

The two did not collide until late that evening, after Cameron had had many drinks. He had not seen Liberty in at least an hour, and he figured she'd gone off with his sister, who had also disappeared. Laila was sitting on her own near the edge of the party, where the café lights were strung to delineate the space from the small expanse of lawn that remained between it and the rise of sand that led to the beach. She deliberately ignored Cameron as he ambled up to her in the darkness. He sat next to her and was silent for a long moment.

"Nice dress," he said at last.

"Fuck you, Cameron," she said, pulling the suit jacket that was draped across her shoulders—presumably Blake's—tighter.

"Loud and clear. Were you hoping I'd pull you off into a dark corner somewhere tonight? Bend you over a barrel in the wine cellar, maybe?"

"You're disgusting. And what I wear is none of your concern. Blake loves this dress, and his opinion happens to be the only one I care about."

This, Cameron answered with a cruel laugh. "I'm sure he does, my dear; I'm sure he does."

~~~

"Can you *believe* her?" Nora said when Laila arrived, pulling her brother in close the moment Larry had been dispatched to fetch them drinks.

"Laundry day?" Leo said, scrunching his nose. His cousin looked dressed for a regrettable night at Bagatelle, not a summer engagement party on the water.

"I can't believe that's what Blake is into these days. I thought he had some class."

"Oh, forget Blake." Leo had no problem taking sides. "You're better off without him, my love. And her."

Leo knew that in reality, his sister missed her cousin. Her betrayal had broken her heart, and then Larry had come in to save the day. Nora had acquiesced to his love then, but she was still bitter.

"It's, like, she doesn't even care! I feel like she wore that dress just to rub it in my face. Like, I get it; you're hotter than me, okay?"

"Oh, stop it," Leo said, putting his arm around her, "she is not hotter than you! You're the most beautiful girl in the room." Of course this was a lie, but it was one he felt obligated to tell. He and his sister's language was one of fantastical stories and hyperbole: it had been since childhood. They always loved each other best and found their ways of reminding one another.

But Leo could feel in the air that night that some era was ending. Liberty, engaged. Nora seemed likely to be next. Larry so loved her, so treasured her. Leo found himself endeared by the oddball fellow, with his lisp and his terrible hair. He'd made such an effort with Leo, reading books Leo liked, remembering all of his favorite foods and drinks in addition to Nora's—always asking after his work. And his *work*—was this all he had left now? His e-mails from his editor at Random House had become increasingly insistent. They'd moved the publication twice now. He'd have to either write it or hire someone soon.

It occurred to him as he watched his older sister—poised in the face of this ostentatious party—that they all had to grow up someday.

ॐ

Laila clung to Blake's arm whenever possible throughout the evening. The dress had been a mistake. Yes, it would have been a touch humiliating to wear a dress Nora had bought her, but as it was, she might as well have been walking through the party naked. She'd caught a brief but unmistakable flash of dismay on her aunt Petra's face as she said hello. But Petra beamed over Blake, as everyone did. So, at least if Laila could keep him close— now, tonight, forever—she could benefit from his golden-boy glow.

"Hey, Katz, how's Mr. Media Titan?" This was Topper, a Harvard friend of Cameron's. Blake introduced Laila, and he gave her a wolfish grin.

"Well, hello," he said.

"Hi," Laila said coldly. Topper launched into a litany of story ideas he felt Blake should consider, and though he didn't say another word to Laila, his eyes were never far from the neckline of her dress. She felt a slow flush of humiliation creep over her.

"Oh, Laila, my darling!"

Her aunt Birdie swept in, looking like the proverbial phoenix, outshining Laila for worst dressed of the party. She clutched her niece's hand.

"I haven't had a moment with you all night! Come, let's get your auntie a drink before I sober up!"

She swept Laila away and nearly collided with a waiter carrying champagne. "Oh, thank goodness!" Birdie said, plucking two glasses from his tray. "This will do for the moment, but do be a dear and get me a martini. Straight up, three olives, oh, thank you, pet."

"Yes, ma'am," the waiter said.

"Come sit down with your poor auntie; my feet are killing me!"

Laila felt relieved to be sitting with her eccentric aunt at the edge of the party. Birdie was always entertaining, but tonight, they were two of a kind—though Laila hoped this didn't portend anything more than a wardrobe mishap for her future.

"Oh, what a beautiful night! I am so thrilled for your cousin, with that dashing fiancé of hers. And *you*, what a catch you've got as well! You're smart, you girls. Smarter than I was. I was a looker when I was younger, you know—not like Liberty, mind you, but still, I should have married then. But no one could keep up with me!" she added delightedly.

"You could still find love, Aunt Birdie. It's never too late," Laila said, only half-listening.

"Yes, perhaps. Maybe one of these gorgeous young bucks here tonight. Put a little pep in my step, what do you suppose?"

Laila laughed. "I think they'd be lucky to have you."

"Yes, perhaps a little boy toy. Indeed." She took a swig of her champagne. "Oh, darling, I'm mostly overjoyed that you're here to celebrate with us. All the little hens back in the nest at last." Birdie reached for Laila's hands, and despite her aunt's tipsiness, Laila detected sincerity in her gaze. "I always missed you, you know. I never approved of how the . . . situation with your parents was handled. What a blasted mess my father could make of things. Though I miss him terribly, I do; I suppose we're doomed to love our fathers no matter how flawed, though, aren't we? And you, you poor thing, you never even got to meet him!"

Laila tried to keep her expression passive as she absorbed what her aunt was saying. Birdie had known all along too. But of course she had—and indeed, this fit into the likely sequence of events Laila had formulated over the months she'd been in New York. Her parents had come to the city. Frederick had taken up with Betsy. The lovers had been discovered, and the lines had been drawn. Gregory had taken Betsy back to Michigan, and his siblings, in their cowardice, had sided with Frederick: the all-powerful patriarch who had grown ever larger and more godlike in Laila's imagination.

By now, Birdie's mood had turned maudlin, and she squeezed Laila's hand in hers: her fingers were slender and bony, and she wore a number of ostentatious cocktail rings—the overall effect was less than comforting and more like having one's hand caught in the talons of a large bird. Birdie.

"But I thought of you. I kept you in my heart, sent out constant good energy to you in my meditations. It was just all so impossible; you understand that, don't you, love?"

"Of course, Aunt Birdie. Please don't worry about it." Why this outpouring now? It must be the impending wedding; it had whipped her into an emotional fervor. Still, Laila couldn't understand, would never completely forgive their collective silence. Why not reach out to her? Her parents were *dead*. Why hadn't the elder Lawrences come for her sooner? Why leave it all to Liberty who knew nothing of the backstory? It seemed unspeakably cruel. But Laila knew better than to lay this at the feet of her eccentric aunt. Instead she simply said, "I only wish I'd gotten to know you all earlier. To grow up being a part of this family, that's all."

"Oh, I know, darling. I wish it too. I'm sure you were the sweetest little thing. But you must understand, the business with Betsy and Papa was bad enough, but then when your mother got pregnant! It would have been such a scandal had they stayed. And anyways: my dear brother, he just couldn't go on living here, knowing what he knew. It was his decision to leave. What more could we do?"

The horizon line seemed to tilt, and Laila felt as though she'd been kicked in the gut. Her mother had already been pregnant when she'd left New York? She'd never really studied the dates on the little cards Betsy had saved, only noting that they were from the year before she was born. But what Birdie was suggesting was something Laila had never considered. She now saw her aunts' and uncles' silence for what it was—fear that their father's indiscretion might have had permanent consequences that went beyond Gregory's estrangement.

"Oh, what a dear fellow you are," Aunt Birdie said, her good cheer restored, as the baby-faced waiter returned with her martini.

"Anything for you, miss?"

Laila shook her head; she'd barely had more than a sip of her champagne. He nodded and disappeared back into the night.

"Well, sweetheart, we mustn't focus on the past, must we? Onward! The future is bright and beautiful."

～ॐ～

"How has your night been?"

"Good; it was so sweet of your mom to throw this party. I love it."

Reece laughed. "Stop it! No security cameras out here, babe."

After the endless rounds of introductions, the small talk, and the speeches, Reece had stolen Liberty away to her guesthouse, where they now sat smoking cigarettes—something they hadn't done since they were teenagers—on the roof. Reece would have attempted to save Liberty from the Stepford wives earlier on in the night, but her own mother seemed hell-bent on presenting her daughter to every single man at the party under the age of fifty—of whom there were a curious amount in attendance. Reece suspected her mother had done some recruiting. The message was clear: she was up next. So she'd grabbed Liberty at the first opportunity, and they'd snuck off to the roof, a beautiful and serene spot where the ocean's roar nearly drowned out the din of the party.

"Okay, it's been exhausting. But I am grateful. I know your mom worked hard."

Reece nodded. The words she'd been mulling all night were at the tip of her tongue. "Cam should have pushed back on this, though."

"I didn't tell him to."

"You shouldn't have to; he knows you hate big parties."

Liberty took a long drag of her cigarette. "It's nice that he's excited, though, right? I mean, I didn't want to be a wet blanket."

Reece could see it then so clearly: polite, easygoing Liberty at the mercy of her domineering mother.

"Just don't let the whole thing get away from you," she said, looking out into the miles of dark ocean before them. "I love my mom, but she's kind of a handful."

Liberty laughed. "Can I tell you something? There were times I wished she was my mom when we were growing up."

"Really?" Reece propped herself up on her elbow.

"Yeah. Don't sound so shocked. You know I love my mother, but she's . . ." Liberty gestured with her cigarette, looking for the right word.

"A Siberian Ice Queen?"

"Well, yeah. And your mom, she was always warm, always inviting. Like, she *cooked* for you guys."

"The hostess with the mostest."

Liberty laughed.

"Well, you didn't see the other side. Elin likes things to go according to plan. *Her* plan, mind you. Cameron is obviously going to be no help, so if she gets too pushy about the wedding stuff, tell me. Okay?"

"Deal," Liberty said, lying back to gaze up at the heavy blanket of stars.

❧

"Leo, you're so bad for bringing that old cougar with us," Nora said, leaning into his side, cuddling against him. They watched as Marissa, one of Elin's tennis friends—newly divorced and in her late forties—tottered off toward the bathroom line, which at this time of night at Pink Elephant was a mile long.

"Why is it okay for you to age up and not me?" Leo said with a smirk.

"It's different," Nora said simply. "Goddamn it," she said, "I'm freezing!"

"Do you want to go inside?" Leo asked.

"No, I like it out here; can we just get that space heater working?"

Leo looked around for somewhere else on the patio to sit, but it was busy, and space was scarce.

"Do you want my jacket?"

"I don't want to cover up my dress! Leo, please."

"Okay," he said. He saw that Larry was approaching, followed by a bottle-service girl, who would certainly be of no use. "Let me go find someone. Here comes Larry; you sit tight."

He made his way into the hazy nightclub where people were moving, sweating, flirting, taking shots, tracking sand in from outside.

"Leeeeoooooooooo!"

He turned in the direction of the voice and saw a very intoxicated friend of his—some model girl he'd met at a dozen parties—standing and bellowing at him from a corner booth.

"Ashley! Hey," Leo said, distracted immediately from his other mission.

"Leo!" she said, nearly tripping over the feet of the other model-y-looking girls, whose long slender legs created a precarious web around their booth's table. *"Hiyyeee!"* She flung her arms around him.

At the center of the klatch of models sat an older man in an expensive linen suit; Leo thought he recognized him. But really, there were so many of these filthy-rich old bastards in places like this, sitting among their collected little harems. Like gorgons.

"Leo," Ashley said, attempting to straighten herself, "you know Simon?"

"Of course," Leo said, leaning forward to shake the man's hand, who remained sitting. "Simon Beauchamp, Leo Lawrence."

"Ah yes," he said, sounding unimpressed. Leo suspected he did not appreciate his diverting Ashley's attention. The other girls at the table seemed nearly inanimate: Leo suspected they'd not yet done as much coke as Ashley clearly had.

"I didn't know you'd be out tonight," Ashley said, practically yelling over the music, "you should have texted me."

"It was last-minute," Leo said, leaning in so she could hear him. He felt Simon's eyes following him. "We were out in South for my sister's engagement party."

"Ohmigosh! Your sister in engaged! That's *amazing*! To *who*?"

"Yeah, it's great. Cameron Michaels. Good guy; we've all known each other for years. . . ."

"Cameron Michaels?" Simon was getting to his feet. He was a tall man, imposing.

"Uh, yes. They've been dating a while."

"And they're engaged?" Simon reiterated. Leo couldn't fathom why he cared.

"Yeah." Suddenly, Ashley or no, Leo wanted to get out of there. "Well, I'd better go back to my sister. Come say hi if you want. Simon, nice to see you."

"Likewise," he said, giving Leo a strange look.

24

THOSE MOMENTS that precede a catastrophe are always the calmest in our memories; whatever quotidian worries we were gnashing between our teeth before are blown to dust in our recollections. Therefore Laila would remember the Tuesday that followed Liberty and Cameron's engagement party as a peaceful one. Blake had gone to the office early, as he normally did; Laila had drawn out her morning over the manuscript she was meant to be delivering notes on later that day. She'd been taking on more for the agency lately in order to make the job seem more legitimate to Blake. He had no tolerance for the idle rich (or in her case, idle broke), and she knew she needed to appear industrious.

That day, she'd decided she would take her pile of critiques directly to Liberty's office herself rather than simply e-mailing them. Now that she lived uptown with Blake, she worked from home more frequently, but she was anxious to see her cousin that day—of course this would seem portentous later. In reality, she'd just wanted to see Liberty to reassure herself; she'd barely gotten a moment with her at the engagement party. She was unnerved by her encounter with Cameron that night. He'd seemed angry that she'd been there, but what did he expect? Did he think he could now claim complete dominion over her cousin's life? Probably so.

Liberty had not been at the office when Laila had stopped

by—she'd been sitting in on a marketing meeting at Simon & Schuster for one of her bigger clients—and the new assistant had taken the notes on her behalf. Laila felt a pang of regret that she hadn't taken the job when she noticed the imperious way the new girl looked at her; the possessive way she rattled off Liberty's schedule for the day. Laila was suddenly nostalgic for the intern position that had kept her at her cousin's right hand.

With nothing to do with the rest of the afternoon, she headed down to the Agent Provocateur on Mercer Street and left with an outré new lingerie set to surprise Blake with that weekend. He was often too exhausted to have sex on weeknights, so she felt as if she needed to raise the stakes over the weekends.

By evening, Laila was curled up in their bed reading a copy of *Vanity Fair*, a glass of wine on the nightstand. Blake often came home late on weekdays. He usually texted her to let her know he'd be having dinner at the office, and he hadn't done so that evening, but this in itself was nothing to worry about. This was simply an inconvenience of being with an important man, and Laila was nothing if not self-sufficient. She had been nodding off a little when she was jolted awake by the sound of Blake's key turning in the front door, by the heavy footsteps that brought him to their bedroom.

"Hi, honey, you coming to bed?" Laila said absently, as he opened the door.

He stood there silently; his face looked pale, and his expression was ominous. Laila felt as though a chill had instantly spread throughout the room.

"What's wrong, my love?"

He would come no farther than the threshold, and he leaned against the doorjamb as though to steady himself.

"You and Cameron?"

And then it was as if time slowed, nearly ground to a halt.

"Liberty's fiancé, Cameron?" She laughed for good measure, though her heart was pounding so loud she felt she could barely breathe. "I barely know him. What about him?"

Blake was alarmingly quiet. He walked forward—near enough to touch her now, excruciatingly close—and handed her his phone. "Scroll to the right," he said.

Laila's hand betrayed her by shaking as she reached for the phone. She could barely steady her finger as it landed on the screen. The first photo was shadowy, but the subsequent images revealed Laila's petite form pressed against the wall of the dimly lit hallway at the Box, and then another with her legs wrapped around Cameron's torso, his face showing perfectly in profile. Laila could feel herself starting to panic. She centered herself and regained her focus, looking back at him as though exasperated.

"It was from before we were together. Are you going to judge me for having a life before you? Talk about unfair."

"Laila, the time stamp. It was while I was in London."

A new wave of dizzy panic swept over her. Who sent that to him? Did it matter?

"What I mean is," she took a deep breath, "it was before we were living together. Before we were serious."

"Laila," he said, stepping toward her, almost menacing. "We talked about this in Montauk. Cheating is the one thing I can't . . . and your cousin's fiancé?" She realized with horror that he was choking back tears. Why now, months after the fact? Why had this invisible enemy waited until now to share the photo? Things were over with Cameron.

"Blake." She reached for him, and he snapped backward. His disgust was plain.

"I can't," he said. "I'm going to sleep on the couch tonight. Tomorrow . . ."

He didn't even need to finish his sentence, Laila knew. She was no longer welcome here.

She got out of bed and followed him into the other room. The chilled air of the AC hit the thin silk of her nightgown. She felt raw.

"It's over? Just like that?"

"Laila, I told you. I can't deal with cheating. You're not who I thought, who I *hoped*, you were." There was no rage in his voice, only retreat, only disbelief. He was becoming more remote by the second.

"But . . ." She wanted to cite technicalities; anything to change his mind. But she wasn't trying to convince a judge. "Blake, I would never do that again. Not now. I didn't really believe that you loved me then; I was scared!"

He was on the couch with his hands between his knees, tears in his eyes.

"Oh, but I did, Laila. I did."

She sat next to him and tried to peel his arms away and kiss him. Sometimes, moments like this could be saved by funneling all the feelings into sex, letting the lines blur between the passion of anger and the passion of lust.

"No," he said, getting up and pulling away as though her touch had burned him. "Actually, I think you should go to your cousins' tonight."

As though she couldn't even be trusted to stay in the apartment. And suddenly she too was desperate to be gone. She dressed hurriedly, grabbed her purse, and left.

So this, then, was the nadir? Blake, her last chance. Gone. She called Liberty, but she didn't answer. She probably had her phone turned off, was absorbed in a book. Laila decided she would go over to her place. It was a Tuesday night; she doubted she'd be out. Laila's mind raced: What had she done? *What* had she done? Then another terrible thought washed over her: What if her cousin had also received the pictures?

Liberty would never forgive her. It would certainly end the engagement. And her relationship with her family? Over. In one night, Laila realized that she might have obliterated every last relationship in her life. She had always *felt* alone, but now she might truly have no one. She barely heard her own voice as she told the cabdriver the address of Liberty's apartment. Her mind spun: That night at the Box, who'd been there? Cece? But no, she was her friend, why would she? And then a detail emerged from the hazy, champagne-soaked memory of the night: in that sea of beautiful people, his face emerging like an augury of doom. Simon. But *why*? Well, revenge was always enough for men like him, wasn't it? Was she imagining that she'd passed by one of those tittering, breakable-looking girls he was with when she was in that hallway with Cameron? She suddenly felt a stomach-churning certainty that she had.

Liberty still hadn't answered her phone by the time Laila had arrived at her apartment. She held on to the hope that her cousin did not know. Laila dialed her apartment from the dingy call box. No answer. She nearly collided with the man who was leaving; Laila's eyes were so blurry with tears that she barely recognized him at first.

"You okay?" he asked, holding the door open for her.

"Yes, thanks." She tried to compose herself. It was the beautiful bartender from Trapdoor. What he'd been doing in the apartment building, Laila had no idea.

As she made her way up the stairs, she started sobbing uncontrollably. She knocked on Liberty's door, but there was no answer. Laila suddenly remembered that she still had her key from earlier in the month, when Cameron had taken Liberty upstate to a B&B for a few days, and Laila had stopped by to feed Catniss.

Laila turned her key in the lock and pushed, calling Liberty's name.

As she opened the door, the world fell out from under her.

25

REECE WOKE to her phone trilling the symphonic ringtone she used for numbers not in her contacts. This was normally her cue to ignore the call, but who would be calling her at 6:30 a.m.? Her alarm would not sound for another hour, and all she wanted was to disappear back into the soft, plush cave of her bedding. She stared at the phone: a 313 number. What? The phone stopped ringing, only to skip over voice mail and begin ringing again. Now her curiosity got the better of her.

"Hello?" she said groggily.

Laila's voice was weak and raw on the other end of the phone. "Reece?"

"Laila, what is it?" she shot up in bed.

❧

Reece later became convinced that she'd known everything in that split second before the words could tumble out of Laila's mouth. Her best friend, the person she loved most, remained in the land of the living only by a small thread.

The family was clustered in the waiting room of the hospital looking shell-shocked. Cameron was already there; Reece had called him on her way. Laila had spent the night at the police station, answering questions. She'd been the one to find Liberty.

Cameron walked silently beside his sister into Liberty's room.

The sight of her friend nearly made Reece's knees buckle. Her face was swollen beyond recognition, and a series of tubes ran in and out of her mouth and nostrils; a cacophony of machines beeped and whirred around her. Reece let her brother fold her into his arms.

"I don't . . . what . . . how?"

"Laila found her," Cameron choked out in his dry and wasted voice. "She was supposed to be with me, but we'd gotten into an argument . . . about the wedding. Oh God, it was so stupid!"

"Who did this to her?" Reece's voice was tinged with rage.

Cameron shook his head. "The police have a couple of leads. Laila was up all night talking to them."

"But why? Why would anyone hurt her?"

Cameron let the unanswerable question hang there.

Reece had a busy day ahead of her at work, but suddenly the idea of being anywhere other than here—by Liberty's side as she inhabited the unknowable space between life and death—felt ridiculous. She called her assistant and told her that she was in the midst of a family emergency and would be out all that day, possibly the next. That it was a *family* emergency felt true. She hardly remembered what it was like not to have Liberty as her closest confidante. In many ways, she'd been more of a sibling than Cameron had; they'd been the witnesses of each other's coming of age. She could not fathom losing her.

The three days that followed were a unique kind of hell, during which the Lawrence and Michaels families shuttled between the hospital, the Jane hotel where they were spending a few fitful hours each night trying to sleep, and the police station where they answered endless questions trying to help the detectives put together a picture of what had happened. A blow to the back of her head had caused an acute subdural hematoma. Given where the police had found her, they surmised that Liberty might have fallen in such a way that her head struck the pointed edge of the kitchen counter. She'd also been struck hard across the face; one of her cheekbones was shattered.

Reece felt comforted by Detective Neely, the officer investigating the case. He was confident and kind, fatherly. Cameron, being Liberty's fiancé, was questioned especially thoroughly, and he was the picture of polite cooperation. Reece knew that this was standard procedure, but it still made her shiver that anyone could think of her brother being responsible. Her heart broke for Cameron. That his last words to Liberty before leaving her had been ones of anger was a regret unimaginable. She could see it in his haunted expression as he gazed at her in her hospital bed.

Their mother, Elin, rose to the occasion with grace as she was wont to do, speaking to the police on multiple occasions, charming them, even. She acted as a surrogate for Ben and Petra, who were so shattered they could barely speak. Petra seemed to have aged decades in a matter of days. It was as though whatever icy reserve had kept her so pristine had at last given way. She was as beautiful as ever, but all of her hard edges seemed to soften at once, and she collapsed into Ben's arms periodically. Nora had come to see her sister the first morning but had become so hysterical that she'd had to leave swiftly thereafter. Leo went with her, shooing the hapless Larry away.

"Why, why would anyone do this to my baby?" Petra asked again and again: to Reece, to the cops, to no one. Elin was her champion: the mothers had grown closer since the engagement, and now Elin handily took the lead with the cops. Reece was proud of her mother, admired her strength, her calm at the eye of the storm.

"The poor darlings have been under so much pressure," Elin told the police, confirming that her son had come to seek her counsel after his argument with his fiancée. "They love each other so much, but being newly engaged, preparing to take on all of this wedding planning, it's stressful! I remember planning our own, goodness, Thatcher and I never fought half so much. And we just wanted them to be happy, of course. We still do!"

Laila kept a near-constant vigil at her cousin's bedside. Liberty had gone into emergency surgery to drain the blood from her brain the night Laila had found her, but she had not regained consciousness, and her prognosis was bleak. Reece knew that Laila was on the outs with her other cousins, and she felt for the girl. If she'd made some questionable choices with men since arriving in New York, well, Jesus, who hadn't? And she was twenty-five, for God's sake; a hall pass seemed in order. Any grievance seemed so petty in light of what had happened.

"I'm going to go get coffee," Reece said to Laila, putting her hand on the younger woman's shoulder. It was the middle of the third—or was it the fourth? The hundredth?—afternoon as they sat with Liberty. "Can I get you some?"

"That's sweet; you don't have to." Laila looked up at Reece with a sad, beleaguered expression.

"You look exhausted," she ventured. Laila's red-rimmed eyes had deep purple circles beneath them, and her skin looked sallow, as though she'd not seen the sun in months. "Why don't I bring you a cappuccino?"

"Actually, that sounds amazing," Laila said.

Reece's coffee mission took longer than expected. A helpful

nurse warned her away from the drip coffee they served in the cafeteria and told her of an espresso stand in the main lobby that was much better. It felt shockingly good to have, if only for a few moments, a simple and accomplishable task. It was a brief respite from the waiting, the interminable hoping that Liberty would recover. Even if she recovered, there was also the horror of how different she might be following such a serious brain injury: the question of how much of her had already slipped away from the world, never to return.

Horrifyingly, the prime suspect who'd emerged was Sean Calloway, aka Bartender Sean, whom Laila had seen leaving the building right before finding Liberty. There was apparently damning enough evidence that he'd been placed under arrest, and having been deemed a flight risk, he was being held in police custody with bail set at $5 million dollars. Security cameras had him entering an hour earlier. He claimed he'd been there to see a friend, but the woman he named claimed to have no knowledge of him other than from Trapdoor, where she and her husband occasionally went to have a drink. The thought that she herself had flirted with this man horrified Reece. How easily we'll look past a person's fatal flaws if their beauty is striking enough. Why he would hurt Liberty was unfathomable; but Reece had been on the earth as a woman long enough to understand that sometimes, this was reason enough. As Reece made her way back down the dreary, antiseptic corridor that led to Liberty's room, she tried to shake Sean's face from her mind but found it stayed stubbornly in place. Of course, now that she thought about it, it was eerie the way he looked at her. Obsessive, even. But how was one ever to suspect what dark thoughts strange men might harbor?

As she rounded the door frame, she heard the familiar sound of her brother's voice, speaking now in a hushed whisper.

"I mean it, Laila," she heard him hiss.

"Cameron," Reece said loudly, announcing her arrival in the room where her brother and Laila stood side by side a mere foot from Liberty's bedside. His face turned toward her, and she caught the tiniest flash of shock before it disappeared, and he came to hug her.

He offered no explanation for what she'd overheard, and the moment disappeared so quickly that Reece wondered if she'd imagined it. She'd barely slept in days; hallucinating did not seem entirely out of the question. Back in the room, the three were once more consumed by their grief over Liberty, who was there in body but already beginning to slip from them.

She did not last the night.

26

"YOU'RE GOING to be great; you look phenomenal."

Laila glowed from the praise of ebullient morning-show host Megan Capshaw, whom she'd only met moments before in the greenroom. Her signature blond bob was inconceivably shiny, and her skin appeared practically poreless, her legendary legs smooth and tan. Laila had chosen her first interview with care. America's Sweetheart and trusted voice of empathy, a doll but a real reporter nonetheless—one people trusted to ask questions that hit just hard enough.

"I'm nervous," Laila said, smiling back at the host from the makeup chair where she was being powdered into near oblivion in preparation to appear underneath the broiling lights of the morning show's set.

"It's okay, everyone is before they go on. But you'll be fine. You're so poised!"

Laila knew that there was no going back from this moment, but she was running out of options. With Liberty's death had gone what seemed like Laila's last shot at being truly taken into the family fold. And for all of her careful planning, and her generally responsible nature, Liberty had not yet made a will—meaning all she owned, including Frederick's vast inheritance, would go to her parents.

Laila had pleaded with Blake to give her another chance, but, though admirably supportive and kind about the family's tragedy, he had made it clear he was done with her. Laila had $500 to her name. It felt as though the rest of the family had practically forgotten that she existed since her cousin's death, so deep were they in their grief. Well, they would remember her now. The highest offer had come from the *Post*, but Laila had chosen the far classier *Morning in America* to give her exclusive interview to. Sean Calloway still sat in prison awaiting trial. After the bail hearing, the press started to dig, and it turned out Calloway had a rather long and damning rap sheet: domestic violence, unpaid child support, assault. The tabloids had a heyday. The headlines were dominated by Liberty for the rest of the summer and into the early fall, but the frenzy wouldn't last: everyone would move on to something else, and Laila's take would decrease in value accordingly. She had only these few cards left, and she didn't mean to waste them.

"And the dress is good?" Laila said now, smoothing out the skirt of her blue cap-sleeved Michel Kors dress. She'd wanted to wear black to emphasize her grief, but black didn't work on television, the producer told her.

"It's perfect! Okay, are you ready?"

"As ready as I'm going to be," Laila said.

Megan winked at her, and with that, she went out onstage to greet the audience, leaving Laila alone in the wings. A producer steered her to a chair where she could watch the monitor as Megan opened the segment. The date at the bottom caught her eye: September 18. Almost a year to the day since she'd arrived in New York. It felt like a century. It felt like a moment.

"By all appearances, Liberty Lawrence led a charmed life. The daughter of real estate scion Ben Lawrence and supermodel Petra

Lawrence, she had a thriving career as a literary agent and was engaged to Cameron Michaels, handsome heir to the Michaels' steel fortune and the brother of her best friend, PR maven Reece Michaels."

The screen showed photos behind her as she spoke, flashing to a paparazzi photo of Liberty and Cameron walking down the street. Naturally, the family had refused to contribute any material.

"But then tragedy struck. On the night of August fourth, Liberty's cousin Laila found her unconscious in her apartment, the apparent victim of a brutal attack. Three days later, she was gone. Here with us today for an exclusive interview, please welcome Liberty's cousin and dear friend, Laila Lawrence."

With this cue, a producer gave Laila the go-ahead to join Megan onstage. They'd chosen an intimate setup for the interview: two armchairs facing each other. Laila could feel sweat collecting at her lower back, where the mic pack was placed. The crowd clapped to welcome her, and she shot them a demure, sad smile as she made her way to her seat.

"Laila, thank you for being here. Let me just say, first of all, how sorry I am for your loss. I know this must be a very hard time for you."

"It is, Megan, but thank you for having me."

"So, tell us, Laila, you'd only recently reconnected with your cousin Liberty, is that right?"

"That's right. Well, a few years ago now."

"Tell us about how the two of you found each other."

"Well, growing up I didn't even know I had cousins. But Liberty sought me out after my mother died. Our fathers had a . . . falling-out with each other, but she wanted to reconnect, especially since both of my parents were gone."

Laila felt a wave of sympathy roll off the crowd.

"Tragic. And was that typical of Liberty? That sort of kindness?"

"Oh yes," Laila said. "She really took me under her wing. She was just incredibly generous."

"You even worked with her, is that right?"

"Yes."

It went on like this for some time, Megan filling in the details of Liberty's life—the charity work, the avoidance of the spotlight, the romance with Cameron—in order to give the audience a sense of what had truly been lost in her death. Laila could feel them responding to her, even though she couldn't see them beyond the bright stage lights. She imagined them turning to one another with sad eyes, shaking their heads at the cruelty of it all. They broke for commercial.

"You're doing great!" Megan encouraged as a small army of quick-moving stylists surrounded both women to powder their noses and readjust any tiny hairs that might have come out of place.

"So," Megan said, leaning forward and placing her chin on her fist after they were live once more, "tell us about the night you found Liberty."

Laila took a deep breath.

"So . . . I'd just had this terrible fight with my boyfriend. Liberty wasn't answering her phone, so I went over."

"And was it unusual for Liberty not to answer her phone?"

"No, she was always putting it on mute while she was working. I didn't think anything of it. I just really wanted to see her."

"So you went to her apartment."

"Right."

"You were close with Liberty."

"Oh, extremely. I wasn't worried about dropping in on her. She was always there for me."

"Now, I know this will be hard, but can you take us through what happened next?"

Laila took a deep breath. If this part didn't sound right, it could turn the whole interview, make it lurid.

"I came in, called her name. At first I thought she wasn't home, but then I went into the kitchen, and she was on the floor. There was a lot of blood."

"And you called the police?"

"Yes. I called nine-one-one."

"Now, you had seen Sean Calloway on your way into the building. And you knew him from the bar, is that correct?"

"Well I wouldn't say I knew him; he was a bartender at this place downstairs."

"The Trapdoor," Megan filled in.

"Right."

"Can you tell me what you remember about meeting him before?"

Laila shrugged. "He'd always been polite, but he was always really focused on Liberty when we were in there. Always staring at her. But you know," Laila gave a sad smile, "that wasn't that unusual; she was so beautiful, everyone stared at her."

"But in this case there was something much darker going on."

"Yes, I never dreamed he was stalking her. The police know from the security camera that someone buzzed him into the building, but no one knows who. Maybe he just buzzed a random apartment and said he'd lost his key or something."

"Have the police publicly confirmed that?"

"No, I'm guessing. I just . . ." Laila squirmed. Helpfully, she began to get teary. "I'm just trying to make some sense of the whole thing, you know? It's just so unfair. She was such a beautiful person. I just keep thinking if anything had gone differently that night . . ."

Megan reached over and squeezed her hand, allowing for a sympathetic pause before the next question.

"Now, Laila, there's something that's come up in a couple of news reports. I want to ask you about it and give you a chance to just put it to rest. I know that some of the papers have been just awful."

A tiny jackrabbit of panic kicked at Laila's rib cage. She'd cho-sen Megan Capshaw for a reason. She wasn't about the "gotcha." She was every politician's first stop on their redemption tour, every starlet's go-to post-rehab. She smiled at her as if to say, *Go on*.

"The court records show that you didn't call the police until about fifteen minutes after the security footage shows you enter-ing the building. Yet you say you called nine-one-one right away. So I'd love to just hear a little bit about what happened in those fifteen minutes."

Laila's mind raced, and then it came to her—a memory clear as a bell. "The thing is, and I haven't shared this with anyone until now, I fainted when I found Liberty. . . ."

And now Laila saw it: Megan wasn't necessarily on *her* side, she was on Liberty's. No one can argue with a dead girl's cause.

"I didn't want to tell anyone because I was embarrassed. I know that sounds silly."

"So you passed out, then came to after fifteen minutes?" What people forgot about Megan Capshaw was that she'd once been an investigative reporter. She'd given it up for the better money and considerably cushier gig of being a morning-show host, but the instincts remained.

"I suppose." Laila shrugged. "What you have to understand, Megan, about going through a trauma like this, is that your memory . . . it's unreliable."

"Well," Megan said, "you're not on trial. And I know you've been enormously helpful to the investigation."

Laila breathed a sigh of relief. Of course Megan couldn't be seen interrogating the grieving cousin.

"So, Laila, the Lawrence family has been extremely private about the incident so far. Tell us why it was so important to you to come here today. What is your message for viewers?"

"I just want girls to know," Laila's mind raced, still off-kilter from the previous question, "that domestic violence can happen to anyone. It doesn't matter your income level or how beautiful or special you are. Which Liberty was—all of those things—but it's such a problem in this country."

Megan looked at her strangely.

"I don't mean domestic violence like she and Sean were in a relationship. They were friends. He was someone she knew and trusted. Which is the case with most assaults, you know? Most women are attacked by someone known to them. It's not the violent stranger lurking in the shadows that we all imagine."

"Indeed. Well, thank you so much for being here."

"Thank you for having me."

❧

"Off the record," Megan Capshaw said to Laila, leading her away from the PAs as they left the stage, "was she having an affair with him?"

Laila looked at her startled. Gone was America's Sweetheart. "With?"

"Sean, the hot bartender? You said *domestic* violence."

"No! Of course not. I mean, if she was, I didn't know about it. That would be so unlike her."

"Well," Megan said, looking pleased with herself, "it's so hard to know a person, though, isn't it?"

❧

That Laila hadn't handled herself perfectly in the interview mattered to no one. She was a beautiful girl in the middle of a criminal case that the whole country was obsessing over. Some people were critical of Megan Capshaw for putting her on the spot and called her exploitative. Soon, the offers were rolling in. *People* wanted to interview her and so did *Vanity Fair*. A talent manager called her, as did numerous literary agents. She was hot, and she was the only Lawrence willing to talk.

❧

"How could she do this to us?" Nora wailed. "After everything we've done for her?"

Reece had watched the interview with the twins at their penthouse. The press coverage had been relentless, and now this. Normally, September was Reece's favorite time in the city: the cheerful return from the beaches and mountains; the good parties again in full swing; fashion week. In previous years, Reece had done New York, Paris, Milan, *and* London: she'd taken Cece with her, and they'd had a ball. This year, other than attending the shows of a few personal friends, she could barely bring herself to leave home other than to go to work.

Now, worst of all, Laila was throwing herself into the media fray with this interview. Knowing they couldn't avoid it, she and the twins had opted to watch it together. Reece thought the interview was perhaps Laila's ham-fisted way of telling them that she needed more attention. Nora and Leo couldn't be bothered with her, and Petra and Ben spent most of their time upstate, avoiding the press. Tuxedo Park was well equipped as a refuge from scandal.

"Now people are going to think she was sleeping with that monster! That it was her fault that this happened!" Nora wailed.

"No one will think that," Reece said. "That's insane!" She put an arm around Nora's shaking shoulders.

"The tabloids will grab hold of anything, you know that," Nora said.

"Laila just wants attention," Leo said. "Next comes the tell-all book, the Lifetime movie, who knows? Maybe Lib's death is Laila's big break." Leo was affecting a cynical tone, but underneath it, Reece could hear a steady current of heartbroken rage. He wasn't wrong. They'd all seen it go down before. People were obsessed with bad things happening to the very wealthy, especially if they were beautiful. Was Liberty destined to that same fate as Patty Hearst and Edie Sedgwick? A footnote in history as a tragic heiress?

In some ways, Reece had not accepted that Liberty was dead. Intellectually she knew, but the heart would hear nothing from the head. Something inside her whispered, *We know the truth; she's not* really *gone.* Being surrounded by the Lawrences—whom she'd sought out during this time—the feeling was especially palpable that Liberty would wander into the room in her unassuming way, book in hand, and ask them what they were all so upset about. She found herself watching the door in anticipation. Surely, surely. But, of course, not really.

"Have you reached out to Laila?"

The twins looked at each other, seemingly annoyed at this rather practical suggestion. They had not.

"Well, don't you think she needs her family right now too?"

"She should have thought about that before she screwed us all over!" Nora said.

Leo shrugged. "She and I were never that close." He gingerly picked up the glass pipe from the coffee table and paused to take a couple of delicate inhales. "I only want to be around people I love right now."

"Me too! You know we've barely been out all month? I'm only even seeing Larry once a week or so," Nora added, reaching to Leo for the pipe.

Reece surprised herself by feeling a great wave of sympathy for Laila. For who had lost more than Laila? She had no parents, no siblings of her own, and now she'd lost Liberty too. The twins had suffered a great loss, but they had each other, and they had their parents, however imperfect. Who did Laila have?

Maybe, Reece thought, Laila had her.

༒

"How are you doing, Mama?" Cece came into Reece's office the next morning and put the coffee she'd brought up—a latte from the Dean & DeLuca below their office—in front of her.

"You're sweet," Reece said with a grateful smile. She took a sip. "Did you see?"

She didn't have to specify what.

Cece cringed. "Yeah, kind of tacky. I mean at least it's Megan

Capshaw. Could be worse? I mean, I wouldn't have done it, but . . ." She shrugged.

"Did she tell you she was doing it?"

"Nah. But I haven't seen her in a while. We've kind of drifted apart, to be honest."

"Have you?"

Cece shook her head. "She kind of went MIA when she met Blake. Which, like, I get it; some girls are just like that when they're in love."

"But she and Blake broke up. . . ."

"I heard that," Cece said. "I tried calling her after Liberty . . . but I didn't hear from her. I don't know."

Reece rubbed her temples with her thumb and forefinger. It was all too much.

"I feel like I should call her. I'm worried she doesn't have anybody."

Cece nodded. "I get that." She reached over and squeezed Reece's hand. "As long as you're taking care of you first."

∼≫∾

"I have to admit, I was really surprised to hear from you," Laila said, sliding into the booth in the corner of Cafeteria across from Reece after the two had exchanged a somewhat awkward hug and some rudimentary pleasantries. It was nearly October, and the days were getting crisper, shorter.

"I've been thinking about you," Reece said with a shrug. "I just figured you could use some support right now. That you could use a friend."

Laila looked as though she might burst into tears. Upon seeing her walk through the door, Reece had known she'd done the right thing in calling her. She looked like a ghost of herself, dark circles blooming under her eyes, her skin pallid and her clothes hanging off her tiny frame.

"I just keep replaying the moment in my head," Laila said, looking down at the table, "and trying to think if there's anything I could have done differently. I know it's crazy, but I feel responsible."

"Laila, no one but Sean Calloway is responsible for Liberty's murder."

The police had warned that the trial would be slow in coming, but no one had any illusions about the trial's going his way: considering the state of the media coverage, the powerful families involved, and Sean's own lack of resources—his exhausted-looking public defender his only ally—his conviction seemed a foregone conclusion by then.

But Reece understood the guilt; she'd felt it herself. How many times had she gone to Trapdoor with Liberty? How had she never seen that something was off about Sean? His looks were a smoke screen. No one could imagine someone so handsome being a murderer. Ted Bundy, people said, but Ted Bundy was no Sean Calloway. And how much worse must it be for Laila, who'd had the misfortune of *finding* her?

"Have you seen the fan sites?" Laila asked.

"I've heard about them," Reece said. There'd been a dozen sites that had popped up where "fans" of Sean could congregate. Just the day before, the *Post* had included an item about a documentary in the works about the phenomenon. *Sean Calloway: Most Wanted.* "It's sick. I don't know what's wrong with these girls."

"And guys," Laila added. A wry smile.

"True. So how are you doing? I've been worried about you."

"You have?" Laila leaned forward subtly.

"Of course I have." Reece felt a wave of guilt. Why had she been so cold to Laila all this time? She'd been a snob.

"Well . . ." Laila twisted her napkin in her hands. Just at that moment, the waiter appeared. The girls ordered a mountain of comfort food—milk shakes, fried chicken, mac and cheese—most of which would remain uneaten when they left.

"To be honest, I didn't think you ever especially liked me." Oh, there it was.

"Listen, I can be a little quick to judge sometimes. It's . . . growing up like we did, you become suspicious of people. But it's not right. And I'm sorry for that. I would really like it if we could be friends."

A smile of such intense gratitude crossed Laila's face that Reece knew she'd done the right thing.

"I think that would make Liberty really happy. I mean, I think that's what she would have wanted."

"I do too."

For a while the girls just chatted, and Reece felt happy to be there with her. They talked about how much they both loved Cece and discussed the latest antics on *The Real Housewives of New York City*, a shared guilty pleasure.

"So are you still going into the agency?" Reece asked.

"Oh, no," Laila said, absently stirring her melted milk shake. "I don't think I could bear it."

"Understandable. So what are you going to do next?" Talking was good, but Reece wanted something she could *do* for the girl.

Laila's demeanor changed. "I don't think you're going to like the answer."

"No judgment, I promise." Of course Reece knew she couldn't

actually promise this. She knew she'd also come to try to protect Laila—and the rest of them—from herself.

"Well, I've had a lot of offers. A book, a documentary, even a reality show."

She didn't need to say what the offers revolved around. They both knew.

"A reality show? Really?" Reece kept her tone light, tried to force a smile.

"Yeah, I know, weird. It's one of those ones where they do televised therapy sessions. Some pop psychologist lady put the concept together. Basically they're looking for 'telegenic' survivors of trauma. Famous if possible."

"Jesus."

"I know. I'm going to pass on that one; don't worry. But the book, that could be more dignified, don't you think? I learned so much from Liberty. It would be a memoir like *What Remains* by Carole Radziwill. Liberty loved that book."

She could feel the girl straining for her approval.

"Here's the thing," Reece said, choosing her words carefully. "If you do one of these . . . projects, Liberty's death, the case, that will be what people know you for. You'll be defined by the worst possible thing."

Laila looked as though she might cry. "I know; I know that. But it kind of feels like my only option right now. Not to be gross about it, but I'm running out of money, and I don't really feel like I can lean on my family right now. I mean, they're dealing with their own grief. . . ."

Reece reached out for her hand. "Listen, I'll . . . we'll help you, okay? Don't worry about that. Just take some time and think about what you really want to do. If you want to work for a literary agency, I have friends at other ones, and I know lots of people in fashion if that's of interest to you; we can find you something."

Reece felt a surge of righteousness on the girl's behalf; she imagined she saw what Liberty had seen. Laila was someone the universe had forsaken: a doomed figure who seemed to lose everyone she might have loved, everyone who might care for her. She didn't know exactly why she and Blake had broken up—only that it had been his doing—the abominable bad luck of its happening the same night as Liberty's death was doubly horrible and seemingly in line with how the universe operated when it made someone its sorry target.

"You're so kind. I see why Liberty loved you so much," Laila said, wiping tears from her eyes.

"I miss her so much," Reece said, "I can barely get out of bed some days. I haven't been able to take her number out of my phone."

"I miss her too. I feel like she was the only one in the family who really loved me."

"I'm sure that's not true." Reece shifted uncomfortably in her seat, because she was certain that in fact it *was* true. For the others, Laila was now an obligation and an increasingly inconvenient one, at that. She'd always thought Nora might be more kindhearted under her spoiled exterior, but now Reece wondered if she'd even really learned to be empathetic at all. Leo just couldn't be bothered to care about much in general and had never been invested in Laila other than as a momentary amusement. Petra might have stepped up under any other circumstances, but she was too shattered.

"I'll help you," Reece said, reaching across the table to take Laila's hand, "I promise."

27

REECE AND Cameron had never been through a true tragedy before: grandparents had passed away and an uncle they'd seen a few times a year. But never anyone so central to their lives, and so young, as Liberty. There couldn't have been anyone whose loss they would feel more—Reece's best friend, Cameron's fiancée—and both of their lives had been thrown off their central axes by her death. Reece had hoped to be able to lean on her brother, but he was heartbreakingly absent: wrapped in his own grief, retreating to his town house alone. The week after Reece saw Laila, when Cameron hadn't answered her calls for days, Reece stopped by unannounced after working a late night at the office, brandishing takeout from Veselka.

"Cameron?" she called out, turning her key in the door. Immediately, she saw something was off. The normally immaculate house was in disarray. She walked into the kitchen, leaving the takeout on the counter. She called his name again, and this time he came down the stairs shirtless and disheveled in sweatpants, several days of blond stubble coating his chin and cheeks. The look did not suit him, for the hair on his face was so similar to the color of his skin that from a distance it made his face look bloated and warped.

"Reece. What are you doing here?"

"Nice to see you too," she said.

"I'm sorry," he said, stepping forward to envelop her in a hug, "I'm just surprised to see you; I didn't know you were stopping by." He didn't smell as bad as he looked, but still a sad, stale aroma clung to him.

"Well, you might if you answered your phone when I called. Anyway, I brought chili from Veselka. Have you eaten?"

He shook his head and leaned over to kiss her on the forehead. The chili was his favorite thing, she knew, along with the giant, squishy rolls that came with it.

Cameron shoved a pile of papers to the side, and they sat down at the countertop.

"Okay, Cam, I have to say, it is a *pigsty* in here. What's the deal?" Reece pulled a wad of napkins from the take-out bag.

He shrugged. "I've been home a lot; I didn't want the maid to be here while I was here. It always makes me feel awkward. Also, I'm not really in shape to see anyone, as you can see."

"Even me?"

Cameron tucked into his chili with the flimsy plastic spoon, not even bothering to use his own silverware; normally he ate even takeout on his fancy flatware. "I just want to be alone."

"Well, I don't," Reece said. "Actually, I want to be with someone who misses her as much as I do. I want to be with someone who understands what I've lost."

"Sorry to be a disappointment, sis." His voice was cold, defensive.

"You know, Mom is worried about you," Reece said, trying for a safer tactic.

"Well, how's that different from any other day?"

"This time, she has a good reason. I'm worried too, to be

honest. Are you seeing a therapist or something?" Reece had seen close-up the changes that Liberty had produced in her brother, how he'd blossomed since returning from London: he was less callow, calmer, more sensitive. She worried this bettered version of Cameron might now be lost forever.

Reece herself was seeing a therapist, of course, someone she'd been to before when she was having trouble recovering from more quotidian heartbreaks and malaise. Everyone in Manhattan had therapists; it was like having a hairdresser. Therapy wasn't helping her much at the moment, but it made her feel as if she were doing something, which was better than nothing.

"Nah."

"So you're just going to white-knuckle it?"

"I guess so."

Reece retreated for a moment into her chili.

"I saw Laila the other day," she said, softly.

Suddenly her brother's gaze became steely. Reece pushed down the memory of walking in on her brother with Laila in the hospital—the flash of momentary fear in his eyes. Why was she thinking of it now? Laila and Cameron had nothing to do with each other, at least not that she knew of.

"*Why?*"

Of course, she thought, he was as unsympathetic to her as the Lawrence family. Resentful of her appearance on the morning show, as glad to discard her as Nora and Leo appeared to be.

"Because she's hurting too. I want to be a friend."

"It's not like you two were friends before," Cameron spat.

"It's different now; you know that. Liberty would want us to look out for her."

"If you say so. What's she up to, anyway?"

Reece groaned, glad to have someone to share this information with.

"She's getting a lot of offers after the morning-show thing," Reece said.

Cameron stopped eating. "What do you mean, *offers*?"

"Tell-all books, oh, and get this, some kind of awful trauma-survivor reality show where they tape them in group therapy or something. I can't believe that such a thing exists, except that I can. The world we live in."

"She can't do that." Cameron's voice was dark.

"I'm doing my best to talk her out of it. I mean, I don't think she *wants* to do any of it. But the Lawrences are shutting her out; I don't think she knows what else to do with herself. And these producers are such vultures, you know?"

"Well, she needs to find something else."

"I told her that. I told her I'd help her." She'd e-mailed Laila about an assistant job opening in her firm just that afternoon. It would be competitive, she'd told her, but she could put in a word. Laila had thanked her and told her she was still putting together her résumé.

"That's not your job."

Reece looked at him curiously. Where had her brother gone all of a sudden? Was he simply so deep in his grief that he could not be reached? She tried to shift the conversation, make small talk, to which she received indifferent grunts. Then she tried talking about Liberty, which was what she really wanted to do.

"You know, Liberty was always so kind to Laila. I realize now that she did so *despite* her family, not because of them. But she was like that. She always found enough room in her heart for everyone. God, that sounds like something from Pinterest, but it's true."

Reece wanted to remember her friend. She needed to remember her friend, accept that she existed now in the past tense, to quit waking up in the morning with the thought that she should call her for lunch today. But the mention of her name shut Cameron down completely.

"Listen, sis," he said, "I'm going to head to bed soon."

"It's nine o'clock!"

"I know, but I'm exhausted. Thanks for coming by, though. Thanks for the chili."

Reece looked at her brother as he stood, threw away the take-out containers, and started to move toward the door. She felt that she'd somehow done and said all the wrong things. Things were never like this between them. Even when her brother had been gone to London for those two years, or when he was off at Harvard before that, they always reconnected in a second; it was always as if no time had passed between them.

"Cam," she said, "please talk to me."

"About what?"

She'd never seen him so cold. It was his defense, she knew. She'd just never seen it raised to this level, and not in her direction.

"About how you feel." She reached out and put her hand on his arm.

"How do you think I *feel*? My fiancée was murdered." His voice was exasperated, as though Reece were being deeply unreasonable, assaulting him with this conversation.

"She was my best friend," Reece said wistfully.

"Is it a competition?" He pulled back from her several inches, and his face hardened.

"Of course not! I'm just saying that I'm hurting too, and it would be nice if I could talk to my brother about it. I loved her too." Now Reece had tears in her eyes. It hit her in unexpected moments that Liberty was *truly* gone, and it was happening now. There would be no end to this suffering she shared with her brother—a lessening, perhaps, a fading, but her death had happened, and it would reverberate throughout both of their lives forever. She knew that her brother's stoicism was a way of denying, or at least delaying, the reality of it all: but in shutting the pain out, he shut Reece out too.

"Well, I'm sorry I can't grieve the way you want me to grieve."

Reece gave up. She would wait for him to soften, for him to come back toward her. She had no choice.

"Okay, let's not *fight* about it. Jesus. I just . . ."

"Listen, it's fine. I'm not mad. I'm just exhausted. I can't do this right now."

In truth, this was a classic move of Cameron's, of most men, really: to act as if normal human reactions, when coming from a woman, were undue burdens to them. It had never bothered Reece until now. She accepted a lackluster hug from her brother and went off into the night.

28

THE PARTICULARLY lovely days of that fall felt almost cruel. The heat and angst of summer receded, and the gentle days, with their golden light, seemed an affront to Reece's senses. Winter would suit her better, and it would arrive soon enough, she knew. But at the moment, the crisp, delightful air was making everyone in New York a little too cheerful for her taste. Without her brother to lean on, Reece turned increasingly to the twins. Being with them reminded her of her friend; Leo more so than Nora. He had a degree of Liberty's wit and warmth, and he had her beauty, of course.

Reece was with them in Tuxedo Park one weekend. She and Leo curled up in the cozy sunroom. It was October now, and the temperature had dropped. The sunroom had become something of a sacred space with Liberty gone. Reece could practically see the two of them as teenagers sprawled out on the window seats, eating a tub of Red Vines: Liberty with her nose in a book and Reece flipping through *Vogue*.

Now they didn't want to leave the place. She and Leo had been holed up there for the better part of the day, breaking only when Leo said he was starving and offered to go get them some sandwiches from the kitchen.

"So what do you hear from Laila these days?" he said when

he returned, handing Reece the roast beef that he knew was her favorite. It was the kind of gesture that might make her tear up given her current state, but she was too distracted by the mention of Laila. She was the only one who still seemed to be on speaking terms with her. In light of what had happened, Nora and Leo might have forgiven her for ever getting involved with Blake—it would have been absurd to let that melodrama overshadow Liberty's death—but the television interview had turned them against her once again. Petra and Ben were similarly appalled; perhaps they would eventually forgive her, but for now they were all living in the omnipresent shadow of Liberty's death.

"Not really, though I think she's living in the West Village now," Reece said. It made her feel guilty to think of Laila on two counts: one, because the Lawrences might feel betrayed that she had any contact with the girl; and two, because she had not actually talked to Laila all that much and knew Liberty would want her to step up.

"Fancy," Leo said, in response. "Pays to sell your family out, I guess. Did she buy a place?"

Reece couldn't believe Leo's naïveté about what a down payment on an apartment in the West Village would actually cost. There had always been so much money that he'd never had to understand where it came from, much less how it was spent.

"No way, not unless . . ."

Leo waited for Reece to continue, but she was momentarily dumbstruck by the possibilities: The book deal? If it was that, at least it would be slow-moving; maybe there'd be time to get her to reconsider. Worse would be something on television: so much more immediate.

"Unless what?" Leo finally prompted her.

She hadn't shared with the Lawrences the fact that Laila had been considering further exploiting the family's tragedy for financial gain. She'd hoped that the girl had had a weak moment in considering these options; that she'd shown a side of herself that perhaps could be kept from the rest of her family.

"The last time I spoke to her, she said she'd gotten some offers."

"What kind of offers?"

She let out a deep sigh. "Book deal; reality show."

"Let me guess: All about Liberty?"

Reece nodded. "She said she wasn't going to take any. But she seemed like she was pretty low on funds."

"Well, obviously she decided to take one of those cretins up on their offers! Or else she has a new, rich boyfriend."

"I suppose that's always a possibility." Reece hoped so, but wouldn't someone have heard if this were the case?

"What are we going to do?" Leo was on his feet now, pacing the narrow room.

"What *can* we do? I mean, it's not illegal to talk about your life experiences, I guess. . . ."

"We could sue her!"

"We don't even know what she's doing, *if* she's going forward with anything." Was this how it would go now? All of them descending further into lurid melodrama? Oh, the tabloids would *love* that, if everyone turned on each other.

"Let's find out, then," Leo said.

"How do you suggest we do that? My efforts to communicate with her have fallen a little short." She had hoped that she'd earned Laila's trust by reaching out, but obviously she had not. Leo was right; there was something more to the situation. Laila never had applied for the job Reece talked to her about.

"Then let's figure it out for ourselves."

"Meaning?"

"There are always ways. We could hire a detective to tail her!"

"Leo. Come on." Reece laughed but couldn't tell if Leo was joking or not. The twins were like this: they were worldly in that they'd traveled all over the planet, met innumerable famous people and titans of business, and yet so childlike in that they seemed to take their cues about how life operated from movies. The movie, in this case, appearing to be *Who Framed Roger Rabbit*.

"I'm serious, Reece, if she's signed on for some tell-all or whatever, I need to know. She can't just . . . profit off of Liberty's death like this. We can't just let it happen!" Leo had abandoned his half-eaten sandwich, and it sat there forlorn at his feet. Reece's heart lurched; it struck her anew that, in losing one person, they had, in fact, lost many. A best friend, a fiancée, a daughter, a sister. The age difference between the twins and Liberty made her an almost parental figure to the two of them, one who was a great deal warmer and more openly loving than their actual parents. Without her, they both felt lost.

"I understand how you feel," Reece said soothingly. "I really do. But Laila's not the enemy. Besides," she said, smiling, trying desperately to lighten the mood, "I wouldn't know where to find a good private eye these days, would you?"

"In fact," Leo said with a mischievous grin, "I would."

She looked at him incredulously.

"My friend Nate, his mother suspected her husband—second husband, Nate's stepfather, not his dad—was cheating on her with his Bikram instructor. So she hired this uptown firm. They got pictures and bam! That sucker was done for. There was an infidelity clause in their prenup."

Reece turned the idea over in her mind, shook her head. "That's crazy." Not to mention that even if they got information, Laila wasn't breaking any laws.

Leo had pulled out his phone and was already firing off an e-mail. "I'll get his name, just in case. Then we can decide whether or not to use it. But once she's out there baring her soul, there will be nothing we can do."

֍

"Oh, darling, isn't that a little dark? You're going to look like a goth."

"It's one of the hot fall colors, Mom." Reece had brought her own nail polish to Haven where her mom had dragged her for mani-pedis.

She'd shown up at her doorstep, a swirl of fresh cashmere in her camel-colored Max Mara swing coat, knowing Reece was home, and announced their appointments.

"It will make you feel better, lovey," she said, removing the sunglasses she was wearing in spite of the overcast day. "You can't just mope around."

Reece went because she knew it would make her mother feel better to take her, not the other way around. Reece held her tongue at *moping*, her mother's dismissive term for what she was actually doing: grieving. Not that she was doing it correctly, but she found she didn't know how to make sense of her life without her friend in it. Every day she woke, and for the first blissful few moments as she emerged from her dreams, she did not live entirely in a world where Liberty was dead. But then her surroundings came back into focus, and it was another long day of putting one foot in front of the other.

At the salon, her mother laughed as she examined the little bottle of dark Essie polish. "Well, what do I know? You're the fashion expert."

Reece smiled, but it stung as it reminded her of the neglected prototypes. Since Liberty had died, all she'd been able to do was drag herself to her day job and back. Truthfully, she wasn't sure she'd ever get back to her own line. Cece had mentioned it once or twice, seemingly in the hope of cheering her up. When it had failed to do so, she'd dropped the issue.

"I saw your brother yesterday. Reece, I'm concerned about him," Elin said as the nail technicians silently went to work on their toes.

"Yeah, well. Don't ask me. He's been shutting me out."

"Well, he's a man, darling. It's what they do. You must keep trying." In Elin's world, the emotional labor of keeping a family together—or a marriage, for that matter—was a woman's work.

"It's not easy for me either," Reece said. She dearly hoped that her mother had not sought her out just to recruit her to cheer up Cameron.

"I know you were close, darling, of course," Elin said. "But he's lost his *fiancée.*"

"I don't think it's a competition," she said, echoing her brother's sentiments.

"Of course not! But I'm only saying. Your brother needs you right now. Whether he realizes it or not. You know you're the stronger one; you always have been."

"Yeah, well. I don't know if that's really the case at the moment."

"Of course it is. I know you think I baby your brother. But it's not because I love him more—Reece, you know that, don't you?"

"If you say so, Mom." Reece smiled at her, teasing her despite the truth of the sentiment.

"I'm being quite serious. You take after me, sweetheart. Made of steel. Cameron is like your father. And we cannot let him collapse in on himself."

Reece looked at her mother and let what she'd said wash over her. Could this be true? Had Elin backed off Reece because she'd never needed her as much? She didn't think of her father as weak in any way, but for a moment she thought of him without her mother, and it was an image she could barely make compute. To think of Elin without Thatcher, on the other hand . . .

"Okay, Mom, okay. I'll try harder."

⁓

Later that week, Reece tried calling Laila again. She was unsure if Leo would ever actually pursue his cockamamie detective fantasy, but he certainly had the means to do it if he wanted, and if there were another option to the cloak-and-dagger, Reece would like to spare them all. Once wealthy people started using their leverage—say, by paying a pricey detective to pry into Laila's life—there was such a long way down to go. Reece didn't want to transgress exactly *because* she knew that they would get away with it. The Michaels and Lawrence families had far more collective power than Laila—right now she was a rogue agent, but they could crush her; ultimately she was at their mercy whether she knew it or not. It was exactly the kind of thing Liberty had hated about her family. They could dispense with anyone who had become inconvenient, silence them, undermine them—as they had with Laila's own parents, Reece imagined. Laila was born an inconvenience to the Lawrence family, daughter of the woman who'd caused all the trouble—Liberty had confided in her best friend when she'd learned of the affair—and she had grown up to become an even bigger one. But Liberty wouldn't want them to disavow her; she'd want her to be looked after, not simply "dealt with."

She got no answer when she tried Laila from her cell. Then, on a hunch, she tried calling her from her landline. It was antiquated to even have one, but Reece had a vintage rotary phone that had once lived in her grandmother's estate and which she couldn't bear to let fall into obsolescence; plus there seemed something romantic about having a landline now that everyone had abandoned the idea. Liberty had referred to it as the Bat Phone. Only a few people had the number, one of them now gone. The number wasn't listed anywhere, came up as Unknown on caller ID.

"Hello?"

"Laila?"

There was a lengthy pause while Laila sorted out whose voice she was hearing and regained her composure. "Reece! Hi!"

"Hi."

"Where are you calling from?"

"My home phone; my cell is being wonky."

"That makes sense. I tried to call you back a few minutes ago, but it didn't go through. Anyway, how are you?"

Reece blanched at how chipper she sounded, or perhaps she was nervous? The two options made her uncomfortable for different reasons.

"Hanging in there," Reece replied, "what's new with you?"

"Nothing much. You?"

Nothing much? Well, what were the chances Laila would tell her this on her own?

"I heard you moved into a new place."

There were a few seconds of pause that lasted an era.

"Yes! In the West Village. I'm so excited."

"Renting or buying?"

"Renting, ha-ha, can you imagine? I'm not that kind of Lawrence. As it turns out, the rent alone is bananas enough!"

Reece let the silence hang there until it threatened to engulf them both.

"It's not what you think."

"I'm so glad to hear that. What is it, then?"

"Well, I do want to tell you, but the contract is just being finalized, and the deal hasn't been announced yet. A book, but not like a tell-all; it's going to be fiction. It's going to be based on, like, a small-town girl comes to the big city. *Not* about Liberty."

"A novel?"

"Yes. Listen, I actually have to run to a meeting in a few minutes. Can I call you later? We should put a lunch on the books."

Put a lunch on the books? "Sure."

They said good-bye, and Reece returned the phone to its cradle. She sat for a moment with the information. A novel? It wasn't beyond the realm of imagination for a bottom-feeding editor to try to make a buck by capitalizing on the infamy of Laila's name, but somehow a novel felt improbable. Let alone one with a large enough advance to enable Laila to move to the West Village. Reece knew enough about publishing from Liberty to know how unlikely this scenario was.

There was something she wasn't seeing. What was it?

Reece tried to move on with her day, but it nagged at her. At last she texted Leo: *Maybe just get that detective's info. Just in case.*

After sending it, Reece felt an immediate coil of shame. What was she doing? How had she become so desperate to know what was going on?

Because her friend was gone, and staying connected to the Lawrence family, even if it meant putting herself in the middle of the imbroglio, was a way of staying connected with her. Liberty had always been her voice of reason in moments like this. These had been their respective roles since forever: Reece was the one who convinced Liberty to take chances, and Liberty was the one who pulled Reece back from the brink of questionable decisions. But what now? Was this crazy or justified? The universe, in taking her friend, had thrown Reece's entire decision-making schema fundamentally out of balance.

It didn't help that her own brother remained absent, and she couldn't shake the feeling that Laila was lying to her. Really, where Laila got her money and what she did with it was none of her business, she knew. Unless where she got it, and what she did with it, hurt her friend's family, or tarnished her friend's legacy. What a cruel thing it was that memories were all that were left of Liberty now; she lived only in the flawed recollections of others—including Reece's own. The idea of her becoming a lurid side note—another murdered rich girl—was too much to bear. Liberty's death was not Laila's story; she did not have the right to capitalize on it.

Reece could barely sleep that night wondering what would become of her best friend's wayward cousin and whether she and Leo ought to push to find out. As it happened, she wouldn't have to wait very long.

29

LAILA HAD figured doing the talk show with Megan Capshaw would have scared the Michaelses into capitulating. But she'd underestimated Elin, though not as deeply, perhaps, as Elin had underestimated her.

Five million: that's what she'd been promised, but of course, that was by the panicked Cameron, who as it turned out had no control over the family's money—at least not the larger sums of it. Even the wealthiest people did not just have massive piles of cash stashed in safes, Laila now discovered. The Lawrences weren't a drug cartel, for heaven's sake; their money was invested, their power more subtle, more dangerous. And this Laila had learned from dealing with Elin.

Cameron carried himself like such a big man, as though with a wave of his hand, the flourish of his signature, a nod of his head— he could make you or destroy you. But it was all a facade; when tested, he'd done nothing but cower behind the proverbial skirts of his powerful mother. In the wake of Liberty's murder, Laila couldn't fathom how she'd ever been attracted to this man. Where she'd once seen strength, she now saw only a childish obstinacy.

The night of Liberty's attack, Laila had arrived at her apartment distraught over Blake. She'd banged on her door but quickly grown impatient and let herself in. She reasoned that even if her cousin wasn't at home, she could take refuge here for the night; she knew Liberty wouldn't mind. That much she'd told the police, and that much was true.

But upon entering the apartment, she'd immediately known something was wrong. She'd called Liberty's name again, and again, there had been no response. But she could hear something, a low keening; an eerie, almost inhuman sound. She walked around the center island that took up much of kitchen. The keening grew louder, clearer. She found Cameron with his knees curled up to his chest in a tight ball, his back against the fridge. It was an absurd sight: a man of his stature trying to disappear into the floor.

The pool of red caught her eye next—still creeping outward a millimeter at a time—and then time had seemed to slow as Laila took in what she was witnessing. Liberty lay at Cameron's feet completely still and bleeding from her head, her face ghostly pale with the exception of a blooming red welt on her cheekbone, her dark hair matted with blood from a wound on the back of her head.

"Cameron," Laila had said in a quiet voice, as though trying not to startle a wild animal. He'd looked at her and for a moment had appeared not to recognize her. Laila walked slowly toward him, averting her eyes from where her cousin lay. His breathing was shallow. She would have imagined herself screaming in such a scenario, but somehow it was all too surreal.

"Cameron, what happened?" she said, crouching beside him. She felt she should fear him given the state in which she'd found him, but just then he didn't seem capable of much. Laila found herself wanting to comfort him.

"I don't know," he said, his voice choked with panic.

"What does that mean, *you don't know?*" Had he found her like this? Gone into shock?

"We got in a fight. She found out about us; someone sent pictures! Oh God. Oh God. She fell. Her head."

So it was as it seemed, Laila thought, not daring to look back at her cousin where she lay, where Cameron had felled her. Simon had gone nuclear, Laila thought, left no chance that the pictures wouldn't destroy her, though he might not have bargained for who else would be taken down in the process. Laila looked back up and realized that the corner of the countertop was bloodied. She crawled on her knees to her cousin's body, focusing directly on the unsullied skin of the wrist that lay splayed closest to her. She placed two fingers on it, and what felt like an eternity passed as she waited to feel a pulse. And there it was, weak but present. Liberty was not yet dead.

"What are we going to do?" Cameron said. Laila turned back to him. Consumed by fear, he looked ten years younger suddenly.

We. Laila turned this over in her mind. So now they were a *we*? The power of the moment flooded her; it was dizzying, this reversal in their roles. Cameron at her mercy. At any other point, she might have enjoyed having the upper hand on him.

"Do you think she'll be okay?" he stammered, and when Laila said nothing, her silence only made him more nervous. His eyes were big and wet, desperate. It was an irrational question, of course, but Cameron appeared as though he were clinging to only a very thin shred of sanity.

"Oh, Cam. No, I don't think she'll be okay." She took his hand, and he clutched hers fervently. "We need to call someone," she added finally.

"Laila, *no*, oh God! I'll go to prison, I can't . . . oh God!" The mention of calling the police seemed to have snapped him back into a frantic reality. Now he was on his feet, his hand wrapped around Laila's forearm. He looked manic, and though his face was pleading, it was impossible not to find him menacing once he was on his feet: all six foot five of him. "Anything you want," he said, leaning toward her, his breath smelling of whiskey, "you'll never have to worry about money. Five million? That's no problem. Okay? Just say you're with me. You *know* I would never have done this on purpose." He choked on his last words. Did he believe that? Laila wondered. She didn't know exactly what had happened, but Liberty did not simply fall, or Cameron would have called the ambulance himself. And her face; he'd hit her. Forcefully enough to have thrown her off her feet.

They'd called Cameron's mother who, according to him, would "know what to do." Her voice on the phone was brutally frank. She told Laila to call the police and tell them she'd discovered the body; she told Cameron to go down the fire escape and to wait in the back alley where there would be a town car in a matter of moments. Laila was electrified with fear, but Elin told her to just make it through the night; she would take care of it. And she had. It turned out that the very wealthy could frame a man for murder relatively easily. In New York, DAs were elected officials, and like any other politicians, a great number of them were wont to be helpful to those who could keep them in power. Sean Calloway—scum, yes, but murderer, no—had, of course, been having an affair with a married woman, which was the reason he'd been in the building that night. And the reason said woman didn't come forward. That she knew he was innocent, that Liberty's true attacker walked free, was a cross the woman was evidently willing to bear. This, Laila could understand, for she too had opted to save herself. She had, she reminded herself over and over, not done any harm to her cousin. She imagined that had she attempted to call the police right away, refusing to go along with Cameron's plan; in the heat of the moment, he might have hurt her as well. For hadn't he proven himself capable of that right before her eyes? The only tiny amount of guilt she felt was in knowing that the last thing Liberty had known of Laila was her betrayal. But this too she would not let take hold: the revelation had not been her doing. If it were up to Laila, she surely would have taken the secret to her grave, as she would perhaps now still do.

Laila had seen Cameron only once since that night, when she was summoned to meet with him and Elin several days later, after Liberty had died. Elin had received her coldly, a paragon of brisk, Waspy efficiency. They sat in the parlor, and once the maid had brought them a round of gin and tonics, Elin got right to it, reaching for her orange Hermès Constance bag and pulling out a check to hand to Laila. All the while Cameron stared out the window as though the whole thing weren't happening. Laila began to wonder why he was even there.

"Fourteen thousand," Laila said, gingerly taking the check from her and examining it.

"It's the maximum that can be given as a gift without incurring huge taxes. For the remainder, you'll be set up as a contractor for the Michaels Foundation. We'll say you're doing," she waved her fingers as though pulling an idea from the air, "marketing work. But this should tide you over for the time being."

Laila wasn't sure she liked the idea of being tied to their family in this way. She'd have preferred to take the money and be finished with it, to move forward and try to forget what she'd done. Onward ever. But she sensed that this was not Elin's first experience with hush money, that the woman knew what she was doing.

"That will take quite a long time to pay out five million, won't it?" she ventured.

At this, Elin laughed. "Oh, my dear, no. One hundred thousand is plenty."

Laila's face fell. Plenty for what? she wondered. For helping someone get away with murder? It certainly wasn't enough to live on in New York for long, though she wondered if that was the idea: give her what amounted to a small fortune, but only if she went elsewhere to spend it.

"That's not what we agreed to, Cameron," she said, and he turned slowly to look at her. Unbelievably, he actually shrugged, as though he had no part in any of this. Now panic crept up Laila's spine. For she wasn't innocent, she knew: she'd perjured herself, obstructed justice.

"Well, that's what we're offering," Elin said.

"And if I don't accept?" Laila said. She was not the one who'd committed a crime—or at least not *the* crime—so how was it that she felt so backed into a corner?

Elin smiled again; this line of conversation seemed perfectly within her comfort zone. "Well, I suppose you'd be wise to consider the consequences of that. Accessory to a murder, extortion on top of that."

"*What?* But . . . Cameron," she spoke as though he was not in the room, "he'd go down too."

"Oh, darling, there will always be ways for us to protect ourselves. But you, on the other hand . . ." She didn't need to finish the thought. "And you should think of your family as well, how they would feel about your part in this. Don't be selfish."

A hundred thousand dollars. Laila took a sip of her drink. It was more money than she'd ever had in her life, this much was true. Had someone offered her this amount when she was first in New York, she would have considered it generous; but for a family like the Lawrences or the Michaelses, it was nothing. A small portion of Nora's closet would have added up to as much. It showed what they thought of Laila—that she was a trifle.

"You know, Elin," she said, "having gotten to know both of your children so well, I wouldn't have thought the Michaelses were the type of family to go back on a deal."

Elin laughed. "There was no *deal*. Cameron was out of his mind; he didn't know what he was saying."

Her gaze was steely. She wasn't really beautiful after all, Laila thought. Her eyes were too small, almost beady, and her forehead was oddly high—it was Thatcher Cameron and Reece had inherited their looks from. Though Elin still left you with the impression that she was beautiful—through her sumptuous clothes, her feline grace—and that was something altogether more difficult to pull off.

"A million," Laila said, trying to keep her thoughts level. How had she walked in feeling as though she had all the leverage only to have it dissipate so quickly? "I know it's not going to hurt you," Laila said, "and I can be out of your lives forever."

"Mom, maybe . . . ," Cameron began, leaning forward into the conversation once more.

Elin leveled a look at him that seemed designed to remind him to let the grown-ups do the talking. He swallowed whatever he'd been about to say. Laila looked at him, but he refused to catch her eye. In profile, she thought that perhaps he also benefited from a similar illusory beauty as Elin, for he did not, in the wan light of the parlor, look so dashing after all.

"This is not a negotiation, young lady. As I said, the checks will be sent to you. Now if you'll excuse me." With that she swept out of the parlor. The housekeeper reappeared and hovered by the threshold as Laila finished her drink.

"So you're just going to let your mother do this?" Laila finally asked, causing Cameron to glance nervously at the help.

"You should go," he said, getting to his feet wearily. He glanced down at her one last time as he walked out of the room, leaving her alone in the parlor.

But Laila had not relented; she'd simply changed her strategy. She'd gone on the morning show to remind Elin that legal matters weren't the only thing at stake. Laila had a story, which that fall was still *the* story, and there were other ways she could do damage to the Michaels family. She hadn't revealed anything, but the reference to domestic violence was meant as a message to Elin. But Elin had not taken it seriously. The only big reaction Laila had gotten was from her own family, who had issued a cease and desist. Now, more than at any other moment, Laila simply had nothing left to lose. She clearly needed to do something that hit a little closer to home for the Michaelses.

Accepting Elin's lowball was not an option. It stung too much, this idea of continuing her mother's tradition of being sent off in shame with the tiniest of consolation prizes: trinkets, minor-league hush money, memories of what might have been. Laila wasn't going down like this. What more did she have to lose?

Dear Reece,

I'm sorry to have been avoiding you, and perhaps this is the wrong thing to do, but I feel compelled to explain. You're not seeing the whole picture and I can see that it's causing you distress. I begged Cameron to tell you himself, but he refuses. I think that his grief over Liberty is compounded by the circumstances that these photos and text messages will explain, and I hope that by telling you all of this, you'll be able to help him truly heal. I don't wish to cause anyone any more pain. Please understand that I thought your brother truly cared for me and I was, I suppose, mesmerized by him. I will regret it forever and my only solace is that Liberty never had to know.

Love,
Laila

Reece got the message on her phone as she came out of the subway; she'd been heading for home, having stayed late at the office as she increasingly did—a vain attempt to distract herself from her reality. She read Laila's message with growing horror and took only a cursory glance at the attachments—a series of text messages between Laila and her brother, and worse, photos of the two of them in an unmistakable clinch—before she shoved her phone back in her pocket. The implications were all too clear. Her brother had not changed for Liberty—Reece saw now how naive she'd been to think he had—and for his side piece, he'd chosen a *family* member of his beloved. No wonder Cameron didn't want to see Reece; he probably felt guilty as hell. Reece felt her throat go tight with rage. She could kill her brother, rip him to absolute shreds. She didn't even have the energy to think what she would do to Laila. How she had abused Liberty's kindness then gone behind her back. As the knowledge seeped into Reece's brain, it began to fill crevices in her memory. The looks she'd caught between the two of them. The time at the Lawrences' upstate house when they had disappeared together. How long had this been going on? How did it start? When did it end—if, in fact, it had ended? And why was Laila telling her? Why had she chosen Reece to unburden her soul upon? Did she truly think that this information would help her in some way? Or was she simply passing the weight of the secret onto Reece to carry?

Her head was spinning. She prayed that Liberty truly had known nothing of this; that she had died thinking the man she loved was faithful and that Laila did not take all of her kindness for granted. What now? She couldn't tell anyone, at least for the moment. She felt desperate to speak to her brother before Laila revealed it to someone else—what if whatever specious logic had compelled her to share this information with Reece also moved her to tell the twins? She was terrified of being implicated by association, that Cameron's betrayal would mean she'd lose the Lawrences forever. Reece changed course and headed for Cameron's town house. She considered sending him a text message, but as Cameron had been so patently avoiding her as of late, she opted for dropping in on him unannounced. Cabs passed her by, but she continued walking. She wore flat riding boots, but her feet ached anyway. She opened the front of her coat; she needed the crisp October air on her skin to bolster her strength.

❧

"Hey, sis," Cameron said casually when he met her at the door, swiftly opening it for her without looking too closely at her face. Had he taken a moment to examine her expression, he would have known something was wrong, but as it was, he seemed to be getting ready to go somewhere. "Come in," he said needlessly as she followed him into the kitchen. She noticed that unlike the last time she'd been here—weeks ago now—his apartment was as spotless as it had been before all of their lives had descended into chaos.

"The place looks good, Cam; glad you let the maid back in."

He pointedly ignored her comment. Though he seemed to have recovered his hygiene standards, he'd remained distant from Reece—and now, of course, she knew why. Elin had been the only one allowed near him, coming to his apartment regularly to check in on him, cook him meals, and dole out other ministrations. She did no such thing for Reece, but then, she never had. Cameron had always been the one she'd babied. Perhaps Elin had been the one to call the maid.

"I can't really hang out; I have to get out the door in a few minutes to head to this work dinner." He went to the kitchen and plucked a half-full tumbler of scotch off the counter. Cameron had never been a teetotaler, but he never used to drink so much on weekdays. Then again, neither did Reece. Lately, she'd found herself pouring wine the moment she walked into her apartment, steadily refilling it until she fell asleep, many mornings waking with an empty bottle on her bedside table.

"I'll take one of those," Reece said now, drily. She hardly knew where to begin. She still did not completely understand what Laila had hoped to accomplish by telling her about the affair. Perhaps Cameron was now ignoring her too—this, in fact, seemed likely—and she was simply lashing out or looking for revenge. Whatever the case, Reece had realized on her walk over that her brother was not the man she'd hoped he was, that she was in uncharted territory with the sibling she'd once idolized. If her brother had done this, what else had he done during the course of his thirty-seven years that she didn't know of? She'd always given him the benefit of the doubt—a benefit he'd proven undeserving of.

"You want scotch?"

"Why not?"

Her brother pulled a tumbler down from the cabinet, and for the first time he looked her in the eyes and saw that she hadn't come by just to say hello.

"Okay, but I only have a few minutes, I'm supposed to meet Bryce at nine o'clock," he said, pouring his sister a double.

"You're going to be late, I'm afraid," she said. Any other time, she would have laughed at herself for the menacing tone.

"Reece . . ." He sounded exasperated. How had her brother grown so far apart from her? She felt as though she were reaching for him across a great chasm, her fingers scrambling in the air, grasping at nothing.

"I heard from Laila," she said, the name alone her trump card. With that, her brother sank silently onto the stool next to her and waited, his eyes blinking with disbelief. "She told me everything. About the two of you, about what you did to Liberty."

She watched as the blood drained from her brother's face. She knew she needed to be quiet now, to let him, no, *make* him speak for himself. She knew her relationship with her brother could never be the same after what he'd done. He'd betrayed the person they'd both loved the most, and, since she was gone, he would never be able to make it right. Liberty would never have a chance to find someone more deserving of her, someone who could love her better. Cameron, who had not yet said a word, got up silently and went to the hall bathroom, from which Reece could hear him vomiting. She fought the urge to go and comfort him, knowing he did not deserve her sympathy; instead she summoned fury, remembering the promise he'd made to her all those months ago that were he to pursue Liberty, he'd do so as a gentleman. He'd betrayed them both.

Cameron walked slowly back into the room where Reece was standing. He took her by the shoulders; his face was ashen.

"You have to believe me that it was an accident. We were having this big fight. . . . It got really heated. She fell . . . and oh God." Her brother dissolved into depthless sobs. He turned away from her, his hands covering his face as if to block out what was happening.

"She fell?" was all Reece could manage. She felt suddenly dizzy, and her brother's movements seemed to slow, as though he were moving through water. They were not talking about the same thing.

"Yes, I promise it was an accident. I don't know what Laila told you, but she wasn't even there when it happened; she came after and . . . I told her it was an accident! Oh God. Then she, she . . ."

Reece was cycling rapidly from confusion to horror to rage to fear. Her brother looked like a desperate, caged animal. She needed to calm him. She needed to not be alone with him here. She didn't think her brother would ever hurt her, but then again, she'd believed he could never hurt any woman.

She steeled herself. He thought she'd already known this information walking in; she had to pretend that she was not surprised. If he realized he'd just confessed unnecessarily, he might panic.

"Reece, Reece." He was now striding back toward her. "You believe me, don't you? That it was an accident? I'd never hurt her, you *know* that! I loved her so much."

Despite the revulsion she felt, Reece let her brother put his arms around her. She rubbed his back and attempted to soothe him. She needed to be away from here. Something crept up in her; had she known something worse had gone on? Had she suspected?

"I know," Reece said, "I know." The words were bitter on her tongue. The life Reece had known—the one where her brother was a good man; where her most darling, lifelong friend was still breathing—was a house burning to the ground before her very eyes.

She was able to calm Cameron enough to cancel his work dinner and to take a Xanax—he was now off in a drugged and dreamless sleep as Reece hurtled uptown in a cab toward her parents' house. She'd called them on her way.

"Mom," she said, "I need to see you. I'm coming up to your house." Her voice shook, and she could barely hold her composure. Her eyes were pumping out silent tears.

"Darling, what's wrong? You're scaring me!" her mother said.

"I can't—I'll tell you when I get there. I just—see you soon, okay?"

She hung up before her mother could say anything else. She could see the eyes of the cabdriver flicking back and forth from the road to her in his mirror. She knew she must be a sight. She prayed he would not ask her what was wrong—she had the wild fear that she might tell him—thankfully he was silent.

"Honey, you're scaring us half to death," her mother said when she arrived at their house on East Seventieth Street. "Tell us what's going on!" Elin had still been awake, but Thatcher had turned in at his customary early hour and was bleary-eyed in his robe as he took his daughter in his arms, kissing her hard on the cheek. He put his arm around her and guided her into the living room.

Her mother, a good hostess even under these circumstances,

offered her wine or chamomile tea. Reece opted for the tea, feeling she needed to be sharp in this moment. Besides which, her head was already swimming from the tumbler of scotch she'd had at Cameron's. Her stomach was empty; she'd planned to order take-out when she'd gotten home, as she often did after such a long day. She'd been flipping through the menu's various options in her mind as she'd come up the subway stairs, just before the e-mail from Laila had blown her life to pieces.

Now, looking at her parents—their worried, expectant faces—she knew that they too were in their last moments of innocence about their son. Reece was torn between her desire to not shatter her parents' world and her refusal to be alone in the hell into which her brother had dragged her. The hell of knowing that he was a monster. And how much worse to know the monster—or at least the man who'd done a monstrous thing—was your son? That you had, in the most literal way, created him?

It struck her anew how much her father—who had his long arm still encircling Reece as they sat on the couch—resembled Cameron. Both men had gotten a pass in life on account of their good looks, their height, and their sports prowess. In a country where white men still maddeningly held the upper hand, they were the ur-example of their species. People deferred to them implicitly, followed them slavishly. But Thatcher was good-natured, easygoing. As far as Reece knew, there was nothing sinister in his past; in fact this was a joke among his friends, who called him the Choirboy. However, who Cameron was, *what* he was, Reece realized, she no longer knew.

She ran through exactly what she would say as her mother was making the tea, and as she did, it hit her with a ferocious jolt: Cameron's alibi. He said he'd been at his parents' home that night, having met his mother for dinner when he had a disagreement with Liberty. Elin had confirmed the story more than once. Reece felt herself go rigid in her father's arms, and she leaned away before he could notice. Did he know too?

"Here you are, sweetheart," her mother said, handing her the steaming mug and placing a dish of cheerfully colored Jordan almonds on the table. Reece sipped the tea in the screaming silence of their vast apartment. So different from her own where the constant, vibrant buzz of the city she loved so much could always be heard. In this apartment, she always felt slightly entombed.

"I've just been to see Cameron," she offered, curling her legs beneath her on the sofa.

"How is he? I've been so worried about him!" Elin's hand fluttered to her cheek.

Her parents hadn't only lied to the authorities—grievous enough—they'd lied to their own daughter. But perhaps they didn't know the whole truth? Reece wished ardently that there was some alternate explanation than the one she kept circling back to. For now that her mind stopped whirring for a moment, she could see it: getting away with murder was something far too sophisticated for Cameron alone to pull off. Her mother, on the other hand . . .

"He told me," she said finally.

"About what, dear?" Elin asked too quickly, too innocently. Her father let out a great sigh, as though wearied by some quotidian fight between his wife and daughter; his "girls." So he, then, also knew.

"You said he was with you," Reece said, looking her mother straight in the eye for the first time since she'd sat down. "That night."

The silence that opened between the three of them could fill a century. Reece felt a litany of accusations bubbling up, but she held back. She sensed her mother would only tell her what she had to.

"Well, we *were* with him that night. He came to us," her mother finally said. "He explained what happened. It was an accident, a horrible mistake. We only did what any parents would do."

Reece felt a rage uncoil deep in her belly. She saw clearly now what she'd willfully ignored: that her parents had been covering for Cameron his whole life. The incidents in high school, the trip to London; all orchestrated to get Cameron "out of a jam," as her father would put it—that Waspy cliché covering all manner of sins.

"You think this is what most parents would do? Cover up the fact that their son *murdered* his fiancée? Perjure themselves? Implicate an innocent man?"

"You're being very melodramatic, Reece," her mother said, in the sharp tone that Reece recognized on such a visceral level from her childhood that it immediately quieted her. "An accident is not a murder. And Sean Calloway is not an innocent man. You've seen the news: spousal abuse, assault, not to mention the kids he abandoned. Sean Calloway is the scum of the earth."

"Could be," Reece said. How could her parents be *defensive* about this? But of course, in Elin's mind, her family ought not to be subject to the same justice as the rest of the world, and there's no reason a lowlife like Sean Calloway shouldn't bear the brunt of it. "But he didn't kill Liberty."

"It was an accident," her father said weakly, "he told us. He was so upset, Reece, you should have seen him. He would never have hurt her. He loses his temper sometimes, forgets what he's doing."

"And London," Reece said, remembering, shaking her head as

the knowledge set in, "you sent him there because of the girl. He did something to her."

"She was trash," her mother said indignantly, "she would have ruined him."

"You never should have let him come anywhere near Liberty," Reece said of her friend, now gone forever, who had loved her and loved her brother, he who had not deserved Liberty or any other woman. "She loved the two of you! You've known her for decades. How can you just let him get away with it?"

"Well, he's not exactly *getting away* with it, you know. There are punishments worse than prison. He's so distraught over all of this," Elin said. "Do you know he can barely sleep? Barely eat? It will haunt him for the rest of his life."

This was a convenient story—that his own feelings were punishment enough—Reece supposed, but it wasn't a realistic one. Cameron might have felt guilty now, but his parents would be there to assuage that guilt, to remind him that it was an accident, treat it as some unfortunate incident propelled by the hand of fate rather than their son's own brutal force. In time—probably sooner rather than later—Cameron would move on to some other girl, one who would have no idea what she was getting into.

"Pumpkin, you don't want your brother to go to prison," Thatcher said. "You might think you do, right now, in this moment. But think about what it would do to our family. We've all been through enough already."

Reece couldn't stomach how her parents were talking about Liberty's death as something that had happened to all of them, as if it were some inevitability rather than something her brother had *done*.

"I have to go," she said woodenly. She had come here thinking she was delivering the most shocking news of her parents' lives. Instead, she'd been on the receiving end of a horrible revelation. And now that the floodgates were opened, Reece realized with a sickening sensation that she'd known all along that something wasn't right with her brother. A thousand tiny incidents came back to her: whispered accusations and closed-door conversations with his parents. It had just been easier to love him than suspect him. But something had always been there—the thing crawling around beneath the bed that she'd refused to pull into the light.

"Why don't you stay the night in your room here, sweetie?" Thatcher said. She and Cameron still had rooms in the house, despite the fact that it was not the one they'd grown up in. Their things had been preserved and reestablished in the new location to remind them that they could always come home. What had seemed sweet suddenly felt sickening to Reece.

Reece shook her head and stood up to leave. Her mother darted in front of her, clutching her shoulders in her soft, manicured hands. Reece stood a few inches taller than her mother, but in that moment felt cowed by her. She'd never seen her mother look so hard and determined. Her countenance was that of a lioness protecting her cub.

"Listen to me, Reece," she said, digging her fingers into the flesh of Reece's shoulders. "You must not say anything to anyone. You're exhausted, and you've had a shock. Go home, and get some sleep. I will come over tomorrow, and we'll talk this all through, okay, my darling?" Now she reached up to smooth her daughter's hair. Reece instinctually melted a little under her mother's touch.

All Reece wanted was to be allowed to leave.

"Okay, Mom. Okay."

30

WHEN CAMERON showed up at Laila's door at midnight, she assumed she knew what he was there for. He would be angry, of course, that she'd told Reece, but it would snap him to his senses. It had to. The public appearance had been for Elin, but she'd been unmoved by it, held her ground. One hundred thousand, not a penny more, she'd told her, and she wouldn't even get the remainder if she didn't shut up and fall in line. But Cameron must have access to at least some money himself, so it was time to put the screws to him. With the initial payment she'd gotten from the Michaelses, Laila had put first and last down on an apartment in the West Village, not far from Cameron. She figured she'd make herself inconveniently close until they came around.

"You look," Laila said, opening the door of her apartment only a crack, "like shit."

"Let me in," he said, and she obediently widened the door. Cameron was still groggy from the Xanax, but he'd woken with a start on his couch less than an hour ago, and the conversation with Reece had come hurtling back to him. He'd come straight to Laila's—this storm needed to be contained. As long as only Reece knew, things would be fine.

"You told Reece," he said finally.

Laila exhaled. She'd only e-mailed Reece that afternoon but had expected this news to ricochet fast, and it had.

"You didn't leave me much choice," Laila said, pulling her robe tighter around herself and settling into the corner of her leather couch, putting distance between her and the pacing Cameron. The couch and a glass coffee table were the only pieces of furniture other than her bed: she'd purchased all three from Crate & Barrel on credit. Fourteen thousand dollars truly didn't get you very far in Manhattan.

"What the fuck were you thinking? That Reece would protect you instead of me? She's my *sister*, and she doesn't give a shit about you."

Cameron glared at her. His eyes looked hollowed and dark, his expression manic. Laila began to wonder if she ought to have let him in at all. She tried not to let her fear show, but he wasn't making any sense. He had that wild animal look to him again.

"What are you . . . ?" Laila began, confused.

"You little mongrel, you really don't understand anything about family, do you? Did you think that Reece is such a Girl Scout that she won't protect her own brother?"

Laila tried not to let the ugly word penetrate. She took a deep breath, composed herself.

"Really, Cameron, it's not like your reputation is all that sterling to begin with. It can't be *that* much of a shock to your sister that you were cheating on Liberty. Though I'd imagine she was plenty pissed off."

Cameron looked at her, bewildered.

"She said . . . ," he ran his fingers through his hair, his face collapsing, "that you told her what we did to Liberty . . ."

"Cameron," Laila said, slowly getting to her feet, "I told her about our affair. Nothing else. I'm not crazy. Jesus."

A blind terror rose up in Laila as Cameron recounted his conversation with his sister that evening. He'd confessed it himself—for no reason, as it turned out. But he'd assumed Laila had told her first; so, then, what was he doing here?

"Cameron . . . ," Laila began, taking a deep breath. He had never looked less appealing to her, with this small and ruthless side of him showing in full view. It was so clear to her that he'd dispose of her at a moment's notice. "Did you come here to threaten me?"

"No, *of course* not. Don't be dramatic. I just want to make sure that you understand how this would all go down if you tell anyone else. For your own sake. You see what's happening to Sean Calloway."

"Reece knows," Laila said, her voice small. She began to shake.

"Stop it," Cameron said, taking her shoulders in his hands and forcing her to face him. "Reece isn't going to tell anyone. She wouldn't. My parents will make her understand. This is how family works. But no more messing around with television interviews and gossip, okay?" he said, now squeezing her shoulders roughly as though to throttle a delicate bird.

"Okay," she said. She needed Cameron to go, that was all. She needed to be alone for a few minutes.

He walked to the door and looked back at her. Was there pity in his eyes? He seemed arrogantly certain that no harm would come to him. Of course, the same could never be said for Laila. And there would be no asking for more money now. The more Laila pushed, the more dangerous she became, the more likely it was that some misfortune would befall her. She didn't belong to anyone or with anyone. She was, just as he said, an orphan, a mongrel.

"Good-bye, Laila," he said.

And he was gone.

❧

Detective Neely was out on a call when Reece arrived at the station. Her parents had offered to call their driver, but Reece had told them it was late; she'd get a cab. In truth, she didn't want them to know where she was headed. She told them she needed to get home to feed Catniss, whom she'd adopted after Liberty's death. But this first, now or never.

"I'll wait," she said to the young female lieutenant who told her Neely was out.

"You sure, honey? It could be a while." The lieutenant looked weary, like this was only one of many long nights she'd worked. Reece felt suddenly ridiculous in front of this woman, realizing that she be might be an imposition.

"As long as it's okay, I'd like to wait."

She shrugged and returned to her work.

Reece knew that she couldn't go anywhere until she talked to Detective Neely. He was the only one she trusted to tell what she'd discovered. She felt certain that whoever else might be in her parents' pocket, he wasn't. He was well-known, had made a reputation for himself as incorruptible. Reece knew that if she left the station now, she might not have the courage to return. She would have to find it in herself to be ruthless toward her brother. Her image of Cameron, whom she'd always looked up to and sought approval from, had disappeared into thin air that night. She now realized he'd been an illusion all along; one she'd held on to selfishly because it comforted her. But the real man, whom he actually was, was dangerous, and had to be stopped.

She waited an hour, maybe more; she had nothing to keep her busy and simply let herself become quietly absorbed in the activity of the station. This was the other side of the city she loved, the one unbuffered by money. Liberty had never ignored it the way the rest of them had, and Reece promised herself that, going forward, she wouldn't either.

"You wanted to see me?" She at last heard the now-familiar voice from above her. Neely was there; his eyes tired but kind.

"Yes, thank you," she said, standing up and offering a hand-shake. "I'm Reece Michaels; we spoke about the Liberty Lawrence case."

"I remember. What can I do for you, young lady?"

She took a deep breath. There was still an off ramp, but it was the very last.

"I have some information that I wanted to share. Could we go in your office?"

Epilogue

IT WAS Laila's first time flying Emirates, and she was immediately comforted by the luxury of their business class. Rather than being crammed in a row, she sat in a neat little pod that would recline all the way back. The last-minute flight to the Maldives was already outrageous, so why not splurge for a little extra luxury? There'd been no real time to plan; a quick Google of which countries had no extradition treaty with the United States had yielded the exotic island nation as the most appealing of the options. She did not see herself thriving in Ukraine or Angola. She'd have enough to pay off the horrendous credit card bill when she sold the pendant, one of the only possessions she hadn't left behind. She suddenly felt as though she had all the time in the world to figure things out.

"Champagne, miss?"

"Yes, please." Laila smiled. The stewards had chic red uniforms, which were far more stylish than any of the rather dowdy alternatives she'd seen on their American counterparts.

"It's well past cocktail hour where we're headed, so why not?" the Frenchman sitting in the adjacent seat said, accepting the champagne. "My seatmate has the right idea."

When the flight attendant glided away, he leaned over and introduced himself. "Maxime."

"Laila," she said. For the first time in ages, she didn't automatically offer her last name. This was a new era in which she didn't need it, would shed it and become the next version of herself. Her seatmate, she noticed now, was handsome, somewhere around forty. He wore a beautiful suit and a Maîtres du Temps timepiece on his wrist.

"What takes you to the Maldives?" he asked. Laila wasn't much of a flyer, but she knew it was perilous to start talking to people when you had a long flight ahead of you, where breaking this first barrier nearly ensures that some level of intimacy will emerge in the hours ahead.

"For an adventure," she said. She liked the look of Maxime; she thought perhaps he was a good omen. She might have been sitting next to anyone, but here he was: no wedding ring, clearly wealthy, clearly interested.

He let out a delighted laugh. "And what will this adventure consist of?"

"I don't know yet; that's why it's an adventure."

"First time?"

"In the Maldives? Yes."

"Well, you will need a tour guide. Someone who's been going there for a decade, before anyone else knew about this little paradise."

"And where might I find one of those?" She was thoroughly enjoying herself now, and as they prepared for takeoff, she and Maxime continued flirting. In her mind, Laila rose above where she sat and looked down on herself: beautiful, young, unencumbered. This girl has only the brightest of futures, and where her past would be lies nothing. She is unstoppable and untethered. She loves no one—or at least, no one still living. Everyone has forsaken her, and she's forsaken them in return. She has defended her own life and slipped from the grasp of those who would do her harm. She's done only what she needed to in order to survive. She is the master of her fate, and she regrets nothing.

Acknowledgments

My deepest thanks to Sarah Cantin, who is an editorial dreamboat for the ages. You helped me bring this novel into being by pushing me to do better and supporting me every step of the way. You are the editor writers hope for when they dream of becoming authors. To my agent, Carly Watters, you are a treasure. I value your keen editorial eye, your steady hand, and your friendship. To my publisher, Judith Curr, I am so lucky to have you. To Albert Tang and Emma Van Deun, your covers are unfailingly swoon-worthy. And to everyone else at ATRIA BOOKS, for your smarts, your enthusiasm, and your hard work, in particular Haley Weaver, Ali Hinchcliffe, and Bianca Salvant.

Also big, big thanks to publicist extraordinaire Crystal Patriarche and her dedicated team at Booksparks, you guys are magic. For the many friends, bookish and otherwise, who have provided so much support to me over the last few years, I couldn't do it without you: Sabrina Dax, Kristina Libby, Margaret Berend, Mo Perlmutter, April Neubauer, Kerri Hatfield, Geraldine DeReuiter, Laurie Frankle, Jo Piazza, Duncan Quinn, Sumako and Maya Kawaii especially. My deepest gratitude to the fabulous ladies of Bookstagram, who have helped me build my fan base, in particular Natasha Minuso and Alyssa Hamilton. To my fellow Seattle

7's, thank you for the community and support. To all my extended family—Roberts, Youngstroms, Glastras, and Dunlops—your support bowls me over, and I'm blessed to have you all. And last, to my mom and dad, you two are the best parents anyone could ask for.

She Regrets Nothing

a novel

ANDREA DUNLOP

A Readers Club Guide

Questions and Topics for Discussion

1. What were your first impressions of the Lawrences (Liberty, Leo, Nora, Laila, Ben, and Petra)? Did your sense of any of their personalities change over the course of the book? How so?

2. On page 62, Laila describes her tendency to transform herself into what she thinks people around her want as "mirroring." Have you ever found yourself mirroring others? Using examples from the book or your own life, discuss whether mirroring seems like an effective tactic for building relationships, or reaching any other goal. Where is the line between trying to fit in and being manipulative?

3. While wealth disparity creates an obvious distinction in power and influence, *She Regrets Nothing* also portrays the way beauty and youth can be strong sources of privilege. What are some of the instances in the novel when the clout of wealth, beauty, and youth are at odds with each other? Do you think one holds more sway over people than the others?

4. There are several examples of the different timelines men and women seem to be given for settling down, from Reece's surprise that her brother Cameron would be interested in having a family when he is "only thirty-six" (p. 102) to Petra's insistence that Nora use a matchmaker to find her a husband since her "options won't get better" (p. 45) now that she is twenty-five. When Nora insists that things have

changed—that men don't only want twenty-five-year-olds, and that women can find good husbands at older ages— Petra suggests everyone is only pretending things aren't the way they were in her day. Do you agree with Petra, or do you think she is overstating the matter? What are some other examples from the book of the consequences of the divergent expectations for men and women?

6. On her way to Thanksgiving dinner with her cousins, Laila reassures herself by mentally iterating some of the glamorous facts about her current life, noting that "as she formed the words in her head, they felt true and not true." What do you think she means by this?

7. As a young, pretty Midwesterner, Laila is seen as naive and unassuming by the more urbane New Yorkers around her. Although at times she takes advantage of the impression people have of her, Laila does express frustration at not understanding the rules of the new social world she is in. What are some of the moments in the book when the reader sees her ignorance? Ultimately, to what extent do you think Laila feigned the role of a clueless small-town girl, and to what extent was that really who she was?

8. The novel seems to distinguish between characters who wear their privilege and status well, and those who do not. What are the hallmarks of each type of person? What are both the external circumstances and innate qualities that seem to make some individuals—Liberty, Reece, Blake—more redeemable than others?

9. Laila is in many ways a fiercely ambitious and emotionally independent woman, and yet repeatedly finds herself financially dependent on the men in her life. Is there power in being a "kept" woman? Which do you think grants greater freedom: working a job that isn't your passion and supporting yourself, or never having to work again but being tethered to a man you aren't in love with?

10. In chapter 18, Leo and Nora imagine leading idyllic "normal" lives outside of Manhattan, conjuring cinematic images of an upper middle–class existence. What would your perfect life be like? Do you think there is an ideal level of wealth that provides comfort and opportunity, but avoids the types of problems Leo, Nora, and Liberty believe having an abundance of money creates? If so, what would that look like, and is it different from the fantasy life you initially imagined?

11. Do you think Laila deserves a portion of the Lawrence fortune? Did Liberty deserve the money? Why, or why not?

12. In the epilogue, Laila envisions herself as a "beautiful, young, unencumbered" girl with "only the brightest of futures . . . unstoppable and untethered. . . . She is the master of her fate, and she regrets nothing." Do you think Laila really has no regrets, or does she just wish to be the girl she is describing?

Enhance Your Book Club

1. Put the "club" in book club—consider having everyone in your reading group come made up in their "Manhattan socialite" best. Put together an outfit fit for an exclusive nightclub in New York City, crack a bottle of champagne to share, or bring some New York-style cheesecake bites to add a flare of luxury to your discussion.

2. At the end of *She Regrets Nothing*, Laila is on a flight to the Maldives to escape New York and make a fresh start. Imagine what will happen in her new life. Will she live with Maxime or find another way to survive in the Maldives without any money? Will she settle down or keep moving, leaving another life behind? Will she ever find a way to maintain the luxurious lifestyle she craves? Will her actions in New York catch up to her, and will she ever regret her choices? Consider writing a denouement that addresses some of these or your own questions about Laila's future, and share with your reading group.

3. Consider reading the *New York Times* opinion piece, "What the Rich Won't Tell You," (https://www.nytimes.com/2017/09/08/opinion/sunday/what-the-rich-wont-tell-you.html). What are some parallels between how the interviewees discuss and/or justify their wealth, and how the characters in *She Regrets Nothing* view their own abundance? What differences do you see? The *New York Times* article takes a strong position on the rhetoric and behavior of the

upper class—do you agree with the author's point of view? How might some of the Lawrences respond to reading this?

4. Visit Andrea Dunlop's website at www.AndreaDunlop.net to learn more about her and her books, and consider reading her debut *Losing the Light* or her enovella *Broken Bay* for another darkly seductive read.